D1011178

SANCTUARY
BAY

Sanctuary Bay
33305234789935
0tfn   2/29/16

SANCTUARY BAY

LAURA J. BURNS
&
MELINDA METZ

 St. Martin's Griffin ≋ New York

This is a work of fiction. All of the characters, organizations, and events portrayed in this novel are either products of the authors' imaginations or are used fictitiously.

SANCTUARY BAY. Copyright © 2015 by St. Martin's Press. All rights reserved. Printed in the United States of America. For information, address St. Martin's Press, 175 Fifth Avenue, New York, N.Y. 10010.

www.stmartins.com

The Library of Congress Cataloging-in-Publication Data is available upon request.

ISBN 978-1-250-05136-3 (hardcover)
ISBN 978-1-4668-6917-2 (e-book)

Our books may be purchased in bulk for promotional, educational, or business use. Please contact your local bookseller or the Macmillan Corporate and Premium Sales Department at (800) 221-7945, extension 5442, or by e-mail at MacmillanSpecialMarkets@macmillan.com.

First Edition: January 2016

10 9 8 7 6 5 4 3 2 1

SANCTUARY
BAY

PROLOGUE

Daddy pressed his finger to his lips, shushing Sarah quiet as he slid the door to the tunnel back on. She wrapped her arms tightly around her knees and pressed her cheek against her arm, trying to pretend she was back in her own room. But it didn't smell like her room. Even the spicy smell of Daddy's cologne had faded now that the tunnel was closed. And grayness was all around her. She was almost four, and that was too old to be scared of the dark. But it wasn't all dark. It was just gray dark.

She tried not to think of monsters crawling toward her. Daddy said there were no monsters. But monsters liked tunnels. They liked little girls.

Sometimes when she was scared she liked to sing the Maggie song. But that was against the rules. She had to be quiet. She had to be still. She had to wait until Daddy or Mommy opened the door and got her.

Thinking about the rules helped. She could almost hear Daddy saying them, as if he was hiding in the tunnel with her. Even though he was way too big. If something bad happens, wait until the room is safe. If you leave the tunnel, put the funny slitted door back on. Run fast. Find a lady with kids. Tell her your name is Sarah Merson. Merson. Merson. Merson. *Merson*. Ask for help.

Her nose started twitching, itching from the thick air. Making her want to sneeze. But she had to be quiet.

Then she heard Mommy screaming. Mommy never screamed. Were the monsters out there and not in the tunnel?

On hands and knees she started creeping toward the slits of light, heart pounding.

"Kt85L is our property," a man said. "You had no right!"

Out there. Mommy on her knees facing the hotel room wall.

Someone's legs. A hand reaching down. A silver bird stared at Sarah from a ring on the finger. Stared with a horrible little black eye. The finger pulled the trigger of a gun.

A bang. Her ears filling with bees. Mommy collapsing on the floor. Red spilling out.

Sarah shoved her fingers into her mouth. Quiet. The rule was be quiet.

Shouting. Daddy's legs running by, out of the room. The bird man chasing. The door banging closed.

Something bad happening.

The room was safe. The bird man was gone. So she had to get out. Mommy was on the floor. Daddy was gone.

She shoved the door and it fell out onto the floor. Near Mommy. Near the red. But the rule was to put the funny door back on. She picked it up and shoved it over the tunnel like Daddy had shown her.

Sarah didn't want to look at Mommy. She looked out the window instead. The window was always open and there was never a screen. Daddy's voice came from the hallway, yelling. Screaming.

Another bang.

Sarah pressing her hands over her eyes. Not looking. Not looking. Something bad happening.

Daddy was quiet now. Something bad. She had to run fast.

Sarah climbed on the chair under the window. The chair always went under the window. She stuck her legs through the window and jumped down. Now run fast.

She ran fast, looking for a lady with a stroller or a kid her age. A mommy would help her. She would say she was Sarah Merson.

Sarah Merson, and something bad happened.

"First time on the water," the captain said.

It wasn't a question, but Sarah nodded as she tightly gripped the rail, the chipped paint rough under her palms. The rolling motion of the ferry made her stomach churn. "First time any-where," she mumbled. Ever since she'd left her latest foster home behind in Toledo, that's all she'd had. First plane ride, first time out of Ohio since her parents died, first Greyhound ride, first boat.

An entire day of firsts thanks to what was probably a clerical error made by Sanctuary Bay Academy. The elite prep school had handed her a scholarship, even though she hadn't applied or been recommended, even though the records from her count-less schools made it sound like community college was her best hope—if she even got that lucky.

The chilly Maine wind blasted across her face, stinging her eyes and turning her kinky hair to a tangled mess. "Do you ever get used to how big it is?" she asked. "The ocean?"

The captain laughed, his red face crinkling. "Try being out in the middle, where you can't see the shore." He swung him-self onto the steep staircase and headed down to the enclosed bottom deck.

Now her only company was a big white dog tied up near a

stubby, rusty metal . . . thing . . . with a thick rope coiled around the base. Her perfect memory would tell her what it was if she'd ever come across it in a book or heard someone talk about it before, but that hadn't happened. The dog's tongue hung out of his mouth happily as they bounced roughly over the water, the ferry leaving thick trails of white spray as it plowed toward Sanctuary Bay Academy. Clearly the dog had more travel experience than her.

She turned around, facing the shore to get a break from the out-to-infinity view. But now all she saw was the rest of the world slowly getting farther away. If her social worker was right, if the scholarship was the real deal, she wouldn't see that world again for almost two years. The academy had a strict policy of isolation.

Not isolation. Total immersion. Nothing but school.

But it still meant no contact with the outside world until she graduated.

"Which doesn't matter," she told the dog. "Seeing as I have no friends or family to miss."

Her last foster family, the Yoders, they'd been okay. Sure, they were extremely white. Big and blond and rosy cheeked and just . . . white. Sarah was sure when they looked at her they saw a black girl with kinky-curly dark hair and a wide nose. But it had been no different when she'd had black foster families. It wasn't as if they saw a white girl when they took in her green eyes and latte-hued skin. But they didn't see themselves, either. They didn't see black. If she'd been one thing or the other, instead of both, would she have found a place—a family—that she really fit with?

She'd never fit at the Yoders. Besides the whiteness, they were just too normal. Three-square-meals-a-day-bowl-a-few-frames-this-Saturday normal. Creepy normal. But she'd liked it there.

No one tried to slide into bed with her. There'd been no hitting or screaming—Mr. and Mrs. Yoder actually seemed to like each other. Decent food. Some new clothes. From Target and Walmart, but new, and hers. Mrs. Yoder had even cried when she hugged Sarah good-bye this morning.

"Maybe she'll miss me," Sarah said quietly. She faced the ocean again, and the dog gave her a wag.

"I'm not petting you," she told it. She didn't have much experience with dogs. It was one of her gaps, or at least that's how she thought of them. She'd lived in so many different homes, with so many different people. She should have experienced more than the average sixteen-year-old, but she had a bunch of gaps. Friends—you couldn't make real friends when you switched schools that often. The ocean—the Maumee River in Toledo didn't come close. Dogs—none, except the one the Weltons kept chained to the front door, and that one wasn't exactly a tail wagger. Parties—she'd never even been invited to one.

Never had a pony or a Lexus with a bow on top for my sweet sixteen, either, she thought, mocking herself. "I just wish this part was over, the not knowing," she said aloud to the dog. She could deal with anything as long as she knew what was going on. It was the not knowing that had her stomach roiling, no matter how many times she tried to tell herself it was only seasickness.

The dog stood up, so it could wag its whole butt and not just its tail. It moved closer, until its leash pulled taut, choking it. "Stupid mutt," she muttered, but it kept on wagging. Okay, fine. Today was New Thing Day, so what the hell. Sarah slowly stretched her fingers out just far enough to brush its head. A second later, her hand was thoroughly slimed.

She smiled, wiping the drool on her jeans. "Thanks for not eating my hand," she told the dog. "I'm weird enough already. I don't need to be known as Stumpy the Scholarship Girl."

Would that be a thing? Would there be a big divide between scholarship kids and everybody else? At her public schools the rich kids had always stayed away from people like her—well, at least at the schools she'd gone to that even had rich kids. But Sanctuary Bay was way beyond that. Her social worker had said students got their pick of colleges after graduation, that the best families in the country sent their kids here. That meant not just rich kids, but outrageously rich kids. Kennedys and Romneys and people like that. Sarah had tried to find information about the school online, a picture or something.

But she hadn't found anything. Maybe since Sanctuary Bay had such an amazing reputation they didn't need to be online. No need to advertise. If they wanted you, they'd let you know.

And they wanted her.

Or they wanted Sarah Merson at least. There had to be another one out there somewhere. A Sarah Merson with fantastic grades and a normal brain and parents who were still alive to help her get into a school like this. A girl who'd never been accused of being on drugs or cheating. A girl no one had ever considered might be "emotionally unstable," to quote Sarah's seventh-grade teacher. That was the girl who was supposed to be on this ferry.

"Maybe they'll never figure out they screwed up. Sucks for the other Sarah, but I probably need it more than her, right?" she asked the dog.

The boat veered to the left, bringing what looked like a row of the world's biggest floor fans into view. They had three blades each and were mounted on enormously tall yellow pillars—she guessed they were about four hundred feet tall—and each pillar was attached to a floating platform.

As they continued steadily toward the platforms, Sarah realized that two people were standing on one of them, inside a small white metal railing wrapped around the bottom of the platform's pillar. One of them pointed at her, and then they both started to wave. Sarah turned around to make sure no one had joined her on the upper deck. Empty.

"You know these people?" The dog whined in response. They were probably just waving to wave.

The boat kept speeding toward the platform. *It must be farther away than it looks*, Sarah thought. Because it looked like they were going to run right into it if they kept going for much longer. She heard footsteps clambering up the metal stairs. "You, let's go," the captain called to her.

Sarah grabbed her suitcase and her backpack. "Wish me luck," she murmured to the dog before she started toward the stairs. The dog wagged, as if to say it was all good. But it wagged at everything. *How could this be my stop?* she wondered. She'd never been on a ferry though. Maybe he was just getting her ready for a stop that was coming up in twenty minutes.

"Anything fragile in your gear?" the captain asked.

"Uh, no. Mostly just clothes," Sarah told him. Foster kids traveled light. The boat veered, pulling up alongside the platform. Now she could see the two people standing by the pillar were around her age, a boy and girl. They were still waving.

"Hi, Sarah! We're your welcoming committee," the boy—on the short side, muscular, cute, close-cropped dark brown hair, Hispanic—called to her.

"So, welcome!" the girl—preppy-pretty, straight red hair, white—added.

She sighed. Sarah always got frustrated when people tried to put her in a black or white box, like it had to be an either/or thing. But more frustratingly, she found herself automatically doing it too. She saw someone and checked off boxes. Size. Age. Race. Attractiveness. Economic status. But race was always there because it was the one box that she never knew quite what to check for herself.

The captain took her suitcase and heaved it over the rail. It landed on the floating platform with a thump. Sarah blinked in surprise. "Nothing breakable, you said."

Sarah managed to nod. She was starting to get blender-brain. It was only yesterday that her social worker had told her about Sanctuary Bay, while Mrs. Yoder buzzed around excitedly. And since then it had been pow, pow, pow—new stuff thrown at her every second. Now she was getting dropped off in the middle of the ocean onto a platform the size of a basketball court.

Oh, but wait. There was a boat tethered nearby on the other side. She'd been so focused on the people and the high fan—a wind turbine, her brain had finally provided when she'd realized she had arrived at a floating wind farm—that she hadn't noticed it. It looked more like a spacecraft than a boat, a spacecraft for James Bond. Low to the water with sleek metal lines, stretching out in two long points in front of a glassed-in . . . she wanted to call it a cockpit, but she was sure there was a better word. One word that definitely applied to the whole thing was magnificent. Just magnificent.

"You want to wear the backpack down, or should I toss it too?" the captain asked after a long pause. Sarah looked over at him and saw that his eyes were wide, locked on the boat beside the platform. So she wasn't the only one who thought it looked like something that wouldn't be invented for decades. The guy who made his living on the ocean did too.

"Toss it," Sarah told him after realizing she was going to have to awkwardly climb down a metal ladder running down the side of the ferry.

"Sarah Merson, come on down," the boy cried in a cheesy TV-show announcer voice, like she was a contestant on *The*

Price Is Right. He gave her a cocky grin. He knew exactly how cheesy he was being and that he was hot enough to pull it off. More than hot enough.

Did rich people even watch *The Price Is Right?* The boy waiting for her at the bottom of the ladder definitely seemed like a rich boy, knowledge of *PIR* withstanding. Except it looked like his nose had been broken at least once, and it hadn't been returned to perfection with plastic surgery. The girl looked rich too. They both just had a well-groomed glow that she'd never seen outside of *Us Weekly.* Not that Sarah was smelly with chipped nail polish or anything. But there was a difference.

Don't stand here staring, she told herself. *You've done this all before.* Not the boat part, but she'd been the new girl too many times to count. And she still hated it. *Don'tfalldon'tfalldon'tfall,* she thought as she stepped onto the ladder, her sweaty palms sliding across the metal railing. She narrowed her focus to the steps until she reached the gently bobbing platform.

"Nate Cruz," the boy said, holding out his hand. She shook it, praying her palms were no longer sweaty. "Junior class president," he added. His eyes were a golden brown, like caramels, his skin just a few shades darker, and the way he looked at her made her feel like she was the only person not just on the platform, but in the entire world. She was relieved when the girl stepped up beside them. Nate's gaze was so intense she felt like she needed a reason to look away.

"I'm Maya," the girl announced. "I don't feel the need to give my title every three or four seconds." She smiled, shaking hands with Sarah too. It was kind of like they were all at a business meeting, or what Sarah imagined a business meeting would be like, anyway.

"She doesn't feel the need to announce her title because she's class secretary, and it's not worth mentioning." Nate shot Maya what Sarah was already starting to think of as The Grin, then wrapped his arm around her shoulders. Maya tried to pull away, but he gave her smacking kisses on the cheek as he pulled her tighter against him.

So that's how it is, Sarah thought. Good to know. She liked to figure out as much as she could about the people in a new place as soon as possible. It made her feel more in control. Nate and Maya a couple. Noted.

Have I said anything? She felt a spurt of embarrassment. Had she just been standing there gawping at the pretty, shiny boat and the pretty, shiny rich kids? *Say something. Anything. Anythinganything.* "I thought the ferry would take me all the way to the school," she mumbled.

"Nope, the school's boat brings students the rest of the way. No need for a regular ferry to Sanctuary Bay," Maya answered. "Once you arrive, you're there 'til grad."

"But don't worry about not being able to leave," Nate told Sarah. "We make our own entertainment."

"We do." Maya gave her words a spin, making it clear she was talking about epic sex. "The only thing I really miss is shopping," she added. "We can get packages every three months, but that just means we get what people think we want. My mom tries, but she's basically hopeless, or else she thinks I'm still in fifth grade. Some of the stuff I get? I'm like—'Seriously, Mom?' Doesn't matter though. There are always people who want to trade."

Sarah remained quiet. She didn't think her first thought, *That's what we call a first-world problem, bitch,* was quite the right way to go about making friends. Instead she turned to Nate. "And you?" Sarah asked. "Does Mommy still think you're a little boy?" The words came out with an edge she hadn't intended.

"I'm past the age of needing a mommy," Nate answered, his

own tone a little sharp. "Let's get to Sanctuary Bay so you can see the place for yourself," he quickly added, the warmth back in his voice. He gave a light rap on the smoked-glass roof of the cockpit. A second later the back slid up, smoothly and soundlessly, revealing six matte-black leather chairs, ones that could easily sit at some swanky bar without looking out of place.

Sarah drew in a shaky breath. She had to stop with the poor-kid attitude. Everyone here was rich—she couldn't be mad at them all, not if she wanted them to accept her. Luckily, if her question had pissed Nate off, he'd only let it show for a second. She got why he was class president. There was something of a politician in him, a calculation under his friendly manner. Again she was being too harsh. It was probably just sharp intelligence.

"Can't wait," Sarah smiled, putting her polite voice back on. "I'm almost insane with curiosity. Do you know there's not one picture of the school online?"

Nate stepped into the cockpit, and stretched out his hand to help her onboard.

"The school has it set up so we can access the Web for research, but that's it. Nothing from us can go out. No e-mail. No way to get on Instagram or Snip-It, so there's no way to post pictures," Nate explained. "We have our own private network though, so we can send stuff to each other, and we have cells that work on-island." He grabbed Maya by the waist and swung her down beside him.

"The Academy wants us focused on school," Maya said as they each strapped into one of the chairs behind the pilot who sat at the control panel. "That's why they have the rule about us staying on campus."

"Total immersion," Sarah said softly, remembering.

"Exactly," Nate replied. "And it works. Sanctuary Bay students get the highest SAT scores in the country."

"And I'm sure Sarah is properly awed by that." Maya smiled at her. "But I'm also sure there are other things she'd like to know about the place."

"Only everything!" Sarah tried to sound eager and perky like Maya.

"Okay, for starters, there are a hundred and eighty-nine students, counting you," Nate said. The hatch glided back into place and the boat began rushing across the water. "Nine hundred raging horses in this baby," he commented. "And it can also run on solar power. Slower, but still."

Maya shook her head. "He's *such* a boy." She didn't sound at all displeased. "The school, Mr. President. We're talking about the school." She turned to Sarah. "First thing you're going to need to decide is if you're with the Puffins or the Lobsters. Those are the two lacrosse teams. Stupid names, I know—they're Maine wildlife. Somebody thought it was clever."

"There are two teams at one school?"

"Have to be," Nate told her. "We stay on the island, so the only way we can play is if we play each other. Just think of it like the Bengals and the Browns."

Sarah's chin jerked up. There weren't that many states with two football teams. "Are you saying that because you know I'm from Ohio?" she demanded, forgetting herself.

Nate gave her The Grin. "Not many states with two NFL teams," he answered, echoing her thought.

"So you did know?"

"You're the new girl. Of course we found out everything we could. With less than two hundred kids, fresh blood is a big deal," Maya said.

Sarah flushed. How much did *everything* include? Her being

a foster kid? Accounts of her random outbursts? The cheating accusations? The ones about drugs?

"So how am I supposed to decide between the, uh, Puffins and Lobsters?" she asked, trying to quiet her rapidly beating heart.

The heat in Sarah's cheeks faded as Maya rattled off the reasons why being a Puffinhead was the *only* option, clearly, since she and Nate were on the side of the Puffins.

"First view of the island coming up," Nate announced a few minutes later.

Sarah leaned forward, wishing the glass wasn't smoked. It made everything appear a little eerie, all shades of gray, even though the day was bright. "I don't see it."

"A little to the left. It doesn't look like much more than a smudge right now," he said.

She turned her head a fraction, and saw a darker spot out in the water. She kept her gaze trained on it, and as the boat sped on, the spot gradually gained size and definition. Rocky cliffs that rose high over the water dominated the island, at least on this side. There didn't seem to be much of a beach, just more jagged rocks. "How big is it?"

"About thirty square miles," Nate answered. "Take you about an hour and a half to walk from the farthest two points, if you could walk in a straight line, which you can't. Once you're off the main campus, there's a big stretch of woods with only a few trails."

More details came into focus. She could see the trees, and among them . . .

Sarah's heart felt like it had been squeezed by an ice-cold hand. Was that the school? She could just make out a brick building almost hidden in the tree line. It obviously used to be fancy, but now sat in disrepair with a crumbling roof and walls smattered with holes where bricks had fallen out, making it look like a smile with missing teeth.

"That's the Academy?" she asked, keeping her voice steady so she didn't betray her unease.

"Oh! Hell no!" Nate quickly answered.

"The school's on the other side of the island. You can't see it yet. It's nothing like *that*." Maya flicked her hand in the direction of the building Sarah had spotted, dismissing it. "You should have seen your face." Maya twisted her mouth into a horrified grimace and bugged out her eyes, laughing. "That's just some old ruin left over from before the Academy was here. You can hardly see it from our side."

Sarah relaxed back into her chair, realizing all her muscles had tensed at the sight of the creepy old ruin. The boat glided into a series of curves as the pilot navigated around the island, and Sarah spotted several cell towers along the shoreline. They made her feel better. Cell towers were modern, not like that decaying old place.

"That's a lot of towers," she said.

"It's a closed system," Nate recited again, as if that explained anything.

The boat powered up to a long jetty made of large flat stones stacked on top of one another and glided to a stop. The hatch slid up and the world exploded into color again. The rich gold of the setting sun turned the perfectly fluffy clouds orange, amber, and pink. The sea held dozens of shades of blue. The stones of the jetty had appeared gray, but now that Sarah could see them without the barrier of smoked glass, she realized they were actually subtle shades of charcoal, lavender, purple, sand, tan, and even a dusty rose.

It was beautiful.

"Thanks, man," Nate said to the pilot, who only nodded in

response. As soon as Sarah, Nate, and Maya stepped onto the jetty, the hatch slid back into place, turning the pilot into a shadowy figure inside. A moment later, the boat was flying across the water, a strange high-tech blip on the ocean.

Maya sighed as she watched it go. "If only we could use it every few weeks for a mall run. We're blocked from online shopping too," she explained to Sarah. "But the school is fabulous enough that missing out is no biggie."

"Your closets are stuffed as it is," Nate said. "She's always begging me to let her store some shoes in mine," he added to Sarah.

"It should be a privilege," Maya shot back. "They're extremely cute shoes."

"My Chucks like their privacy." Nate started down the jetty after grabbing Sarah's suitcase and backpack. Was it weird to let a stranger haul your crap? Maybe he was just being a gentleman, as Mrs. Yoder would say.

Sarah watched him for a few seconds, carrying her bags like they were weightless.

"Coming?" Maya asked.

"Yeah. Sorry," Sarah answered, heading across the stones after Nate, Maya trailing behind. At the end of the jetty, more of the same stones had been used to create long, high steps up the side of the cliff. A small brown rabbit skittered out of the way as Sarah started to climb.

The cliff was so steep that Sarah couldn't see what lay above until she reached the second step from the top. Then her whole field of vision was filled with a wide, vividly green manicured lawn, leading to the most beautiful building she'd ever seen. Her eyes flitted about, trying, and failing to take everything in all at once. Stone base, red brick walls, four stories high, with window upon window, tall and crisscrossed with white latticework all the way across the first floor, Greek columns flanking both sides of the glass entrance doors. Two wide staircases, also of stone, ran in graceful curves from the lawn up to the wide veranda that wrapped around the entire building. A balcony followed the line of the veranda on the floor above. Arched niches held classical statues of white marble. A bell tower rose out of the center of the white roof, a chimney on either side of the roof continuing the symmetry that the whole structure possessed.

Nate glanced over his shoulder. She stood rooted in place, unable to take the last step. There was too much to see. "Now *this*," he said, "is the school."

"No fucking way." The words escaped before Sarah could stop them. *Classy, Sarah. Real classy.*

"Fucking way," Nate replied. He smiled, not The Grin, but something softer, his eyes intent on her face.

If she'd seen a picture of the place online, she wasn't sure she would have gotten on the plane, no matter how big of a life-changer the school was. This place wasn't meant for someone like her.

"Don't you want to see the rest?" Maya piped up from behind.

Sarah was still trying to see all of *this*. *You can make me relive this moment as much as you want,* she told her freaky brain. She took the last step, breathing in the smell of freshly mown grass, her eyes still flicking over the school. Two three-story wings stretched out from both sides of the main building, columns alternating with the huge windows on both of them.

Don't go falling in love with it, not until you're sure you are staying, she told herself sternly.

A flash of movement and color caught her gaze, a long banner unfurling from one of the smaller windows on the third floor of the east wing. The fuchsia cloth kept unrolling until it was only a few feet above the veranda. Vivid yellow letters in a vertical row spelled out WELCOME, SARAH!!!

She suddenly felt like she needed to sit down in a small quiet room by herself for at least a few minutes, just to breathe. To digest everything that had happened since five this morning when the social worker picked her up to drive her to the airport.

"I think we've been outclassed as the welcoming committee," Maya commented as they headed down the path that led across the huge lawn. "Here comes Karina. She's one of your suitemates, Sarah. And that banner came out of the window of your room."

Sarah watched as a petite girl with long dark hair took the steps from the veranda to the lawn two at a time. She reached them before they were even halfway across the lawn. "I've been standing by the window for an hour to get that timed right," she exclaimed.

"Yeah, thanks for making us look like slackers, Kar," Maya teased. "Let me state the obvious. This is Sarah Merson. Sarah, meet Karina Sharma."

"That was amazing. That banner. Thanks so much," Sarah said. She'd started at new schools what felt like a thousand times and the most she'd ever gotten was a tour from a kid who worked in the office.

Karina gave her a fast hug. Sarah felt herself stiffen, and hoped Karina hadn't noticed. "Just wanted you to know we're happy to have you here, like Jamiroquai dancing and tetherball happy." Sarah had no idea what that last part meant, but she got the idea, and anyway, Karina was talking too fast to try to interrupt with a question. "'We' being me and Izzy, your other roommate," Karina continued. "I've been here since I was a freshman, but Iz just started last year. She's a senior. I'm a junior like you."

"Your lung capacity must be phenomenal," Nate commented

as they started walking again. "You got all that out without taking a breath."

"I'm phenomenal in a wide variety of ways, Cruz. Are you only just starting to realize that?" Karina winked at Sarah.

She's gorgeous, Sarah thought, sneaking a glance at her new roommate. *Not just pretty, gorgeous*. East Indian, Sarah was pretty sure, with skin almost the same shade as her own, and eyes such a deep brown they were almost black. Every guy there probably got palpitations when she walked by.

After they climbed the stairs to the main entrance, Karina took Sarah's suitcase from Nate, swinging it away when Sarah reached for it. "You two are dismissed," she told Nate and Maya.

"We were going to give Sarah a tour," Maya protested.

"Nope! She's probably tired, and I'm taking her to our room, letting her sit down, and getting her a beverage of some sort," Karina answered. "You can do an official tour later. Or just let Izzy and me show her around." She pulled one of the glass doors open and waved Sarah in first.

"You good with that?" Nate asked Sarah.

"Sure." It sounded great actually, as close as she was going to get to sitting in a small, quiet room by herself right now. She needed it more than ever. Her senses were on overload as she took in the elaborate wallpaper of the—again her vocabulary failed her. Sitting room? Waiting room? Lobby? Whatever the room should be called, it was huge, with a ceiling that went up two floors. A mammoth fireplace dominated the far end of the room, and there were clusters of furniture—chairs, love seats, sofas—on Persian carpets that almost created small rooms within it. The colors and patterns complimented each other, but didn't match. It was as if everything was special, one of a kind.

"Don't worry," Nate said quietly as he handed over her backpack. "In a few days you'll feel like you've been here forever."

Again, he'd known what she was thinking. "That's not possible," Sarah murmured. She started to turn away, but Nate still held one of the backpack straps.

"It is. But only if you leave all your crap behind," he said, his voice so low only she could hear it, eyes locked on hers, like he was trying to give her a coded message. "Sanctuary Bay is who you are now."

Sarah stared at him, surprised. Nate's intense look vanished, and The Grin reappeared. He released the backpack. "You have an appointment with the dean at six. I'll come by your room and escort you over."

"Thanks," Sarah said as he walked away.

The dean. If Sarah could get through that meeting without getting sent back home, her whole life would change—as long as she left all her crap behind, apparently. *Sanctuary Bay is who I am now.*

"Okay," she told Karina. "Show me everything."

2

"To our room!" Karina exclaimed. She took Sarah by the arm, steering her toward a wide polished wood staircase with the same gentle curve as the brick steps leading up to the school's door. "Oh my gosh, so, I'm insanely curious about you. I want to know *everything*. But I can go first if you want."

"You go," Sarah answered. "I want to know everything too." She *did* want to know about her new roommate. But she also wanted time to figure out what she wanted to say about herself.

"Well, I'm from L.A. My dad's in the Biz. Movie producer.

My mom's a lawyer slash 1950s housewife." Karina came to an abrupt halt. "Okay, I know I said no tour, but you have to see the Board. One of them at least." She released Sarah and turned toward the wall, where what looked like a large flat-screen TV was mounted. It showed a close-up of the rocks on the jetty, wet with sea foam.

"Calendar," Karina said. The picture of the jetty disappeared and was replaced by a calendar of school events. Sarah had only managed to read a few words when Karina said "menu" and a list of that night's dinner specials came up.

"Pasta: shrimp and scallops fresco," Sarah read. Seriously? Karina continued, "My messages," filling the screen with a row of texts. "How does it know it's you?" Sarah asked.

Karina shrugged. "I suck at understanding that stuff. It might as well be little fairies inside. Some kind of facial recognition software, I guess. The Boards all recognize you, no matter where you are on campus. They know everything about everyone." She ran her finger through the air, making the messages scroll. "Uh-oh. One from Ethan." She pinched her fingers together and the picture of the jetty returned. "My boyfriend," she explained. "He can be a little obscene. I love it though! I'll read it later. Why are we standing here? Up to the room!" She started up the stairs. It took Sarah a second to follow her, semi-stunned by the rush of information.

"We're on the third floor in the east wing," Karina said over her shoulder. "Izzy's up there, so you'll meet her in a minute. Preview—she's from Boston." She said it like Sarah was supposed to get more than Izzy's hometown out of what she'd said. "You know, old money, regular visits to the Museum of Fine Arts, DAF to the BSO, all that."

She might as well be speaking Chinese, Sarah thought as they reached the top of the staircase and started down a long hallway. She didn't ask for a translation though. Sarah was good at figuring things out on her own. All it took was paying attention—she could remember all the details.

"I hope you don't mind, but Izzy and I did a little decorating on your part of the room. It's such a pain to have to do it the second you arrive. And anyway, you'd have to wait forever for a package, since you didn't bring that much with you." They started up a second staircase.

Not much, Sarah thought. *Only everything I possess.*

"Just a duvet and some pillows and a lamp and a couple other things," Karina continued. "We're the third one down," she told Sarah they reached the third-floor landing. When they got to the door, she pressed her fingertip against a small silver pad and Sarah heard the door unlatch. "Dean Farrell will take your fingerprint when you meet her later," Karina said. "They use fingerprints for everything here. Checking out books and lab equipment, opening doors, paying at the dining hall."

Between that and the Boards, they can pretty much track every student every second of the day. The realization gave her an itchy sensation between her shoulder blades, like someone was staring at her.

"Hey, Izzy, we're here," Karina called, pushing open the door. The first thing Sarah noticed was the way the small living room smelled—like lavender and vanilla. Then she noticed the colored strings that looped around the ceiling. They held dozens of photos clipped to them with clothespins. Either Karina or Izzy—or both—was a creative type. A black tree had been painted on one of the sky-blue walls.

A door opened, pulling Sarah's attention away from the room, and a girl stepped through. Were there any ordinary people in this school? Izzy was as gorgeous as Karina, if in a completely different way. Your basic all-American boy's wet dream, blue-eyed with wavy blond hair that fell to the middle of her back, swim-suit model body, long legs, big boobs.

"You survived Hurricane Karina, I see," she smiled, then crossed over to Sarah and shook her hand. "I'm Isobel Trescott. Izzy."

"Hi." Sarah made a mental note to shake hands and give her last name the next time she met someone. Nate had done that too, and Nate seemed to understand a thing or two about fitting in. People here shook hands, so if you wanted to seem like one of them, you shook hands.

"I'm not a hurricane," Karina protested. "I'm simply enthusiastic."

That was for sure. But Sarah kind of liked it. Having two girls that *enthusiastic* in the same room would be too much. But one of them meant there was no pressure to keep a conversation going.

"I'll notify Merriam-Webster that one of their definitions is wrong," Izzy said, smiling affectionately.

"Izzy thinks enthusiasm is low class. It's the Boston thing," Karina teased back, warmly.

Karina pointed at Sarah. "I promised you a beverage. I could make Barbacoas. They're practically my signature cocktail."

"Garnished with, if you can believe it, beef jerky," Izzy said. "Californians have a million ways to fuck up a drink."

"You don't have to have one. I'm almost out of mezcal anyway. But this is a special occasion. Sound good, Sarah?" Karina asked.

"Um . . ." She didn't plan on meeting the dean—the school had a *dean*—drunk off her ass.

"Diet Coke?" Izzy offered.

"That sounds good. Maybe I could try the other thing later," she told Karina.

"You'll love it. I promise," Karina replied. "Oh! You haven't

even seen the bedroom yet! We share. There's only one bathroom too, sorry. But we make it work." She started toward the
door Izzy had come out of.

One bathroom. Three people. Sounded like a pretty good
ratio to Sarah, but she forced the thought away. It was part of
the crap she had to leave behind. Poor people shared bathrooms.
Rich people apparently thought sharing was something to apologize for.

Karina threw open the bedroom door. Sarah shivered when
she stepped through.

"I know. It's freezing in here," Karina said, noticing. "But we
made sure you have lots of blankets."

"There are cold spots all over the school," Izzy added as she
headed toward the mini-fridge in the corner. "The island bedrock goes really deep, and it makes it hard to keep the building
warm."

"Why would the bedrock have anything to do with the heat?"
Sarah asked skeptically.

"It's not the rock, it's all the caves and tunnels down there,"
Izzy said. "The whole place is filled with holes, and the cold just
sort of seeps out from the tunnels in some places. I'm not sure
the school even knows where all the passages are. I don't think
they want to know."

"That's right, I didn't tell you yet!" Karina cried out. "The
school is built over the remains of a POW camp from World War
Two. At one point it got blasted to bits by a bomb, and the whole
operation was moved into the bomb shelter underneath. They
made it bigger, carved rooms right out of the stone. Nazi soldiers were kept here during the war. Actual Nazis. Their cells
are still down there."

"That can't be true. The East Coast was never bombed during World War Two," Sarah protested.

"Right, and the government never covers *anything* up," Karina said sarcastically.

The room felt even colder to Sarah now, and she wrapped her arms around herself. The school was so beautiful, every detail perfection. The discovery that something foul lay deep underneath was disturbing.

Like there wasn't something foul right in my face in half the places I've spent my life, she thought. Compared to them, hell, compared to pretty much anything, Sanctuary Bay was a paradise, no matter what lay hidden underneath it.

"Obviously you know more than that I come from Toledo," Sarah told Nate as he walked her to the Administration building for her meeting with the dean. "You know I'm a foster kid, and all the rest, right? That's what you meant by 'my crap.' I have to pretend none of it ever happened."

She'd been thinking of his words all afternoon, and she needed to know exactly what he'd meant. Mr. Class President had seemed to guess what she was thinking more than once, and that bothered her. Every time she went to a new place, Sarah made sure to figure out where she stood and where everyone else stood. But she didn't particularly like the feeling that somebody else was doing the same thing to her—that had never happened before.

Nate didn't answer fast enough, so Sarah rushed on. "Does everyone know, or did you and Maya get a special briefing since you were coming to meet me?"

"Actually, by 'your crap' I meant your attitude," Nate replied.

Sarah was so surprised she stopped walking. "Well, that's blunt."

Nate shrugged. "You have a chip on your shoulder. About

being a foster, being poor, being whatever else you think makes you different. I can practically see the resentment."

"Wow," Sarah said. "I thought I was pretty good at hiding it."

"Nope," he replied. "Your face was judgmental when Maya was talking about her care packages."

"Sorry," Sarah muttered. "It wasn't her, she was nice, but you guys are so out of touch with reality. As if not shopping is some kind of huge hardship—"

"This is exactly what I mean," Nate cut her off. "Sanctuary Bay is a clean slate, Sarah. You can be whoever you want to be."

Sarah sighed, defeated. "Only somebody who has everything can say that. People like me don't get a clean slate. People like you—"

"Why do you think I can spot your resentment? I spent the year before I came here couch surfing," Nate said. "I moved on whenever somebody's parents got tired of feeding me."

Sarah stared at him.

"Dad was out of work for three years before he took off, and afterwards Mom liked to take it out on me, so I left," Nate explained. "My life was shit. The scholarship to Sanctuary Bay changed everything."

"I . . . thought you were like everyone else here," Sarah faltered. "I'm sorry, I'm such an idiot . . ."

"Look, the people at this school will end up running banks. And universities. And *countries*. I want to be one of them," Nate said. "Don't you?"

"I do." Sarah felt a rush of desire so strong she could barely breathe. "God, I really do. This place could give me a whole different life."

"Then drop the attitude. Don't resent them. *Learn* from them." He started walking again. "Come on. You don't want to be late."

Sarah fell in next to him silently. They didn't say another word until they were at the door of the dean's outer office. She was still struggling to take in what he'd told her, reconciling it with the polished, confident guy she'd thought she had pegged the second she saw him.

"Thanks . . . for bringing me over," Sarah said. She wanted to thank him for telling her about himself, but she couldn't find the words.

Nate nodded. "You deserve this opportunity, Sarah. Throw the crap away and take it," he replied softly, opening the door for her.

Sarah's eyes stung and she had to blink fast to clear them. She'd heard stuff like that before, from social workers and school counselors and Mrs. Yoder. But it felt different hearing it from Nate, from someone who actually got it, got *her*.

There was no receptionist behind the desk, probably because it was almost six o'clock on a Saturday. She watched the grandfather clock in the corner until the minute hand was straight up, then walked over to the dean's closed door and knocked.

The door swung open and Sarah stuck out her hand, doing her best impression of Izzy, and Nate, of someone who knew they deserved to be here. "Hi, I'm Sarah Merson."

Dean Farrell smiled and shook her hand, and Sarah quickly ran through her usual checklist. White. Thirties. Black pants. Fitted black jacket. Black-rimmed glasses. Mint-green pumps with seriously high heels. Short black hair that showed off a pair of diamond studs. Red lipstick.

The pants and jacket were sort of severe and professional looking. But the shoes were fun. Sexy, even. Did that mean confidence? The hair wouldn't take much time. Did Dean Farrell make practical choices? But she cared about how she looked, and she had the kind of face for short hair. Had to be ambitious to get this job by her age. And smart. Probably went to one of the colleges these kids were trying to get into.

Sarah had changed out of the clothes she'd worn to travel and done what she could to tame her hair. After the plane, bus, ferry, and boat, she'd needed to. She was just in khakis and a long-sleeved T-shirt. But it was no secret to the dean that she was poor.

Dean Farrell motioned her into one of the chairs over by a low sofa, and took the seat across from her. She could have chosen to sit with a desk between her and Sarah, but she hadn't, and Sarah figured it was some kind of welcoming behavior to put the new student at ease.

If this was all a screwup, now was when she'd find out.

But the dean didn't say anything about how she was so sorry but there was this other Sarah Merson who should have received the scholarship. Instead, she talked about how impressed she was with Sarah's test scores and her exceptional aptitude for chemistry and how she knew Sanctuary Bay was going to offer Sarah the chance to shine.

As the dean reached up to adjust her glasses, the sleeve of her jacket moved, revealing a silver bracelet, just a linked chain with a single charm in the shape of a heart.

Sarah's gaze caught on the heart, and—

She was in. Sitting in the car on the way to a new foster home. On the I-90. The seatbelt pressing lightly across her chest. The sun glinting off the social worker's bracelet, a silver chain with a heart charm. Tasting a cherry Life Saver. *Feeling* it on her tongue, down to a thin sliver, the edges almost as sharp as glass. "Last Friday Night" playing on the radio. Her foot tapping to the beat, even though the song annoyed the hell out of her. The social worker saying, "We could stop at Tim Horton's. I know you love those Maple Dips." Sarah answering, "I guess. It's not like . . ."

And she was out.

Sarah's body gave a tiny jerk. She flushed when she realized she'd murmured those last words aloud. She'd worked so hard to break that habit, and she mostly had. The stress of meeting the dean must have shook her up more than she realized.

Sarah felt frozen, stuck in place while her body adjusted to reality, to the fact that she was sitting motionless, not in a car going sixty-five. It was 2016, not . . . She tried to place the memory, but couldn't. Too many trips in that car. Too many stops for doughnuts. Too many moves. Maybe she wouldn't mind having her freaky memory thing if more of her memories were good.

Finally she felt her mind clear and her body relax. The memory surge was over. She raised her eyes to Dean Farrell.

The dean was staring back at her.

I guess this is where I get off the Sanctuary Bay ride, Sarah thought. *I couldn't even make it a whole day.*

"What just happened?" Dean Farrell asked, eyes scanning Sarah's face.

"I . . . I don't know," Sarah mumbled. Should she describe the memory issue? Talk about how Mrs. Yoder was convinced it was epilepsy and the foster mom before that had thought it was demons? How half her elementary school teachers had thought she had a learning disability and the other half had thought she was just doing it for attention? "I, um, I space out sometimes. I'm sorry."

"Well, you've got to be exhausted from the trip," Dean Farrell replied with a casual shrug that didn't match the way she'd been staring when Sarah came out of the surge—like Sarah was an exotic bug she wanted to stick a pin through. "I'm sorry we had to rush you here so quickly. A spot opened up unexpectedly, so we wanted to bring you in now instead of waiting until next fall since the semester's barely started."

Sarah just gaped at her. That was it? No interrogation? Usually when she had a memory episode in front of an adult, they freaked out. They wanted answers—are you sick, are you on drugs, did you pass out, was that a seizure? They never wanted the truth, that occasionally instead of just remembering something, Sarah got thrown back into the moment itself, living that memory as if it were happening all over again, every sound, every sight, every single sensation and detail.

"Let's finish up quickly so you can go get some rest," the dean said cheerfully. And then, as if nothing had happened, Dean Farrell began talking about what classes Sarah would take. She had Sarah press her finger on a touchpad so the door to her room would recognize her, gave her a cell phone that could be used only on the island, and said that Sarah should feel free to come to her if she had any problems. Then another handshake and meeting over.

Sarah walked slowly on her way back to the main building, trying to accept that she was official now. She was really going to go to school here. *Live* here. Learn to become one of these privileged people, just like Nate had said. When she reached the dorm room door, she put out her hand to knock, then stopped herself. This was her room. Because she lived here. She pressed her finger against the small silver pad next to the door and heard it click open.

Karina bounced out from the bedroom. "How'd it go? I'm sure it went great. What kind of shoes was Farrell wearing? She's such a shoe whore. Not that I don't love a nice shoe myself. I very much do."

"They were pumps. Light green." Sarah was probably

31

supposed to know the brand, but she didn't bother looking at stuff she couldn't have.

"Probably the new Louboutins. He's into that color palette right now. I wonder if she has a personal shopper send her care packages."

"The teachers can't leave either?" Sarah asked, surprised.

"All part of the total immersion the school is so proud of," Izzy told her, appearing in the bedroom doorway. "They think teachers will impart knowledge and wisdom to us if they are forced to spend time with us outside class."

"Well, Mr. Fisher *does* impart some insane weed," Karina said.

Sarah's eyebrows shot up. "Oh, yes, drugs have infiltrated our sacred Sanctuary, even with virtually everyone here twenty-four/seven," Izzy said, laughing at the look on Sarah's face. "Think prison contraband." Which explained Karina's alcohol stash. "Even the support staff has to stay on the island as long as they work here. Continuity is part of the whole 'new educational system' that's supposed to make us all superior in every way colleges care about."

"Oh," Sarah said. "Uh . . . sucks for them, I guess." Though she couldn't imagine many better places to live than this, it seemed like it was trendy to complain about being stuck on the island.

"We should head to dinner," Karina said. "The dining hall is a ways behind the main building. It's not far, but it gets cold at night, so grab a jacket."

Sarah wondered if she'd get to the point where Karina's mothering would piss her off. Right now she actually appreciated being told what to do. And she was glad both her roommates seemed to assume they'd be eating together, at least tonight. For once, she was at a new school where she wouldn't have to figure out where it was acceptable for her to sit in the cafeteria. Accidentally sitting in someone's regular seat wasn't a good way to introduce herself.

Izzy moved out of the doorway to let Sarah and Karina into the bedroom. Sarah's suitcase and backpack had disappeared from where she'd put them on her bed. "Oh, I unpacked for you," Karina said, following her gaze. A hot burst of anger mixed with shame shot through Sarah. Who did this girl think she was?

She took a deep breath in, and let it out slowly. If she followed Nate's advice to not judge, she would just accept that Karina was being friendly.

"Which I told her was *completely* inappropriate," Izzy said, reading Sarah's expression. She sat in her desk chair and smiled. "That being said, I want your leather jacket."

Sarah was confused. Her leather jacket? The one she bought for six bucks at Goodwill without even switching tags? Izzy stood up and opened her closet. It was stuffed. She flicked through the hangers and pulled out a gray sweater, holding it out to Sarah.

It took less than a second for Sarah to place it—she'd seen that sweater in a magazine at the library. She could picture the entire page layout, the headline, and each item shown. This sweater had been worn by an Asian model with her hair in a high ponytail. The text next to the photo said, "Alexander Wang. Chunky open-knit cardigan. $625."

Sarah sank down onto her bed. People actually bought things like that? One sweater for hundreds of dollars? She'd always assumed the clothes in magazines belonged to movie stars only, not regular humans.

"Trade?" Izzy asked.

"You don't have to if you don't want to," Karina said. "But we're always trading stuff here. It's one of the few ways to get new things before package day."

Sarah frowned, trying to think it through. Trade her six-buck jacket for a six-hundred-and-twenty dollar sweater. Was it some kind of pity move? Or would it turn out to be a trick?

"My jacket's from Goodwill," she said. What was the point in trying to pretend she wasn't poor as dirt? They'd seen her stuff. They knew. "It would take about a hundred of those jackets to make a decent trade for that sweater."

"Right, it's vintage," Izzy replied.

"I used to love finding great vintage stuff." Karina checked her cell as she spoke. "There was this great place, the Super Thrift Store in North Hollywood, that I'd go to. My mom hated when I'd come home with anything. She was afraid the clothes would have bedbugs."

"The jacket has a stain on the sleeve," Sarah told Izzy.

"What you mean is that it's *distressed*." Karina plopped down next to Sarah. "Make her give you two sweaters. Boston thinks she'll look like a badass in it."

"Let me try it on at least," Izzy said. "And for the record, I am a badass, in whatever I happen to be wearing."

"Fine." Sarah gestured toward the closet, keeping her expression neutral. Izzy opened it. A lot more hangers than clothes.

Izzy slipped on the jacket and buttoned it. It was big on her. On Sarah too. It was a men's, sort of in the style of a blazer. Izzy didn't look like a thug in it. It actually looked great on her. Not quite as loose as on Sarah because of the boobs, and the black leather made her hair look even blonder.

Karina pointed at her. "Yes to the dress!"

"I don't always listen to Karina, because, really, who can with her output, but I do listen to her on fashion. So, trade?" Izzy asked.

"Trade," Sarah agreed. Maybe it was pity, Izzy being charitable. But maybe she actually wanted the jacket. Even if she was trying to give Sarah something nice, that didn't have to mean she was patronizing her. Being cautious, questioning motives, that had been part of surviving in the old world, but not here.

Izzy tossed her the sweater. It was so soft in her hands that it made her want to press it against her cheek. She shrugged off the urge, pulling it on. $625. $625. $625! Nothing was that soft or pretty. She shot a glance at herself in the long mirror. The sweater did something to the plain navy tee and khakis. It made them into an "outfit."

"Yes to the dress," Karina said again, smiling at Sarah. "Now let's go. I'm starving." She put on her own jacket. It looked a little military, with double rows of buttons running from the waist up and epaulets on the shoulders. Sarah might not know what to call the room downstairs, but epaulets she knew.

"Do you have your cell?" Karina asked.

"In my pocket. Do I need it for something?" Sarah asked. It wasn't like anyone had the number. She realized she didn't even know it. She'd have to get it off the phone later.

"You need it for everything," Izzy said. "Just like your smart-phone."

Yeah, right. Just like that thing she'd never had. They'd seen her clothes and shoes and even her ratty underwear, but they still didn't get it. The fact that there existed people who couldn't afford phones had probably never occurred to either one of them. The unfairness of that sent a rush of anger through her, and she had to struggle to let it go. Maybe it would get easier.

Izzy led the way down to the first floor. *She's the alpha dog,* Sarah decided. Izzy was quieter, but Karina seemed eager for people to like her and Izzy didn't seem like she cared, which gave her the upper hand. Not that she was mean or anything. She'd been completely cool and friendly to Sarah, and she and Karina seemed to get along really well. But, yeah, Izzy was alpha, and Sarah wouldn't try to change that. It was always safest to let the power stay where it was.

They were right about it getting cold at night. When they stepped outside, Sarah was really glad she was wearing the sweater. In Ohio, September was one of the hottest months, but not here. She was also glad the path that led across the huge back lawn had small lights running along either side. Because it was dark, even with the lights emanating from the school. No streetlights out here. No cars driving by with headlights shining. The stars were brighter though, piercingly bright.

"Tonight there's hot caramel custard soup as one of the desserts. I know soup dessert sounds gross, but it is sooo good. You have to try it," Karina said.

"You realize you're treating Sarah like either she's five or she's a puppy. I'm still trying to decide which," Izzy teased.

"I'm sorry!" Karina immediately said. "I wasn't trying to be all controlling or whatever. It's just you're new, so you don't know about the dessert or how cold it gets or any of that."

"It's all good," Sarah reassured her, and realized she meant it. "You've both been great. Fixing up my part of the room and taking me with you tonight, and the banner. Everything."

"Awwww. You're welcome." Karina beamed.

"Everyone's going to want to hang with you," Izzy replied. "You have to understand how incredibly sick we are of each other, at least some of the time."

"Other new kids started at the beginning of the semester, didn't they?"

"Well, yeah. But mostly first years, so that doesn't count," Izzy said.

"Especially first-year boys," Karina chimed in. "Most of them are shorter than me. And that's short. And anyway, the difference between a fourteen-year-old and a seventeen-year-old, even not counting that girls are so much more mature, is ridiculous. I should think of who to introduce you to. I think Brian and Emma just split and—" She stopped midsentence. "I'm doing it again. I'm going to stop." She grinned at Sarah. "Unless you want my help finding a guy."

"Maybe later," Sarah answered. A guy was the last thing she needed to add to the mix. She was on sensory overload already.

"Karina can't believe anyone would want to be single for even a day," Izzy said.

"Why be single when you can be in love?" Karina countered. "Ethan makes everything better. Bad things aren't as bad, and good things are awesome."

"What kind of insane drugs does Ethan impart?" Izzy asked.

"Our roommate here doesn't like my boyfriend. But that's because she refuses to get to know him," Karina told Sarah.

"I know enough," Izzy shot back.

It was the first time an exchange between them had any kind of edge. Sarah wondered if there was history there, something that had happened between Izzy and the boyfriend. Had he hit on her or something? Or could Izzy have some kind of secret crush on him she was overcompensating for?

"We're here," Karina said, as they reached the door of a building at the edge of the woods; it looked like mostly pine trees from here. The dining hall was built out of logs, appearing almost like it had grown naturally from the ground.

Sarah thought she'd seen enough to stop expecting the school to be anything like what she'd seen in Ohio. Still, she'd thought a cafeteria was a cafeteria. Long tables. Fluorescent lights. Kind of a faint sour smell, and a stronger disinfectant smell.

Not here. It was like a restaurant with cozy booths and small tables, and low lighting. It smelled like pine needles and polished wood and good food. The center of the room was dominated by a fire pit on a circle of the same rocks that made up the jetty. A copper hood caught the light of the flames.

"Maya and Taylor are already here," Karina announced, waving. "I asked a couple of friends to eat with us, so you could meet some people," she added to Sarah. "Do I need to apologize again?" she asked Izzy, speaking all in a rush the way she always did.

Izzy laughed. "You're being Karina. You shouldn't have to apologize for that."

"Good. Guilt makes my stomach hurt, and I'm hungry."

They wove around the tables heading toward a long buffet. Sarah was conscious of a lot of curious glances, some more obvious than others. She was tempted to throw her arms wide, spin in a circle, and tell them to get all their looking over with at once. But she didn't. Obviously. First day, make that first weeks, you laid low, took in everything you could, tried to figure out how things worked, and didn't call attention to yourself— at all.

She picked up a china plate from one end of the buffet table and studied the array of food. Not the pasta, she decided. She loved shrimp and hardly ever got to have it, but pasta was messy. She wasn't going to end up in front of a bunch of strangers with a noodle sliding down her chin. She went with the meatloaf instead.

"They serve drinks at the table," Karina said when they reached the end of the buffet. "And the desserts will be out in about half an hour."

Sarah got what felt like her hundredth introduction when they sat down at the big circular booth in the corner. Taylor— white, sandy brown hair in a smooth ponytail, the kind of makeup that looked like no makeup, just natural flawless skin— was a junior too. She'd also chosen the meatloaf, and was eating it with chopsticks. Was that a thing? Was Sarah supposed to be doing that? She did a quick table check, but she and Taylor were the only ones eating it, so she couldn't be sure.

"What's with that?" Izzy asked, nodding toward the chopsticks. Okay, so it wasn't a thing.

"I heard if you eat with chopsticks, you'll naturally lose weight. It's because you eat smaller bites, so you eat slower and that gets your digestive juices flowing," Taylor explained. "I'm definitely eating more slowly."

"I'm sure your roommates will appreciate you switching over from the scarf and barf method," Izzy commented, raising an eyebrow. She took a big forkful of her pasta and didn't drop any on her chin.

"So, Sarah, you met with the dean, right? Did you figure out your class schedule?" Maya asked, shooting Izzy a disapproving look. It didn't seem to have any effect on Izzy. Sarah wondered what it would feel like to be that kind of girl. She didn't want to care about being approved of, but it made life workable. Survivable.

"We figured out a tentative one," Sarah answered. "But she said I could make changes if I needed to, once I got a feel for the classes." The dean had set up another meeting with Sarah after her first week to talk about if her classes were what she'd called "challenging and stimulating enough." At her old schools, the only time Sarah had talked to a principal was if she was in trouble.

"What are they? Maybe we have some with you," Maya said.

Sarah started listing the classes she'd be taking. "Ethan's in that one!" Karina exclaimed when she got to Advanced Chemistry. "Want me to have him send you his notes?"

"Sure. That would be great, especially since everyone's already weeks ahead of me."

Karina pulled out her cell. "Text Ethan," she told it, then left a message about the notes.

"I can give you my American Renaissance Lit notes," Maya volunteered.

"Thanks," Sarah said. Was this more of Maya's student government welcome? Or were people really just that nice here? Izzy was the only one who had shown even a little edge.

"On it." Maya pulled her own cell out of her purse. "Send Sarah all American Renaissance notes," she instructed it. "The cells are connected to our laptops," she told Sarah.

"Sarah Perlberg or Sarah Merson?" a smooth female electronic voice asked.

"Merson," Maya told it. "They'll be there pretty much now," she told Sarah.

"It can do that?" Sarah asked.

"The cells can do everything. I'm in that class too," Taylor said, "but my notes suck. I should make Maya send me hers too. She copies down practically every word."

"Ms. Coté pulls most of the exam questions out of her lectures," Maya replied. "And not everything she talks about is in the textbook." As she continued to explain the value of her detailed notes, Sarah noticed a guy—white, tall, lanky, dark hair, couldn't tell about the eyes yet—approaching them. He fisted his hand in Karina's long hair. She tilted her head back and had time for a pleased smile before he leaned over the side of the booth and kissed her. Not just a quick hello. A *kiss*. It went on so long a couple of guys at a nearby table started to hoot encouragement.

Finally, he pulled away, then circled around and sat down next to Karina. "This is girls' night," Izzy told him.

"Oh, you finally made time for that castration appointment, Iz?" he shot back. Blue. His eyes were a vivid, icy blue. And his

40

black lashes were crazy long. He had features Sarah had heard described as "fine"—sculpted lips, prominent cheekbones and chin, and a long, somewhat narrow nose. Unlike Nate's, that nose of his didn't look like it had ever been broken.

Karina gave him a playful shove. "Bad."

Izzy smoothed one of her perfectly arched brows—with her middle finger. The guy—who had to be Ethan—grinned at her, then jerked his chin at Sarah. "That the new girl?"

Clearly not a first-and-last-name-with-a-handshake type. "Sarah," she told him.

"Well, Sarah. Welcome to the Sanctuary Bay Academy," he said sarcastically. "Prepare to embrace the suck."

What was that supposed to mean?

"Nice," Maya muttered. Taylor seemed too focused on getting her meatloaf into appropriately small bites to follow the conversation.

"I'm *always* nice," Ethan agreed.

"Out of my seat," a girl—white, skinny, brown hair—ordered Ethan. She looked like she shopped out of the Official Hipster Catalog in her thick-framed glasses, Strawberry Shortcake tee, skinny jeans with a few carefully placed patches, and clunky grandma beads. "Out of my seat," she repeated when Ethan didn't move.

"Settle down, Specs, I'm going." He kissed Karina again, then took his time sliding out of the booth.

"Your boyfriend's kind of an ass," Taylor remarked. So she *had* been listening. She glanced over her shoulder, watching Ethan saunter away. "Nice butt though."

"Don't listen to him about the school," Maya told Sarah. She paused as they gave drink orders to one of the servers. Once he left, she continued. "Ethan's one of those people who thinks it's cool being a hater."

"You don't even really know him," Karina protested.

"Of course I know him," Maya said.

"It's pretty much unavoidable," Izzy agreed. "Living on an island and all."

"I'm going to go wait for the caramel soup. I'll get you one, Sarah. They're better nice and warm." Karina stood up, even though she hadn't gotten through a quarter of her dinner.

"Stand by your man," the hipster girl crooned with a twang. "I'm Tif, by the way," she said to Sarah, a little twang still in her voice.

"As in Tiffany. She's from Georgia," Izzy added, as if that explained everything.

"Atlanta, okay. Not some pea farm." Tif sounded annoyed. She must have forgotten hipster chicks didn't care about shit. "And people from all over the place are named Tiffany. It's a normal name."

Maya took over the conversation, giving Sarah a rundown of the clubs she could join and the school activities coming up. As she was finally wrapping up the rah-rah, Karina returned with a tray holding four bowls of dessert. "I figured you didn't want one, since you can't eat it with chopsticks. But if you do, I'll go back," she said to Taylor, seeming to have returned to her cheery self.

"I'm good," Taylor answered.

The caramel soup was the most delicious thing Sarah had ever put in her mouth. Enough time at this place, and her brain would be stuffed with memories she'd be happy to replay forever.

"Back to our room for chick flicks and Barbacoas?" Karina asked when they'd all finished.

"Um . . . I sort of said I'd meet up with Nate," Maya confessed.

"Girls' night is sacred," Karina reminded her. "We agreed that it had to be, otherwise someone would always be in a relationship and we'd never be able to get all of us together at the same time."

"What I meant was that I said I'd meet up with Nate because I have to study. Studying has to come before girls' night, and I didn't get my calc homework done," Maya said.

"That's what the young people are calling it these days?" Izzy teased. "Let her go, Kar. Getting done . . . with homework is important."

"Oh, fine," Karina said. "But next week—"

"Next week I promise. Just not on Saturday night again." Sarah stood up so Maya could get out of the booth.

"I actually have to go too." Tif got to her feet and brushed her bangs out of her eyes. "Don't complain," she said before Karina could get a word out. "Big delivery of lawn fertilizer came in this afternoon."

"I kind of want to hit the gym," Taylor said, with an apologetic smile. "I skipped this morning, but I promised myself I'd go sometime before the end of the day."

"Oh, go. The three of us are plenty for girls' night," Karina decreed. "Sarah, you get to pick the movie."

"Please not *Safe Haven*," Izzy begged as they started for the door. "We've seen it a million times, and it's never gotten any better."

"You don't have a romantic bone in your body," Karina said. "Not even one of the little pinky bones. I mean that dance at the diner? Swoon!"

"Never seen it," Sarah admitted.

"Then we have to watch it! You'll love it. Everyone does, except Izzy. Oh, let's take Sarah the long way back. I want her to see Suicide Cliff," Karina said.

"Suicide Cliff?"

"It has an amazing view," Karina explained. "I caught Tif humming 'Heart's Content' one day with this dreamy smile on her face," she continued, hopping back to talking about the movie.

"Does Tif work on the grounds or something?" Sarah asked. "Why does she care about a fertilizer delivery?"

"Remember before when I said school was sort of like prison?" Izzy asked with a sly smile.

"Well, Tif is like our Red on *Orange*," Karina jumped in. "She's the one that can get you stuff from the outside."

Karina had started talking in L.A.-speak again, but Sarah figured she understood the important part. "So the weed and the booze come in with legitimate shipments from outside, like lawn fertilizer."

"Our girl's quick," Izzy said as they walked. "The gardener has someone on the mainland who'll add things to the regular order. A few other employees at school do too. It's not just drugs and alcohol. On the island, people want everything from the real world. Movies and music, we can stream from the school database. But that leaves a lot. Nail polish. Clothes. Favorite food is a big one. There's a guy here who would die without his Chile Limón Doritos. They have chips and stuff at the coffee place, but not his precious Doritos."

They had a coffee place on campus too?

"How do you pay, though? It's not like you show up here with wads of cash that will last until graduation." Or did they? "And I doubt the gardener takes AmEx."

"You know how we get packages from our parents?" Izzy said. "There's always stuff we don't want. Some of it's stuff the various sources do. Or if not, it's stuff they can sell."

Jesus, what exactly were parents sending?

"My mom sent a Coach bag I wouldn't be caught dead carrying. She thinks we like exactly the same things," Karina told her, as if she'd heard Sarah's silent question. "That's kept me in treats for months."

"Tif takes a little cut for delivering everything and collecting payment. It's not like everyone at school can keep showing up at the gardener's shed. It's a nice deal for her. Her care packages wouldn't get her far. But hey, there's still barter for people without sufficient funds. Writing essays works. People here are smart, but that doesn't mean they aren't lazy. And BJs work for everything."

Sarah caught Karina shooting Izzy a sharp look, as if trying to remind her that their new roommate was someone who'd have to pay with her mouth if she wanted anything from the outside. "Here's the overlook I wanted to show you," she said to Sarah, veering off the path. "Watch the edge. No lights out here."

Sarah and Izzy followed Karina out near the edge of a cliff. The moonlight shone down on the water, creating a streak of silver, and across the jagged rocks where the waves broke into explosions of white spray.

"It's so beautiful, but sometimes I can't look at it for long," Karina said, her voice low and serious. "Sometimes when I stand here I get this crazy impulse to jump." Izzy instantly placed her hand on Karina's arm. Karina laughed. "Don't worry. It's not like I'm going to. But you know how sometimes you get a crazy thought, like what would happen if you put your hand in the garbage disposal? And then you can't stop thinking about it. And it's like a part of you is attracted to the idea."

Sarah backed up a step, her gaze now drawn more to the sharp, deadly rocks. A low moan filled the air, and she jerked her head toward Izzy, sure she was messing with them. But then she heard the sound again, and it definitely didn't come from Izzy.

"Did you hear that?" Sarah whispered, trying not to sound terrified.

"It's the ghost," Karina said, still staring down. "One of the POW prisoners escaped from his cell. He managed to get topside. When the guards came after him, he kept running. He had to know he was going to die, but he just kept running. He landed right down there. It's his spirit you hear. That's why it's called Suicide Cliff, because of him. I hear his ghost all the time."

"Well, that's what some people think the sound is anyway," Izzy said, rolling her eyes, and Sarah let out a breath she hadn't even realized she'd been holding. Izzy didn't believe in the ghost story, and that made Sarah feel better, even though she didn't believe in ghosts, period. She used to when she was little, because she wanted her ghost parents to come visit her. But they never did.

They stared down at the rocks for another moment, then Izzy added, "Some people say it was one of the patients from the insane asylum on the other side of the island who escaped and killed herself here." Sarah's breath caught in her chest again.

"There's an insane asylum on the other side of the island?" Sarah's voice came out in a squeak.

"Oh, not anymore," Izzy replied. "It was built back in the 1910s, for the mentally disturbed rich. Or just annoying family members the robber barons didn't want to deal with. The buildings are still over there, but they're falling down." So that's what Sarah had seen from the boat. The welcoming committee clearly hadn't wanted to tell her anything that would make the school sound less than perfect. "It was closed up back in the early thirties," Izzy continued. "They did horrible things to the patients. Starvation treatments. Days in tubs full of ice. Months strapped to beds. Forced sterilization. I know I'd rather take the dive onto the rocks than live through that."

The moan came again, low and plaintive. The back of Sarah's neck prickled as the small hairs there rose in response.

"It sounds like a woman to me," Izzy said. "Her spirit may have been trapped here for all these years."

"Or the sound could be made by the wind blowing through the caves." The voice came from right behind Sarah and she jumped. She looked back and saw Ethan. He put his hand on her shoulder. His thumb brushed against the side of her neck, and a jolt of hot electricity shot from her heart to low in her belly. "Easy, new girl. This place is so boring people have to make up stories to keep themselves entertained."

He pulled his hand away, and Sarah involuntarily moved her own hand over the warm spot it had left.

"But I can think of better ways to amuse myself, can't you, Karina?" He grabbed her by the hand and jerked her tight up against him. She giggled.

Izzy gave an exaggerated sigh. "So much for girls' night."

"Do you mind?" Karina asked Sarah.

"Go," Sarah told her. "You've spent half the day babysitting me."

"It's not like that," Karina protested.

"Go," Izzy said. "It'll save me from *Safe Haven*. And you'll only sit around the room texting him all night if you don't."

Ethan backed toward the path, without releasing Karina.

"No worries," Izzy told Sarah. "I'm between boys at the moment, and there are a variety I haven't tried yet. When you're in the mood, we can go shopping together."

3

Sarah stared up at the bedroom ceiling, the only sounds Izzy's steady breathing and the soft hum of the ocean. She lightly smoothed one finger over the inside of her right elbow. Ages ago, she'd trained herself not to fall asleep in a new place. When she was little and she started to doze off, she'd pinch her arm, right on the tenderest stretch of skin.

It wasn't like being awake protected her from anything. But somehow it was worse waking up to beer breath in her face, a hand sliding under the covers. When she knew it was coming, she could pull herself far away, deep inside herself. And when she was older, bigger, when she knew it was coming, she could grab whatever weapon she'd managed to find—kitchen knife, rock, anything.

Most places her vigilance turned out to be unnecessary. A foster dad came after her a couple of times when she was seven, and another place a foster kid had tried some stuff when she was eleven. But her perfect memory could replay each episode so well that it was hard to shake the fear. And after what had happened to her parents, it wasn't as if she had started out fear-free.

So every time she moved to a new place she never really slept for at least the first few nights, until she figured out if she was in danger or not. Or until she was so exhausted that the pinching, or, later, the massive amounts of caffeine, wouldn't work anymore.

She knew she was safe here. Only she, Karina, and Izzy could get past the fingerprint scanner on the door to the suite. She didn't know her roommates well enough to truly trust them, but she did trust that they wouldn't try to hurt her while she slept.

Except she couldn't sleep. She'd trained herself too well. Maybe she should go out into the living room and watch TV or something. She could do that here—there were no rules. She didn't have to worry that she'd get thrown out of the place if she bothered someone.

Or she could take a bath in the deep claw-foot tub. The bathroom was on the other side of the living room. The sound of the water running wouldn't wake Izzy up.

Or she could get her laptop—*her* laptop!—and read the English notes Maya had zapped her.

Or . . . she could just go to sleep. She felt the ache of fatigue in her burning eyes and heavy limbs. She'd hardly slept last night. She'd felt secure at the Yoders', but knowing she'd be leaving for the school the next morning had kept her mind racing. Then there'd been the hours on the plane, bus, ferry, and boat.

Sarah rolled onto her back and pulled the covers up a little higher, grateful to have heavy blankets to protect her from the cold spot that came from deep under the school. Where the POW camp had kept the prisoners. Like the prisoner who had hurled himself over—

Stop it. Going over the stupid ghost stories Karina and Izzy had told her was not going to help her drift off. She closed her eyes and concentrated on her breathing. In, out. In, out. The smell of cedar mixed with something spicy—cloves, maybe—filled her nose. It was a good smell. In, out, in, out.

Weird. That wasn't how the suite had smelled when she first came in. She remembered noticing the scent of lavender and vanilla. Must be plug-in air fresheners, with a different fragrance in the living room and this one. Although she hadn't noticed a difference in the rooms' odors earlier.

No thinking, she reminded herself. *I'm just supposed to be breathing.* In, out. In, out. Each breath brought her deeper into that spicy scent. Cedar and—

And she was in.

In the grayness, following Daddy's rules. Being quiet. Being still. Hiding. Waiting until he or Mommy opened the tunnel door. Smelling the musty tunnel, the spicy scent of Daddy's cologne fading.

She was trying not to think of monsters crawling toward her. Daddy said there were no monsters. But monsters liked tunnels. They liked little girls.

Thinking about the rules helped. She needed to keep remembering the rules. If something bad happens, wait until it's safe. Then run. Run fast. Find a lady with kids. Tell her your name is Sarah Merson. Merson. Merson, Merson, *Merson*. Ask for help.

Her nose twitching, itching from the thick air. Making her want to sneeze. But she had to be quiet.

Then Mommy screaming. Were the monsters out there and not in the tunnel?

She had to move. On hands and knees, creeping toward the slits of light, heart pounding.

Seeing her. Mommy on her knees facing the hotel room wall.

Someone's legs. A hand reaching down. A silver bird staring at her from the ring on the finger. Staring with a horrible little black eye. The finger pulling the trigger of a gun.

A bang. Her ears filling with bees. Mommy collapsing on the floor. Red spilling.

Sarah shoving her fingers into her mouth. Quiet. Being quiet. Daddy's legs running by. The bird man chasing.

Something bad happening. Feeling a hand on her shoulder.

And she was out. Sarah jerked up off the bed, searching wildly for anything she could use to attack.

"Sarah, Sarah, it's okay. It's me. Karina."

There was a delay between hearing the soft words and comprehending them. "Right, okay," Sarah answered, keeping her voice low the way Karina had. She twisted her head to the side, trying to wipe her face on the shoulder of the oversized tee she slept in.

Had she been crying for real? Or just in the memory surge?

"Come on. Let's go out to the living room for a minute. Izzy's asleep," Karina whispered.

Sarah glanced at Izzy's bed. Karina was right. Izzy lay on her stomach, one arm thrown out. It was hard to imagine someone sleeping so peacefully right next to the hell Sarah had been going through.

She slid out of bed, her heart still pounding like it was going to rip free from her chest.

"That must have been some nightmare," Karina said after she shut the door behind them. She switched on a floor lamp, leaving the living room dim.

Sarah sank down on the sofa. She didn't think her legs would carry her any farther. She couldn't bring herself to look at Karina. First a surge in front of the dean, and now this. She'd known this girl for less than twenty-four hours, and already she'd ruined things with this psychotic meltdown.

"I'm fine," Sarah said. "You can go back to bed."

Karina sat down beside her. "I wasn't in bed yet." She was still wearing the clothes she'd had on at dinner. Pay attention. Focus. Be normal. "I just got back from hanging with Ethan," Karina continued. "You were kind of . . . thrashing around. I didn't know if I should wake you up, but it looked so horrible. And then I realized your eyes were open. I thought for a second you'd woken yourself up, but you were still dreaming, almost like in a trance. You looked like you were . . ." Her voice trailed off. "Like you were fighting with something," she added after a moment.

"Sorry," Sarah told her.

"Don't be stupid," Karina said gently. "There's nothing to be sorry for. You know what we should do? We should watch cartoons. When I have a nightmare I hate to go back to sleep right away. I need to get something happy in my head first." She used her cell to click on the TV. "The school has an insane library of stuff we can stream. Music too." She hit another couple of buttons and started to scroll through a list. "Oooh! *Maggie and the Ferocious Beast*! I haven't seen that show in forever, since kindergarten probably. Did you watch it when you were little?"

Sarah felt a small smile tug at her lips. "Great googly moogly." She'd actually watched that show in the Before. Before she was a foster kid. Before her parents died. Back when things were good.

"We have to watch one. Izzy would have a fit." Karina broke into a wide smile. "But Izzy is asleep." A few seconds later, the theme song to the cartoon started to play. Sarah could have sung along. She remembered every word, along with the words to every other song she'd ever heard. But she thought she'd remember the *Maggie* song even if she had a normal brain. It had come on at lunchtime, and she and her mom had always watched it while they ate.

"I remember this one! Can you believe it? It's the one where—"

"The Jelly Bean Team gets their own train," Sarah finished for her.

"Yes!" Karina clapped her hands. "The Jelly Bean Express!" She grabbed one of the pillows off the sofa and held it cuddled against her, and for that second it was easy to picture her as a little girl with her favorite stuffed animal.

Sarah and Karina watched for a few minutes in silence. Then, eyes still on the TV, Sarah spoke without thinking for once. "It wasn't actually a nightmare," she confessed.

"What?"

Out of the corner of her eye, she saw Karina turn toward her. But she couldn't bring herself to look back. Eyes on the three-horned polka-dotted cartoon beast, she went on, "It was a memory. Of when my parents died. They were both killed on the same day, when I was really little."

Karina let out a gasp.

Stop talking. You don't talk about your parents getting murdered so soon after meeting someone. But something about Karina felt so comforting, so accepting . . . But that didn't mean she wanted to know all the horrific details of Sarah's life.

"Oh my god, I'm so sorry," Karina said softly. "What made you think of that?"

The air freshener smelled like my dad's cologne, Sarah imagined herself saying. *It triggered a memory surge that put me right back into that hotel room watching them die.*

But she couldn't. The surges—they were too strange. It was bad enough she'd just spewed the news about her dead parents. "I'm not sure," she said finally. "Maybe just the stress of being in a new place. It doesn't matter anyway. It was a long time ago." She shrugged. "Listen, I'm fine now. You can go to bed. I'll just watch a little more *Maggie*."

"You are *not* fine," Karina protested. "If my parents—" Her cell buzzed, and she pulled it out to look at it. "Oh."

"What?" Sarah asked.

"Um . . ."

"Karina?" Izzy emerged from the bedroom, yawning. "Let's go." She waved her cell in the air.

Karina shot a glance at Sarah. "I'm so sorry," she murmured. "I hate to leave you when you're so upset."

"Leave me?" Sarah repeated, baffled.

"Yeah. I—I mean we—have to go." Karina stood up. Izzy, still in her pajamas, was already at the door. "I'm really sorry."

"Where are you guys going in the middle of the night?" Sarah asked.

"Watch another *Maggie*, it'll make you happy before you go back to bed," Karina said, forcing a smile.

Izzy gave Sarah a little wave, and then they were gone, leaving Sarah alone.

She stared at the door for a long moment, trying to process what had just happened. Where were they going? Why hadn't they invited her?

Because they've known me less than a day, she thought. *I can't expect them to include me in everything just because I was assigned to their room.*

Still, she felt lonely and embarrassed. Why had she told Karina about her parents? They were probably talking about how weird she was on their way to . . . wherever they were going.

Sarah clicked off the TV and wandered slowly into the bedroom. She put her cell on the little bedside table—black with an intricate pattern of leaves, flowers, and diamonds in white. Her roommates took this kind of stuff for granted, and she was almost afraid to even touch any of it.

"I've got to sleep," she said to the empty room. She'd been awake for almost twenty-four hours, and her mind felt foggy. "Maybe that's why I had the bad surge."

The room still smelled like cedar and cloves. Sarah didn't want the scent to hurl her back into the night of her parents' murders again. She hurried to the window and opened it, letting the smell of the ocean in. She leaned on the windowsill for a moment, the fresh air filling her nostrils. The view was incredible, over the lawn stretching out to the edge of cliffs and a glimpse of the ocean beyond. So far, the ocean was her favorite thing about this whole place. She loved the sound, the constant gentle shushing.

As she turned away, she thought she heard a new sound mixed with the whispering of the waves. She jerked back around, holding her breath.

Yes. There it came again. A keening cry, soft, but definite. Sarah leaned out the window and craned her neck so that she could see the spot Karina and Izzy had shown her earlier. Suicide Cliff. She pictured a woman in a long white nightgown running toward the edge, her arms bound across her body by a straitjacket. She wouldn't even be able to throw out her arms as she plummeted, not that anything would prevent her from being killed when she hit the rocks.

She gulped.

Remember what Ethan said, she thought. Wind in the caves. It's a completely logical explanation.

That sound, though. It seemed filled with sadness and longing and pain. It was hard not to believe it was something more, something unearthly. This was definitely not going to make getting to sleep any easier. Sarah pulled back and shut the window all the way, but she could still faintly hear the ocean, the cries. Not cries, she told herself again. Wind in the caves.

She was about to turn away from the window again when she saw shadows racing across the lawn. Sarah pressed her hands on the cool glass, staring hard. People, the shadows were people. Maybe twenty of them.

As one, they all dropped to the grass, still moving, but now crawling on their bellies. "What the fuck?" Sarah whispered. About half a minute later, they were up again, running. Moving like they had a single brain. She couldn't look away, watching until they circled around the edge of the building and out of sight.

Away from the window, Sarah ordered herself. She couldn't take any more creepiness. She rushed back to bed, squeezed her eyes shut, and wished Karina and Izzy were here.

But she was all alone.

Sarah found her steps quickening as she happily headed to chemistry class on Monday. It was her favorite subject, and she rocked it. She could recall all the facts she needed to ace most subjects as long as she'd done one pass through the textbook, but chemistry she actually loved. It was precise. Complex, but if you understood the rules and formulas, predictable in a way most things weren't.

Like her roommates.

When Karina and Izzy took off in the middle of the night without bothering to tell her why, Sarah figured it meant they were done being tour guides for the new girl. They were friends with each other, and she was just their roommate. Which was fine—Sarah liked to know where she stood with people, and bad or good didn't matter.

But when she woke up Sunday morning, they were both back in the room and acting like nothing had happened. She'd slept late, something she hadn't expected to do, and Karina and Izzy had waited to have breakfast with her. After that they'd walked her around the campus, showing her the lacrosse and soccer fields and the track. The outdoor track. There was also an indoor one, in what they called the sports center. The center also had a rock-climbing wall, two basketball courts, a bowling alley, a coffee place with a billion designer coffee drinks and juices and snacks, and an Olympic-sized pool, not much use to Sarah, who had only mastered the dog paddle. She could deal with the Jacuzzis in the locker room, though, *very* easily deal with those. There were saunas too, but her hair didn't appreciate steam.

Her roommates had even shown her where her classrooms were, including the little studio where she and her piano tutor would be meeting first thing in the morning. Dean Farrell had insisted she get some kind of "musical instruction." All Sarah had ever had was two days with a plastic recorder in third grade.

Then Karina and Izzy had taken her over to the theater where the drama types put on two plays a year. There was a huge screening room in the building's basement—with a popcorn popper and actual real butter. By the end of the tour, Sarah understood exactly why even the most privileged kids didn't have a problem spending years on the island. Well, except Ethan. She hadn't forgotten the "prepare to embrace the suck" warning he'd given her.

The entire day, Izzy and Karina had acted as if Sarah was their new bestie. She'd gone along with it, and she hadn't asked about where they went the night before. But the fact that they didn't mention it, either, made it clear they didn't want Sarah to know.

They didn't trust Sarah. So she couldn't trust them.

The teacher and two boys were already in the chemistry room when she arrived. "You must be Sarah," the teacher—Hispanic, built like a wrestler, longish brown hair curling around his collar—said, then grinned. "Have I impressed you with my deductive abilities?"

"Absolutely," Sarah answered, unsure what else to say.

"Diaz doesn't have much to brag about," one of the guys—black, older than Sarah, with a beard—commented.

"Only my deductive abilities, my muscled physique, my full head of hair, and—"

Beard kid laughed. "What'd I tell you?" he asked Sarah, clearly not worried about interrupting. "Number three, and he's already at possession of hair."

"Dr. Diaz does have good hair," an Asian girl, pretty with dangly earrings almost down to her shoulders, said as she walked over to one of the four lab stations and sat down.

"A for the day to Eliza!" Dr. Diaz called out.

The other guy spoke up. "Paying for compliments." He shook his head, sending his longish red hair swinging. "Sad. By the way, nice shirt, Dr. D!" His voice was bright with faux enthusiasm. The shirt was a basic one-pocket tee, navy blue.

"A for the day, Bryce," Dr. Diaz announced. "Anything you'd like to say, Sarah? While I have the grade book open." Not that he did.

"Um, are there assigned seats?" she asked as a few more kids wandered in, including Logan from her English class that morning.

"Take this one." Dr. Diaz pointed to a seat at one of the front two stations. "Your lab partner will be Ethan Steere."

"Lucky girl," someone murmured from behind her, the two words infused with sarcasm.

"If he shows," Beard guy said.

"No need to go to class when you're a member," Eliza said under her breath. "Which is guaranteed if you're a Steere."

"And we're back to that secret society shit. You're obsessed." Logan rolled his eyes.

Sarah had no idea what they were talking about. She was stuck on the name Steere. As in *Steere*? Could Ethan really be part of that family? Her see-it-remember-it memory supplied her with an abundance of info all at once: Grace Steere, leader of the World Health Organization. Winston Steere, her brother, CEO of LJ Martin Levitt. Sam Steere, their cousin, who had his own show on MSNBC. Michael Steere, another cousin, co-founder of Space Station Technologies. She'd seen three of those four names in one place. The *Forbes* list of the most powerful people of 2014. Most powerful in the world. And there had been three more Steeres in the top fifty. Was Ethan part of *that* family?

The overhead lights flashed blue. The school used that to signal the start of class instead of a bell.

"Okay, today we're going to do something a little different," Dr. Diaz said. "We're going back into the big lab, and I want each team to choose a piece of equipment and experiment with it. What *doesn't* it do that would be cool? We're too tempted to be limited by the equipment we have. But if the technology exists, it means that the work that requires the technology already exists. To make breakthroughs we might need to start with our own equipment." He paced as he spoke, his teasing tone gone. He sounded intense and passionate. "I want you to be revolutionaries. I want you to create revolutions. Come up with a modification for your piece of equipment or come up with a whole new piece if you want. Today's an outside-the-box day." He looked over at Sarah and smiled. "Okay, let's get going. And have fun!"

He strode over to a metal door in the back of the room and pressed his finger against the pad to open it. Sarah followed the other kids as they headed in. When she stepped through the doorway, she stopped so abruptly someone ran into her. Sarah glanced over her shoulder. "Sorry," she told Eliza, moving out of the way, her gaze returning to the lab as she matched pieces of equipment she'd only seen in pictures to the real things—an X-ray microanalyzer, a multi-wavelength ellipsometer, and—what she was pretty sure was—a microprocessor-controlled potentiostat.

It took her a second to realize that Dr. Diaz was standing next to her, grinning. "Kind of a nice setup, huh?" he asked.

"Kind of," Sarah repeated in awe.

"Why don't you play around with the STM," he said. "We did an experiment using it last week. This will give you a chance to catch up. There are instructions in the binder next to it, but let me know if you need a hand."

Great googly moogly. The expression had been stuck in her head ever since her interrupted late-night cartoon binge with Karina. But it fit perfectly. She was going to get to use an STM, a fucking scanning tunneling microscope! It could show the individual atoms on the surface of a sample. With the STM, she could do more than look at atoms, she could move them around, *manipulate* them to create a chemical reaction. When she reached the table holding the scope, she couldn't bring herself to touch it, even though she'd lusted after it from the first time she heard about it. It was small. At only eight inches high, compared to the three-and-a-half-foot-tall electron microscope Bryce and his lab partner were using, it didn't look all *that* different from the 30x compound microscope she'd gotten to use at her various schools. But it was worlds away. *Galaxies* away.

Sarah sat down and picked up the binder. *That* she could touch without worry. She didn't want to do anything with the STM until she'd read every word, even though she'd already read everything she could find and probably knew enough to take the scope apart and put it together. She flipped to the first page and read the table of contents, then turned to the next page, which gave the history of the STM. "In the early twentieth century, the developments in quantum mechanics—"

A loud banging on the lab door interrupted Sarah. Dr. Diaz walked over slowly, taking his time, and opened it. Ethan, possibly one of *the* Steeres, came in. He didn't seem at all embarrassed or apologetic about arriving late.

"Diaz," he said as he passed the teacher.

"Steere," Dr. Diaz replied. "You want to fill us in on what you were doing that kept you from being on time? Not that we aren't delighted that you've decided to show today."

"I was in the tunnels under the insane asylum, looking for an escape route," Ethan replied. That got a few snickers, but most people in the class were already caught up in the assignment. Really into it, in a way Sarah hadn't seen much at her old schools.

"Well, you'll be happy to know that when you do make it to class, you won't be without a lab partner anymore. You'll be working with our new student, Sarah Merson. Since she wasn't here for the experiment analyzing a sample with the STM, I'm having her use it today. Fill her in on what she missed. And she can fill you in on today's assignment."

Ethan gave a noncommittal grunt that could mean "fine" or "that sucks" or just "I heard you," and joined Sarah in front of the microscope. He barely even glanced at her. "Put on gloves for starters. And don't breathe on any of the system parts," he said.

Sarah's back stiffened. She knew that. Breath had billions of organic substances. "Hi," she snapped.

Ethan turned to her, plastered a huge fake grin on his face, and said, "Hi! Are you enjoying your time at our wonderful school so far?"

Sarah rolled her eyes. "Do you want to know the assignment or what?" she asked.

"Sounded like my assignment was babysitting you," he replied, dropping the faux enthusiasm. "The first thing you need to do is make the tip. You take—"

"I got it. While I do that, you can start thinking about a way the STM could be improved, something that could lead to a scientific breakthrough." She couldn't keep the excitement out of her voice.

"Look at you. All eager beaver." Ethan sprawled in the chair next to hers. She couldn't help noticing his shirt ride up, showing a sliver of hard belly above his low-slung jeans. He noticed her noticing, and one side of his mouth curved up in a self-satisfied smile.

She took her time moving her gaze away. She wasn't going to let him think she cared that he'd caught her looking. "If advancing our understanding of the world is so boring, why are you here? There are people who'd kill to be in this lab, getting to use this equipment," she shot back in an even voice.

Ethan slapped his hand against his chest. "You've wounded me, but in a way that has opened my eyes. My life will be much more meaningful now that I've befriended a poor but scrappy girl to make me appreciate everything I have."

She *had* sounded like that. Crap. "I have not befriended you." Sarah pulled a pair of latex gloves out of a box on the lab table. "And you know nothing about me."

His ice-blue eyes slowly ran from her off-brand sneakers to her $9.99 haircut. He didn't say anything, but he smirked, like he knew everything he needed to know. Why was Karina with this asshole?

"You can also think of a completely new kind of equipment." Sarah snapped on the gloves. She'd read a breakdown of how to make a tip for the STM and how to prepare a sample. It flashed through her brain vividly, along with the ads that had been scrolling down the side of the screen on the library computer she'd been using at the time.

First she had to prep the tools—wire cutter, tweezers (pointed and rounded), flat-nose pliers. She took them from the drawer to her left. Now she needed the ethanol. Not on the table. Not in the drawer. She glanced around the lab, trying not to be too obvious.

"Need help with something, Sofía?" Ethan drawled.

"It's *Sarah*," she told him snidely. "And no." She'd just spotted a row of cabinets along the far wall. She figured the basic supplies would be there.

"Says 'Sofía' back here." Suddenly his warm fingers were on the back of her neck, sliding under her collar, tucking the tag of her Sofía T-shirt back into place. Sarah froze, praying he didn't know that Sofía was part of Sofía Vergara's exclusive clothing line for Kmart. Flushing, she scrambled to her feet and hurried across the room. She was relieved to find that she'd been right about where to find the ethanol and other stuff she needed.

"So where were you really when class started?" she asked Ethan when she returned to the table. She wanted control of the conversation.

"In the tunnels under the insane asylum, looking for an escape route," he answered, in the same flat, matter-of-fact voice he'd used with Diaz.

4

"Want to get together later and study?" Ethan asked, falling into step with Sarah as they left chemistry a couple of weeks later. He'd started following her out when he bothered to show up to class, and Sarah figured it would be weird not to walk to lunch together, since they pretty much always ate at the same table.

Sarah hadn't thought she would still hang out with Izzy and

Karina once they were done helping her get settled. But they'd made her a real part of their group of friends, including her in everything—including eating basically every meal together. They both still disappeared in the middle of the night once in a while, but they hadn't gone together since that first strange night. A couple mornings a week Izzy was up and out of the room before Sarah and Karina woke up. Karina called it Izzy's "secret assignation," and Sarah figured she didn't need the details.

She glanced over at Ethan. He was almost painfully good-looking—and knew it. Still, sometimes when she was with him, she got a crazy impulse to reach out and trace the perfect shape of his upper lip with one finger.

"By study, you mean you copy my lab notes from the times you were searching for escape routes?" she asked, ignoring the impulse. He still hadn't admitted the real reason he showed up late—or not at all.

"Pretty much," he replied, as they headed to the back exit.

Sarah wished she could just zap him the notes, but she didn't use her laptop in chem lab. Pen and paper was easier because she liked to add sketches of what she was looking at under the 'scope. "Yeah, okay," she answered. He was Karina's boyfriend. And he was her friend. Kind of. In the way an obnoxious guy who was part of your actual group of friends was your friend. It was hard to believe she had a *group* of friends. She'd barely ever managed more than one before the social worker showed up and moved her again. But nobody was coming for her at Sanctuary Bay. She couldn't leave even if she wanted to.

They walked outside and started toward the dining hall. Sarah caught sight of the trees near the path vibrating. Almost immediately, the Puffin lacrosse team burst out of the woods and charged toward the school. She didn't see anyone give a signal, but as one, they dropped to the ground and began doing burpees in perfect unison. It was the lacrosse players she'd seen from her window her first night here. She'd found out their coach believed in workouts at odd hours. He also believed that his team should think of themselves as one being. They had to eat every meal together—and they did that in sync too, every fork up and down at the same time—study together, and socialize together.

The Lobster coach was just as crazy—or crazier—in his own way. There were rumors about him forcing his players to endure extreme physical and psychological pain so that nothing they experienced on the field could distract them. He was supposed to be a genius at discovering their deepest fears and then making the players experience them again and again until they were inoculated against them.

Both coaches mixed up special protein drinks—each with a carefully guarded recipe—for his team. You never saw a Puffin or a Lobster without a sports bottle in the team colors.

"Coffee place at seven?" Ethan asked. He flicked the end of the red scarf Izzy had loaned her. Red and white were Lobster colors, and her roommates were both Lobster fans, which made Sarah's team affiliation a no-brainer. "Obviously you're going to the *big game*." He made it sound like some archaic ritual that he was way too intelligent to believe in.

"Yeah, okay," she said again. "Seven."

"Not so many big words," he begged. "You've got to remember my parents bought my way in here."

Sarah just shook her head. He thought he was being funny, but his parents probably had bought his way in. Not that he was stupid, but he was a slacker, who probably wouldn't have made the cut without the family cash. They could afford it. Turned out he was one of *those* Steeres. After that first class she'd typed "Ethan Steere" into Google and up came a thousand pictures of him at political rallies, red carpet premieres—there was an Oscar-winning actor Steere in the mix too—and fancy charity events. Sarah had never gone to anything that could be called an event. But she was here. At Sanctuary Bay. That was enough. "Since your parents spent the bucks, maybe you should, I don't know, try to make it worth their while," Sarah suggested.

Ethan shrugged. "They'll make whatever donation it takes to get me into Harvard. Got to keep up the family tradition."

"Just flunk out then, if it doesn't make any difference. You hate it here," Sarah snapped. He didn't make that any kind of secret. "Stop going to class completely. Fail every test." He constantly pissed her off, beautiful lips, amazing blue eyes, long, lean body, and all. She could still barely believe that this school had wanted her, but she'd taken Nate's advice and squashed her resentment. The kids here generally seemed to get how good they had it at the academy. Unfortunately Ethan still brought out all her crap, as Nate had called it. He was a rich, entitled idiot and he didn't even know it.

"Flunking out is not part of the Sanctuary Bay educational system," Ethan said.

"So you tried it?"

"Among other things."

"You're an overprivileged, inbred asshole, you know that?" Sarah burst out, unable to contain herself. "You have no idea what the real world is like. You're shitting away a chance other people would kill to have."

"My world is as real as yours is, Sarah," Ethan shot back.

"Whatever. You don't care, why should I? Find some other place to get your notes."

"Not a problem." He held the door to the dining hall open with exaggerated politeness.

Sarah hesitated, frowning, but she couldn't keep just standing there. She brushed past, and the sounds of clattering plates, rushing footsteps, and barked orders enveloped her. Students in long white aprons and hairnets dashed between tables, slamming food down.

"What's going on?" she asked, forgetting for a second that she didn't really want to talk to Ethan ever again in life.

"What do you mean?"

"I mean this." She waved her hands at this chaos. "Why are kids doing the serving?" She noticed the buffet table was missing too.

"Didn't think you'd object to—whatchacallit?—Honest work," Ethan replied.

"That's not what I—" But Ethan was already gone, striding toward their table. Sarah stood still for a moment, confused. The dining hall had always had waiters before, but real ones, not students. Why had it changed?

Slowly, she made her way over to the usual table. Karina, Izzy, and Tif were there with Matthias, a guy from Sarah's history class. Taylor had started eating at another table about a week ago, and Matthias had started eating with them instead. Nobody said why, and Sarah didn't ask. She'd never really known Taylor that well, so why make it an issue? "Why'd they change things around?" she asked her friends.

"Huh?" Tif used one fingertip to push her hamburger off the bun. "Any of you carnivores want it, it's up for grabs." A second later, one of the younger student servers shoved hamburgers in front of Sarah and Ethan, then trotted off as someone from the kitchen yelled, "Move your asses!"

Looks like the daily specials have disappeared too, Sarah thought as she took a bite of the hamburger. Maybe the school always switched things around.

"You think you can sit down next to me like nothing

happened, without even attempting a lame apology?" Karina demanded, glaring at Ethan. "I'm not expecting you to fill my mailbox with orange Tic Tacs or ask if your Boy Scout troop can marry us. I do realize you are, in fact, you, but come on."

Obviously Sarah wasn't the only one who received Ethan's special asshole treatment lately.

"I won't apologize for not agreeing with you, especially when I know, I *know*, that you don't give a rat's ass either way," Ethan retorted. He took a bite of his hamburger.

"I do care. And that you don't know I care is an even bigger problem," Karina cried out, and Matthias began slowly banging his head against the table. Sarah didn't blame him. Karina and Ethan had two modes at meals—basically molesting each other between bites, or fighting.

"Do a couple for me, would you?" Izzy asked. "I don't want to mess up my hair." Matthias agreeably gave a few more head bangs.

"If you would ever listen to me for even two seconds—" Karina began.

Ethan grabbed the half burger left on his plate. "I'm done." He stalked away, leaving Karina fuming.

"I don't understand you, and I'm unusually clever," Izzy told Karina. "Explain to me what you're doing with that guy. He's such a poser. Not to mention you fight every four seconds. And he makes you miserable most of the time. Please, just explain to me."

"I can't explain it to you, because you've never been in love," Karina replied. "Probably because you're so *clever*. You're all brain and no heart."

"And you're like one of those battered women who stay with their abusers," Izzy retorted. "Because they looooove them. All heart and no brain."

Karina gasped. Sarah felt herself stiffen. "Fuck you, Izzy," Karina whispered, all her usual animation drained away.

"Wow, you changed my mind with that well-reasoned argument." Izzy's lips curled into a sneer.

Sarah's gut clenched. She was used to fighting, but usually she didn't care about the people involved. Izzy and Karina had both been really nice to her, and the two of them were usually so close.

Matthias shoved the last of his burger in his mouth. "Gotta get a little studying time in before calc," he mumbled and bolted.

Sarah wished she could go with him. Instead she sat there, trying to come up with something to say that would smooth things over. Nothing came to her. Tif didn't seem to be having any luck either. She just kept chewing on a bite of hamburger bun even though it had to have disintegrated by then.

"Hey, girlies." Nate dropped into the chair vacated by Ethan, putting him between Sarah and Karina. "What's the what?" He gave them The Grin. Sarah smiled back, relieved to have somebody new at the table who might help diffuse the badness. She hadn't talked to Nate too much since that first day, but he'd made sure to check on her a couple of times.

"Just a little discussion on the meaning of love," Tif answered, pushing her black-framed glasses higher up on her nose.

"Can we talk about lacrosse instead?" Nate slowly began to unwind the scarf from around Sarah's throat. "I get that you want to bond with your new roommates." He slid the scarf free. "But the choice of a lacrosse team can't be made lightly." He took off his own scarf, black and white, Puffin colors, wrapped it around her neck, and studied her intensely for a long moment. She flushed as her heart began to beat rapidly and warmth spread throughout her body. "Suits you. That's all I'm saying."

"As our class president, shouldn't you support the Puffins and the Lobsters equally?" Izzy asked. Sarah could still hear a slight strain in her voice.

"I'll provide beers equally to both sides at the Puffin victory party to be held in my suite after the game," he promised, then stood and headed to another table, Sarah's scarf still in his hand.

"He likes you," Karina said when Nate was out of earshot.

"Yeah. That thing with the scarf? *Sexy*." Tif stared after Nate.

They had to be wrong. Although she agreed about the scarf thing—*damn*. But Nate was one of the most popular guys in school. That kind of guy and Sarah? No. "He only talked to me for five seconds," she protested. "Which brings the total to thirty seconds, other than when he and Maya met my ferry. You know Maya? His girlfriend?"

They all stared at her.

"Maya and Nate? They're not together," Tif said. "Not unless they're keeping it some big secret."

Izzy chimed in before Sarah could object again. "I'm no expert on love, my heart being made of ice and all." Izzy shot a hard look at Karina. "But I concur. Nate definitely likes you."

"How's your crazy roommate?" Ethan asked as he dropped into his chair the next day in chemistry, early for once. They were the first ones in the room.

Sarah gave a noncommittal shrug. They were fighting now, but tomorrow—or in an hour—he and Karina would be back together, based on everything Izzy had said and what Sarah had seen so far. It was always a bad idea to get in the middle of an on-and-off relationship.

"You're not speaking to me? Out of sisterly solidarity with Karina or because you're still pissed that I'm not taking full advantage of everything the luck of my birth has given me?" His blue eyes were bright with amusement.

She *was* still disgusted with his sense of entitlement. But she wasn't going to let him think she cared enough to still be angry.

"I'm not getting into some thing between you and Karina, that's all," she answered. She was also really, really trying not to get into some thing between Karina and Izzy. They'd gone to the game together, and it was okay, since there wasn't a lot of talking time, but at the party in Nate's suite they'd avoided each other. And Nate? The guy who supposedly liked her? He'd brought her a beer—that's it. He seemed to be everywhere at once, making sure everyone was having fun, except for those long slow dances he'd had with Maya, half of them to fast songs. He was nice to Sarah, but only in the way he was with everyone else. Obviously Karina, Izzy, and Tif were imagining things.

"Fair enough," Ethan said. "Hey, I was thinking, since you don't want to give me notes, how about if I bought them? I get some nice stuff in care packages, so I can trade for pretty much anything you want."

"Of course. *Of course* you think that would be the solution. You know, not everything can be . . ." Her words trailed off as she noticed the smile tugging at Ethan's lips; goddamn those perfect lips of his. "You're messing with me."

He laughed. "You just make it *so* easy. And you're cute when your eyes get all squinty and mad."

"They don't get squinty," she muttered.

He leaned closer and studied her face. "You prefer beady? Or maybe—"

His cell burped, just as Sarah's gave a beep. She hadn't customized the ringtones yet. She pulled it out of her pocket and tapped the screen to open the new text. Ethan got his open a few seconds before she did, and the little moans and gasps from her cell echoed the ones from his.

At first Sarah thought somebody had managed to send a porn clip to everyone, but then she realized the woman she was looking at was a teacher she'd seen in the halls. And the other woman getting down and dirty with her was Maya. Maya from the boat. Maya, Nate's girlfriend.

"Nice technique," Ethan observed, grinning.

"Seriously? That's what you think when you see this?" Sarah cried.

"Am I about to get yet another lecture on the correlation be-tween wealth and the lack of morals?" he asked. "I don't see you turning it off."

She *had* been staring as her brain processed. Maya and a teacher on the desk in a classroom. "I'm just—"

"Ho-ly shit," Bryce said as he walked into the room, cell in hand. Eliza was a few steps behind him, staring at her cell too. "What is it about a freckled ass?" Bryce continued. "It makes me want to play connect-the-dots with my tongue."

Eliza slapped him on the back of the head, and Sarah looked back at her cell. "Who was filming this?" she asked. "It's like they don't even know they're being watched." She glanced around the chemistry room. Were there cameras hidden somewhere?

As she returned her gaze to her phone, the screen went black. "Now I know why Ms. Winston never flirted back," Logan said, waving his cell as he came in. "She's on the other team."

"Yeah, that's it," Eliza snarked. "There's no other possible rea-son for a woman not to flirt with you."

"Where's the rewind?" Bryce asked.

Nate. The thought exploded in Sarah's mind. He must be mortified. She tried to imagine how it would feel to find out your girlfriend was cheating on you, everyone titillated by the sex or gossip or both, staring at you, trying to gauge your reaction. Had he had any idea something was going on with Maya? He and Maya had just been all over each other at his party.

"It's probably because Ms. Winston is judging the next debate," Eliza commented.

"Oh come on," Bryce scoffed. "She's a total TILF."

"No other reason necessary," Logan agreed.

"Maya's never gone girl before," Eliza said. "I think there's definitely another reason."

"What does the debate have to do with anything?" Sarah asked Ethan.

He shrugged. "I don't follow the soap opera that is Sanctuary Bay."

He really can be a superior snot, Sarah thought. *I bet he's as curious as everyone else, but doesn't want to admit it.*

Eliza answered for him. "Ms. Winston is judging the debate on Friday, and Maya's going up against Derick Kuok, and he's never lost."

"You think Maya would screw somebody just to win?" Maya was a rule-following, good-girl type. And boffing a teacher was not exactly rule-following, good-girl behavior.

"Maya's killer competitive," Logan said. "And the debate coach is worse than Coach Edwards." Worse than the Lobsters' coach? That was saying something.

"Oooh, or maybe it's a secret society thing," Eliza went on, eyes wide. "They must have crazy pranks. The Skull and Bones society at Yale makes its members do insane stuff before they graduate and become presidents and moguls and whatnot."

Logan snorted. "That whole thing is a myth."

"No, it's not. I heard it's called something like the Wolf Den. Only a few people get invited to join each year."

"Anyone else need more proof than a rumor?" Logan asked, glancing around. "You believe in the POW ghost too, Eliza?"

Eliza shot a speculative glance at Ethan. "What do *you* think?" she asked him.

Sarah turned to watch him along with everyone else. If there was some elite club that guaranteed postgrad wealth and power, she wanted in, and Ethan would know about it.

"I think Maya's just getting her rocks off," Ethan replied.

Eliza rolled her eyes. "Maybe. If there *was* a secret society here, I should be in it. So it probably doesn't exist."

The blue light flashed to signal the start of class. Dr. Diaz and the last few kids came in a few moments later. "I have your tests graded," Dr. Diaz said, dropping his battered leather satchel on his desk. He pulled out a stack of papers. "Nice work, all of you. Although it looks like I need to spend a little more time going over SN2 reactions," he added as he began passing out the tests.

"Come on, Diaz. You're not actually going to pretend that we haven't all just seen that sex tape," Bryce said.

"That won't be covered on the next exam," Dr. Diaz replied. He put Sarah's test on the table in front of her, facedown. She flipped it over. Perfect score. Pride swelled inside her. Her memory gave her a massive advantage, but it wasn't as if she had the answer to all the possible stereoisomers of a specific molecule stored in her brain. That came from understanding the concepts, not memorization.

Her happiness drained out of her when she saw the note Dr. Diaz had scribbled at the top of the page: "Sarah, please see me after class." She knew what that meant. She'd dealt with it before. He thought the charity case couldn't possibly have gotten a hundred without cheating. She'd thought he was different. So in love with the subject, so eager to pass his enthusiasm on to them, to make them believe they had it in them to be original thinkers with the capacity to make a scientific leap that could change everything. But he was just like her old teachers. He didn't think someone like her could be anything but average—if she was lucky.

But she'd aced that test. Even if he decided to give her a big, fat zero for cheating, she knew that she'd gotten the A because she'd deserved it.

It seemed like hours before the pink light flashed, indicating the end of class. "You coming?" Ethan asked.

"I'll see you over there. I need to ask Dr. Diaz a question."

"Just make sure to keep your pants on," Ethan teased, letting his eyes run down her body in such an intimate way he might as well have been peeling her clothes off. To her annoyance, Sarah felt her skin flush in response. She couldn't think of a good comeback before he grabbed his backpack and headed for the door.

At least she knew what she wanted to say to Dr. Diaz. "I didn't cheat," she announced as soon as everyone else had gone. "Not that anything I say will convince you. You've made up your mind." He looked startled.

"Back up. Who said anything about cheating?" he asked.

"That's what you want to see me about, right?" Sarah picked up her test and pointed to his note. "I'm sure you've read my file, and there's plenty in there about what a huge cheater I am. You know foster kids can't actually achieve anything. We're all damaged losers, right? Attitude problems, drug use, learning disabilities, we've got them all."

"Back up," Dr. Diaz said again. He walked over and sat down in Ethan's chair. "Where are you getting this? All my note said is that I wanted to talk to you."

"About how I could have possibly gotten a perfect score."

"Sarah, for someone with such an aptitude for science, you're awfully good at jumping to conclusions. Your test did make me want to talk to you, yes, because I'm curious about what plans you have after graduation. If you're interested in majoring in chemistry or considering med school in the future, we ought to discuss the classes you should take in your senior year. If there's anything you feel shaky on that's a prerequisite, I could help you get up to speed. I know you switched schools several times, and even for an excellent student that can leave gaps."

Sarah let out a long sigh that felt like it came from deep in her belly. She opened her mouth to answer, but didn't know what to say. Guess I'm not done leaving all my crap behind, she thought ruefully. "Sorry."

"Can you tell me what all that was about?" he asked gently.

"It's just . . . It's happened before. When I've done really well on a test," she said. "Some teachers assumed I cheated. Even though I would read chem books for fun. The first time I was sitting next to a kid who got a hundred too. A kid who every-one knew was really smart with a nice PTA mom. The teacher was sure I copied. Then it got in the file."

"And the file followed you everywhere. I won't lie, I saw it," Dr. Diaz said. "But what I got from your records was that you were strong and determined, as well as exceptionally bright. You had so many strikes against you, changing homes, changing schools, but it didn't stop you from achieving."

Sarah hesitated. Should she tell him about her memory? "Thanks," she said. "But I . . . I didn't have trouble with school-work even though I changed schools so much. I have a kind of strange brain. I can remember basically everything, all the text-books, and that helps."

Dr. Diaz narrowed his eyes, studying her. "When you say you remember *everything* . . . "

"Everything I've read, everything that's happened to me. Even stuff from when I was really little," Sarah explained. "I told the teachers that all along, but they said it had to be my imagination, that I can't possibly have memories from when I was two or three. I do, though. Vivid ones. I remember the tag on this stuffed animal I had, even though I lost it at the playground when I was in preschool. It said, 'Under penalty of law, this tag not to be removed except by consumer. All new material consisting of polyester fib—'"

"One second." Dr. Diaz got up and rooted around in his backpack.

"I guess I could have memorized that off some toy last month. It doesn't prove anything. But I remember it from when I was a kid. Before I'd even heard the word 'polyester.' Before I knew how to write. I remembered the shapes of the letters, and later, when I knew how to read, I understood what it had said."

Dr. Diaz sat back down and handed her a paperback called *The River Why*. "Ever read this?"

"Never even heard of it," Sarah answered.

"Great book. Covers all the big stuff—philosophy and fishing." He opened it to a page in the middle and handed it to her. "Read a page for me."

"You mean out loud?"

"No, just to yourself. I want to try a little experiment. If you don't mind," he added quickly.

"You don't believe me."

Dr. Diaz sighed. "I'm not doing too well with you, am I? I believe you. I believe everything you've told me. I think you might have something called hyperthymesia, perhaps combined with an eidetic memory."

"Eidetic is a photographic memory. I've definitely got that. But what's hyperthymesia?" Sarah asked. She remembered every word she'd ever seen, but she'd never seen that one.

"It's where a person can recall every day of their life in extreme detail," Dr. Diaz explained. "The temporal and the parietal lobes are significantly larger in people with HSAM, hyperthymesia, than those in the average person. They're the parts of the brain linked to autobiographical memory."

"Sounds like me," Sarah said.

"I've never met someone with a brain like yours. Honestly, I'm curious to see it in action, that's all. It's the scientist in me, or the doctor, I guess. You know I'm also the school doctor, right?"

"Yeah." Sarah had read the bios of all her teachers on the school intranet and so knew them by heart.

"I didn't mean to sound like I was doubting you. It's not that."

"It's okay." She'd never had a teacher apologize to her before.

"I've read that having an exceptional memory can sometimes be a burden. That people can get a little lost in their memories," Dr. Diaz commented.

"Tell me about it," Sarah said with a laugh. Now that she knew he didn't think she was crazy, the words rushed out. "It can be intense. Sometimes it's like I'm reliving the memories, with full-on smells and tastes and sensations. They almost overpower me. In my file it says people thought I was on drugs or having seizures, but that's why. I have some . . . not good memories, and when they come back, sometimes I react like they're actually happening again. Anyway . . ." She turned her attention to the book, read a page, then handed it to him, and began to recite.

"Word perfect," he said. "So was it like you were seeing the words again?"

She nodded.

"Fascinating." He smiled. "I hope you don't feel like a lab rat."

"As long as my eyes haven't turned pink, I'm okay," she said. "Actually, it's good to talk about it this way, like it's science, instead of like I'm a freak."

"I'll tell you something I've figured out as a high school teacher and as a former teenager. Everyone feels like a freak sometimes, especially at your age," Dr. Diaz said. "It gets better, but it never completely goes away. I speak from experience."

Sarah tried to keep the skepticism off her face. Ethan was too arrogant to think of himself as a freak. Izzy was too. And Karina? How could someone so beautiful, somebody everyone in school loved, feel freaky? Or someone as popular as Nate, even with his screwed-up, pre-Sanctuary Bay life?

Dr. Diaz grinned. "Some people have a better façade than others, but get to know someone, really know them, and you'll see." He stood up. "Go eat lunch. I've kept you too long. We'll talk about your college plans another time, anytime you want. I'm around. As you know, we're on an island."

"Okay. Sounds good." Sarah grabbed her stuff and started toward the door.

"And Sarah," Dr. Diaz called after her. She looked over her shoulder. "We can talk about other stuff too. Like if your memories start feeling overwhelming. Or if you just need help navigating Sanctuary Bay."

"Thanks," she said, and she meant it.

Sarah glanced at the Board in the hall outside her last class. There were more kids around it than usual, snickering at the latest messages about Maya and Ms. Winston. It was all anyone had been talking about.

Don't they get that these people are real? she wondered. She kept thinking about Nate. She hadn't seen him since the text bomb. They didn't have any classes together, and he was a no-show at lunch.

She couldn't resist pulling her cell from her pocket when she reached the main staircase. As she climbed, she opened the map. There was a function that could show the location of anyone at the school. She hesitated. It felt like an invasion of privacy. But everyone else seemed to use it all the time.

When she reached the first landing, she lowered her voice and said, "Locate Nate."

"Basement stairwell main building," the cell replied.

Sarah glanced down at the screen. There was a purple dot, her, and then a yellow dot, showing Nate's location near the main entrance.

Then he vanished.

Sarah blinked in surprise. "Locate Nate," she said again.

The cell was silent for a long moment, her own purple dot pulsing alone on the screen. Finally it spoke. "Student offline."

5

Sarah shoved herself out of bed. She'd tried mind-over-bladder to convince herself she didn't have to pee so she could stay snuggled under her comforter, but it hadn't worked. *Something's off*, she thought, frowning as she started for the door.

She was alone. Karina's bed was empty. So was Izzy's. Did they sneak off together again? Were they back to being friends? She grabbed her cell off the night table and checked the time. Almost one. She hesitated, then said, "Locate Karina."

A yellow dot appeared on the screen, moving across the back lawn toward the dining hall. At least it had come up. Nate's had never returned after it vanished from the screen earlier. "Locate

Izzy," she said. A second dot appeared next to the first. What were they doing out there in the middle of the night?

None of my business, she thought. She hurried to the bathroom, grimacing as her bare feet found one of the floor's icy cold spots, then returned to her room. Her empty room.

Seriously, where were they? They told her everything else. Why would they sneak out without her? Sarah's mind buzzed with possibilities, but nothing made sense. The whole school had thrown her off balance lately, from the unexplained dining hall changes to the student-teacher sex. Not to mention Nate's on-and-off flirting, and Ethan's annoying hotness.

But Izzy and Karina were the worst part. She liked them. She wanted to trust them. But how could she when they didn't tell her the truth? Sarah hated uncertainty. She needed to know where she stood with people; it's how she survived.

"Screw it," she muttered. She yanked on a pair of jeans and one of her old sweatshirts. The pale gray sweater that used to be Izzy's would be too easy to see in the dark. As soon as she jammed on her sneakers, she left, her eyes glued to the dots moving across the screen of her cell. Karina and Izzy were at the edge of the woods.

Sarah trotted down the two sets of stairs and out the back exit. The teachers took turns as dorm monitors, but they were all pretty lax about it. Maybe they figured there wasn't much trouble to get into on an island.

Frost had covered the grass and moisture soaked through the thin canvas of her shoes in seconds. She shivered. She was crazy to be out here at this hour. She should go climb back under her warm covers and leave her roommates alone to do . . . whatever it was they were doing.

But she kept going. Even when she entered the woods and

realized the trees were so thick in places she didn't have a glimmer of moonlight to guide her, she continued. Finally, when she'd walked the forest equivalent of a couple of blocks, the dots on her cell stopped.

Sarah slowed her pace as she closed in on them. Each time a pine bough slapped at her or her foot landed on a stick, she was sure they were going to hear. And what then? How would she explain being out here? Why *was* she out here?

Because it's too fucking weird for the two of them to be in the woods in the middle of the night, that's why, Sarah thought. She had to know what they were doing.

She crept forward. A yellow light glowed from between the tree branches, and she heard a soft scraping sound followed by a muffled thump. Sarah inched closer—scrape thump, scrape thump—and saw that she'd almost reached a clearing. She pressed her body tightly behind the rough trunk of one of the pines.

Torches. The first thing she saw was actual torches with flames. Three of them were stuck into the ground, casting a flickering light over a clearing around an enormous pine tree, one that towered over the others. Izzy and Karina stood beneath it with Nate. The scrape and thump she'd heard was someone—a guy Sarah didn't know—digging a deep hole, long and narrow.

Sarah's heart lurched against her ribs. A grave.

Maybe the cat she'd seen hanging around the Admin building had died and they were burying it, she thought wildly, desperate for some sort of normal explanation. The hole was too big for a cat though. Way too big.

Suddenly another sound came from the forest. Footsteps.

Sarah pressed herself closer to the tree trunk, the coarse wood biting into her flesh even through her sweatshirt. Four boys appeared from the shadows at the far end of the clearing. On their shoulders, they carried a coffin.

As they moved across the clearing past Sarah's hiding spot, she heard a scratching, scrabbling sound, followed by a muted scream. Someone was in there! Sarah's eyes darted back to Izzy, Karina, and Nate. They just stood there. No horror on their faces. No cries of protest.

They only watched, calm and silent, as the coffin was lowered into the grave, the screams from inside growing louder, and as the boy with the shovel began covering the coffin with earth. Burying someone alive.

Sarah stumbled away from the tree, horrified. She had to get out of here. But her feet crunched on a broken branch on the ground, and Nate's head jerked in her direction. Terrified, Sarah froze. Nate's caramel eyes met hers, no trace of warmth in them. He signaled to two of the boys who'd carried the coffin, and they started toward her.

Sarah whipped around and ran, but they were on her in seconds. One of them yanked her hands behind her back and tied them together. "Get off me!" Sarah screamed. Something was tossed over her head, then a wad of cloth was jammed into her mouth. A pair of hands grabbed each of her shoulders, and she was half pushed, half dragged through the woods. She fought, twisting, trying to dig her heels into the ground, but her sneakers just slid on the slippery pine needles, and the boys were too strong.

It wasn't until the ground smoothed out that she was even sure they were taking her in the direction of the school. They had to be moving across the back lawn now. But even if she could scream, there was no one to hear her. It was too late for anyone to be out. Except the people who'd snatched her.

What were they going to do to her? She'd seen them bury someone alive! Would they kill her too?

The guys slowed, and Sarah heard a door open. Were they taking her back into the school? Maybe they would just throw her in her room and tell her to keep her mouth shut if she didn't want to end up in a hole in the woods too.

But instead of pulling her over to the stairs and up, she was yanked through another door not too far from the first one. "Stairs," one of them grunted. Soon she was being roughly steered down a set of steps, then across a wide room. Their footsteps echoed.

They stopped, and Sarah heard a key jiggling in a lock, then a squeak of hinges. "Stairs," he said again. The hands on her shifted. It felt like only one person was behind her now, with one hand digging into each shoulder.

"I'll go first," one of them said. They started down again, the air growing colder and colder, chilling her through.

These steps were bumpy and uneven under her feet, unlike the first set. While the room had felt cavernous, the stairway felt narrow and claustrophobic. Her arms brushed against the walls. They were wet, and there was the smell of decay. Where the fuck were they?

The steps ended and she was taken down a hallway. She heard a metallic clang, and then she was shoved, hard, sending her sprawling to her knees. "Wait here until we figure out what to do with you." There was another clang, and the sound of footsteps moving away.

Sarah used her tongue to work the wad of cloth out of her mouth, choking and coughing. She jerked her head back and forth until her head covering fell off. It was somebody's jacket.

Sarah struggled to her feet. It was hard without being able to use her hands for support. She stood in a ragged stone cell with a door made of rusty bars. A large, tarnished lock held it closed.

Panic started to overwhelm her, but she forced it down. *Hands first*, she told herself. She tried to get control over her ragged breathing as she gently twisted her wrists back and forth. Slowly, steadily, the binding was loosening. A few more twists and it fell to the floor, also stone. The whole cell had been hacked out of a massive hunk of rock.

That first day Karina had mentioned something like this. Sarah took a deep breath, and each of Karina's exact words came back to her. "The school is built over the remains of a POW camp from World War Two. At one point it got blasted to bits by a bomb, and the whole operation was moved into the bomb shelter underneath. They made it bigger, carved rooms right out of the stone. Nazi soldiers were kept here during the war. Actual Nazis. Their cells are still down there."

So that's where she was, trapped under the school. She circled the small room. Damp, phosphorescent patches of mold gave the walls a faint, sickly yellow glow and a tiny sliver of moonlight beamed in from a slit high above her. *The room must go straight through to one of the cliffs over the ocean*, she thought. Not that it was of any help to Sarah, but it was something.

Avoiding the mold, she sat down in the middle of the cell. She needed a plan. Nobody would hear her scream, not with the ocean pounding against the rocks. But eventually someone would come for her, unless they decided to let her starve down here. Which maybe they would, since they'd already buried somebody else alive.

She shivered. No, she couldn't think that way. Someone would come for her. And they'd have to come into the cell to get her. The door wasn't that wide. Maybe two of them could get through at the same time. She needed some kind of weapon. Her eyes darted around. All this stone, but not a loose rock anywhere.

Maybe she could convince them she wouldn't say anything, that she wasn't a threat. She could tell them the truth. That the school was her one shot at a decent life, that all she wanted was to graduate and she wouldn't do anything to screw that up, including running to the dean with a story she probably wouldn't believe.

Nate was class president. Karina was the daughter of a Hollywood power couple. Izzy was the daughter of high-level Boston society types. Who would believe Sarah's word over theirs?

Nobody.

And maybe, for once in her life, that was a good thing. She was powerless. If she could make them see that there was no way she could hurt them, they'd let her go. They could move the body. There'd be no evidence that she could point to. Except that there'd be a person missing, but that wasn't any kind of proof. It could've been some guy who worked in the kitchen that nobody even knew. Or a janitor. Someone unimportant. Someone no one would care about. Someone like her.

No one will come looking for me, Sarah thought. Izzy and Karina can say I fell off Suicide Cliff, and that will be that.

She pushed the thought away. She had to focus on staying positive.

So that was the plan. She'd start talking as soon as she heard someone coming toward the cell. She forced herself to believe—even though they had thoroughly conned her—that Karina and Izzy wouldn't hurt her, not if they didn't have to. Nate either.

She shifted, trying to get comfortable on the hard floor, and something moved under her butt. She reached down, pulling free something long and narrow. A branch? She held it up to the faint light. A bone.

Sarah hurled it at the wall, unable to stop a horrified scream from clawing its way out of her throat. Maybe it was a prisoner's. It could be decades old. She had no reason to think there'd been another student left to die in the cell. She leaned forward, studying the bone from a distance. It looked old and human. *From a prisoner*, she told herself. *It's definitely from a prisoner. That's what makes the most sense.* She wrapped her arms around herself as tightly as she could and pulled her hands inside the sleeves of her sweatshirt, but a shudder still ripped through her body.

Sarah squeezed her eyes shut. Maybe it would help if she didn't have to look at her prison. *Wait!* Her cell. She could call someone for help. She pulled her cell from her pocket. "Call Dr. Diaz."

No signal.

Of course. Even with all the cell towers, there wouldn't be a signal this far down into the stone of the island.

A groan suddenly echoed, pulling her from her thoughts. It wasn't like the moans she'd heard that night on the cliff. It was possible to believe those low, soft sounds could be wind in a cave. This groan was human. She was certain of it.

Was it the spirit of the man who'd become so desperate he killed himself? Was that why it was freezing down here, because so many men had died down in these holes, their spirits trapped in the prison that had held their bodies? If one ghost could make a cold spot, why couldn't hundreds turn the whole area icy?

Her whole body started to shake, so she hugged herself tighter, taking a deep breath. Her imagination was taking over. She wasn't in danger from the spirits of the dead. She was in danger from cold-blooded killers. The moan came again, and Sarah couldn't stop her thoughts from ricocheting back to the prisoner. Had he died instantly, smashed on the rocks? Or had the ocean sucked him away while he was still alive? Had it taken hours for him to drown, his bleeding body growing weaker and weaker as he struggled to the surface again and again for another breath?

At some point exhaustion must have claimed her because when she opened her eyes, the pale light of early morning shone down into her cell from the narrow opening high above her. How long were they going to leave her here? Her eyes caught on the bone. Had they decided not to come back until she was dead, until the flesh had rotted off her bones?

Sarah pushed herself to her feet, her legs cramped from hours on the cold, hard floor. For the first time, she could see the details of her surroundings. Despite the chill, droplets of sweat slid down her back.

What had happened here?

Someone had been tortured, had his mind completely destroyed. Every centimeter of the stone walls and floor had been carved with jagged, meandering letters and numbers, some crossed out with long, deep slashes.

One section was a calendar. Another might be a poem. Sarah wasn't sure. The way the lines of words were arranged made it seem likely, but they were all in German so she couldn't be positive. And etched into the floor, right along the base of the wall and running the entire circumference, was the same word, over and over and over, sometimes big, sometimes small, sometimes almost illegible.

Bromcyan.

Bromcyan.

Bromcyan.

She crouched down and traced one of the "B"s. Her fingertip ran over something sharp. Sarah leaned closer. Something was imbedded in the stone, something small and pale. She pried it free, holding it up to study it. It was a piece of fingernail stained with blood.

Bile rose in her throat. Could these words have been *clawed* into the stone? Was that even possible? How desperate would someone have to be to do that? To dig that word into the wall so many times. Bromcyan.

I have to get out of here. Now.

Sarah felt like she was trapped, not inside a stone cell, but inside an insane mind. And if she had to stay there much longer, she'd go insane herself.

6

Sarah sat with her eyes closed, but now that she knew the words were there, it was like she could see them, feel them, everywhere. They're from a long time ago, she told herself. The man who wrote them is dead. She couldn't help feeling like it was the same prisoner who'd killed himself. The room vibrated with desperation and despair and psychosis. Death would have felt like relief to any man trapped in here.

The man was a Nazi, she reminded herself. *I'm feeling all this pity for a Nazi.*

Maybe Bromcyan was the name of his town in Germany. Or the name of someone he knew that died. Or that he killed. The way the word repeated meant it had to be deeply meaningful to him. But none of that stopped her horror—whoever he'd been, he'd lost his mind here.

Maybe Bromcyan was his last name. Maybe he was trying to hold on to his identity, his sense of self, as the insanity began to take hold. Sarah felt like she was exposing herself to his insanity, poisoning herself, with every breath.

When were they going to let her out of here? And what were they going to do?

She slowly looked around the cell again, this time ignoring the strange markings on the wall. Had she missed something she could use as a weapon? There was the bone. She could inflict pain with that somehow. Or . . . What else? She could tear up her sweatshirt and use the bone to shove pieces of cloth through the small slit in the rock. If someone on the outside saw them, maybe—

Crazy. No one would see them. All that was down there was spiky rocks, not soft sand that anyone would want to stroll on.

The sound of approaching footfalls interrupted her thoughts. Two figures in dark hooded robes that brushed the floor moved up to the cell door.

Her executioners.

"Look, I don't care what you did. Being here, at this school, is a way to change my life. That's all I care about. I'm not going to tell anyone anything," she babbled. "Just let me go and I'll pretend none of it ever happened."

Neither of them answered. One slid a key—an old-fashioned one with three teeth and a curlicue handle—into the lock and opened the door. They both rushed in. Sarah lunged for the bone, but didn't reach it before they each grabbed one of her arms.

The boys—Sarah was almost sure they were boys—marched her down a narrow corridor in silence. They turned a corner and entered a large room carved out of the rock. Torches burning in holders on the walls revealed two lines of figures, all in maroon— the color so dark it was almost black—hooded robes.

"I already told these two, I don't care what you did last night. I won't say anything. Izzy? Karina?" She searched for a sign of recognition among the hooded people. "You know me. You know what my life was like before I came here. All I care about is graduating and getting a chance at something better. Even if

I did say something, who would believe me? No one." She could hear the panic rising in her voice, and swallowed hard.

She scanned the room, searching for an escape route. Her eyes locked on a towering form at the far end of the room. It was made of bones, hundreds of them, some stained with dried blood the way the fingernail in her cell had been. A cluster of skulls had been lashed together to create a giant head. The mouth, open in a howl, was lined with teeth made of jagged rocks. Bones had been roped together with seaweed to form arms, and the enormous fingers were made of ribs. More seaweed wrapped around the bones creating the torso, and there were ragged pieces of cloth and leather tangled in it. Sarah realized one was a red armband with a swastika on it, and a shudder ripped through her.

Dread overwhelmed her as she was forced to kneel before the grotesque figure. At eye level she saw a dull gold pin on one of the strips of cloth, a bird on the top, another swastika below that, and a submarine at the bottom. The whole thing was ringed with a garland of leaves.

German U-boat insignia, she guessed. The cloth is scraps of a German prisoner's uniform. It reminded Sarah of an immense voodoo doll or something from an ancient Druid ritual. Except for the Nazi stuff. Paying attention to the details helped push down her terror.

A chant started up behind her. "Heil, Jager! Heil, Jager! Heil, Jager!" The words grew louder, turning to shrieks, as a new robed figure arrived. His or her robe was different. More elaborate. Black velvet, and hooded, with a belt made of seaweed studded with what looked like human teeth.

The figure stopped next to Sarah, and faced the lines of chanting people. "Heil, Jager! Heil, Jager!"

The hysteria in their voices set Sarah's heart skittering in her chest. They sounded frenzied, like a mob barely under control.

All she wanted to do was run. Adrenaline was surging through her body, but she didn't see any exit in front of her, and behind her were those rows of crazed people. If they attacked, she'd never get by them.

The black-robed figure raised his hands, and the crowd instantly went silent.

"Why do we gather here today?" The voice was a booming echo.

Nate.

Before last night, he'd seemed like a guy who had turned his life around, someone who'd made her think it might be possible for her too. Why was he involved in this? Why were any of them?

"We gather to renew our spirits and our strength," voices answered solemnly, as if the stone room was a church.

"And what is it that has the power to renew our strength?" Nate demanded.

"Blut und Knochen," came the reply.

"Yes, *Blut* and *Knochen.* Blood and bone." He used two fingers to beckon someone forward. One of the maroon-robed followers approached and held a clay bowl at the base of Sarah's throat. Her heart seized.

Enough.

Sarah leaped to her feet. Immediately dozens of hands were on her, pushing her back to the ground, pinning her ankles to the stone floor, clamping both sides of her head, restraining her hands behind her back. The bowl was repositioned at the base of her neck.

Nate turned and bowed low to the horrendous sculpture, then straightened. He reached into the bone chest and withdrew a knife, the blade jagged on both sides, reminding Sarah of the serrated teeth of the thing's mouth.

"We honor the sacrificed by taking their blood and bone into us, and they gift us with the vigor and vitality of the spirit released," Nate intoned. He stepped up to Sarah and rested the knife against her throat. She tried to jerk her head away, but the hands holding it were like a vise. Her breath came in harsh gasps, each breath drawing her throat harder against the knife.

He was going to slice her throat. They were going to drink her blood out of the bowl. Then gnaw on her bones. And no one would know. No one would even care that she was gone. She had no parents, no family, nobody to notice that Sarah Merson had vanished from the earth. She squeezed her eyes shut, promising herself she wouldn't cry. And she didn't. Even when the blade pierced her flesh, and a trickle of her blood ran down her neck and into the bowl, she still did not cry.

"If we drink of your blood, you will become one of us," Nate told her. "You will become part of the pack. But first you must prove yourself worthy. You must trust us with your darkest secret. It will be recorded in the sacred scrolls, along with the secrets of every member from now to the very first pack."

Pack. He'd used that word twice. Sarah brought back the words Eliza had spoken: "Maybe it's a secret society thing. They must have crazy pranks. The Skull and Bones society at Yale makes its members do insane stuff before they graduate and become presidents and moguls and whatnot."

Was that what this was? A secret society? Was what she'd seen in the woods a prank?

Sarah struggled to get her breathing under control. They weren't going to sacrifice her to their freaky god. She was safe.

She'd read an article in a magazine once about secret societies throughout history. It talked about the Skull and Bones, plus the Freemasons, Rosicrucians, the Illuminati. Groups of influential people bound to one another in secret, able to achieve incredible success in everything they did. What Eliza said was true—the members of these societies went on to be the most powerful people in the world. This was a secret society, one at the most exclusive school in the country, and they wanted *her* to join. The school was a ticket to a better life. But the society would be a ticket to something phenomenal.

Nate flicked one finger, and the bowl was pulled away from Sarah's throat. She was lifted back to her feet. "Will you make your confession? Or will you leave now and never speak of this again?"

"Confession," Sarah answered. If that's what it took to get in, she'd do it.

"Confession." The hooded figures repeated in low whispers.

Nate put his hands on her shoulders. The low-hanging hood hid his eyes, but he gave her a reassuring squeeze as he turned her to face the group. "Begin," he instructed.

What was she going to say? What was her deep, dark secret? That she shopped at Walmart—when she got to buy something new? That she'd gotten bounced from home to home because . . . because who knew why? Because she wasn't good enough. Because she was damaged.

"Begin," Nate said again, a harsh edge in his voice now.

"I'm a freak." The words rushed out, surprising her. "My brain. It's not normal. I remember everything. Even from when I was just a baby. No one believes me, but it's true. Sometimes it's not even like I'm remembering. It's like, like I'm thrown back in time, back into something that happened to me in the past. I can see it all, but not just that. Smells, tastes, sounds— whatever I experienced then, I experience again. There are times I think I'm crazy. More times, it's others who think I'm crazy. Or lying. Or on drugs. So, not such great recommendations for my college application, right?"

She gave a slightly hysterical laugh. No one responded. They were waiting. What else did they want? She went for the darkest moment of her life.

"When I was not even four, I saw my parents murdered right in front of me. I remember every detail. I've *experienced* it again, and again, and again. People say it's impossible. They say there's no way a three-year-old could remember anything. But it isn't. Not for me." Her voice began to waver, but she pressed on. "It was like an execution. This man made them get on their knees and shot them. I don't know why. And so I don't know who my parents really were. You don't get shot like that, all cold and professional, if you're just Mr. and Mrs. Suburbs, right? And my dad had told me to hide in the air-conditioning vent. He made sure I knew what to do in every hotel room we went to. Like he knew it might happen. We kept moving from place to place, and he set up all the rooms the same way and made me go over the rules. So, that's my secret. I'm a freak, with a freak brain, who had parents that might have been truly bad people." She choked in a breath, her whole body suddenly feeling drained, spent.

"We accept the confession." Nate stepped up next to her. "If you join us, Sarah, you will never be alone again. We will be your family and you will be ours."

She would have connections to the people in this room for the rest of her life. They would help her create a life she hadn't even dreamed about. She nodded. "I want to."

"First, you must pledge your loyalty. Do you vow to put the commands of the Jager before your own desires?" Nate asked.

"I do," Sarah answered. The air around her felt like it was

crackling with electricity. It was as if the attention everyone was focusing on her had taken on a physical form.

"Do you vow to put your brothers and sisters, your packmates, before all others?"

"I do," Sarah replied. They had chosen her, and she would never forget that.

"Do you vow to guard the secrets of the Wolfpack, including its very existence, from all others?" Nate, her Jager, asked.

"I do." She would never betray them. Betraying them would be betraying herself.

"We honor our newest Wolfpack member by allowing her to take the Blutgrog with us. She honors us, by sharing her blood." He raised the clay bowl up to her lips. Dazed, Sarah realized it was filled with liquid, dark and oily, the drops of her own blood somewhere in the mix. Nate rested one hand on her head. "Drink and be one with us."

Sarah didn't hesitate. She opened her lips, allowing some of the liquid to be poured into her mouth. It sent a bolt of fire down her throat and into her belly as she swallowed. Instantly, the hands released her, and someone helped her to stand.

Every sensation became magnified. Her heartbeat turned to a drumbeat in her ears, and she could feel it pulsing in her throat, inside her wrists, behind her knees. She could feel the blood cells bouncing off her veins and arteries running through her entire body. The awareness of the individual hairs on her head made her scalp prickle. The seams of her jeans felt like thin metal wires running up and down her legs. The inside of her sneakers felt porous. And she swore she could even feel the individual molecules of air brushing against the inside of her nose, tickling when they reached her lungs.

She could feel *everything*.

And the smells! She could smell the salt and rot of the seaweed, the metallic tang of the dried blood on the monstrous sculpture, the chalky scent of old bones, a dozen kinds of perfume and cologne, the musty odor of mold and mushrooms.

Nate returned the knife to the chest of the monstrous sculpture. Then he threw back his hood, took the bowl, and drank. Sarah couldn't stop staring at his face. His pupils were surrounded by a beautiful starburst of brown that was a few shades deeper than the caramel color of the rest of his irises. There were tiny creases at the edges of his eyes, smile lines. His lower lip looked so soft, so puffy, that Sarah had to press her teeth together to stop herself from leaning forward and biting it.

"What is *in* that stuff?" she breathed.

"Ground bone from the POW prisoners, and their dried blood," Nate replied. It should have repulsed her, but it didn't. Nothing did. Even the mold on the walls now seemed miraculous, with its strange illumination.

"And a lot of alcohol," someone shouted from the back of the room.

"Bone, blood, and a few other odds and ends." Nate smiled at her. "Welcome to the Wolfpack, Sarah. I knew from the moment I met you that you should be one of us. You made it happen a little faster than I planned when you saw our mission last night."

"Tell me that wasn't real," Sarah breathed.

"He was completely safe. He had an air tank," Nate reassured her. "We give each other missions, challenges, to push us to grow and evolve. Luke needed to face his deepest fear, and last night we gave him that opportunity." Nate turned and handed the bowl to the next closest person. David! Her piano tutor, she realized as he threw back his hood to drink. The stubble on his cheeks and chin—so many shades, mahogany, tan, black, even a little rust—were illuminated by the torchlight.

"Welcome, Sarah," he said, then passed the ceramic bowl along, the folds of his maroon cloak rustling with the motion. A droplet of the murky liquid remained on the side of his mouth, and Sarah wanted to wipe it away with her thumb. She wanted to touch everything, taste everything, smell everything, experience everything. Her senses were insanely sensitive. The world was new and wondrous, and she couldn't wait to explore it. *Not just the world*, she thought. *Me.* She felt reborn.

Sarah's attention was caught by the motion of a hood being pulled back, the folds of the maroon cloth lovely as flower petals. She didn't know the girl, but she knew of her. Grayson Chandler, a swimmer who everyone predicted would make the Olympic team after graduation. Sanctuary Bay had a coach who was a former Olympian himself. "Welcome to the pack," she told Sarah, her eyes warm. Sarah's gaze ran over the cords in Grayson's neck, the hollow of her clavicle. She could stare at that little bit of smooth skin for hours, especially the way she could see Grayson's pulse beating there, a rhythmic, dancing beat. But Grayson was already passing the bowl on, and Sarah's gaze went with it. A huge grin broke across her face when the next member of the Wolfpack was revealed.

"Karina!" she cried out, so happy to see her friend after thinking such horrible things about her.

Karina grinned back. "It was so hard not to tell you!" she exclaimed. "But you're here now, Sarah, and we are going to have sooo much fun."

Sarah could listen to Karina talk forever. Her voice was like music as it ran through different tones with her animated exclamations.

Karina drank, then passed the bowl on. Another girl Sarah recognized, but hadn't ever spoken to—Hazel Cerff, president of the senior class. Definitely some heavy hitters in this group.

So why had they picked *her*? Sarah swallowed, enjoying the slick, slippery slide in her throat. Well, why not? She had to stop letting her past make her question everything good that happened to her at Sanctuary Bay—wasn't that basically what Nate had told her on the first day?

Hazel held the bowl up toward Sarah, offering her a toast, then drank. Sarah knew the next person—Logan from English and chem. And the next—Izzy! She was so relieved to know her friends were really as great as she'd thought. Looking at their faces, she could tell how happy they were to have her there. The pink in Izzy's cheeks was lovely against her perfect skin. "You're so pretty, Iz!" she exclaimed, then felt herself flush, the warmth in her face as pleasurable as sinking into a warm tub.

"You too, gorgeous," Izzy said, with a knowing smile. She drank and passed the bowl on. And it turned out Kayla Austin was under the next hood. Kayla was in English with Sarah and Logan. She was an amazing poet, and her dad was the creator of Snip-It, a new social media site that had swiftly put all others in the distant past. Her mom had founded a charity to eradicate hunger in the U.S. Sarah hadn't been able to resist Googling people in her classes once she found out that Ethan was one of *those* Steeres. The results had been mind-boggling and intimidating.

But now she was being treated like an equal. Invited into the group.

It got harder and harder to pay attention. She was on sensory overload, the textures, colors, the scents and sounds. Just being in her body was almost overwhelming, her hair brushing against the back of her neck, the way her ribs expanded with each breath, the way her muscles contracted and released when she turned her head. She tried to force herself to at least remember every person there. They were her family now. An amazing family. They were all so accomplished. All the connections to the rich and powerful and brilliant she'd ever need could be found right here.

After the last person drank, the group burst into a chorus of wolflike howls. Sarah threw back her head and joined in. It seemed as if blending their voices blended their spirits. She could almost feel all their heartbeats along with her own, the air they breathed out entering her own body. *Seriously, what was in that Blutgrog stuff?*

Who cares, she decided, and howled again, the vibrations inside her throat thrilling her.

Nate held up his hands again, and the room went silent. "There's one thing left for Sarah to do before she's a full member of our pack," he announced. "She needs to complete a mission. Any ideas?"

Izzy's voice rang out before anyone else's could. "I say she goes up to Ethan Steere in the hall, grabs his ass, and kisses him—with tongue," she shouted. That got a round of hoots and laughter. "And she can't give any explanation. At all," Izzy added with a glint in her eye. "You have to walk away without a word, Sarah."

Sarah glanced over at Karina. Her face was pale and her lips were pressed together. Not a happy wolf. Things were still tense between Karina and Izzy, apparently. Was this just a way for Izzy to give Karina a screw-you?

"We need a second," Nate said. He didn't look especially happy either. Maybe he was interested after all.

"I second!" Logan called out.

"Complete the mission to complete your initiation," Nate told Sarah, a slight frown on his face. "Of course, we'll need some witnesses."

Sarah shot another look at Karina. Her worry must have

shown on her face, because Karina smiled, a smile that seemed forced, but still a smile. "It's okay," she mouthed.

"You all know how to find Ethan. I'll do it right before first period." Sarah wanted to get it over with. "Be in the hall if you want to see it."

"We can't all be there," Nate said. "That would look suspicious."

"I'll get the evidence on my cell," Logan volunteered.

"Perfect," Izzy said.

Sarah didn't like being used as a pawn in some game Izzy was playing with Karina. But she couldn't refuse the mission. She'd just been given lifelong membership in a group with all the coolest, most popular, most connected kids in school. She couldn't turn her back on that.

Besides, it was just a kiss, right?

Sarah headed straight for the bathroom the second she got back to the dorm room. She definitely needed a shower before she kissed anyone. Nate had made them leave the subbasement a few at a time, and she'd been in the first group. Neither Izzy nor Karina had left with her, so she had the suite to herself.

She chose a creamy scrub made with finely ground peach kernels and olive seeds from the unbelievable selection of bath products in Karina's collection, trying to ignore the guilt over using Karina's stuff to prep for kissing Karina's boyfriend. *It's not really for Ethan*, she told herself. Her night in the POW cell hadn't left her smelling all that great. After all, she didn't want him to pull away before she even had the chance to fulfill her mission. Because that's what it was. Not a kiss. A mission. And Karina understood that.

If Karina had a problem, it would be Izzy. She was the one who'd thought of the stupid mission. Sarah pushed the friction between her roommates out of her head and let her heightened awareness of the shower absorb her. Of all the great things about Sanctuary Bay—and her very generous roommates—shampoo was near the top of the list. Having shampoo and conditioner had made wrangling her hair so much easier. There'd been one foster home where she'd had to wash her hair with a bar of soap. Disaster. But now she could get thick Magic Marker–sized ringlets going without much hassle.

How long will the Blutgrog effects last? she wondered. It was hard to keep her mind on serious things. Toweling off turned out to be an experience close to ecstasy. She wasn't going to be much good in classes if she kept getting lost in random sensations.

When she walked into the bedroom, she saw that both roommates had returned. Karina's eyes were locked on her cell in a way that made Sarah sure she was trying to avoid talking to Izzy. And Izzy watched with an amused expression on her face, like she was aware she'd gotten to Karina and was enjoying it.

Sarah grabbed her favorite jeans—from Goodwill, but they fit perfectly. Why was she even thinking about what she was wearing? Her stomach tightened as she imagined grabbing Ethan and kissing him. How would he react? Probably with some kind of snarky comment that would make her feel like an idiot, but that wasn't too much to ask in payment for belonging to the Wolfpack.

"You look good," Izzy told Sarah coyly after she'd pulled on a snug long-sleeved tee. "Don't you think, Kars?"

"Absolutely. As always." Karina tossed her cell aside. "I'm

taking a shower." She stripped, threw on her robe, and stalked out of the room without another word. Was she only mad at Izzy? Or at Sarah too?

She couldn't worry about it. Sarah pulled on her sneakers and grabbed her backpack. "I guess I'll go kiss Ethan."

"With tongue. And don't forget you have to grab his ass," Izzy reminded her in a playful tone.

"Yeah, and thanks for that," Sarah told her.

"I did you a favor!" Izzy protested. "Compared to some of the other initiation missions people have been given, you got off easy. Kissing a jerk isn't so bad—we've all done it. Karina does it routinely."

Sarah sighed. This mission was clearly Izzy's screw-you to Karina, and Sarah had to figure out how to keep herself out of it. Laying low was the best way to handle the situation, most situations, in fact. All she had to do was get through it quickly and not say too much.

"Later," she said, heading for the door.

"Have fun," Izzy called after her. "He's a jerk, but I bet he's a decent kisser."

Sarah waved in response. There was no good answer that let her walk the line between Karina and Izzy without taking sides. As soon as she was out in the hall, she checked her cell for Ethan's location. He was down in the Humanities wing. She noted that Logan was nearby, already in place to record the encounter. "Okay. Good to go," she muttered.

She hurried down both flights of stairs, popping a cinnamon Life Saver as she went even though she'd just brushed her teeth, then strode purposefully to the west wing. *Get it over with and move on*, she thought.

She spotted Logan first, then Ethan a second later. He was

by himself. Good. She didn't allow her pace to slow. She ignored Logan, who gave her a thumbs-up as she passed. She walked directly up to Ethan. He said "Hi." She didn't say anything. She reached around, grabbed his butt in both hands, and went up on tiptoe—he was so tall—for the kiss.

He pulled his head back before she reached his lips, and stared down at her, his face expressionless. She noticed he had a ring of gray around his blue eyes and his butt was nicely muscular in her hands and that he smelled like freshly sharpened pencils and oranges. Sarah inhaled deeply, then shook her head. She couldn't just keep standing there *noticing*. If he pulled away completely and walked off, it was going to be a hundred times harder to make a second attempt.

Sarah slid her hands up his back and knotted her hands in his hair—so thick and silky—then pulled his head down to meet hers. This time he didn't move back, letting her capture his lips with hers. She didn't have to worry about getting him to open his mouth. His tongue was already brushing against the seam of *her* lips, urging her mouth open, then his tongue was inside, tangling with hers, his hands on her waist, pulling her body flush against his.

New sensations flooded her. The hard muscles of his chest. His heart beating against her chest. One of her hands slid from his head to the back of his neck, the skin there so smooth. Her tongue was in his mouth now, his teeth slick and hard, the inside of his cheeks warm and soft.

She heard a small sound, almost a gasp, and realized it had come from her. That realization broke the spell the sensations—that's all it was, over-the-top sensations created by the Blutgrog—had cast over her. She released him and backed away, her fingers pressed against her lips.

"Sarah—" he began.

She turned and ran before he could say more. The second she rounded the corner, hands grabbed her. David and Kayla. They pulled her into the nearest stairwell, and she was immediately engulfed in a group hug by at least half the Wolfpack. Someone gave a low howl in her ear, his breath hot.

"We are going to party so hard to celebrate. Friday night," Nate promised, tightening his arms around her. "You haven't partied until you've partied with the pack."

"Great," Sarah managed to say, her lips still burning from the kiss, her legs trembling. *The Blutgrog*, she told herself. *It's that drink. It makes everything more intense.*

I'd be feeling this way no matter who I kissed.

7

The effects of the drink had worn off a little before she headed to chem, so that was something. She wouldn't be completely distracted by breathing in the sharp-pencils-and-oranges smell of Ethan while they listened to Dr. Diaz lecture. Make that sharp-pencils-and-oranges-and-delicious-boy smell. During the kiss, she'd been close enough to Ethan to smell his skin, soapy clean and a little musky.

She stared at the door to the classroom apprehensively. Hopefully he'd be a no-show. Or late. Late would mean no time for talking. Would he ask her about the kiss? What was she supposed to say? She couldn't tell him the truth. Maybe she could say she'd been lusting after him since the day they met, and she had to see what it was like to kiss him. He'd believe that. His ego was big enough.

Steeling herself, she walked in and took in a sharp breath of relief at the sight of Ethan's empty seat.

"How's it going, Sarah?" Logan asked as she sat down. He gave her a we've-got-a-secret smile. After only one night, her circle of friends had expanded exponentially.

"Great. All great. I feel great," Sarah babbled. Maybe the Blut-grog hadn't worn off *quite* as much as she thought. The feel of her tongue forming those words—too many words—made her want to giggle, but she managed to restrain herself. She couldn't go around giggling like a fool.

"Greetings," Dr. Diaz said, coming in just as the blue light flashed. "It's time for . . . Chemistry Visionary of the Week! Up today—Carl Wilhelm Scheele. This guy, he was apprenticed to an apothecary when he was younger than you. He spent his spare time and his nights studying chemistry. A few of you look like you might have been following his example last night." He gave Sarah a pointed look. "After all, I can't think of any *other* reason my students would be staying up 'til all hours."

That got a few laughs. Dr. Diaz continued. "Scheele had only rudimentary equipment, we're talking mid-seventeen hundreds here, the knowledge of chemistry and science he was working with didn't give him much. But, he discovered oxygen!" Dr. Diaz did a little jump and fist pump. Sarah snorted. He was such a dork, but she loved how he got so into his lectures. "It came out of his observation that . . ."

Just then Ethan opened the door. Sarah focused all her attention on Dr. Diaz, but couldn't help but be hyperaware of the exact moment Ethan sat beside her. Heat crept up the back of her neck as the scent of him invaded her nostrils, every odor distinct. Pencils. Oranges. Soap.

At least he can't talk to me, she thought, and after a few moments she was able to drag her attention back to chemistry. She typed in every word Dr. Diaz said, even though they were locked in her perfect memory. The activity calmed her. She caught Ethan glancing at her several times. But she studiously ignored him.

The flash of pink light came way too soon. Her heart felt heavy in her chest, each beat an effort. She turned to Ethan hesitantly.

"Going to lunch?" was all he said.

"Yeah."

And they walked out together, like always.

The silence stretched out between them. Ethan yawned loudly.

What is he thinking?

"Sorry I'm boring you," Sarah muttered.

He shrugged. "It's not you. I just suffer from terminal ennui. I have everything, so I want nothing. Oh, wait—that's your line."

Sarah shook her head. "You're not going to drag me into this argument again."

"But I'm so spoiled and unappreciative," Ethan sounded half amused and half pissed off. "Whereas having nothing until now makes you appreciate everything." He flung his arms wide. "All the wonderful *stuff.*"

"It's not about stuff, it's about a chance to have a decent life," Sarah snapped.

"Bullshit," he said. "You want the house, the car, the clothes with the right labels. You're just too self-righteous to admit it."

"Sure, I want the stuff. Like hair conditioner," she snapped. "Like clothes somebody else hasn't worn first. Like a door with a lock in a place that's mine. But mostly what I want is to be treated like a human being, not a piece of trash."

Oh god, why had she said that to him of all people.

"Thank you for another stimulating debate, Sarah. See, this

is why it's good that the school has a mix of students from all backgrounds." Sarah recognized that last part from the Sanctuary Bay intranet. Ethan pulled a half-open roll of cinnamon Life Savers out of his pocket. "Want one?" he held it out to her.

She took one without thinking, relieved he hadn't glommed on to what she'd just said. And suddenly, she was in.

Tasting cinnamon Life Saver. Feeling the slickness of Ethan's teeth under her tongue. Smelling soap, oranges, pencils, and *him*, Ethan. Feeling his muscles, her legs beginning to tremble, her mouth opening in a gasp.

And she was out. Praying she hadn't actually let out that gasp. She shot a glance at Ethan. He was looking back at her, a half smile quirking his lips. He'd given her that Life Saver just to mock her, she realized. Just to remind her of what she'd done. Sarah bit down and cracked it in half, then ground it between her teeth and swallowed.

"Want another one?" he asked. "You like this flavor, right?"

Sarah didn't answer. Instead, she hurried the last few feet to the dining hall and scurried inside, leaving Ethan to catch the door. No servers today. No clattering dishes or running feet. The buffet was in place as it had been the first few days.

She headed toward the usual table and saw Karina walking toward them with a tray. When they reached her, Ethan took the tray, set it down, then grabbed Karina by the waist and lifted her up for a kiss. She wrapped her arms around him.

"Aren't you glad there's lunchtime entertainment?" Izzy asked as she stepped around them and sat down.

"Yeah. Fun," Sarah murmured, ordering herself to look away. But she couldn't, at least not until Ethan's eyes opened and met hers as he continued kissing Karina.

By the time the pink light flashed at the end of her last class, Sarah was exhausted. The Blutgrog from the initiation ceremony had drained out of her system and she felt sluggish without her heightened senses. Or maybe she was sluggish because she'd hardly slept last night. Whatever the reason, she just wanted to go to bed.

But before she'd gotten very far down the hall, Dean Farrell called her name. Sarah glanced at the dean's shoes so she could report to Karina—pale gray suede, pointy toe, conservative looking until you saw that the wedge heel was python print.

"I'm glad I ran into you," the dean said. "How's it going now that you have a few more weeks under your belt? Do you have a minute to talk, or should we set up a time for you to come by my office?"

"Now would be—" Sarah broke off as the scent of cedar and cloves assaulted her, the smell that had triggered the memory of her father on her first night. Dean Farrell's perfume must be a similar scent. "Um, now wouldn't be that great," she said quickly, breathing through her mouth so she wouldn't get hit with the odor again. "I can call your office and set up something," she added, backing away.

"That would be fine." Sarah could feel Dean Farrell staring at her curiously as she rushed away. But she had to get somewhere safe. She pressed her hand over her nose, as if she was about to sneeze. The scent was still overwhelming somehow. Where was it coming from?

The chemistry room was just down the hall. Sarah picked up speed, breaking into a trot. She'd told Dr. Diaz about her memory. It would be okay if she lost it in front of him. But it was too late. Three steps away, the scent got her. And she was in.

In the grayness, following Daddy's rules. Being quiet. Being still. Hiding. Waiting until he or Mommy opened the tunnel door. Smelling the musty tunnel, the spicy scent of Daddy's cologne fading.

She was trying not to think of monsters crawling toward her. Daddy said there were no monsters. But monsters liked tunnels. They liked little girls.

Thinking about the rules helped. She needed to keep remembering the rules. If something bad happens, wait until it's safe. Then run. Run fast. Find a lady with kids. Tell her your name is Sarah Merson. Merson. Merson, Merson, *Merson*. Ask for help.

Her nose twitching, itching from the thick air. Making her want to sneeze. But she had to be quiet.

Then Mommy screaming. Were the monsters out there and not in the tunnel?

She had to move. On hands and knees, creeping toward the slits of light, heart pounding.

Seeing her. Mommy on her knees facing the hotel room wall.

Someone's legs. A hand reaching down. A silver bird staring at her from the ring on the finger. The finger pulling the trigger of a gun.

A bang. Her ears filling with bees. Mommy collapsing on the floor. Red spilling.

Sarah shoving her fingers into her mouth. Quiet. Being quiet.

Daddy's legs running by. The bird man chasing.

Something bad happening.

In the hallway, another gunshot.

And she was out. It took her a moment to realize she was sitting in a chair in the chem room, Dr. Diaz standing over her. "Please tell me I didn't start crying."

He didn't say anything. Sarah sighed. "Please tell me a limited number of people saw me."

"I got you in here pretty fast when I heard you. I don't think you'll be the newest gossip item on the Boards." Dr. Diaz handed her a piece of filter paper. Sarah stared at it, then realized she was supposed to use it as a Kleenex. She wiped the tears and snot off her face, and crumpled the filter in her fist.

"Want some strawberry juice?" Dr. Diaz asked. "It should be almost ready." Without waiting for an answer, he headed toward the door to the big lab. Sarah followed, feeling awkward and large after spending those moments in her little kid body. "Put a drop of liquid nitrogen in a couple of beakers and swirl it around," he instructed.

As she did, her heart rate normalized. Dr. Diaz opened the centrifuge and pulled out a jar filled with a deep pink liquid on a diagonal. The other half of the jar was filled with a denser liquid that was a dark rose color. "You got those beakers chilled?" he asked.

"Um, yeah." Sarah hadn't really thought about why he'd wanted her to use the liquid nitrogen.

"Excellent. You are in for a treat. With the 'fuge you get a silky juice with a really intense flavor." Dr. Diaz put a piece of filter paper over the top of the jar and poured the liquid into one of the beakers, then repeated the process with the second beaker. "Cheers," he told her.

Sarah clinked her beaker to his, then took a sip. Dr. Diaz was right. It was intense—strawberry squared—and almost too sweet. "Keep going," he urged. "You still look a little shaky. You could use the glucose." She took a longer swallow. "So I'm guessing I just saw the side effects of your remarkable memory."

"That was an especially bad one," Sarah told him. "Sometimes the memories just hit me. I'll see or taste or smell something, and *wham*! It takes me over. Entirely. And suddenly I'm living the past, completely unaware of the present."

"So you're reliving, not just watching the events play out." He took a swallow of his strawberry juice and gave a long "Ahhh" of satisfaction.

"Yeah." He was trying to make her not feel like a freak. And it was working. "It was a memory from when I was really little. One of the ones people are always telling me I shouldn't be able to have because I was so young. They shot my mom in the head, then my dad ran and the guy followed him. I heard another shot, so I knew they killed him too."

She rolled the beaker between her palms. "Later, when I was older, I searched for mentions of a murder like that in the news. There was nothing. I don't know why they were killed, but it wasn't random."

"After we talked last time, I read up on eidetic memory and HSAM," Dr. Diaz said. "One article mentioned that there are some cases where the subject remembers dreams as vividly as their waking moments. It can be hard for such people to tell if they're remembering something that really happened, or if they're remembering a dream."

"You don't believe me." She put the beaker down. "You think I'm remembering a nightmare, not something that really happened."

"Sarah, someday you're going to start giving me the benefit of the doubt," he told her. "It's not that I don't believe you. I just think it's worthwhile to explore all the possibilities. Scientist, remember?"

"But when I dream, I just dream like a normal person," Sarah protested. "I don't smell things or feel them the way I do in that vision of the day they died."

"The thing is, people like you store memories in a different way, even in a different part of the brain. Maybe those sensations are recorded even though you don't remember having experienced them when you wake up."

"I guess it's possible," Sarah said slowly.

"It seems like a plausible dream for a little girl dealing with the death of her parents, being sent to live with strangers," Dr. Diaz said. "I'm sorry for that, Sarah, that you lost them so young."

The warmth and sympathy in his voice made her eyes sting and her throat tighten. "Thanks," she answered, her voice hoarse.

"Hey, you think we could figure out how to make a Frappuccino with some of this stuff?" He gestured to what had to be a million dollars' worth of science equipment.

Sarah laughed. Her instinct to head for the chemistry room and Dr. Diaz had been a good one. "We have the technology, that's for sure."

"Ready for your first party down in the den?" Izzy asked Sarah on Friday night.

"Since neither of you will tell me what the parties are like, how can I answer that?" Sarah said.

"They're always a little different," Karina replied. "But they're always fun!" She took a pair of earrings from the top drawer of her nightstand and waved them at Sarah. "Put these on. They're perfect with that sweater."

After a lot of protesting, Sarah had finally agreed to let Izzy loan her a sweater for the party. It was cream-colored, long-sleeved, with a V-neck that was lower than what Sarah usually wore. The earrings would be great with it. They were beautiful, long with a gentle S shape, and sparkly with jagged crystals in purple, green, lavender, ruby, and pale blue. When Sarah held them up next to her face in the mirror, she had to admit she loved the way they looked against her dark hair.

"Put them on," Karina urged. "We need to get going."

"Okay, okay." Sarah smiled as she put them in. "Ready," she announced, and together they all headed down to the door near the school's back entrance. Karina pressed her fingerprint on the pad next to the door. Somehow one of the pack members had hacked the system and added everyone's fingerprints to those accepted by the door pad.

After they went down the first set of stairs and crossed the cavernous furnace room, Sarah got the honor of unlocking the door to the subbasement, because she'd just gotten her key. She felt a little thrill of anticipation as she started down the rough wooden stairs.

"Wrong way," Izzy told her as she started to turn left at the bottom. "We only use the Bone Man room for ceremonies. The robes too."

"For parties and other social stuff, we use the den," Karina added. She moved into the lead, and they followed a twisting corridor, until they reached a room about as big as the coffee shop. It was much warmer than the rest of the subbasement, probably because the damp stone walls had been covered with thick Oriental rugs. The room was lit with dozens and dozens of candles.

Small groups of kids lounged on piles of cushions scattered all over the floor. "Hmmm. That looks interesting." Izzy nodded toward a tangled heap of very long leather strips that were a couple of inches wide. Sarah couldn't believe her eyes hadn't gone there first.

"You don't know what they're for?" Sarah asked quietly, hoping it wasn't a stupid question.

"No, it's a new addition," Izzy said. "Nate's a genius for coming up with ways to keep the parties lively."

Lively? Sarah shot another glance at the leather strips. *It's not another initiation*, she reminded herself. *I'm already in the group.* Still, a little apprehension mixed with her excitement.

"We need drinks." Karina raised her voice. "Who wants to bring three gorgeous girls some drinks?" she called. Four boys were instantly on their feet, including Logan. "What'll it be?" one asked. Sarah hadn't officially met him yet, but she thought his name was Cody.

"Martinis," Izzy replied, dropping down onto a cluster of pillows. "Okay?" she asked Sarah and Karina.

"Sure," Sarah said, and Karina nodded, as they joined Izzy on the floor. At least her roommates were getting along tonight. Sarah continued to look around the room. More people had arrived. She thought it was close to being the whole group, about twenty in all. Something on the wall across from her snagged her attention. "You guys have a flat-screen down here?" she exclaimed.

"We have everything you could possibly want," Karina assured her.

"I thought there wasn't any electricity," Sarah said.

"The candles are for atmosphere," Izzy explained. "Thanks, boys," she said as their drinks arrived. Sarah took a small sip. She'd never had a martini before. She wasn't sure she liked it, but she was willing to give it more of a try.

A long howl interrupted the buzz of conversation in the room. Sarah turned toward the sound. Nate was in the rough stone doorway holding the ceramic bowl from Sarah's initiation in both hands. "I don't think it's a full moon, but I feel my wolf coming out!" Nate shouted.

Everyone howled in response. Sarah threw back her head and let her voice blend with all the others. Nate wandered from group to group, bringing the bowl to the lips of each member of the pack. Sarah's stomach tightened when he reached her. Nate's intense gaze always made her feel as if he was looking deep inside her, seeing much more than her face, taking in her secret wishes, fears, and desires. He'd always been able to understand her, from day one. She stared back at him as she took a swallow. The taste—what she could identify—was a mix of mushrooms and berries and alcohol. Nate smiled at her before moving on to Izzy. She felt his smile brushing across her face as the Blutgrog took hold.

She let herself sink into the sensations. Branching lines of warmth pulsed through her body. She became acutely aware of her mouth, her tongue lightly touching the soft roof, lips meeting in a light touch. Aware of the small tinkling sound made by the crystals of her earrings as she turned her head slightly, of the gold wires running through the tiny holes in her earlobes. Aware of the colors in a single candle flame, gold, yellow, cream, a bit of blue.

"I bet you're all wondering what these are for," Nate said when everyone had drunk. Sarah focused on him, trying to concentrate on his words. He tapped the pile of intertwined leather strips with one foot.

"I know what I'm hoping," Logan yelled.

"Here's the deal. Guys grab the end of a strip with a knot in it and tie it around your wrist. Girls do the same thing, except use the end with no knot. When you find out who's tied to you—well, you take it from there. Just have fun and be safe." That got another round of howls. When Sarah howled along, it felt as if she were already tied to everyone in the room, their joined voices connecting them.

Nate held up his hands, and the room went quiet. "There are black strips, red strips and green ones. Girls who want girls, use the green, either end. Guys who want guys, same thing with the red. Experimentation, as always, is welcome."

Sarah felt a little nervous as she approached the strips. There were a bunch of guys in here she'd never even spoken to. A bunch of hot, smart guys handpicked to be in the group, she reminded herself. She smiled as Karina helped her tie the end of a black strip to her wrist. The leather was cool and pliant. She wouldn't mind it wrapping around her entire body.

As she tied one to Karina, she suddenly thought of Ethan. She wanted to ask Karina if this was weird for her, but she seemed fine with it. She turned to Izzy to see if she needed help. Izzy held the end of a black strip and a green one. "I'm trying to decide if I'm feeling adventurous," Izzy explained, then dropped the green strip. "Maybe another night."

"Go time!" Nate yelled.

Sarah felt a tug on her wrist, but she had no idea who was doing the tugging. The strips were too tangled. "I think I need to go over yours," she told Izzy, and Izzy crouched down so Sarah could step over her strip. A jerk from the other end of her strip suddenly took the slack out and brought her tight up against a guy with short blond hair, her chest pressing against his back, her nose at the base of his neck. She vaguely remembered his name being Luke. He laughed and so did she. "Um, I think I need to squeeze in front of you. I don't have enough rope to go anywhere else," Sarah told him.

"Do whatever you want. I'm at your service," he replied.

Sarah inched around him, her leather strip loosening just a bit. Then she noticed that Grayson had been pulled up against him on the other side. This was going to be tricky. She had to cross in front of Luke to get more slack, but Grayson was standing super close, facing him, and there was only a little gap Sarah could squeeze through.

"You have room," Luke said, and she could feel the tiny vibrations of his voice inside her ears. She giggled. It felt like he was tickling her without even touching her. The Blutgrog was incredible stuff.

She wasn't convinced that there was enough room, but she began wriggling between them, her back to Luke. "Hey, new girl," Grayson purred. Their faces were almost touching, so Grayson closed the small distance and kissed Sarah on the cheek, smiling as she pulled away.

Kissed by an Olympic hopeful, Sarah thought giddily.

Slowly she managed to work her way past, feeling Luke hard against her butt as she did. She gave her hips a little wiggle in response. She'd never felt like this, so accepted, so connected, so desired.

She continued weaving through the jumble of bodies, light-headed with sensory stimulus—fingernails lightly sweeping across the skin at the small of her back where her sweater had ridden up, hands running through her kinky hair, her own hands exploring, stroking a stubbly cheek, the hollow of a throat, the curve of a waist.

The leather strip between her and *him*, whoever he was, was really loose now. She had to be getting close. Her heart began beating faster, the heat lines running through her body becoming almost electric. A few couples had already broken free of the twisted web. Sarah could see Karina and David lying in a pile of cushions near the door. He was using their leather strip to blindfold her, and she was laughing, head tossed back. Ethan would—

The thought shattered as arms wrapped around Sarah, one just under her breasts, one across her belly. "Found you," a low voice growled huskily in her ear. Nate. She twisted around to face him. God, he was beautiful, all blocky jaw and bumpy nose, and hard body. He made her think of a boxer. The candlelight reflected off his dark hair, his caramel-colored eyes gleaming.

She ran her hands over his biceps, lightly squeezing, confirming he was just as muscular as she thought. "And now that I've found you, exactly what am I going to do with you?"

"Don't you mean what am *I* going to do with *you*?" Sarah untied the leather that bound her. "Uh-uh," she impulsively told Nate as he started to unfasten his. He looked surprised, but intrigued. She added an extra knot to the leather secured around his wrist, then used the loose end to lead him over to an unoccupied pile of pillows. She hesitated a fraction of a second, then put her hands on Nate's shoulders, turned him around, and tied his hands together behind his back. He wasn't the Jager right now. Or the class president. Or the most popular guy in school. He was hers.

Again, Sarah moved her hands up to his shoulders, letting her thumbs caress the sides of his neck, running over cords of muscle, fine little hairs. She almost became lost in the intensity of her perceptions, but she caught herself and pushed down gently with her palms. Nate obediently dropped to his knees. Sarah knelt behind him, spreading her legs so that she held his body between them. His neck . . . she still hadn't finished exploring it. She lowered her mouth and ran her tongue across the edge of his hairline, loving the faint taste of his sweat, a tiny bit salty, a tiny bit sweet, but mostly just clean, like water. Nate let out a long, shuddery breath. Sarah smiled against his warm skin, then gave him a little nip, enjoying the give of his flesh under her teeth.

She wanted more, more of him. She slipped her hands around him, running her palms under his shirt and over his bare stomach, tracing the muscles that defined it. His body jerked when her pinky dipped into his belly button. It jerked again when she slid one hand higher and let her fingernail flick across one of his nipples. She could experiment like this all night,

119

feeling his textures, tasting him, discovering his most sensitive spots.

But Nate had managed to work his hands free. He swiftly turned around to face her, grabbed her by the waist, and let himself fall back on the cushions, taking her with him, giving her hundreds of new impressions to absorb now that her body was stretched out against the length of him—his fingers sliding under the waistband of her jeans, his heart thundering against her chest, her own heart pounding on the other side, his mouth on hers.

It was almost too much, too intense, too powerful. Sarah shuddered underneath Nate, her world narrowed to the sensations he was creating in her. Who cared about the rest of the world when she had this?

8

The lights came up in the theater and Izzy and Sarah started sidestepping their way out of the row of seats. "Karina would have loved that movie," Izzy said. "All fate and destiny and true love."

"I texted her to meet us, but I didn't hear back," Sarah said.

"I guess this is one of the rare nights she and Ethan have managed not to piss each other off. Did you see that card she made him? She's the absolute perfect girlfriend, always doing romantic things. I think that's partly why I hate that she's with Ethan. He takes it all for granted," Izzy commented.

Sarah was glad to hear Izzy say something nice about Karina

for a change. They'd been sniping at each other for weeks. "Maybe he . . ." She trailed off as she spotted Nate walking up the aisle. "Hi, Sarah," he said.

"Hi." Hi. That was all she'd come up with.

"Hi, Izzy," Izzy said.

"You didn't give me a chance," Nate protested. "Bye, Izzy." He waved as he passed. "And Sarah."

Hard to believe I spent hours making out with him, Sarah thought. When she saw him in the halls or the dining hall, it was like they barely knew each other.

That's how the Wolfpack parties work, she reminded herself. Like with Karina. She'd spent hours on that homemade card for Ethan. But that didn't mean she didn't have a good time with whoever she wanted to down in the den.

"So you didn't like the movie?" Sarah asked. She didn't want to think about Nate anymore. It made her kind of crazy.

"Not enough explosions." They pushed through the double doors and out into the corridor. "Huh. Guess I was wrong about Ethan and Karina being together," she commented.

Sarah followed her gaze, and saw Ethan coming out of the coffee shop. Alone. As if he felt her looking at him, his head snapped up and his eyes met hers. He finished the coffee, crumpled the paper cup, tossed it in the trash, and headed straight for her.

His long strides covered the distance between them quickly. His expression was intense, almost angry. He didn't say a word when he reached her. He just grabbed her butt and jerked her tight against him, then bent his head and kissed her.

Even without the Blutgrog, Sarah felt the kiss in every part of her body, heat radiating through her. She knew she should pull away. This was Karina's boyfriend, and she wasn't on a mission. But before she could make her feet move, Ethan broke the kiss, then turned and walked away. Sarah stared after him, brain spinning. What was— Why—

"How do *you* like it?" he called, not even bothering to look back.

"*Well*," Izzy said after a moment. "Your mission was, what, two weeks ago? Doesn't seem like Ethan's been able to get it out of his head."

"He's a jackass," Sarah snapped. "That was just his idea of payback."

Izzy looked at her doubtfully, her eyes curious.

"I haven't had another mission since then," Sarah blurted out, desperate for any way to change the subject. "What happens if you screw up on a mission or can't take it or something?"

Izzy waited until they were outside to answer. "I don't know. It hasn't happened since I've been in the pack. We're good at getting one another through missions. Now," Izzy raised an eyebrow, "let's talk about Ethan."

"What do you think Karina tells him about the nights we're in the den?" Sarah asked.

"We both know that's not what I meant," Izzy said.

Sarah picked up her pace. It was cold walking back to the dorm. "Seriously though, he has to wonder why there are so many nights she can't be with him. She must always have to make up excuses."

"Haven't you noticed? Karina's good at making stuff up," Izzy replied.

Sarah wasn't sure what Izzy meant, but she left the comment alone. She didn't want to side with either roommate against the other. "I can see why people in the pack end up together. It would be a lot less complicated," she said as they reached the main building.

Izzy smiled, pulling off her knit hat as they stepped inside. "Is there someone you'd like to get less complicated with? Someone named Nate perhaps? Or else . . ."

"Or else what?"

"I thought, and was suitably horrified, that I saw a spark between you and Ethan back there," Izzy said. "Something more than payback."

"No," Sarah said quickly. "And not just because he's Karina's boyfriend. I called him an inbred overprivileged ass once, and my opinion hasn't changed." Even though the overprivileged ass had almost turned her body liquid with that kiss.

"And Nate?" Izzy asked. They started up the curved staircase. "Don't think I haven't noticed that you two ended up together at both the parties we've had since you joined."

"But that's random. We never know who we're going to end up with," Sarah protested.

"Oh, I don't think you're giving our Jager enough credit. He comes up with those little games we play. You really think he can't rig the outcome if he feels like it?" Izzy asked.

"But he doesn't really talk to me outside of the pack," Sarah said. "You saw him at the theater. I got two whole words from him."

"Perils of being class president. Got to always be making the rounds, not letting anyone feel ignored. Or favored. But the pack is more important to him than anything. So if he spends time with you there, that means something."

The pack was more important than anything to Sarah too, and she knew it was probably for the same reason as Nate. The Wolfpack was their ticket to a far better future than either of them would ever have had on their own. "It *is* pretty incredible. It hasn't even been a month since my initiation, but I feel like I've known you all forever. And for me, that's . . ." She grew quiet, realizing she'd been about to reveal more than she planned. "It's great." She busied herself pressing her fingertip against the door pad and opening the door.

Izzy took off her coat as she headed into the bedroom. She got a bottled water from the mini-fridge and offered one to Sarah. Sarah shook her head. She was still too cold from the walk home. "That's not what you were going to say." Izzy stretched out on her bed. "You feel like you've know us forever and for you that's . . . what?"

Sarah smiled, amused in spite of herself. She could never get anything past Izzy. The girl noticed everything. *Well, why shouldn't I tell her?* she thought, sitting on her bed. *I already made my big confession to the pack. I'm not supposed to have secrets from them; I'm supposed to trust them with my life.*

"I was going to say that for me, feeling so close to everybody in the pack, it's . . . new. I got moved around so much as a foster kid. And neither of my parents had any family, at least none that ever showed up after they died."

Izzy nodded. "I'm sorry about your parents, Sarah. I can't imagine what that would be like. I should have said something before. It was just hard to figure out what the right thing to say would be."

"Thanks." Sarah switched the conversation away from her parents, afraid she might get teary. "In the foster system, it wasn't just that I never had a real family. I never got to make real friends, either. Even when I was little, parents didn't want their kids hanging out with someone like me." She tried to laugh but it came out strangled. "I can't blame them. I wasn't always exactly clean. My clothes smelled. I looked like a girl who might give your kid lice. Hell, I probably did to at least a few."

"I can blame them. Assholes," Izzy said, outraged.

A real laugh escaped Sarah. "Thanks. So being part of the

Wolfpack . . . it'd be cool for anyone, but for me it hardly feels real. I still can't even accept that I'm actually one of you."

"One of *us*." Izzy kicked off her sneakers, letting them fall on the floor at the foot of her bed. "You idealize us too much. Not that we aren't fabulous." She gave her wavy blond hair an exaggerated flip, but then her expression turned serious. "But you're not the only one with a fucked-up past, you know. There's me, for one."

Sarah didn't reply. As nice as Izzy was being, she still didn't get it. Nothing she'd experienced as a privileged Boston girl could ever compare.

"I'm not talking about only getting to invite fifty people to my thirteenth birthday party or whatever it is you're thinking," Izzy said.

"I wasn't—"

"Yeah, you were," Izzy cut her off. "You know why I'm at Sanctuary Bay? I killed someone. *Killed*. And how did my parents deal with it? They shipped me here and pretended it didn't happen. Wrote a big check. Covered it all up. Even though it wasn't my fault. It was an accident."

Sarah was stunned. "What happened?" she asked tentatively.

"It's such a cliché. I was date-raped." Izzy's words came out flat and clipped. "Or I would have been date-raped, anyway. It was this guy Gavin, I knew him from school. My parents were out and we were hanging at my house. It was the first time we were ever alone together. I was fifteen. He was seventeen. And I was so thrilled he wanted to be with me, even though I was younger. We started kissing, and it was great." Her voice started to get higher as the words tumbled out. "I want to say I knew right away he was scum, but I didn't. I was really into it. He was such a good kisser. Then he started unbuttoning my jeans, and I put my hand down to stop him. It was going too fast for me. But he wouldn't stop." She paused and looked at Sarah, but her thoughts were somewhere else, back in that room with Gavin. "I just wanted him to get off me. So I shoved him. We were on the couch, and he fell off, hitting his head on the coffee table. It was a Gilbert Poillerat with a pink marble top and wrought-iron base." She laughed. "I can't believe I'm telling you that like it's important, but the table was just so hard, that's the point. There was blood everywhere, and I couldn't stop it. It happened so fast. Suddenly he was . . . dead. He was still warm and everything, but his eyes were empty. He was gone."

Izzy had started to hyperventilate. It was almost like she'd fallen into one of Sarah's memory surges. "You're okay," Sarah said. "You're okay, Iz. Sit up. It'll be easier for you to breathe."

Izzy kept panting, her hands curled into tight fists. Sarah got up and hurried over, reaching for Izzy's arms to help her. But the second Sarah touched her, Izzy lashed out, viciously knocking her away. Sarah stumbled backward, unable to catch her balance and fell to ground. Izzy let out a shriek. "I didn't mean it!" she cried. "I didn't mean it, I swear! Are you okay, Sarah? Oh my god, I'm so sorry. I wasn't trying to shove you." She scrambled onto the floor next to Sarah.

"I'm fine," Sarah assured her. Izzy pressed her hands over her face. "Everything's fine," Sarah crooned over and over, until Izzy's breathing began to slow down. Sarah reached over to Izzy's nightstand and picked up her water. "Take a sip."

Izzy pulled her hands away and took a long drink. "Sorry," she said, sounding more like her usual self. "I have a little case of PTSD. I thought I had it under control. I have a therapist here who's been working with me—that's where I go those early mornings. Sanctuary Bay is known for its excellent psychiatric department. Cutting-edge treatments, all that. It's another reason my parents sent me here. Not that I tell anyone that, and miraculously it's not one of the things everyone finds out at this place. They managed to handle that too. My parents excel at making ugliness go away. That's as much what Sanctuary Bay was about as the psychiatry success rates. They were furious with me."

"Even when they knew what happened? That you were defending yourself?" That seemed impossible to Sarah. These were Izzy's real parents, her flesh and blood, not some strangers making extra cash by giving her a place to sleep. "Assholes."

"They were embarrassed. Humiliated. I wasn't the perfect daughter they could show off and brag about anymore. There was no trial, none of that. Just a nice settlement for Gavin's family and a nice school for me." She took another swig of water. "Fucked-up past. I told you."

"We could form a club," Sarah said. She kept her voice light, but she was staggered. Nothing ever seemed to bother Izzy. She was all about maximum pleasure and minimum drama. And now it turned out there was all that horror and pain underneath her smooth and beautiful exterior.

"You'd be in a club with an accidental murderer?" Izzy asked, using the backs of her pinkies to wipe mascara streaks from under her eyes.

"If you'll be in a club with the kid who smells," Sarah told her.

Izzy smiled. "It'll be all the best people."

Karina pulled her cell out of her pocket and checked it, then set it down on the coffee table in the living room.

"If you do that again, I'll be forced to diagnose OCD," Izzy commented. She glanced at Sarah. "Second opinion?"

"You *have* been looking at it a lot," Sarah said. "Even though we both did test texts and calls."

"Why are you two always ganging up on me lately?" Karina complained.

"We're not," Sarah told her. At least she hoped not. Sarah still loved Karina, but it was true she and Izzy had gotten closer since their talk. And they hung out together more often, since Karina was off with Ethan a lot of nights.

"No judging." Karina pointed at Izzy, then Sarah, then she checked her cell again. And they all laughed together. "If that boy doesn't call or text in the next ten minutes, he can forget about getting any for a long time."

"And you won't have to suffer, because you'll still have the pack parties," Izzy said. "Lots of yummy boys to scratch any itches."

Karina wrinkled her nose. "Don't be gross."

"You don't look like you think it's gross when you're sprawled out on the pillows in the den," Izzy teased.

"But no judging," Sarah added quickly. Karina obviously enjoyed herself with whatever wolf boy she ended up making out with, despite her claims to be madly in love with Ethan, but now wasn't the time to say so. Not when Karina already felt ganged up on.

"No judging from me," Izzy agreed. "I'm an advocate of taking advantage of whatever goodies are available. I just wonder how it goes with all that true love between you and E."

Me too, Sarah thought.

"The Wolfpack is the Wolfpack," Karina said. "And why do you care, Iz? You hate Ethan anyway." She checked her cell again.

"I don't," Izzy shot back. "Just curious, that's all. You know I have trouble understanding all this love stuff with my heart of stone."

Karina shot her a glare, right before her cell buzzed—along with Sarah's and Izzy's. Karina opened her text fastest. "'Now,'" she read aloud, her eyebrows drawing together. "'Bone Man room.'"

"What do you think's going on?" Sarah asked. Usually the Wolfpack texts just said a time, nothing else. Sarah had never seen one that said "now" before. And they only used the Bone Man room for ceremonies, always scheduled days in advance.

"Probably just one of Nate's moves to keep us off balance," Izzy suggested.

"Ethan is now officially out of luck," Karina said as she stood up and started for the door, Sarah and Izzy right behind her. It was earlier than meetings were usually called—and before curfew—so they had to be careful going through the door that led to the first basement. No one outside the pack could see that door being opened or there would be questions.

They lingered in the hallway until the coast was clear, then hurried through the door and down to the subbasement, quickly putting on their ceremonial robes, which were stored in one of the old cells. Throwing up their hoods, they joined the lines of pack members on either side of the room.

No one spoke as they waited for the Jager to appear. No one moved. The ceremonies always had a formality, a gravity, but tonight Sarah could feel a new tension in the group. *What are we here for? What was so urgent we were called together with no warning?* Sarah wondered, staring down at the floor. Her hood dropped so low it was hard to see anything else.

The tension grew with each moment they waited. A girl gave a nervous giggle, then went silent so quickly it was as if a hand had been slapped over her mouth. Sarah's scalp had started to itch, and a spot near the middle of her back. Trying not to fidget, she shut her eyes, hoping that would help. But instead, it just made her more aware of every tiny irritation in her body.

She opened her eyes, focusing on the details of the floor's rough stone, the slight differentiations in the gray color, a chip in the rock here, a crack running through there. She heard a faint rattling sound, then a metallic squeal, and a muffled moan.

She continued to face forward. They were expected to remain in place until Nate arrived. The rattles grew louder, the muted cries more agitated. Wheels entered Sarah's field of vision, bouncing over the stones, one of them turning in the wrong direction, causing the high metallic shriek. She lifted her head until she could see a larger slice of the room from under her heavy velvet hood. The wheels belonged to a gurney, being pushed past by two pack members. On top of the gurney, a sheet covered a squirming body.

"Heil, Jager! Heil, Jager!" The chant began from those closest to the entrance. When Nate strode past Sarah in his black robe, she joined in, her shout adding to the frenzy of sound. He took his position in front of the terrifying Bone Man sculpture and raised his hands. Immediately the chanting stopped.

"What is owed to the Jager?" Nate called out, his voice easily filling the large room, echoing off the stone.

"Loyalty unto death," Sarah answered in unison with the others.

"What is owed to the pack?" The moaning from the gurney continued under Nate's strong voice and the answering pack.

"Loyalty unto death."

"Those are the first of our sacred edicts. What is the third?" Nate asked, his voice loud but controlled.

"We stand alone. We trust no one but our brothers and sisters."

"We stand alone," Nate repeated. "We trust no one but our brothers and sisters. And yet one of our own has broken the vow. One of our own has put another before the pack. One of our own has chosen to trust another, an *outsider*, with our secrets. And now one of our own must pay the price. Come closer to witness the punishment required by our laws."

There was a soft whispering of robes as the pack gathered in front of the Bone Man. Nate gave a signal to the figures on either end of the gurney and they rolled it into place before him. Sarah pulled her hood back a fraction to clear more of her vision. A fire had been lit in a copper bowl resting inside the Bone Man where the heart would be.

Nate pulled back the sheet in one long, smooth motion, revealing Grayson Chandler tied down on a filthy mattress. Naked. Her flesh covered with goose bumps, nipples erect. Eyes wide with terror, she twisted her head back and forth, trying to spit out the wadded ball of cloth that had been stuffed in her mouth and tied in place with more cloth.

Sarah stumbled back, horrified. Izzy caught her by the arm, holding her steady. "We will not banish our sister from the pack. We will be merciful. We will punish her, because it is required of us," the Jager intoned.

Nate signaled to another member, who handed him the bowl of Blutgrog. He brought the bowl to each member of the pack, letting them drink. His hands were completely steady when he lifted the bowl to her lips. She reluctantly swallowed. She didn't want to experience this more intently. She didn't want to experience it at all.

When each member of the pack had drunk, Nate turned and removed a length of iron from the fire blazing inside the Bone Man. It took Sarah a second to notice the shape of a wolf's head glowing deep red at one end. It was a brand.

Grayson began thrashing as much as she was able while still restrained on the gurney. Sarah's stomach gave a slow, sickening roll as she saw that the rough ropes had rubbed away the skin on Grayson's wrists and ankles, leaving the flesh raw and bleeding. With her Blutgrog-enhanced senses, Sarah could smell the sharp, coppery odor of blood. When she breathed in, she could almost taste it on her tongue, along with the acrid fear sweat pumping out of Grayson's body.

Izzy was still holding her arm, and Sarah could feel her friend's pulse beating in her fingertips, much more slow and even than Sarah's own erratic, racing heartbeat.

"Let this mark be a reminder that speaking of the pack to an outsider is verboten," Nate cried. "Let this mark be a reminder that only those of us initiated here in this room before the Bone Man can be trusted."

Instinctively, Sarah jerked her head to the side so she wouldn't have to watch the brand come down on Grayson's stomach. But that didn't stop her from hearing the sizzle, from smelling the smoke and the frying-meat scent of Grayson's burning flesh.

Somehow Grayson managed to free herself from the gag, and Sarah was sure that even without her phenomenal memory she would never be able to forget that scream. Nate flicked his hand, and Grayson was rolled out of the room, still screaming, the broken gurney wheel squealing in accompaniment. "Now we begin again, our pack cleansed," he told them, pacing between the two lines of robed members.

Sarah took a deep breath, filling her nostrils with the scent of chalky bone, old blood, and rank seaweed coming from the towering Bone Man icon. Cleansed. She felt sick from what they had just done, but the pack had to be kept secret.

"Why do we gather here today?" the Jager called.

"We gather to renew our spirits and our strength," Sarah said.

She forced the image of Grayson's thrashing body, the memory of her scream, and the smell of her burned flesh out of her mind.

The two members who had left with Grayson returned to the room, taking their place in line. Where was Grayson?

"Our disgraced sister rests in body, but we know now that she is forever here in spirit. Tonight all members of our pack are present. Our pack. It *is* ours. *All* of ours." Sarah felt that electric energy in the room again. The energy of a group with a singular focus. "Never forget that you have brothers and sisters. Never forget that you are part of something much larger than your-self."

As if she could. No one in this room, at this school, had a family, not truly. What they had was the people gathered around them right now. For the years they were at Sanctuary Bay, family was only care packages, if you were lucky. There was no way to keep up friendships with people from before.

"As a reminder of this, our great blessing, we will perform the next mission together. It is assigned to all of us," the Jager con-tinued. "When we have completed it, I know we will be stron-ger than we have ever been. The weakness that led our sister to stray will be removed." He let out a howl and they all joined in. Sarah could feel the tiny bones of her inner ear vibrating with the sound, and her larynx vibrating as she joined in the cry.

Nate raised his hands for silence and a hush fell. "The mis-sion will take place on Halloween night. On that night we will join in an act of sacrifice. On that night we will take a life, to honor what the pack has given us and to bind us."

Sarah's mouth grew dry. He means an animal, she told her-self. He has to mean an animal. Or maybe it will be like when Luke was buried alive. It won't be for real.

"Together we will offer up the most precious gift—a human soul," Nate told them.

Sarah felt like the tendons in her knees had been severed. Somehow she managed to remain standing. No one protested. Why wasn't anyone saying no? Why wasn't anyone saying this was fucking crazy?

Why wasn't she?

She opened her mouth, but no sound came out.

Nate's voice was clear and strong and compelling as he continued. "And when we have made this sacrifice together, we will be closer than any oath or vow, no matter how sacred, could make us. We will be as one, one brain, one heart, one body, one pack."

"One pack," they all repeated.

"One pack," Sarah whispered.

9

Three days before I'm supposed to help kill someone, and I'm drinking beer at a bonfire, Sarah thought. *How fucked up is that?*

The answer: Very. Very, very.

There had to be a catch. Nate had said they were sacrificing a human *soul*. So maybe that didn't mean someone would actually die.

Ethan kicked her foot. "No doing chemistry equations in your head, or whatever it is you're thinking about," he said. "This is a party. Or is that something else you never experienced out in the real world before you were saved by Sanctuary Bay?"

"Stop being such a porcupine," Karina said affectionately, wrapping one arm around Ethan's waist, while she roasted a marshmallow with the other.

"Porcupine isn't the animal I was thinking of," Izzy commented with a little shrug.

Tif and Matthias ran back up to the fire. "My feet are actually blue," Tif said as she rolled down the legs of her jeans and held her feet out to the fire.

"Maine. October," Izzy said. "Logic."

"I told her," Matthias answered, digging his bare feet into the rocks. Sarah had always thought beaches had sand—that's what they looked like on TV. But the beach here was entirely made up of small, smooth rocks.

"You told her, then you went in the water yourself. Yeah, that makes sense," Izzy said.

"I grew up in Maine," Matthias reminded her. "I'm conditioned, unlike our little magnolia here."

"This bonfire open to anyone? Or is it invitation-only?" Nate sat down without waiting for an answer, The Grin on his face. Olivia, a girl from the pack Sarah hadn't gotten to know too well yet, sat down next to him.

She frowned. Were they a thing? *He's always with* me *at parties*, she thought.

"Our bonfire is your bonfire." Karina rotated her stick to get her marshmallow golden brown all over. "It's not like the beach is big enough for two of them anyway."

They were gathered on the one tiny strip of beach that wasn't off-limits to students. It ran along for only about fifty feet on either side of the jetty.

"There's a great beach on the other side of the island, near the old asylum," Ethan said. "Of course, we're not allowed on it. Just another one of the school's stupid rules for the sake of rules. There's no reason we shouldn't be able to use it."

"Really? How did you find it? There's that big hedge blocking the way over there." Olivia took a beer from the cooler.

"A hedge isn't enough to stop Ethan," Karina answered for him.

"There shouldn't be *anything* blocking the way," Ethan said. "Why do we need to be hemmed in here?"

"Maybe because the ruins of the asylum are dangerous and could collapse on anyone stupid enough to go over there," Nate shot back.

"Then they could say that," Ethan replied. "They could treat us like the intelligent people they know we are, instead of like prisoners."

"Prisoners? Prisoners with a movie theater, and an Olympic-sized pool, and a—" Nate began arguing before Sarah had the chance. Prisoners? Seriously? She rolled her eyes. Every school had rules.

"Ooh, a pool and a theater," Ethan was saying sarcastically. He shook his head. "What is it with everyone here? All it takes is some nice stuff and your brains shut off? You'd probably all have jumped into a van with a pedophile holding a bag of candy."

"I do love a nice Reese's Peanut Butter Cup," Matthias joked.

A couple of people laughed, but not Sarah. Ethan had been handed so much in his life it had completely warped him. It made her crazy.

Nate glared at Ethan. "This school isn't handing out candy. It's handing out an education. My life would be shit if I hadn't gotten a scholarship here, and I'm not ashamed to say it." There was real anger in Nate's voice.

"My life's shit here," Ethan said. He sounded angry too.

Izzy leaned close to Sarah. "I was right. He's not a porcupine. He's a moose. Nate too. And they're smashing their antlers together trying to impress you," she whispered.

"What? No way," Sarah whispered back.

"Every time one of them makes a point, they look at you to see your reaction," Izzy insisted.

Izzy noticed everything. *Could she be right?* Sarah wondered. Ethan *had* kissed her. Although he'd certainly kissed Karina a bunch of times since then. And Nate had, if Izzy was right, arranged to be with her at two pack parties.

"Then we have different definitions of shit," Nate said to Ethan, then glanced at Sarah.

"No, we don't," Ethan snapped. "You're just letting a bowling alley and some gourmet coffee cover up the smell." He looked over at Sarah.

She glanced back and forth between the two glaring guys. Was this really about her?

"I probably would have dropped out of high school if I hadn't gotten to come here. No point in finishing without college, which I wouldn't have been able to afford." Nate jumped to his feet. "With Sanctuary Bay on my application and recommendations from the teachers here, I can get in anywhere. And that ain't shit." He stalked away.

Sarah stood and started after him. "Of course, they're perfect for each other," she heard Ethan say edgily. "Poverty makes them *so* much more mature than the rest of us."

"I'm sorry about all that," she told Nate when she caught up to him down at the edge of the water. He didn't look at her, just stood staring out at the ocean, hands jammed in his pockets. "Ethan's an entitled idiot."

Nate didn't answer.

"It's the same for me with this scholarship," she said. "I tell myself I would have found a way to go to college without it. But I don't know if that's true." She took a deep breath. "Sanctuary

Bay overlooked some stuff in my transcripts that most places wouldn't. They took a chance on me. They changed my life."

Nate turned to face her. "You're amazing, and you deserve everything this place can give you. *Everything.* You did it, Sarah. You didn't let your past hold you back."

"That's because of you," she said. "You took a chance on me too, the very first day I got here. You told me the truth about yourself and that made me see things differently."

"I could tell you deserved it," he replied. "And you deserve even more. That's why I wanted you in the Wolfpack. The friends you make there are different from other friends, because of what we go through together."

"I know. I've never had anything like it before."

"And our packmates?" Nate said. "Think of the kind of families they have, the kinds of jobs they'll get after college. There will be doors open for you—for us—all over the place. Wolfpack members rule the world. I'm serious. Business, entertainment, politics, science, sports, media, there are Wolfpack alumni everywhere, at the highest levels, and after college, we're going to be there too."

Conviction charged his voice, glowed in his eyes. He believed what he was saying with every molecule of his being. Listening to him, Sarah did too.

"That's what you said when I first met you," she remembered. "You asked if I wanted to run things, and I did."

"See?" Nate gave her The Grin. "I pegged you for the pack right from the start."

Sarah smiled back, so glad he'd wanted her. "But we're not really going to kill someone, are we? I know you say going through so much together creates a bond, but . . ."

"For you and me, the Wolfpack is different than it is for everyone else. They have all the connections they need. We don't.

We're not from this world." He reached out and smoothed her hair away from her face. "All I can say is that you want to be with the pack on Halloween night. *I* want you there."

Then he cupped her face in his hands, and kissed her, soft and sweet. It was the first time he'd kissed her outside one of the Wolfpack parties. It felt different out in the real world. It meant more. It wasn't just about fun.

Sarah slid her arms around Nate, and he deepened the kiss, his tongue exploring her mouth slowly. It was nothing like the hard, demanding kiss Ethan had given her that night after the movie. *Ethan?* Why was she thinking about Ethan? But now that she was, she couldn't stop. Was he watching from the bonfire?

Or maybe he's making out with his girlfriend, she thought, ashamed of herself. *With my friend, Karina, nicest girl around. What did Matthias call her? The Sweetheart of Sanctuary Bay.*

Sarah forced her attention back to Nate. It wasn't hard. Nate was difficult to ignore. She let her tongue flick against his, pulling him closer against her. He kissed his way down to the hollow of her throat, then back up to her ear. "Promise me you'll be with us on Halloween," he whispered, his breath warm against her skin. "It won't be the same without you. And you'll regret it if you aren't there. Trust me."

She wanted to believe him. She wanted the advantages the pack would give her. "I do. I will," she whispered back before he again captured her mouth with his own.

Sarah's legs trembled beneath her ceremonial robe as she stood in the Bone Man room on Halloween night. She thought she could trust Nate, but she couldn't help feeling unsettled about what was going to happen tonight.

"Heil, Jager! Heil, Jager!"

Nate had appeared in the doorway holding the bowl of Blutgrog over his head. When the pack went silent, he called out the words that opened every ceremony. "Why do we gather here today?"

Sarah responded numbly. *We aren't going to really kill anyone,* she kept telling herself. All she had to do was follow instructions until it was revealed that the sacrifice was only symbolic or something.

"We will need strength for what we must do tonight," Nate said once he reached the end of the usual call-and-response. He threw back his head and took a long drink from the bowl, then offered it to the person at the top of one of the two lines flanking the room. The hooded figure drank, then uncovered his face. Luke.

He drank, then held the bowl up to the next person while they drank. Grayson. Sarah was happy to see her here again—she hadn't been around since they branded her. Grayson brought the bowl to the lips of the person on her other side. Grayson's eyes were wide and fearful, the whites glistening with a slight orange tint in the torchlight.

The bowl traveled down the row until it reached Karina, who then held it while Sarah drank. The shift in Sarah's senses happened almost instantly, as always. Her fingertips now registered the tiny irregularities and roughness of the bowl's finish. She could smell Karina's shampoo, the vanilla scent of her lip gloss.

When she turned, Izzy's perfume, spicy and woodsy and mixed with the sharpness of sweat, overwhelmed her. Sarah could hear how rapid Izzy's breathing had become. Izzy, always so in control, seemed as agitated as Sarah felt. When she raised the bowl to Izzy's mouth, a vibration ran through the ceramic. From what, she wasn't sure. Tremors from Izzy's lips, or Sarah's fingers, or both?

When the ritual was complete, Nate strode to the front of the room. He reached through the ribs of the Bone Man and pulled out the metal bowl that had held the fire on the night of Grayson's punishment. Something inside it rattled as he turned to face the group.

"Tonight we will take a life together—and tonight, one of us will die."

The atmosphere in the room changed instantly, became charged like the air before a thunderstorm. One of *them* was going to die?

"For a sacrifice to be meaningful, what is sacrificed must be beloved. Each of us is beloved to every member of our pack," the Jager continued. "Tonight one of us will be sacrificed to make the Wolfpack stronger. We will honor the one who offers their life for the group forever. And the rest of us will be forever bound by taking a cherished life on this sacred night." He held up the bowl reverently. "Inside are stones. All are black, except one. The pack member who chooses the white stone will be revered as our sacrificial victim."

Still holding the bowl aloft, he walked back to the other end of the room. When he reached Luke, he nodded. Luke reached up and took a stone from the bowl.

Black.

The Jager moved to Grayson. Tears now streaked her cheeks. She took in a long, shuddering breath before raising her hand to take a stone.

Black. Grayson let out a relieved sob, knees buckling.

The Jager continued down the lines.

Black.

Black.

Black.

With each black stone, Sarah felt hysteria gripping her tighter and tighter. All the fears of not belonging came rushing back like mocking voices in her mind. Nate wanted her here tonight—was it a setup? Had they asked her to join them only to use her as a human sacrifice?

Black.

Sarah's pulse thundered in her ears. It was Karina's turn. She laughed a little as she thrust her hand into the bowl. She rolled the stones under her fingers, taking her time selecting one.

I'm next, Sarah thought panicked, her heart beating erratically.

Karina opened her hand, her laugher stopping abruptly.

White.

10

We're not really going to kill Karina. We're not, we can't, Sarah told herself as she walked through the woods with the rest of the group. The Blutgrog had turned each heartbeat into a drum strike that vibrated through her entire body, but the sound that pierced her, that threatened to shatter her, was Karina's soft crying. Karina didn't struggle as she walked, didn't try to free herself from Harrison and Luke, who each held one arm. But she hadn't stopped crying since the moment she drew the white stone.

Nate led the way to the clearing at the heart of the woods, the one where she'd seen them bury Luke. They called this place the Pine Tree, even though the forest was full of pines. This one was the biggest tree Sarah had ever seen, big enough that it blocked the sun so nothing grew underneath it. The clearing was wide, the ground a bed of soft reddish-brown pine needles. The moon hung low in the sky, huge, full and heavy, a deep orange color, as if it had been dipped in blood. The torch Nate held aloft glowed with almost the same color. He gestured to Luke and Harrison.

They pulled Karina up against the massive tree. Using a strip of black leather, they tied her wrists to an iron ring that had been screwed into the thick, dark trunk, high over her head.

It was one of the same leather strips they'd used at the first party, Sarah realized. This was going to turn out to be a game. It would probably even end with a party. The pack—her friends, her family—wouldn't kill anyone. Especially not Karina. Everyone loved Karina. It was impossible not to.

"Come to me," the Jager ordered, and the pack gathered around him in the center of the clearing. "We will honor Karina in our hearts and in our history for her sacrifice. We will also honor the pack member who takes her life. It is something we do together, but only one of us can pull the trigger." He handed the torch to Luke and pulled a handgun with a wooden grip and a long metal barrel from the depths of his robe.

Nate let the pistol rest in his palm as he held it out to them. "Who will take the honor? Who will act for all of us?"

"This is how Nate became the Jager," Izzy whispered into Sarah's ear. "I heard there was a sacrifice before I joined, and Nate was the one who did it."

Sarah tried to picture Nate, sweet, understanding Nate, shooting someone in cold blood. She shivered. *It could just be a rumor,* Sarah told herself. It had to be. Yet she knew that Nate was willing to do whatever it took to be a part of the Wolfpack, the best of the best.

Is that why he wanted me here? she wondered. *Does he want me to take this pistol and put myself in line to be the next Jager?*

She couldn't do it. Neither could anyone else.

For a moment, the only sounds were Karina crying, Sarah's pounding heart, and the crackle of pine needles as someone shifted from foot to foot. Then Hazel spoke up. "Couldn't we choose stones again? Or something like that?"

Hazel's voice shook with fear. She didn't seem to think it was a game. Sarah's heartbeat grew painful, as if an iron fist was squeezing and releasing it, over and over. A hard little seed of fear in her chest had started sprouting thorns.

"I thought you all understood why we had to do this," Nate said, disapproval lacing his voice. "We must—"

"Oh fine, I'll do it." Izzy snatched the pistol. She took a step away from the group, turned toward Karina, raised the gun, and fired. Brilliant white light from the muzzle illuminated Izzy's face. She was smiling.

"*No!*" The explosion of sound propelled Sarah into motion. She launched herself at Izzy and tackled her to the ground, sending the gun flying. "What did you do?" Sarah screeched. She grabbed Izzy by the shoulders, pinning the taller girl to the ground. "What did you do?"

"I did what had to be done," Izzy replied calmly.

Sarah stared down into Izzy's eyes. They were expressionless and empty. An icy chill of shock ran up her spine. She forced herself to move, to stand on shaking legs, to look around. She and Izzy were alone in the clearing. Everyone else had run. Even Nate. Even *Nate*.

Sarah turned toward Karina. Her head had flopped to one side, throwing her hood off. Her long dark hair fell over part of her face, but Sarah could see the dark irises of her eyes. They stared sightlessly, and her mouth hung open, as if she had died midscream. Sarah's throat made a soft clicking sound as she fought down bile.

"You killed her. You *killed* her!" Sarah accused, whirling back toward Izzy, who now stood picking at a bit of dirt caught in the velvet nap of her robe.

"So? It's not like I haven't done it before." Izzy shrugged. "It was actually easier this time. You know, there's such a taboo against murder, but then you do it, and you realize, it's not that hard. You can do it again."

"What?"

"It changes you," Izzy said. "Must be why I was the only one with the balls to pull the trigger."

"But that—that other time was an accident. You were fighting off a rapist," Sarah protested.

Izzy twisted her mouth to the side, thinking. "Maybe. I mean, he certainly wanted to do me, and he didn't care what I wanted. But I knew exactly how sharp the corner of the table was. I knew the tabletop was made of marble. And I took very careful aim, and he hit that corner perfectly."

Sarah just blinked at her. "But . . . Karina. Why would you kill Karina?"

Izzy smiled. "You sound so surprised. I told you the truth. You knew why I was at this school. You're the only one who knew—well, except Karina." She glanced over at Karina's body, hanging limply by her hands, still tied to the iron ring. "But I guess she doesn't count anymore, dead and all. Anyway, someone had to do it. That's what we came out here for."

"No. It was just supposed to be a . . . a game, like a mission, like when Luke was buried alive," Sarah argued weakly. "Just pretend."

"Talk to Grayson about *pretend*," Izzy said. "Although that brand is cooler than a tattoo, in my opinion. Much more original. No, you can tell yourself we didn't really plan to kill Karina, but you know that's not true. Admit it, you were relieved I did it. It meant you didn't have to. But you're as guilty as I am. You heard the Jager. We all did this. *Together.*"

Sarah stared at her wordlessly. What was there to say?

Izzy smoothed her wavy hair into place. "I'm heading back. You coming?" She strolled away without waiting for Sarah's response.

It took Sarah almost a full minute to realize she was standing alone in the woods with a dead body. When it hit her, she ran blindly through the dark, pine branches slapping at her, scratching her face and hands, the only parts of her body unprotected by the robe.

She raced from the woods, across the back lawn, and up to the main building. She yanked open the door and started to slam it behind her, stopping herself just in time and shutting it quietly. She couldn't get caught coming inside when a body would be found soon. A body. How could she be thinking of Karina as *a body* already? Tears stung her eyes. She took a few steps, then stopped abruptly. She didn't know where to go. Not back to her room. *Their* room. Hers and Karina's and Izzy's. She couldn't go there. She never wanted to see Izzy again.

The den? No. The rest of the pack—including Nate—had run off and left her.

Dr. Diaz. He'd helped her before, he'd help her now. She pulled her cell out of her pocket. "Locate Dr. Diaz," she whispered, her voice shaking.

"Teachers' quarters," the cell replied cheerfully. Sarah glanced at the dots on the screen—she'd never been to the teachers' area before. Dr. Diaz's dot was two floors above the sitting room near the front entrance. She raced up the main staircase and followed the blinking yellow dot up another set of stairs and down to his door. She tapped on it, and he didn't take long to appear.

One look at her face was all he needed. "What's wrong?" he

asked. "What happened?" He held the door open wider and she hurried inside.

Sarah opened her mouth— What was she supposed to say? How could she tell him what had happened? What they'd done? She let out a shaky sob.

"Sit down," Dr. Diaz told her.

Sarah let him lead her over to the chair in front of his desk. She sat down. A little muscle beneath her right eye had begun to twitch.

"You're starting to worry me, Sarah. I need you to talk." Dr. Diaz pulled an armchair over next to her and sat. "Please, tell me what happened. Let me help you. Did you have another memory surge?"

She wanted to tell him everything. But she wasn't going to bring the Wolfpack into this. She couldn't. Without them she might lose too much.

Dr. Diaz took her arm and laid his fingers on her wrist, eyes on the wall clock. "Can you tell me your name?" He didn't sound freaked out now. He sounded calm. Professional. Like the doctor he was.

The doctor voice snapped her out of her shock. Sarah pulled her wrist away. "I'm fine. I, you were right; I just had one of my memory things. I'm okay now." She stood up.

"Are you sure? What's with the robe?" Dr. Diaz asked.

The robe? The ceremonial robe! Sarah still had it on! She hadn't even thought about it when she'd come tearing up here. How could she explain it?

"I, I . . . We killed Karina!" she burst out, her calm resolve shattered by his question. The words were like a tidal wave now, unstoppable. "I'm in this secret group. The Wolfpack. We decided to sacrifice someone. I thought it was just a, just pretend, a twisted game. But there was a gun. And—"

Dr. Diaz was on his feet. "Where was this?" he asked.

"In the woods."

"You need to show me. Now," Dr. Diaz told her. Sarah blinked. "She might still be alive," he explained. Could she be? Sarah hadn't gotten close to her. She'd seen Karina's limp body, her unblinking eyes, her mouth open in an endless scream. "We need to go now," Dr. Diaz ordered.

"Okay." Sarah shoved herself to her feet, tearing off the robe. She'd be able to run faster in her jeans and sweater. And maybe Karina was alive. It was dark out. Maybe Sarah hadn't seen right. Except that the moon was so full, the light from it so bright. Pushing the thought away, she raced back down the stairs, Dr. Diaz right behind her. Together they ran out the rear exit, down the path across the lawn, through the woods.

But when they reached the clearing, it was empty.

There was no gun lying on the ground.

There was no body hanging limply from the tree.

There weren't even any footprints in the pine needles.

11

"Let's just get you back to your room," Dr. Diaz said. But everything had changed. He didn't sound like himself, not even his ultraprofessional doctor self. His voice was different—*careful*. Like she might explode.

"I swear to god she was here, she was dead," Sarah whispered, her eyes flicking from the iron ring in the Pine Tree to the spot on the ground where Sarah had tackled Izzy. There was no sign of a struggle. "I'm not crazy," her voice broke.

Dr. Diaz took her arm and gently steered her back through the woods. "Try to think, Sarah. Were you and your friends doing anything you shouldn't have been?"

You mean like murdering someone? she thought wildly. That little muscle under her eye was twitching again, faster now.

"Did you do any drugs?" he pressed.

"No," she said automatically.

He sighed. "I'm not asking as a teacher, Sarah, I'm asking as a friend. I won't tell anyone. But if you took something, it's possible that a drug might've caused your memory to get confused. A mind-altering substance mixed with a brain like yours, well, that could get complicated."

"You think I imagined it?" she asked, trying to focus on her feet, on stepping over branches and not slipping on fallen leaves. Normal things, not murderous things.

"Truthfully, I don't know. But I think there are drugs that cause hallucinations, hallucinations anyone might find vivid and real. I tried a few of those, years ago. Once I came out of it, I knew I'd been tripping, as we called it back in the day." He smiled, but it looked forced. "But for you, even later you might not be able to distinguish a hallucination from reality, because your brain stores data differently."

Sarah thought about it. She was almost certain that the Blutgrog was a drug, not just alcohol and berries or whatever. It had always made her feel strange, always made the rest of the Wolfpack lose pretty much every inhibition they had. But it had never caused hallucinations. The things the Wolfpack did were very real. Like branding Grayson. Horrific, but real. She and Izzy and Karina—*Karina*, her name was a surprise punch to the gut—they'd talked about Grayson's punishment afterward. They'd all had the same experience, and hallucinations didn't work like that.

And Sarah had always felt extraordinarily clearheaded when she drank it, all her senses heightened, her reality amped up. Her *reality*. She shook her head. "No drugs."

They tramped through the woods silently until they finally hit the smooth expanse of the back lawn. "Okay, not a hallucination. A dream then," Dr. Diaz said thoughtfully. "Bleeding into your perception of reality. You think you're remembering the truth, but you're only remembering a dream? We talked about how that can happen to people with extraordinary memories."

"I don't know," Sarah murmured, lost in thought. Nothing like that had ever happened to her before. In a surge, she felt as if she was inside a memory, that the memory was happening in the present. The memory could feel real, but she'd never felt that a dream was real. She'd never confused them.

But maybe Dr. Diaz was right. Maybe her brain processed data differently than other people's, even in a dream. It made more sense that the whole thing had been a horrible nightmare. Izzy wouldn't have killed Karina. Or acted so casually about killing that boy, that had devastated her. "Maybe you're right—" She stopped abruptly, a realization slamming into her.

"But you saw me in the robe. We wear robes for the ceremonies. I didn't dream that I put it on," she pointed out. Right now she needed to think like the science geek she was. Neither the hallucination theory or the dream theory made sense. She wished they did, but they just didn't. She'd had Blutgrog a ton of times by now, and it had never made her sleepy or given her hallucinations.

"I'm not saying everything was a dream. You could have put on the robe to meet with your friends, then you could have fallen asleep without undressing," Dr. Diaz suggested as they stepped inside the building. "You thought you were playing a game.

Maybe you did, and parts of the game even ended up being incorporated into the dream."

But why would tonight be the first time in her whole life where a dream felt like a memory?

"We both saw the clearing, Sarah. There was no indication that anyone had even been out there earlier tonight."

They reached the main staircase and began to climb. He was right. No footprints. All the pine needles undisturbed. A wave of dizziness washed over her, and for a moment she felt her grip on reality shift.

"Get some sleep, Sarah." Dr. Diaz's voice startled her. She glanced up, realizing they were at the top of the staircase. She needed to go down the hall to reach the east wing. Dr. Diaz needed to go up the next staircase that started a few feet away. "The morning always brings clarity. We can try to figure this out tomorrow."

"Okay." In a daze, she took the first step. "Thanks."

She didn't look back, but she knew Dr. Diaz stood there watching her. He was worried. *Well, not as worried as I am*. The image of Karina's lifeless eyes rose up again, and Sarah clenched her teeth, willing herself to stay here, in the reality of this present moment. She couldn't risk remembering too clearly—the shot, the scream, the way Karina's long dark hair fell over her face and just stayed there, her eyes staring from behind it. If she let that memory take over, she'd go mad.

"It's not real," Sarah whispered. "There was no body."

But it *was* real. She was sure of it. She knew herself. She knew her brain.

Karina was dead.

"You're going to sleep through your first class, lazy." Izzy's voice filtered through the layers of sleep into Sarah's consciousness. "It's almost eight thirty."

I'm late, Sarah thought, panicked. She sat up in bed, her heart pounding, trying to remember where she was supposed to be.

"Don't worry, you're way ahead of Karina," Izzy went on.

Karina. Shrill scream. Dead eyes. Body slumping forward, stopped from falling only by her hands tied to the iron ring. *Stop. Stopstopstop.* Sarah was fully awake now, all her energy focused on keeping herself *out* of the memory of Karina. Not that she could stop a true memory surge, but she could try to stop herself from thinking about all the unspeakable details of the night before. She turned horrified eyes on Izzy.

Izzy smiled and cocked her head toward Karina's bed. "She's not even back yet."

Sarah didn't have to look to see that the bed was still made. She knew Karina hadn't slept there, because Karina was dead. Izzy had killed her.

"Can you imagine how late she's going to be? It's not like she can go straight to class wearing the same clothes. Our Karina's not the walk-of-shame type." Izzy turned toward her mirror and pulled out a tube of Chanel lip gloss in the palest pink, the gold band under the cap catching the light. Focusing on the details helped Sarah keep her mind where she wanted it, away from Karina's face, drained of life.

"What? What are you talking about?" Sarah finally managed to squeak.

"Karina." Izzy met her eyes in the mirror. "She obviously must've taken it to the next level with Ethan. She never came home last night. And Ethan isn't the letting-the-girlfriend-sleep-in-his-room type, even though he has a single. Wonder how she pulled it off."

Sarah stared at her roommate, speechless. *What's going on? Am I dreaming?* she wondered frantically. She pinched the spot on the inside of her elbow and an arrow of pain shot up her arm. Not dreaming. Her mind replayed the words on Izzy's lips last night: "I took very careful aim, and he hit that corner perfectly."

That conversation had happened. Body or no body. Footprints in the clearing or no footprints. It *had* happened.

"Iz . . ." Sarah trailed off.

Izzy raised her perfectly arched eyebrows, waiting. After a moment, she shook her head and laughed. "You're really out of it today—maybe you had a little too much fun last night." She tossed the lip gloss on her dresser, grabbed Sarah's leather jacket, and headed for the door. "See you. Don't be too late!"

When she was gone, Sarah sat very still for a long time, trying to process things. Karina was dead. Izzy shot her while everyone watched. Sarah remembered every single second of the horrible incident. But Izzy didn't seem to remember it at all. Or else Izzy was the worst human being in the entire world, somebody who not only thought it was okay to murder your roommate in cold blood, but who also thought it was fun to spend the next morning acting like it never happened. Did she expect Sarah to go along with her? Was this her attempt at getting away with it?

Without looking at Karina's bed, Sarah got up and pulled on her ancient Target jeans and a black top. She automatically reached for the sweater Izzy had traded her, but her hand stopped before touching it. She couldn't wear Izzy's clothes, not anymore.

It was cold outside, and her ratty old Goodwill sweatshirt wouldn't help much, but Sarah didn't care. She hurried out of the suite. All the happy memories she'd had there were tainted now. She had to get away.

"We've got to hurry if we don't want to miss English," Maya said as soon as Sarah stepped out the back door.

Sarah jumped in surprise. Had Maya been waiting there for her? They didn't usually meet up to walk to class.

"I can't believe I overslept!" Maya continued.

"Me too," Sarah muttered. But she might as well let Maya drag her to English. Ms. Coté, the teacher, would drone on about Emerson, and Sarah could tune out and try to figure out what was going on. After all, she'd already read all the assigned essays and criticism. She would also remember every word of the lecture today, even if she didn't pay much attention—the same way she remembered everything that had happened last night.

They had gone into the woods.

They had tied Karina to a tree.

And Izzy had shot her.

Dead.

"Hey, Merson, is that a little beard burn on your face?" Kayla asked in a loud whisper, giggling as soon as Maya and Sarah entered the room. Logan, sitting next to her, made kissing sounds and laughed.

What?

"I'm going to sit with them," she told Maya. Maya rolled her eyes, but didn't try to follow. Nobody was supposed to know about the Wolfpack, but somehow it always seemed as if nonmembers could tell when they weren't wanted.

Sarah took a deep breath and headed for her friends. Logan grabbed his jacket off the chair next to him so she could sit. Both he and Kayla were grinning as if there was nothing wrong.

"As I was saying," Ms. Coté gave Sarah and Maya pointed looks. Maya looked abashed. But an angry teacher didn't even register on Sarah's radar this morning, not when Karina's dead eyes kept flashing in her mind. "I want you to break into groups of three or four. There are books of nineteenth-century art on the shelf. Take one, choose a landscape, and discuss it in conjunction with Emerson's 'Nature.' I'll give you half an hour, then we'll hear a short summary of your conclusions."

Sarah, Logan, and Kayla immediately pulled their desks together. She sighed with relief. She wouldn't have to suffer through class until she could talk to someone from the Wolfpack. Logan shook his head when Taylor tried to join them. "Full up." She looked like she wanted to argue, but jerked her desk over to another group with a huff of irritation.

"Have you heard anything? What's up?" Sarah whispered.

"Nate's dick!" Logan joked. Kayla smacked his arm, but she was giggling.

"Excuse me?" Sarah knew her voice had an edge to it, because they immediately stopped laughing.

"Oh, don't be embarrassed. We tease everybody who decides to do sexy times at the meetings," Kayla said. "Usually Nate doesn't get into PDAs unless we're in party mode, but I guess you made him get over that."

"That's not the only thing she made him do!" Logan cried. Ms. Coté shot them an angry look as she slammed one of the art books, which none of them had bothered to fetch, onto Logan's desk.

"God, you're disgusting. That doesn't even make sense," Kayla told Logan, lowering her voice a little. "Anyway, it's not like we did much official meeting stuff."

"What are you guys talking about?" Sarah asked.

"You and Nate getting busy during the movie in the den last night," Logan replied. "Oh, I'm sorry. Did you even know there was a movie on? You were a bit . . . distracted."

"A movie?" A rush of dizziness made Sarah's brain feel like it was shutting down.

"Yeah, *The Conjuring*. That opening scene?" Kayla gave an exaggerated shiver. "I hate anything with creepy dolls."

Sarah felt like she was losing her mind. She didn't know exactly what she'd been expecting, but this was not it. The two of them were acting as if Karina's murder didn't matter at all.

"You mean you all went back to the den and watched a freaking movie after that?" she practically shrieked.

A few kids glanced over at them, and Kayla's eyes widened. "Quiet!"

"Everyone took off. I had no idea where you guys were," Sarah said, lowering her voice a notch. "If you saw Nate getting busy after that, it certainly wasn't with me. How sick are you people?"

Kayla and Logan stared at her, confusion in their eyes. "Sarah, what the hell?" Logan whispered. "After *what*?"

"After . . . after the sacrifice," she whispered. She couldn't bring herself to say Karina's name.

Logan's eyebrows drew together in bewilderment. "What sacrifice?"

Sarah's mouth felt dry. There wasn't a flicker of fear or guilt or remorse on either of their faces. They were acting just like Izzy, like it was a normal day. Like nothing had happened.

"Don't you remember we were supposed to make a sacrifice on Halloween, to bind us together as a group?" Sarah pressed, desperate for someone to remember what she did. "We drew stones. We went out to the woods."

"I remember doing the opening ritual," Kayla murmured. "But then we put the movie on."

"No. We went out to the Pine Tree," Sarah insisted.

"We did not. It was raining. Who wants to go out and get soaked?" Logan replied.

"Seriously. I would've ruined my leather skirt," Kayla said.

It wasn't raining last night, Sarah thought. It was a perfect, star-filled sky last night. There weren't even any clouds blocking that huge orange moon. And this morning? No puddles. No damp lawn.

"What about Karina?" Sarah said. "Don't you remember anything about her?"

"I think she was there." Logan shrugged and shot a questioning look at Kayla.

"We were all there, weren't we?" she asked, her expression vague. "I don't think I talked to her, though."

"Me either." Logan suddenly seemed interested the assignment, flipping intently through the paintings of landscapes.

Am I losing my mind? Sarah wondered. The rain. She had to remember the rain. That was a fact. Not what she believed. Not what anyone else believed. A fact. It did not rain last night.

And that meant they were lying to her. They were both lying to her.

Could this be some elaborate prank? Some other part of her initiation? Maybe that was the theory she'd been looking for. Nate could have ordered everyone in the pack to tell the same lie. He could have staged a murder, then made everyone pretend they'd spent the night watching a movie. Sarah felt a jolt of raw hope.

The rain detail was weird, but she pushed it out of her mind. It was one of the Wolfpack pranks. For the first time, she began to feel calmer.

After English—and her, Logan, and Kayla making fools of themselves trying to recap their "discussion" of the essay and painting—she checked her cell. Nate was at the Sports Center. Sarah caught up to him just as he was heading inside.

"Sarah, hey!" He smiled, his brown eyes fixing on her like she was the only person in the world. "What are you doing here?"

"I'm, um . . ." As usual, Nate's unwavering gaze unsettled her, got her heart beating a little harder. "I was looking for you."

"Good," he said, his smile growing wider. He reached out and slipped his arm around her waist, pulling her in for a quick, body-tingling kiss. Sarah stiffened. Was he going to act like everything was normal too? Didn't he get how twisted this prank was, how watching Izzy "kill" Karina had nearly destroyed her?

"You're freezing," Nate murmured, his lips brushing against hers as he spoke. "Come inside." Wrapping his arms around her shoulders, he guided her into the marble lobby of the Sports Center. It was warm inside, but he kept holding her anyway. She ignored how good it felt, how comforting, to soak in his closeness, and gently extracted herself.

"Nate, listen. I need to talk about last night," Sarah said. "I can't stop thinking about what we did, and I have to know . . ." She let her words trail off.

"It was phenomenal," he murmured. "I'm going to have to watch that movie again though. You had me way too distracted."

Distracted. The same word Kayla and Logan had used. He was keeping the sick joke going, telling her the same story.

Like an alibi.

The thought slammed into her.

This morning she'd thought maybe Izzy was trying to get away with Karina's murder by pretending it never happened. What if that's what the whole pack was doing? Not pulling a prank on Sarah, but creating a group alibi.

Sarah felt like she'd been shoved into the icy ocean. She'd been trying so hard to come up with a way that Karina could still be alive, to convince herself that she hadn't seen what she knew she had.

"I can't stop thinking about it either," Nate added earnestly. His smile was gone, but he still stared at her intensely, his eyes doing that thing where they rapidly flicked back and forth in tiny motions, like whatever she was going to say or do deserved every ounce of his focus and concentration.

It would make sense for Nate to handle the cleanup in the woods, she realized now. That's what he did. Take charge. She could picture him getting rid of the evidence, creating a cover story. But that didn't mean he should be lying to her.

"Nate, be serious for a minute. We should we tell somebody," she said. "Maybe you can keep things quiet for a little while, but that can't last. We'll be in even more trouble if we're not the ones to admit it."

Nate looked surprised. Then he threw back his head and laughed. "I don't think we'll be in too much trouble," he said. "And everyone probably saw us, so there's nobody to tell." He leaned in for another kiss, but Sarah shoved him away.

"How can you laugh?" she cried, baffled.

"Oh. Sorry." He stopped and put on a serious expression again, but within a few seconds his trademark grin was back. "I can't help it, Sarah, I had fun. I don't care if people know that I like you."

"What are you talking about?" Sarah practically screamed. She couldn't take one more insane conversation.

"Last night," he said. "Down in the den? The whole pack was there. Did you think nobody would notice us kissing?"

Sarah stared at him, not saying a word. His arms had found their way around her again, and she could smell his soap—a heady, musky scent. "Kissing?" she finally asked.

"Among other things." He moved closer, pressing her against his chest.

"I, um, my memory is a little hazy," Sarah lied. "We were watching one of the *Saw* movies, right?"

"You remember even less of the movie than I do." He nuzzled

her neck. "We were watching the *The Conjuring*. Or not watching." Nate pulled his head back and looked down at her, his eyes penetrating. "That's what happened, Sarah. We all watched a movie in the den."

His voice was so firm, so sure, so confident. He seemed so much more certain of his memories than she was of hers.

Slowly, Sarah nodded. She could picture the den, its walls draped with Oriental carpets and its floor covered with cushions. She could picture the huge TV on one wall, and the Wolfpack scattered around the room, laughing and talking back to the movie. She could feel Nate's lips on hers, his hands moving over her body as they lay on a pile of pillows in the dark corner.

But Karina's dead eyes didn't fit into that memory. Had her special snowflake of a brain short-circuited? Izzy had been so normal this morning. Logan and Kayla too. And Nate was a hundred percent regular Nate, intense, but he was always intense. Karina *could* have stayed over at Ethan's . . .

"I thought we were supposed to do a mission with the pack, though," Sarah said, backing away enough to make him stop touching her. How was she supposed to think with Nate touching her? "For Halloween, remember?"

"Is that what's bothering you?" Nate shook his head, leaning close again, sliding one hand from the base of her neck to the small of her back, creating a hot shiver in its wake. "Sarah, we did the opening ritual. Nobody was into going outside last night, it was raining. It wasn't your fault for keeping the Jager too busy."

The tingling heat he'd started up in her body suddenly cooled. He was lying to her. She'd let herself get sucked into the fantasy that the night before had been spent making out with him in the den.

"I have to go," she blurted out, jerking away from Nate's embrace.

"Come find me at dinner!" he called after her.

Sarah waved without looking back. She couldn't risk getting drawn back into Nate's orbit right now.

She pulled out her cell. "Locate Karina."

"Student offline," it announced.

She wrapped her arms tightly around herself. What did *that* mean? Dead? Or actually offline? Or maybe down in the den where there was no signal? If she'd been right, and the rest of the Wolfpack was pranking her, then Karina would have to stay out of sight. She would be hiding somewhere.

But Karina's dead eyes. Her slack body. Could that really have been faked?

"Locate Izzy," she said.

"Student offline," the cell replied.

Alibi or mind game? Karina alive or dead?

If the story was an alibi, why had Nate and the pack left her out? She was part of the family, why didn't they tell her what to say?

But she hadn't been with the rest of the pack after Karina's murder. She hadn't been there when Nate gave out the instructions. She'd freaked out and run off on her own and outed the Wolfpack to Dr. Diaz. She'd broken her vow to her family, and now they were all in on a plan that didn't include her. Did they know she'd told Dr. Diaz? Would she be branded just like Grayson?

How could she have been so dumb? It had never even occurred to her to go looking for the rest of the Wolfpack after they took off. But if she was committed to the group, really committed like she vowed to be, wouldn't that have been her first instinct? Wouldn't she have gone to them instead of Dr. Diaz?

All morning they've been trying to give me our alibi, Sarah realized. *Nate and everyone else, they came up with a cover story for us, and they've all been telling it to me. They've been showing me what to do. I'm supposed to say the same thing. If anyone asks, we were all watching that movie in the den, and I was making out with Nate.*

They were one another's alibis. If they all stuck together, no one would be able to disprove their story. It was exactly what the Jager had said—doing this awful thing would make them closer as a group.

Except that meant Karina was really dead. Unless Sarah was being hazed. Or maybe her loyalty to the pack was being tested? Sarah felt like her head was about to crack open.

She took a shaky breath and made a decision. When she was with the Wolfpack, she would speak the lies she'd learned from them. Down in the den, movie, making out, Karina there. *Karina there.* But she promised herself, she promised her roommate, her friend, her pack sister, that she would find out the truth.

No matter what.

12

Sarah rested her hand against the cold metal of the door. The den had been one of her favorite places on campus, a place where she felt completely accepted and loved—where she felt safe. Her pack had always welcomed her here. So why was she so afraid to open that door now?

Because if she didn't, Karina could still be alive.

Sarah could still imagine Karina down in the den, reading magazines while the prank on Sarah played out, letting out a giggle every time she thought of the look on Sarah's face. But if Karina wasn't there . . .

She couldn't stand in front of the closed door forever. She'd promised herself she'd find out the truth. Checking the sub-basement was the first step. Still, she took the two flights of stairs slowly. She checked the cells first, then the Bone Man room, even though there was no way Karina would sit around in that creepy place, then she walked to the den.

The TV was off. The sofas and piles of pillows were empty.

On the pile of pillows in the corner, that's where she'd been making out with Nate last night. The movie playing, the laughter and screams of her packmates, all dull background music while his hands roamed over her body.

Sarah shook her head. That hadn't happened. They kept saying it, but it wasn't true. She could picture it so perfectly, but she remembered everything that had ever happened to her, and it just hadn't.

She glanced around the room again. Karina wasn't there.

Sarah felt despair rise up in her belly, and she shoved it back down. She wasn't giving up yet. If Karina was hiding out, there was one other place she might be.

"Ethan!" Sarah yelled, not caring if anyone heard her. She banged on his door. "Ethan, I know you're in there!"

The door flew open so suddenly that she almost fell into Ethan's arms. He wore boxer-briefs and nothing else, and his dark hair was wild. Sarah's cheeks heated up and she looked away. "Is Karina here?" she asked. Ethan's room was the obvious place for her to hide. Karina wouldn't even need an excuse.

"No." Ethan pulled the door open wide enough for her to see his whole room. It was a mess—piles of dirty clothes, stacks of books about to topple—but he was the only one there.

"Then what are you doing in here?" she demanded.

"Well, Officer, I was taking a pretty epic nap, but I'm afraid I don't have anyone to back me up on that story," Ethan said sarcastically.

Sarah pushed past him and glanced around his room, searching for any sign of her roommate. "Karina didn't come home last night. Izzy figured she stayed with you."

"She didn't." The sarcasm vanished from his voice. "And you still can't find her? Did you ask your cell?"

"It said she's offline, and I haven't seen her all day," Sarah told him. "I'm . . . I'm afraid something happened to her." She left it at that, afraid to betray the pack again.

"Wait. I thought you girls were doing something together last night," he said, studying her face.

"We were in the library studying." Ethan would never go to the library, so there was no way he would find out it was a lie.

"I thought you said she didn't come home."

"Right. Well, we had a fight," she lied. "Izzy said some crap about how you're a horrible boyfriend, and Karina got mad and stormed off."

Ethan scratched his flat belly. "So the usual?" he said. "What were you doing during this fight?"

"I was on Izzy's side," Sarah said.

He laughed.

"We figured Karina went to find you after she left. Like I said, she never came home." Sarah pushed down the image of Karina's dead eyes.

"Let's go." Ethan stood up and grabbed a T-shirt off the back of his desk chair.

"Go where?" Sarah forced herself to watch him as he pulled his jeans up over his lean hips. She knew he'd make fun of her if she was too shy to watch him getting dressed.

"Go find Karina." He put on his boots, then glanced at his cell.

"Let's get out of here before lunch period ends. It'll be easier to get off campus with everyone milling around."

She'd almost forgotten it was a school day. English felt like forever ago. For a moment, she had a crazy desire to go to her next class, pretend everything was totally normal. She wanted what being in the Wolfpack would give her, that life Nate had described. If she just went to class, just followed along with what Nate said, maybe she could keep that life.

It wouldn't be hard to convince herself that she'd been in the den, making out with Nate . . . She could almost feel it, almost hear the sounds of the movie . . .

"Are you coming?" Ethan asked.

Almost.

"Yeah. I'm coming."

Sarah stopped short when Ethan started across the lacrosse field. Behind the stands, there was a hedge higher than their heads and so thick she couldn't see the other side. He was leading them to a dead end. "Are you screwing with me?" she asked. "I thought you wanted to find Karina."

"I do." Ethan didn't even glance back at her. He kept walking right toward the hedge. "I marked it with an old piece of brick," he muttered. Eyes on the ground, he veered a bit to the right. "Here."

"What are you talking about?" In spite of herself, Sarah walked over and looked. A piece of red brick sat half buried in the dirt at the base of one of the bushes. "And this means what?"

"It means the path leads here. Or led here, I guess." Ethan dropped onto his belly and army-crawled toward the hedge. "You might get leaves in your hair," he called back.

Sarah watched his legs disappear beneath the massive bushes.

What he said hadn't made any sense. But nothing had the entire day. She'd been knocked completely off-balance and couldn't seem to find a way to recover.

"I'm not waiting, Sarah." Ethan's voice sounded muffled.

Feeling like an idiot, Sarah dropped to the ground. She couldn't see anything but leaves in front of her face, and as she crawled forward on her stomach, she had to just hope that she wouldn't smack face-first into the trunk of the bush. If it had a trunk. She hadn't read anything about evergreen shrubs, and there hadn't been much ornamental vegetation in the crappy Toledo neighborhoods she'd lived in.

Small branches whapped her in the face, so she closed her eyes and kept moving until she didn't feel them anymore.

"I think you're safe now," Ethan said, sounding amused. He didn't seem at all worried they wouldn't be able to find Karina.

Sarah opened her eyes—and gasped. In front of her stretched a wild, overgrown field with weeds and grass at least a foot high. All the school lawns and sports fields on the other side of the hedge were emerald green and perfectly cropped, but here it looked like the no-man's-land on the side of an interstate.

"Welcome back to reality. You're always talking about it, so I'm sure you'll be comfortable here." Ethan held out his hand to help her up, and Sarah took it, too thrown by the landscape to reply. "Sanctuary Bay Academy doesn't bother with the world outside its boundaries."

He set off across the field, and now Sarah could see that there was indeed a path through the weeds—a narrow dirt path, the unplanned kind made by people walking. There had been a path like that across the patch of land between the 7-Eleven and the bus stop at her second-to-last high school. Everyone had been too lazy to stick to the sidewalk on their way to buy Slurpees after school.

"Who made the path?" she asked after a minute. There were so many other questions, but for some reason that was the one that bothered her.

"Don't know. It was here when I got here," Ethan replied. "Not that I found it right away—it leads straight to the asylum, but it kind of dumps you in the middle of nowhere at the edge of the school. I always figured there must've been something else there before the Academy. That the path used to lead to something other than a giant hedge, but the school just dropped some sod on top of it and that was that."

"Asylum?" she asked uncertainly.

"That's right, Sarah, we're going to the nuthouse." Ethan didn't bother to look back at her. He didn't care whether she followed him or not.

Sarah let the silence stretch out while they tramped through the field. *What's missing is garbage*, she suddenly realized. Usually on unused land, among the overgrown grass and weeds there would be litter. Here there was only pristine but crappy-looking nature. It made the whole empty field seem creepier somehow. Emptier. Sarah drew her thin sweatshirt tight around herself. The wind was cold. They had to be heading toward the water.

"I thought we were looking for Karina," she finally said. Not that they would find her, since she was dead. Sarah pushed that thought away. She didn't know for sure. She had to keep reminding herself that she didn't know what the truth was. There had been no body.

"That's right. If she's not at school, she'll be here." Ethan stopped and gestured down at the building that stood in front of them. Sarah gasped in surprise. Two seconds ago there had been nothing but grass and sky, and suddenly there was a two-story-high brick ruin beneath them.

"We're on a hill," Sarah said, shaking her head to clear out the dizzy feeling this place was giving her. The building was tall, but even the roof was below where they stood. "Or is it a cliff?" The ground at her feet dropped down sharply, and the brick building stood at the bottom of a chasm she hadn't even noticed. "I would've walked right off this drop-off."

"Yeah, the weeds block your view of it," Ethan agreed. "First time I came here, I fell and slid all the way down to the asylum. It was fun. I broke my arm."

"This is the old insane asylum?" Sarah stared at the crumbling building. It was much bigger than just the ugly tower she'd seen from the boat on her first day. It was easily as big as the Sports Center—or at least it had been before half of its walls fell down. "They built it in a hole?"

"It's more like a notch, actually," Ethan said. "The drop-off is steep, but at the bottom the ground is flat again, and it stays flat all the way out to the bluffs. So the asylum isn't in a hole. It's more like the Sanctuary Bay Academy is up on a mesa."

"I saw part of it from the boat, but the rest was hidden by the trees, I guess. I had no idea this was all still here, rotting away," Sarah whispered. She wasn't sure why, but it seemed wrong to talk loudly.

"You probably saw the ruin, the one up here," Ethan said. "That was doctors' quarters or something, I figure, because it's not down in that hole where the patients were. It's that way, near the edge of the cliff."

Sarah squinted into the distance, following his gesture, and she could just barely make out the brick tower.

"That one is fenced off because it's crumbling. I don't go in there because I don't want to end up crushed to death. I'm not as stupid as your boyfriend thinks." Ethan pointed to the ground at his feet. "The path leads to these stairs. I figured that out *after* I broke my arm."

Sarah glanced down, startled. She hadn't even seen the narrow staircase that led down the hill. It was a rickety, ancient-looking wooden structure that hugged the wall of the drop-off. "This place is freaky," she said, gripping the splintery railing tightly as she climbed down after Ethan.

"My theory is that they chose this island because it had a natural little shelf where they could trap the lunatics," Ethan said. "They couldn't get up this cliff except by these stairs, which were locked." He jumped off the bottom of the staircase, making the whole thing shake. "See? Iron gate."

Sarah was too busy trying to figure out how to get down the last two steps, which were broken nearly in half, to look up.

"You have to jump." Ethan's voice held a challenge.

"Fine." Sarah didn't give herself time to hesitate. She simply stepped off the side of the steep staircase and dropped to the ground. The impact sent a shock wave up from her knees to her back. It was only four feet or so, but it still hurt. To cover, she turned to examine the gate. It was made of rusted iron, and had an old lock in place. "Why couldn't they just climb up onto the steps from the side?" she asked. "The same way we got off?"

"Twelve-foot-high bars." Ethan pointed to the dirt next to the staircase, where a section of iron fence was lying. "The stairs rotted away enough that the fence fell off."

The bars each had a sharp spike on the top. Sarah felt a wave of horror. "So the inmates were trapped at the bottom of this . . . notch. With the cliffs and the ocean on one side, and this hill they couldn't climb on the other side."

"Well, it *was* an insane asylum," Ethan pointed out. "I'm sure they didn't want the crazies wandering all over the place."

"God, you're such an asshole," Sarah exploded. "We're talking about people. Human beings."

He shrugged. "I suffer from compassion fatigue. We go in over here."

"Wait, what?" Sarah called, hurrying after him as he headed toward the brick building. There were windows on the first floor, and none on the second floor. Rusted iron bars covered the broken glass of the ancient windows. "What do you mean, you go in?"

"Karina and I. We come here sometimes to . . . have our privacy." He smirked. "She enjoys getting loud."

Sarah winced. This place was horrifying—it was nothing more than a crumbling old prison where people were locked away without windows, trapped on an island, and stuck in a hole with no escape. "You guys use this as a romantic getaway? That is truly messed up."

"Nobody from the school would ever find us."

"How did you find it, then?" she asked. Ethan led the way to a place where the brick had collapsed, creating a hole in the wall. He stepped inside. Sarah followed, shivering a little as she left the sun behind.

"My first try at looking for an escape route meant heading toward the water," he said. "It's an island. Every way off is going to involve the ocean. So I spent my first six months at Sanctuary Bay exploring every inch of the coastline. It's hard to miss this place."

The room they stood in was some kind of wardroom—rusting metal beds lined each side of the long, narrow space. But Sarah was too busy staring at Ethan to take it in. "*What?*" she cried. "Are you telling me you were serious all this time? You've been looking for an escape route for real?"

He stared at her, shaking his head. "Haven't I told you that about a million times?"

"Well . . . yeah," she said. He had. It simply hadn't occurred to her to believe him. She'd figured it was just part of his I-hate-this-school shtick, which she also didn't really believe. It had always seemed like one more way for spoiled Ethan Steere to feel that the best things in the world still weren't good enough for him.

"I haven't found a way off yet," Ethan said, "but I have managed to spot a few places where I can be alone. Off the grid, like here. It's not escape, but it's . . . temporary escape, I guess. Mental escape."

"From what?" Sarah asked, baffled.

"Sanctuary Bay. All the *activities* and made-up lacrosse games and rah-rah stuff." He ran his hand through his hair and gave a little shudder. "Sometimes I just need to get out of there, be where I can think my own thoughts, you know?"

"I guess," she answered, although until today, she'd never wanted to leave the campus.

Ethan headed deeper into the room, his eyes scanning the decaying mattresses, the jagged, broken bed frames.

"Why did you come here in the first place if you hate it so much?" Sarah pressed. "There's got to be a thousand kids like me who would die for a chance to go to Sanctuary Bay. Who would love to take your spot if you don't want it."

"You think I had a choice?" Ethan gave a bitter laugh. "I'd gladly let the plebes take my place if I could just get off this damn island. Alive, I mean."

"Is that supposed to be a joke?"

"You tell me. My brother never made it." Ethan stopped walking and stood still, his back to Sarah. Something about the hunch of his shoulders made her want to go over and hug him.

"I didn't even know you have a brother," she said.

"I *had* a brother." Ethan turned and looked her in the eyes. "Philip. He was five years older than me."

Sarah was transfixed by the sound of his voice. It sounded hollow, like it belonged to someone else.

"What happened to him?" she whispered, almost afraid to hear the answer.

"I don't know. He got on the ferry when he was fourteen, and he didn't get off of it when he was eighteen. Everyone else did—I know, I was there. My parents and I stood on the dock watching every single Sanctuary Bay graduate walk down the gangplank, but Philip didn't show. When we asked the school, they said he got on the ferry to go home. They said he finished the immersion program, he got accepted to Yale, he graduated, he got on the boat . . . and that's it. Nobody knows anything else."

Sarah let out a sharp breath. "I'm sorry," she said.

Ethan raised one eyebrow, and suddenly his lips quirked into a knowing smile. "You think he fell off the ferry and drowned," he said.

"Um . . ." Sarah grasped for something to say, anything that wouldn't sound terrible. She knew what it was like when people refused to believe you. "I don't know what else to think."

"That's because you trust them." Ethan spun around and began walking through the room again. "Karina's not here. We have to look farther inside."

"I trust who?" Sarah asked, trailing after him. "The school? Why shouldn't I? Why shouldn't *you*? I mean, I guess they're negligent if they let someone fall off the ferry and they don't even notice it." She frowned. "But that doesn't mean they'd lie about it. They told you what they knew."

"They told my father, and he told my mother, and she told me. Who knows if I ended up hearing anything the school really said? If they even said anything at all," Ethan muttered.

"Stop walking," Sarah commanded him.

Ethan glanced back at her, surprised. She saw a flash of anger in his blue eyes, but he stopped anyway. "Sorry, can't you walk and talk at the same time?" he asked. "They really shouldn't have cut funding to the Head Start program."

Sarah didn't want to get sucked into one of their snarkfests. "You're talking about your dead brother and looking for your maybe-dead girlfriend. You can take two seconds and stand still while you do it," she snapped.

"My maybe-*dead* girlfriend?" he repeated.

"No. I just mean . . . I didn't mean that. He's missing. She's missing. I don't know what I'm talking about," Sarah fumbled. "I only wanted you to stop and explain this to me."

"Fine." He sighed. "All I know is that I said good-bye to my brother when I was nine. He was my best friend and my idol and he never, ever treated me like an annoying little kid, even though I probably was."

"Probably," Sarah agreed, before she could stop herself.

He shot her a sharp look, but he kept talking. "I didn't understand the full-immersion thing then. I was too young to really get that I wouldn't hear from Philip for years. He obviously understood, because he cried when he hugged me good-bye. And after a while, I started to realize that I didn't have a brother anymore. Not in the way that counts, anyhow."

"I never thought about that," Sarah admitted. "I don't have any family, so the immersion doesn't matter. I just thought about how it would affect the students here, not about how their families back home must feel."

"Yeah, well, their families feel awful," Ethan said. "Every

three months my mom would send off a care package—I'd always go help pick shit out—but there was never anything that came back for us. It was like mailing a box off into the void. We had no way of knowing if the stuff got to Philip. We had no way of knowing if he was even still alive, except for the report cards the school sent. Hell, those could've come from a chimpanzee playing with a computer for all we knew."

"Wow. When you put it that way, I'm kinda surprised everybody's folks keep sending the packages so regularly," Sarah said. "It's an entirely one-way relationship."

Ethan shrugged. "My mom never stopped."

"Maybe the time seems shorter to parents," Sarah suggested. "You were just a kid—four years seems like forever to little kids."

"It is forever. I don't even remember what Philip looks like," Ethan murmured, his voice barely above a whisper. "I remember facts about him—his hair was reddish, he loved the Red Sox, he would do physics equations for fun. But I don't remember *him*."

"I . . . I can't imagine that," Sarah admitted. "I remember everything. I have an eidetic memory. It's when—"

"I know what it is," Ethan cut her off, snapping out of his sadness.

"I also have this thing called HSAM, where I can remember an insane level of detail about everything that's ever happened to me."

"I didn't know that about you," he said.

"You're upset because you forgot your brother, but sometimes I wish I *could* forget my parents. They died when I was three, but I still remember everything about them. People say that's impossible, but it's not."

"Doesn't that make you feel better, to remember?"

"No. It's worse. They still feel real to me, as if they're still here. Because I remember them like I saw them yesterday. But I didn't. And they're not." Sarah tried to shake off her thoughts. "We're talking about you, though. And Philip."

"Actually we were talking about me and my escape wish," Ethan said coolly. "You asked why I want off the island, and I'm telling you it's because I think Sanctuary Bay killed my brother. Or kidnapped him. Or . . . something. I don't know what."

"Why are you here though, if you think they're so bad?" she asked.

"I never wanted to be here. Two months after Philip fails to show up, my dad comes home one day and announces that Sanctuary Bay wants me. Like it's a good thing."

"Even after Philip?" Sarah frowned.

"Yup. I freaked out. My mom got hysterical. Dad acted as if we were both crazy. He just kept talking about how it was the best school in the entire world." Ethan gave another bitter little laugh. "I figured I was safe—my mother had to be sedated, she was so upset at the idea of me going here. She kept screaming that she wouldn't lose another son."

"Understandable," Sarah said.

"Then a week later, she packed my suitcases and told me I was leaving for Sanctuary Bay in the morning. Like it never happened. Like Philip never existed, like she'd never been hysterical, like she had never fought with my dad about it," Ethan said. "It was the most bizarre thing I've ever seen in my life, the most horrible. It was my mom but not my mom, you know?" He paused for a moment. Sarah had the urge to touch him again, but didn't. "All the way to the ferry I tried to talk her out of it," he went on. "I kept reminding her of how she'd reacted a week before. She just smiled and ignored me and then kissed me good-bye."

"Why'd you get on the boat?" Sarah asked.

"I was fourteen and my parents had gone insane," Ethan replied. "Exactly what option do you think I had?"

Sarah didn't answer. Her own experience coming to Sanctuary Bay had been so different, it was hard to know what to think.

"So, about my maybe-dead girlfriend," Ethan said. "You want to tell me what you're talking about?"

"I just meant she's missing," Sarah said again, trying to sound convincing.

"Great, so let's go find her. Can I walk now? You done grilling me?" he asked.

"Yes. Sorry." Sarah took a shaky breath. She hadn't thought things could get more intense after last night, but hearing Ethan's story had brought it to a whole new level. "Where are we going now?"

"I told you, farther inside. Karina likes the stairway in the old lobby, because there's a great view of the water from there."

Sarah trailed after him, wrinkling her nose at the musty scent in the air. She would've expected the crumbling walls to let in the smell of the ocean, but instead it just smelled like animal droppings and mildew. "I can't believe you guys hang out here voluntarily," she muttered. "You're weird enough, but Karina likes things to smell nice. And not have rats."

"You clearly haven't had good enough sex. Karina's not here for the nice atmosphere."

Sarah ignored the dig, but felt her face flush. "If she's here right now, she's not here for sex with *you*," she pointed out.

"If she's here, she's trying to make me worried so I'll come find her . . . and then we'll have sex. Not sure if you've noticed, but your roommate thrives on drama, even if she has to create it herself."

Karina did have a flare for the dramatic. She started just as many fights with Ethan as he did with her. Maybe they both liked making up. *Be here*, Sarah silently begged. *Be here, Karina. Be here to laugh at me for the great prank you pulled. Be here to make out with your boyfriend.*

Ethan moved aside a heavy board that hung from one rusty hinge—which used to be a door, Sarah guessed, judging from the thick metal dead bolt attached near the top. *The lock is on the outside*, she thought with a shiver. It was there to lock people in the room, to trap them there.

They went through a short hallway, rounding a bend where another door had stood. The next room was bigger, with marble on the floor and a once-grand doorway on the ocean side. It had partially collapsed, and the columns that had stood on either side of it were covered in bird poop. "This was the lobby?" Sarah guessed. "The part they let visitors see."

"That's my guess. It had a higher roof and nicer materials. And check out the stairs." He pointed across the open space to a wide, curving staircase that swept up into the darkness above.

"It looks like something in a mansion," Sarah said. *And a little bit like something from our school*, she thought.

"The asylum was paid for by a consortium of New England's wealthiest families," Ethan told her. "They funded it, then they sent their crazy relatives here and washed their hands of them." He grinned. "The good old days."

Sarah rolled her eyes, knowing he just wanted to get her mad.

"So the part the rich families saw was gorgeous, but the inmates slept in that awful room," she said. "Typical."

Ethan let her little jab at rich people go. He went over to the stairs and started climbing.

"Are they stable?" Sarah asked, alarmed.

"Karina and I have given them a few good workouts," he said suggestively. "Nothing ever fell down, so I think it's okay."

Sarah glared at his back as she followed him up, a strangely jealous feeling she tried to ignore shooting through her.

She stopped halfway up at a large window that looked out over the ocean. She leaned on the windowsill and gazed out. The glass was long gone, and the sea breeze felt refreshing on her face. From here, she couldn't even see the island beneath her. The building was so close to the bluffs that all she saw was gray-blue water.

"Karina isn't here." Ethan said from behind her.

"No," Sarah agreed, without looking at him.

"You didn't think she would be." It wasn't a question. "You want to tell me what really happened last night, Ms. Memory?"

"We had a fight," Sarah insisted. She couldn't tell him about the Wolfpack. "Honestly, I got kind of drunk last night, and that screws with my memory. Sometimes I can't tell if something's a memory or a dream." *That's what Dr. Diaz thinks, anyway.*

"Why did you say Karina might be dead?" Ethan pressed.

"I told you, it was because we were talking about your brother maybe being dead. I meant missing. What's upstairs?" Sarah asked. "There were no windows. Is it more ward rooms?" She pushed past Ethan on the stairs and jogged up. The top was hidden in shadow. *No window means no light,* she realized too late.

"It's nothing you want to see." Ethan had come with her. Sarah felt a rush of relief to have somebody else here in the darkness.

"Why?" she whispered.

"These were the treatment rooms." Ethan stepped around her and led the way down the dim hall. He stopped in a doorway and pulled out his cell. The light cast a dim glow that was almost swallowed up by the darkness. Sarah took hers out too.

"Is that a tub?" she asked, peering into the room.

"It's for hydrotherapy," he explained. "They used to force people to take baths as a way to calm them."

"Right. Sometimes they kept people in the baths for days," Sarah said, stepping closer to the large metal tub. Secured on either side were rotting leather straps where a patient's wrists would go. She shivered, backing away. She didn't need to see any more of this room.

They continued down the hall. The next room looked like a dispensary, with glass-front cabinets lining one wall. Only a few shards of glass remained. Big wooden filing cabinets ran along the opposite wall, so massive they looked like they should have fallen through the moldering floor.

Sarah gave the floor an investigative shove with her heel. Seemed stable. She stepped inside and eased open the door of one formerly glass-front cabinet. It was filled with small metal canisters—each one bearing a skull and crossbones symbol printed on the peeling paper label.

"But this is marked as poison," Sarah said. "Why would there be poison in a hospital?"

"I think you're using the term 'hospital' pretty loosely," Ethan replied. "I doubt anyone really cared much about keeping the inmates healthy."

"Their families would've cared if they were being poisoned," she said.

"Maybe." He sounded dubious. He took a canister from her hand and squinted at it. "Malaria."

"That's not a poison, it's a disease." Sarah gasped. "Oh, but malaria was used as a treatment for neurosyphilis! I read about that. They would give people malaria and hope that the high fevers would fry the syphilis from their brains."

"I guess they could have been trying to help some people."

"Except for the ones who died of the malaria . . . ," Sarah said. "There's a lot of other stuff in here too." Some of the thick glass bottles had labels still attached, but most of the words had faded beyond recognition. There was one she was pretty sure said "Opium" and another that said "Bromcyan."

Sarah stared at the label, stunned as if she'd taken a jolt of electricity to the heart. Bromcyan. The word she'd seen carved over and over in the POW's cell, the word she'd thought might be the prisoner's name.

Had he known it was the name of a drug? Why would he have become so obsessed with it? Obsessed to the point of madness. Had they given it to him? What could it have done to him to make him spend all that time scraping it into the walls, and even the floor, of his cell?

"What's with you?" Ethan asked.

"Nothing," Sarah said. "I was just thinking how, um, a lot of old psychiatric treatments seem like torture, but they led us to where we are now. Think about it: chemo is poison. Maybe someday in the future people will be horrified we used it." She shrugged. "It's the progression of science." She was babbling, but telling him about the POW cell would mean talking about the Wolfpack, and she couldn't go there. Not yet. He was an outsider.

"It's ancient history," Ethan replied, bored. "We're looking for Karina. She's not in here."

"She's not here at all, then," Sarah said, feeling her hope die with a stab of disappointment.

"There's one more room we can try." Ethan sounded hesitant. "Maybe I'll go alone."

"What? Why?" Sarah asked.

"Um . . . it's personal. And weird." Ethan headed back out into the hallway, the light of his cell bouncing along with him.

Sarah thought about the poison bottles and the tub with restraints next door. Who knew what else was up here? "Nope," she called. "I'm not staying alone." She jogged after him, but he had vanished in the darkness of the hall.

Sarah's cell gave off barely enough light to see a foot in front of her, so she slowed her pace. She didn't know the place as well as Ethan did. It was impossible to tell how long this passage was, or how many doors lined the sides. There seemed to be a lot of different treatment rooms, but she didn't see the light from Ethan's cell in any of them.

"Where did you go?" she called. "Ethan?"

The air felt heavy, as if it had been trapped here, stagnant, for decades. Sarah felt the hair on her arms stand up. This place wasn't right. The yawning, shadowed doorways led into even darker rooms filled with who knew what. More tubs? More restraints? Something worse? "Ethan!" she yelled again, starting to panic.

Why weren't there any windows up here? she wondered. Did they not want screams reaching the outside? She'd heard stories about how a lot of old institutions abused their inmates. Had that happened here, in these blackened rooms?

Something skittered across the floor in front of her, and Sarah screamed.

"A rat," she said out loud. "It's just a rat."

The next door on her left loomed up, a square of darker black against the gray of the hall. Sarah peered inside, and there was Ethan. Finally.

"I can't believe you took off like that," she snapped, starting toward the light of his cell. "Did you not hear me scream?"

"I also heard you say it was just a rat." He strode toward her. "Karina's not here. Let's go," he said quickly.

But it was too late. Sarah had already seen the table he stood next to. The strange, old-fashioned lamps hanging from the ceiling made it clear this was an operating room. The table had metal straps bolted to the side, all of them upright now, but Sarah got an immediate mental image of how they'd be fastened down over the person on the slab. "They performed surgery on inmates?" she asked. "For what? Lobotomies didn't start until the 1930s, and this place was abandoned by then."

"Can we just go?" Ethan said.

"And why would they need to strap people down? Did they not use anesthesia?" She continued. "What kind of surgery would a mental patient even need?"

"I think they sterilized them." Ethan's voice was low. "Most likely against their will."

Sarah sucked in a breath. "Because they were mentally ill. The asylum wanted to keep them from breeding."

"People did a lot of awful things in the past, things no doctor today would even consider," Ethan said. "At least, not if they wanted to keep their license."

Sarah frowned. "Why would Karina be in this room?"

"Look, she has a dark side, okay?" Ethan sounded embarrassed, an emotion Sarah hadn't even thought he could feel. "She liked it in here."

"You mean you guys . . ." Sarah glanced at the table in distaste. It was almost impossible to imagine Karina in here, or even her with a dark side. Karina was . . . sunny. A sunny Southern California girl.

"I told you it was *personal*. Let's get out of here," Ethan said. "This place gives me the creeps."

They had only taken two steps toward the door when Ethan stopped her abruptly. Footsteps. Right outside the room.

13

Ethan grabbed Sarah's arm, his fingers digging into her flesh. With his other hand, he turned off his cell. Confused, Sarah did the same. He pulled her to the side of the door, against the wall, just before the beam of a flashlight cut through the room.

"School security follows me sometimes," Ethan whispered, his mouth against Sarah's ear, his breath hot on her neck. "Be chill."

She nodded, desperately trying to not inhale his pencils-and-oranges scent, still unsure why they needed to hide from security. She'd never heard of a "Don't leave the school grounds" rule. Of course, it had never occurred to her to try. It probably hadn't occurred to anyone but Ethan, since leaving involved crawling through a hedge.

"Clear," a voice said from the hallway. "Must have been rats."

The flashlight beam swept across the room again. The light caught one of the shards of another grouping of broken-glass-fronted cabinets, shining light directly into Sarah's eyes.

And she was in. Light from the muzzle of the gun flashing over Izzy's face. Izzy smiling. Aiming the gun at Karina. Sarah screaming. "No!"

A hand clapped over her mouth and she was out. No. Sarah felt the world go spinning around her. She wasn't out or in. She was out *and* in. The woods mingled with the dark of an OR, and Karina's eyes were still there—*her dead eyes*—but it was Ethan's hand on her mouth. There was no clear break between her memory and the present. Confusion flooded her body, and Sarah retched.

"Whoa!" Ethan snatched his hand away, and Sarah stumbled to her knees.

Footsteps came running toward them in the dark. Sarah couldn't think of anything besides breathing. Where was she? In the woods with the Wolfpack, or in the asylum with Ethan?

"Sarah, what the hell?" Ethan's voice cut through the chaos in her mind. "What's going on? Are you okay?"

She clung to his voice, using it to pull her out of the memory. And she was out, finally. "Yeah. I just—"

"What are you kids doing in here?" The two security guys appeared in the doorway, flashlight beams focused on Sarah and Ethan. The light hurt her eyes and she flinched without meaning to.

Ethan stepped in front of Sarah, blocking the light. "Nothing," he said. "We were just messing around."

"You can't be here, and you know it, Mr. Steere," the bigger of the two men growled. "This time we're going to—"

"But we're just doing research," Sarah said, impressed that she'd managed to think so quickly after that surge. It had only lasted moments, but it had felt as if she'd never escape it. Climbing to her feet, she held up her hand against the flashlights. "Can you lower those?"

"Excuse me?" The big guy sounded a bit thrown, but he pointed the light at the floor. "Research?"

"Yes. For Dr. Diaz," Sarah improvised. "He wants our chem class to focus on the proper usage of psychotropic chemicals, and there are some examples of improper storage out here. We told Dr. Diaz we'd collect the samples so he could reference them in class."

"Just look at them," Ethan said, smoothly picking up on her

line. "In the cabinet there, unsecured." Sarah was relieved that there were old medications in these cabinets too. "Some of them were marked poison, but the storage method allowed the medicines to seep out into the atmosphere as they decayed."

Sarah had to bite her lip to keep from laughing, but the mention of poison seemed to do the job.

"It doesn't matter. You can't be in here. This structure isn't sound," the big guy said, his tone less angry than before. "Let's go."

"We're going to have to confirm your story with Dr. Diaz," the second guard added as they all headed down the grand staircase. Sarah felt a huge sense of relief just to be back where the sunlight reached them.

"That's okay. Dr. Diaz will confirm it," she said, hoping that it was true.

"I didn't mean to get you involved," Sarah said the instant Dr. Diaz closed his office door behind the departing security guards. "I was trying to keep Ethan from getting in trouble. He was only out there because he was helping me."

"Wrong. I was there looking for Karina. You're the one who insisted on coming with," Ethan argued.

"You were helping me by looking for her," Sarah pointed out.

"Karina?" Dr. Diaz's eyes narrowed. "Is this about last night, Sarah?"

"He knows about last night?" Ethan asked, turning to Sarah, annoyed. "He saw the fight in the library? How insane did this fight get?"

"A fight? Sarah, you didn't say anything about that." Dr. Diaz sounded concerned.

"I . . . We . . ." Now Ethan was going to find out about the Wolfpack too. Sarah closed her eyes and pictured Grayson's face as the branding iron seared her.

"What the hell is going on? What happened to Karina?" Ethan demanded.

"I'd like to know that, as well. If this is some sort of stunt that your little group is pulling, Sarah, it's gotten out of hand." She cringed. Dr. Diaz had never acted so much like a teacher before. Instead of the friendly, easygoing man she was used to, she was facing yet another disapproving adult. One who suspected that she was doing something wrong.

"It's not. Or if it is, they're pulling the stunt on me too," Sarah answered. She opened her eyes and forced herself to meet Dr. Diaz's gaze. "I'm really scared that what happened last night was real. I don't know how else to explain where Karina is."

"And Ethan? What's your part in this?" Dr. Diaz asked.

"I slept until about noon and woke up to find my girlfriend gone. *Maybe dead*, right, Sarah?"

She sighed. There was no way to keep her Wolfpack vow and keep her sanity too. And she needed help. "Karina and I—and Izzy—are part of a secret society. I was initiated last month. They made me promise not to tell anyone."

Ethan snorted. "The Wolfpack?"

Sarah gaped at him. "How do you know about that?"

"They asked me to join last year. I laughed in their faces," Ethan said. "Can't say I knew Karina was in it, though."

"She is. Was." Sarah frowned. "The pack does a bunch of missions. Some of them are stupid—"

"Like kissing your roommate's boyfriend?" Ethan interrupted edgily.

"Yeah." She blushed. "And some of them are kind of dangerous. Last night, for Halloween, we were supposed to commit a murder together. It was going to be a way to bond us all for life. We had to sacrifice one of our own."

"Excuse me?" Ethan cried. "Murder?"

"It was just a joke," Sarah said quickly. "At least I thought so. Karina got picked to be the victim and we took her out to the woods and tied her to a tree. I figured that was it—we'd just scare her and let her go. But then Izzy . . ."

"Izzy shot her," Dr. Diaz finished for her. "That's what Sarah remembered."

She shot a glance at Ethan. His body had gone rigid, and his jaw was tight. "But we went back and there was no body," she told him in a rush. "Dr. Diaz came with me. There was no body! No sign of anything!"

"No. There wasn't," Dr. Diaz agreed.

"And today everyone else in the pack acted like none of it ever happened. Even Izzy! Nate said we all just watched a movie. The other people I talked to said the same thing." Frustrated, Sarah kicked at the leg of her chair. "It's making me crazy. They all had the same details—which movie, how Nate and I . . . I mean, nobody could answer me when I asked where Karina was. They all just said she was watching the movie too, but no one actually remembered talking to her."

"So you're the only one who remembers the murder." Ethan's hands were clenched on the arms of the chair.

"*If* it was a murder. Maybe it was a prank. Maybe they're all messing with me. I don't know," Sarah told him. "I've always trusted my memory. But today I keep getting these weird little flashes of what they described, us all down in the den watching a movie. And there's no proof of anything else. But I remember seeing Izzy shoot Karina last night. Maybe it was faked, but I saw it."

"Sarah, last night I thought you had too much to drink and

that you were confused," Dr. Diaz said. "But the fact that Karina is still gone troubles me."

"Can't you find out where she is? If a student is missing, the school has to search for her, right?" Sarah asked.

"Tell that to my brother," Ethan muttered.

"I'm going to call Dean Farrell about it right now," Dr. Diaz promised.

She nodded, standing up to go with Ethan. Dr. Diaz sounded perfectly calm. But she saw his expression as she pulled the office door shut behind her. He was afraid.

"We have to keep looking, but I don't know where else to try," Sarah said. "I already checked the den where we meet."

"That's fine with me, Sarah. I'm done with you anyway," Ethan snapped, walking off at a fast pace.

She watched him for a moment, then ran to catch up. "Why? You want to find Karina as much as I do. You have to keep helping me. There has to be something else we can do."

"Were you ever going to tell me the truth?" Ethan demanded, whirling around so quickly that Sarah stumbled backward as he got right up in her face. "You thought you could just lie about what happened, and I'd go along with it like an idiot?"

"No! I didn't want to betray my friends," she protested weakly. "I took a vow."

"Your friends think killing someone, or pretending to, is some game, but you're still willing to lie for them," he said, disgusted. "Screw you."

"Ethan, wait. I wasn't lying. Well, not really," she said. "I lied about us being in the library and Izzy and Karina fighting. But I'm not sure that anything happened. The rest of the pack says we were in the den watching a horror movie, and that we didn't go out anywhere or do any kind of crazy murder ritual. Doesn't that sound more plausible than what I remember?"

He didn't answer. He also didn't walk away again. "You said you remember everything. You said you trust your memory."

"My memory is perfect, but it's really weird. It's not just that I can remember everything," she said. "Sometimes I get these, I don't know, visions from the past—like, I remember things in such detail, with smells and sounds and feelings, that when the memory comes it seems more real than what's happening right now. It used to be hard for me to tell which was real, until I learned to recognize it. That's what happened when I freaked out in the asylum."

"Okay . . . ," Ethan said doubtfully.

"Diaz told me that my memory means my brain processes input differently than other people's do. He said my brain might not even recognize the difference between the memory of a dream or a hallucination and a real memory. I never felt like I couldn't tell the difference between a dream and reality, but if my brain can't recognize the difference . . . maybe my memory isn't as perfect as I always thought." Her voice broke, the realization making her feel like the earth was crumbling out from under her feet.

"So maybe this memory you have about killing Karina was a bad dream, but you keep remembering it as if it was true," Ethan said. "Got it."

"Maybe. Maybe my brain is in meltdown. What I'm saying is that I wasn't lying to you," she replied. "I'm just not sure what happened. I have something that feels like a memory, but everyone else who was there has a different story. All I know for sure is I'm worried about Karina, and I don't know where she is, and I don't really trust the Wolfpack anymore, and I need some help." Sarah drew in a shuddering breath. "I keep seeing her eyes. Karina's dead eyes," she whispered.

Ethan's face paled.

"I don't want it to be true," Sarah said, a sob escaping her. "Oh, god, I just want it to be a bad dream, but she's gone. She's gone."

"Okay. It's okay." Ethan reached out and pulled her into his arms, holding her tight. The last of Sarah's resolve broke, and she burst into tears, clinging to him.

"I'm sorry," she mumbled against his chest.

"No worries. I'm scared too," he said.

Sarah took in several deep breaths, willing herself to stop crying. The tears still came, but she managed to get control of the sobbing. "It hasn't always been this bad. I think maybe the Blutgrog screws with my memory." It definitely screwed with the intensity of her sensations. It could be screwing with her brain in other ways too. "It's this drink we start the Wolfpack meetings with. It's supposed to be made with the old blood of the POWs, but it's basically grain alcohol."

"Nice." Ethan shook his head. "No wonder you're hallucinating." Ethan's arms loosened slightly, and Sarah suddenly became very aware of the fact that he was holding her, her chest pressed tightly against him, their bodies entwined. She pulled away so fast that she almost fell over.

"Okay. I'm done with the freakout," she said, wiping her cheeks. "So will you help me?"

"Yeah." He smiled, a real, genuine smile. Sarah wasn't sure she'd ever seen one on his face before. "And then after we find Karina, we can work on figuring out what happened to my brother," Ethan said. "You're the only one I've ever told about him."

"Oh?" She wasn't sure why she felt surprised, but she did. Why would he tell her something he hadn't even confided to Karina? As far as she knew, Ethan didn't even like her, let alone trust her enough to share such a painful family secret.

"I tried, when I first got here," Ethan went on. "I didn't say he never came home, I just asked all the seniors if they remembered him, but they didn't."

"Most of his friends probably graduated with him," Sarah guessed. "What about the teachers?"

Ethan sighed. "They just talked about how brilliant he was. Nobody had a clue he was missing."

"If he fell off the ferry—"

"If he really fell off, the school should've had a huge memorial for him," Ethan cut her off. "Everyone here should've known about it whether they were friends with him or not."

Sarah blinked in disbelief. "You're right," she said.

"Instead I'm supposed to believe that they told us he disappeared but didn't bother to mention it to the teachers who'd just handed him his diploma right before he got on the boat?"

"No. That doesn't make sense." Sarah frowned.

"The truth is here. Somewhere. I just have to find it." Ethan's gaze bounced around the marble hallway as if it were a cage.

"I'll help you." Sarah reached for his hand and squeezed. "We'll help each other."

Ethan nodded. "We know one thing for sure: Karina hasn't been around all day. Locate Karina," he told his cell. "Just in case," he added to Sarah.

"Student offline," the cell responded.

"The cells don't work in the den," Sarah said. "But I checked down there."

"They don't work in the asylum either, but we checked there too." Ethan was silent for a moment then said, "I want you to take me there, to the tree. You said you tied her to a tree."

"Dr. Diaz and I already went back to—"

Ethan interrupted her. "I don't care. I need to see it."

———————

"So they all had exactly the same details?" Ethan asked as they walked through the woods.

"Yeah."

"And you think they might all lie?" Ethan probed.

"They might," Sarah admitted. "The Wolfpack values loyalty to the group above everything else. You put the other members above yourself. You do what you're told. You protect the group. I even thought maybe Nate came up with a story to give the Wolfpack an alibi for Karina's murder."

Ethan raised one eyebrow.

"I know, I sound paranoid," Sarah said. "But covering up a murder is a good reason to come up with a mass lie. And there was something rehearsed about what they all said—everybody kept using the same words, about me and Nate being . . . distracted."

"But you don't remember this . . . distraction?" he asked.

"No. And I really believe I would if it were true." She felt her cheeks grow warm. "Unless the Blutgrog has started eating my brain or something." She rubbed her face with her fingertips, as if that would help her think more clearly. "But even if the pack is lying, it might not be to cover something up. Like I said, they love playing games, giving out missions. They could all be screwing with me."

"And people do this voluntarily?" Ethan sounded disgusted.

"At least it would mean Karina is okay," Sarah replied. She stopped, trying to get her bearings. The forest looked different in the daylight, and navigating it wasn't something she had a lot of experience in. "I know the clearing is close. There's an incredibly tall pine tree, and the clearing is underneath it."

"There." Ethan pointed to the left. "I know the Pine Tree.

It's massive." He led the way through the underbrush, holding branches so they wouldn't snap back and hit Sarah in the face.

"Ethan . . . I'm sorry," she said.

"For what?"

"For being a bitch to you all this time. I thought you were an ass."

"Don't go getting mushy on me," Ethan replied. "I'm still an ass."

She smiled.

"Here we are." He surveyed the clearing. "Looks the same as always."

It did. The thick carpet of orange-brown pine needles was smooth, as if no one had been here in weeks. Sarah's pulse sped up as she tried to ignore the memory trying to overtake her. The shot ringing out, echoing through the trees. Karina's head snapping back, then slumping forward, her eyes dead. Her eyes . . .

"This ring in the trunk. Did you guys do that?" Ethan's voice brought Sarah back to the present.

"The iron ring? Yeah. I mean, we used it to tie Karina's hands to the tree. I don't know who put it there." They moved closer to the huge pine.

"It's been there as long as I've been here. I always wondered what it was for," Ethan said grimly. "So Karina was here, with her arms up over her head." He ran a finger along the circumference of the ring.

Sarah nodded. "At least in my memory." And deep down in her gut, she felt it was true, the way her memories always were.

"I don't see any blood on the ring, or the tree, or the ground. Wait—" He knelt suddenly, staring at the base of the huge trunk. "What is this?"

Sarah bent down next to him and examined the weird little lump of yellowish gunk stuck to the wood. It was tiny—maybe half an inch long—and rounded as if it were a cylinder. "Part of a candle?" she guessed. "Or is it some kind of sap from the tree?"

"I think it's a bullet," Ethan said slowly. "It's made of wax."

"Okaaaay . . ." Sarah frowned. "How is it a bullet if it's wax?"

"I used to go on these crazy vacations with my family when I was little, and one time we were at a resort where they had lessons for the kids all day—you know, to keep them out of their parents' hair?"

Sarah nodded. There was no point in explaining that she hadn't even known kids were allowed at resorts and she wasn't entirely sure what a resort was anyway. She'd assumed it was a beach and sunsets and massages, based purely on the ads they put on city buses. But if there were children and lessons, well, she obviously hadn't gotten the whole thing right.

"One of them had a circus school, and Philip used to take trapeze classes and tumbling, things like that. I bribed one of the instructors to teach me trick shooting," Ethan went on.

"While you were a kid?" Sarah cried.

"It's not like my parents knew about it," Ethan said. "Anyway, we used wax bullets in the guns. That's what made it *trick* shooting. When you see somebody shoot an apple off a guy's head or whatever, it's not a real bullet."

"You're saying that's what this is? A fake bullet?" Sarah reached out and picked up the blob of wax. It was tiny and nondescript. She wasn't sure she really believed it was a bullet and not just part of someone's birthday candle. But it was the only thing in the entire clearing that was out of place. "The only reason a bullet would be here is if somebody shot a gun, at the tree."

"At Karina tied to the tree, you mean," Ethan said. "You're not crazy, Sarah." He put his hands on her shoulders. "Your brain isn't malfunctioning. It did happen the way you said."

Sarah nodded. She felt as if her feet were back on solid ground again. "A fake bullet means it's all just a Wolfpack prank."

"No reason to use wax if you're trying to kill someone," Ethan agreed.

"She looked dead, though, Ethan. The way her head was slumped over, her eyes . . ."

"It would hurt like hell to get hit by anything moving that fast, even if it's not a metal bullet. Maybe it knocked her out?" Ethan said. He put the bullet in his pocket. "Where did the gun come from?"

Sarah thought about it. "Nate. I don't know where he got it from, he just had it."

"Fine. Nate pulls out a gun loaded with trick bullets, Izzy takes it and shoots, and Karina drops dead-ish. What happened then?"

"Everyone took off, except me and Izzy," Sarah said. "I was horrified about Karina. Izzy just made fun of me."

He stared at her, shocked. Sarah bit her lip. "Yeah, Izzy was . . . unhinged afterward," she said. "She said we were all responsible for the murder, even if she was the only one brave enough to pull the trigger."

"Obviously she was in on it."

"Yeah, if it's a Wolfpack mission," Sarah said. "This morning she acted like she didn't remember anything, just like the others."

He shook his head, disgusted. "What happened after Izzy made fun of you for being upset?"

"She left," Sarah answered. "Then I left to go get help. When I got back with Dr. Diaz, Karina was gone."

"And she still is." Ethan rested his hand against the trunk of the tree where Karina had been. Sarah looked away. The moment felt too intimate. They'd found answers out here, but still not the answer they needed. Where was Karina?

Sarah's cell buzzed the minute they stepped out of the woods onto the back lawn of the school.

"Nate called a meeting for midnight," she said. "God, I don't even want to see any of them ever again." Then she stopped, suddenly feeling as light as a helium balloon. "Wait. This is it!"

"This is what?" Ethan asked.

"The end. I'll go to the meeting, and Karina will pop out," Sarah said. "This is when they'll tell me the whole thing was just a mission, a trick on me! We'll probably end up having a huge party." The relief was so strong that she almost felt dizzy. "And it'll be over."

She could see Ethan's shoulders relax. "That makes sense. Twisted sense, but still."

"I'll call you as soon as the meeting's over," Sarah promised. "Oh! Diaz. Shit. He was calling Dean Farrell—do you think he told her already?"

"Uh, yeah, it's been over an hour," Ethan said. "But I can go tell him it was just a prank."

"Do you think he told her about the Wolfpack?" Sarah asked, sudden terror filling her. "They'll hurt me if they find out I told anyone."

"Lovely," Ethan muttered. "Listen, I'll talk to Diaz and we'll figure it out. We might have to tell the dean you were hallucinating on cold medicine or something, but we'll make sure she thinks the Wolfpack isn't real."

"Thank you," Sarah said. "Really."

"No worries." He turned away.

"And Ethan? You can't tell anyone. Don't even tell Karina I told you about the Wolfpack," Sarah begged. "Please?"

"Fine. I promise," Ethan said. "But you should seriously think about whether these are the people you really want as friends."

"Your girlfriend is one of them," she retorted.

"And *I'll* be seriously thinking about *that*," he said.

At midnight, Sarah took her place in line in the Bone Man room. It was so hard to stand still. When were they going to bring out Karina? Maybe she was already in line! Sarah couldn't wait for things to be back to normal.

Ethan had texted, letting her know the Dean Farrell situation was taken care of—Dr. Diaz hadn't managed to get the dean on the phone. Sarah felt embarrassed now that she'd ever involved anyone else. But she knew they wouldn't rat her out. Dr. Diaz would probably just want to explore her episodes more. And Ethan didn't trust anyone who worked at the school. He'd never go to the dean for anything.

Besides, he wouldn't risk getting me hurt, Sarah thought. She didn't always like him, but she realized with some surprise that she did trust him.

"Heil, Jager!" The chant began and Sarah eagerly joined in. Before long, the ceramic bowl was held to her lips, and she happily took a drink of the Blutgrog. Tonight was going to be perfect for super-sharp sensations. She was sure they'd have an epic party as soon as they told her the truth.

Nate paced up and down between the two lines of pack members. "Tonight all members of our pack are present. Our pack. And it *is* ours. All of ours," he said, his voice deep and booming.

"Never forget that you have brothers and sisters. Never forget that you are part of something much larger than yourself."

Sarah frowned. He was repeating himself, giving the same speech he'd given two meetings ago. She almost snorted. This was taking it too far. But she'd let the pack have their fun.

"As a reminder of this, our great blessing, we will perform the next mission together. It is assigned to all of us," Nate went on. "When we have completed it, I know we will be stronger than we have ever been." He let out a howl and they all joined in, Sarah loudest of all.

The Jager raised his hands for silence. "The mission will take place tomorrow night. Tomorrow night we will join in an act of sacrifice. Tomorrow night we will take a life, to honor what the pack has given us and to bind us."

Sarah felt a wave of dizziness. The hot robe, the dank smell of the room, the closeness of everyone around her, and Nate's words—all heightened by the Blutgrog—flowed together into a memory of that other meeting. Her stomach lurched. She wasn't going to just stand here and reexperience the beginning of the worst night of her life.

"Together we will offer up the most precious gift—a human soul," the Jager told them.

"Okay, stop. You got me good!" Sarah burst out. "Now bring out Karina and crank the music!"

Everybody turned to her, shocked. Dead silence followed her outburst.

Nate flew at her. "You do not speak while the Jager speaks."

Sarah stepped forward to meet him, yanking back her hood. He stopped short. "Enough, Nate! Mission over, okay?" She felt a spurt of anger. "You put me through hell, you know that? It's time to end the game."

"Sarah," he said. "Return to your place. *Now*. And I'll think about how you should be disciplined." The rest of the pack remained quiet. All held their positions in line, facing forward, motionless.

"How much longer are you going to go on?" she demanded. "Should I tell you the rest of the speech?" She raised her voice, addressing the whole pack. " 'When we have made this sacrifice together, we will be closer than any oath or vow, no matter how sacred, could make us. We will be as one, one brain, one heart, one body, one pack,' " she quoted Nate. "Isn't that right, *Jager*?"

Nate gaped at her.

"I get it, okay? You're repeating the same mission again. You're pretending it never happened, just to make the prank even more extreme," she said. "But it really is enough. I went crazy all day searching for Karina." She looked up and down the lines. "You here, Kar?" she called, raising her voice.

There was no sound. No laughter. Nate slowly lowered his hood. His caramel eyes were wide. "Sarah? Wh-what are you talking about?"

Several other members, including Izzy, pulled their hoods off too. They looked puzzled.

The lightness in Sarah's body disappeared. "I'm talking about how you all tried to convince me Karina was dead. Last night we dragged her to the Pine Tree. She was the sacrifice Nate was just talking about. Izzy shot her with a wax bullet, and you've all been pretending you don't remember, trying to make me think I'm crazy . . . or something . . ." Sarah trailed off, her eyes darting around the room. Breath suddenly shallow, she waited for someone, anyone, to acknowledge that they knew what she was talking about.

Nate's eyebrows drew together in confusion. Grayson and Luke glanced at each other, and Luke shrugged. Everybody seemed baffled. Sarah felt the hair on her arms stand up. Something wasn't right. If they were still pulling a scam on her, there should be at least one person who gave it away, intentionally or not.

"Izzy," she said, whirling around to look her roommate in the eyes. "You remember what happened to Karina. I know you do. You were the one who pulled the trigger."

Izzy took a step back, her face pale. "I . . . I have no idea what you're talking about, Sarah," she whispered.

Sarah stared at her. The sneer on Izzy's full lips as she said they had all killed Karina flashed through her mind.

But that Izzy wasn't here. This Izzy's lips trembled, and her blue eyes were frightened. She looked so confused. They all looked so confused.

"You really don't remember?" Sarah asked. "Karina in the woods, tied to the Pine Tree?"

"I haven't seen Karina in a long time," Izzy said slowly. "I think she must've run away or something."

"Maybe she went home," Harrison suggested.

"Home? Nobody's allowed to go home," Sarah said.

"Well . . . maybe it was an emergency," Nate said haltingly.

"Why does it matter?" Kayla asked. "I thought we were getting a mission."

Sarah was speechless. The rest of them looked back at Nate, waiting for the mission. As if everything Sarah had said didn't matter. They weren't acting like Karina was dead or even like she was missing. They were acting as if it didn't matter at all, as if they didn't care about Karina, even though she was one of their own, even though the Jager had just given a big speech about how they were all brothers and sisters.

They don't even seem to remember her that well, Sarah thought. It's like their brains turn off whenever I make them think about Karina.

"The mission will be a sacrifice," Nate said, though his voice didn't sound so commanding anymore. He seemed like regular Nate now, not the Jager. "A true sacrifice, a terrible sacrifice."

"No," Sarah said, more quietly this time. "We are not going to sacrifice anybody." Whatever was happening, she wasn't going to let it go any farther.

"Sarah. You have to stop interfering," Nate protested.

"This mission goes too far," she replied. "We're not murderers." She stepped out of line, into the center aisle where only the Jager was allowed. "Murder isn't what we stand for, and it won't bond us for life," she told her packmates. "It will scar us for life. It's a line nobody should ever cross, because once you do, it changes you." Her eyes found Izzy's.

Izzy gazed back blankly, no trace of recognition at the words she'd said in the woods. Sarah felt a cold, numb feeling settle in her gut. Izzy didn't remember what she'd done to Karina. None of them did. They genuinely thought this meeting was the first time a sacrifice had been discussed.

"We're not murderers," she said again.

Izzy nodded. So did Cody. A low murmur ran through the room, and she saw several people agreeing.

"You're right, Sarah," Nate said. "No sacrifice."

There was a long silence. Nobody seemed sure how to act. After a moment, people began shedding their robes and filing out.

A shudder ran through Sarah's body, and she sank down to the ground. What was happening?

"Sarah?" Nate sat down next to her, his gorgeous face etched with worry. "I hope you don't think I was serious. I'd never kill anyone."

"Then what were you talking about?" she asked. "Because honestly, Nate, I am utterly baffled. If the mission you were just talking about wasn't really to murder somebody, what was it? A mind game?"

"What? No." He studied his fingernails for a minute, lost in thought. "I would have stopped it before things got out of hand," he finally said.

"You mean before one of us got picked? After we dragged them out to the woods?" Sarah asked. "After we tied them to the Pine Tree?"

Nate's leg began bouncing up and down, fastfastfast. Sarah had seen the nervous tic before, but never from Nate. Other people got nervous. Nate was always smooth and in control. She stared at his leg, fascinated.

"I don't know what you mean," he said. His leg bounced.

"There's an iron ring in the Pine Tree. You tie the sacrifice to it," she said.

Nate's leg bounced faster.

"You get out the gun. You get out the wax bullets, so you can fake the whole thing, right?" she asked.

"I don't know." His leg moved so fast it was more like vibrating than bouncing. Sarah watched it. Watched him. Unflappable Nate.

"Tell me, Nate, where does the sacrifice go afterward? Do they go hide somewhere?"

"I don't know," he said, "but we are all as one. Brothers and sisters."

"Right. Except when we kill one of our own," Sarah pressed.

"One pack, one mind. Brothers and sisters." Nate's leg moved furiously. His eyes were fixed on the floor, unfocused. "The Bone Man calling."

"What?" she asked. "You're not making sense."

"Bone Man." Nate's entire body began to rock back and forth. He was freaking out—and it freaked her out. "Bones and blood man. Blood Man."

"Nate." Sarah reached out and took his hand. "Nate?"

Suddenly his head snapped up and he met her gaze. His leg stopped bouncing. His brilliant smile appeared, and his laser-like intensity was back. "I have to go." He got up and headed for the door without a backward glance.

"Where are you going?" Sarah demanded.

"I just have to go," Nate replied. Then he was gone.

14

The next morning, the first thing Sarah saw when she opened her eyes was Karina's bed. She stared for a few seconds, trying to will her roommate to come back from the bathroom, yawning, and drop to the ground for her yoga stretches just like always. But she knew it wouldn't happen.

Then she looked over at Izzy's bed. It was empty too, but the covers were thrown back. Sarah was glad Izzy had taken off early. She couldn't deal with another surreal conversation. What she needed was someone she could trust. She needed Ethan. She'd sent him a text update last night, and they'd agreed to meet up first thing this morning.

Sarah scrambled into her clothes. When she reached the

coffee place, Ethan was already there. He'd staked out a small table all the way in the back. She hurried over and sat down across from him, realizing a Nutella latte, her favorite, was already waiting for her. She glanced at him curiously before smiling to herself and taking a sip.

"So, if it wasn't a prank," he said, "where's Karina?"

Sarah shrugged helplessly. "They . . . barely seemed to remember she existed."

"Because they're playing you," Ethan said. "They're trying to mess with your head."

"No, that's the thing. You didn't see them. It was freaky. They can't *all* be such good liars or actors," Sarah protested. "Nate was the weirdest. He got agitated and became . . . I don't know, nonsensical. And Izzy! I know her, Ethan. I know her secrets. I would know if she was lying."

"Well, she either lied last night or she lied the night you took Karina to the Pine Tree. You said she actually bragged about killing Karina," Ethan said. "Which is it?

Sarah hesitated. The night she'd shot Karina, Izzy had been *alive* somehow, animated in a way Sarah had never seen before. "Honestly, that night in the clearing I felt like I was seeing the true Izzy for the first time," she admitted. "But last night, when I looked her in the eyes, she really had no idea where Karina was."

"Well, I'm going to talk to her. I'll get the truth," Ethan announced, getting to his feet.

"She's not going to tell you anything she didn't tell me," Sarah said.

"She shot my girlfriend. I'm talking to her." Ethan pulled out his cell. "Locate Izzy."

"Administration building courtyard," the cell replied.

Ethan glanced at Sarah. "You coming?"

Sarah grabbed her latte and stood. She definitely wasn't going to let him talk to Izzy by himself. "She's probably going to therapy. She has early morning appointments a couple of times a week. Did Karina ever tell you Izzy's getting treatment for post-traumatic stress?"

"It's not working. She's still nuts," he deadpanned.

"You know, whenever I start thinking you might actually be a decent person, you say something to convince me you're a jerk again," Sarah told him as they walked.

"I like to keep you on your toes."

"Mental illness is an *illness*."

"No shit. But PTSD doesn't make you calmly grab a gun and kill someone, and that's what you said she did," he argued. "Do you see her anywhere up there?"

"No." There were only a few people out this early, none of them Izzy.

Ethan checked his cell, and frowned. "Not there."

"Where is she?"

"No, I mean, she's not on the map. Her dot disappeared," he said.

Sarah's stomach clenched. "Is it a cell screwup?" she asked.

He hit a few buttons. "You're on there," he said. "And Mr. Fisher's dot is moving toward the dining hall just like he is."

"The Wolfpack meets in the basement of the main building, and that doesn't show up on our cells. If the Admin building has a basement, maybe it doesn't either," Sarah suggested.

"I've seen a staircase around the back of Admin," Ethan said thoughtfully. "I never bothered going down. I was looking for ways out, not deeper in." He led her around the building to a narrow walkway blocked by a wrought iron gate. A sign on it read NO ADMITTANCE.

Sarah hesitated.

"Really?" he asked her. "Because of a sign?"

"Sorry. Habit," Sarah replied. "When people always expect you to be a fuckup, you tend to follow all the rules just to prove them wrong."

"Sounds boring." Ethan flipped up the latch and opened the gate.

"How was that not locked? The security at this school is so random," Sarah said as they started down the walkway. "Like the door to the subbasement where the Wolfpack meets. It has a regular lock, no fingerprint pad."

"Yeah, the student areas are high tech, but a lot of the things I've found off the grid are barely any tech at all." He opened the door at the end of the walkway. "Case in point." They started down the stone steps. "Guess they expect us to be good little boys and girls and stay where we belong. Or else they don't want to spend money on the staff areas, since staff don't pay tuition."

"Well, there are nicer spots on campus." The concrete stairway was steep and long. And cold. It obviously led to a subbasement. "I . . . I think I was wrong about Izzy going to therapy," Sarah said.

"Unless her therapy is in a janitor's closet or whatever they keep down here," Ethan said.

The last ten steps were almost completely dark. Then the staircase ended at a closed door. Sarah pulled it open slowly, unsure what to expect.

A tunnel made of textured stainless steel stretched out in front of her. Brilliant lights ran down either side, high on the walls. About six feet away, something that looked part car and part train sat between two rubber bumpers that lined each side of the tunnel. It was like she'd stepped into the future.

"Is that a monorail?" Sarah asked. She'd seen a picture of one in an ad for Disney World once. "A mini one?"

"Holy shit. They have something like this at Heathrow, but what is it doing under the school?" Ethan asked.

"It's like the boat," Sarah said.

"Yeah, but the boat's part of the package to impress the parents. 'A Black Diamond yacht will transport your child to the Academy.' Nobody said anything about this." He ran his fingers through his hair. "Ready to take a ride?"

Sarah stared at him. She was ready to turn around and run. "But we don't even know if Izzy came down here."

"There's no other reason she'd be off the grid," Ethan said. "But even if she's not, I'm finding out where this thing goes. This might be where I finally learn what's really going on at this school."

Sarah hesitated, then nodded. He was right. Whatever was down here, they had to know what it was.

"Do you know how to drive it?" she asked.

"If it's the same as the one at the airport, it drives itself."

Of course it does, Sarah thought. She followed Ethan over to the little car, so sleek, with rounded edges. Sensing movement, both doors slid open without a whisper of sound. They stepped inside. There was a short row of seats on one side. The other side held a padded bench, with restraints. Sarah's body went cold. What was *that* for? She sank down onto one of the seats with Ethan beside her. When he grabbed her hand she was more grateful than she'd ever been in her life.

After a low warning chime, the doors closed, and they began to glide through the tunnel in their pod. Sarah thought they must have gone at least a couple of miles before they reached the other end and the doors swished open again. A few steps led up to an ordinary-looking door.

"Here we go," Sarah said, reaching for the handle. As her fingers brushed the metal, a scream split the air.

Sarah jerked the door wide. Another hallway stretched out in front of them. The screaming continued. "Izzy!" Sarah gasped. She and Ethan both took off, sprinting down the empty hallway in the direction of the scream.

The hall turned sharply, and when Sarah rounded the corner, she saw a door about a hundred feet away where the screaming was coming from. Ethan reached it first. He yanked the door open into a big room, with overhead fluorescent lights and a few carts full of surgical instruments. A row of computers lined one wall, the monitors scrolling names of medicines or chemicals—dopamine, 5-hydroxytryptamine, oxytocin, GABA, acetylcholine, 3-bromcyan, norepinephrine, somatostatin—

Sarah's attention snagged on "3-bromcyan." *Bromcyan.* That drug again!

"What are you doing here?" somebody cried.

A man stood in the back of the room, dressed in scrubs like an OR nurse. He moved toward her, and that's when Sarah saw the tubes running from the computer to the table behind him. To Izzy, on the table.

Izzy lay flat, pinned down with metal bars like the ones in the old asylum. Her wrists were restrained with leather straps, and her head had been turned to the side and locked in place with a tight strap over her forehead. There were electrodes on her temples and some sort of port at the base of her skull. A thin silvery tube led from there to the computer.

She was screaming.

"Oh my god!" Sarah cried. "Izzy!"

She raced for the table, and began working on one of the wrist restraints before the nurse could stop her. Ethan struggled with the restraint on Izzy's other wrist. Izzy's shrieks echoed off the walls, piercing and feral like an animal in pain. Sarah managed to free one of Izzy's hands, and she began clawing at the strap over her head.

"Stop! Get away from her." The nurse grabbed one of Sarah's arms, tugging hard. Sarah flipped her wrist around, got a grip on the guy's arm, and jerked him toward her, kneeing him in the balls.

The nurse went down with a cry of pain. Sarah whirled back toward Izzy. Ethan had freed the other wrist restraint. Now Izzy clutched at the head strap with both hands, twisting her torso in agony, her hips and legs still held down by metal bars.

"I'm not sure if I should pull this out." Ethan hesitated with his fingers inches away from the tube feeding into the port at the back of Izzy's head.

Chemo patients had ports installed sometimes, but the tube plugged there didn't look like any IV line Sarah had ever seen. "Do her legs first. I'll try to get her head loose, then maybe we can figure out the best way to deal with the tube."

From the corner of her eye she saw the nurse haul himself up on one of the surgical carts. He hit some kind of button on the wall. "Hurry! He set off an alarm," Sarah warned. "Izzy, calm down," she said. "We don't have much time. Let me get this off." She ran her fingers over the strap around her roommate's forehead, trying to see where it connected. Izzy clawed at her, nails digging into Sarah's hands, scratching hard enough to draw blood. Sarah cried out in pain.

Ethan grabbed both of Izzy's hands so Sarah could keep working. "It's okay, Izzy," he said in a soothing voice. "We're going to get you out of here."

"Get away from her," the nurse panted, still doubled over in pain.

"Shut up, you sadist," Sarah snapped. She dropped to her knees and peered under the table. There! A buckle to hold the strap tight. Sarah reached up and worked it loose.

That was all Izzy needed. The instant the strap loosened, she shoved it off her head and sat up straight, still screaming. Ethan struggled to keep his hold on her. "Easy, easy," he said.

"Iz, you have to calm down," Sarah pleaded, getting to her feet. "We'll take off those metal straps somehow, but I need to get a better look at the tube in your—"

Izzy wrenched one hand away from Ethan, wrapped the strange-looking tube around her hand and yanked.

Sarah cringed and closed her eyes for a second, half expecting blood to come gushing out of the port along with the tube. When she opened them again, Izzy was working on the metal restraints. Ethan had let go of her other hand and was trying to help. If pulling the tube had hurt her, it was impossible to tell. The screams hadn't changed—still shrill and nearly unbearable.

Why is she still screaming? Sarah thought, growing frantic.

"Let me help. Security's going to be here any second." She reached for the metal bar holding Izzy's hips down.

Izzy backhanded her across the face.

Sarah's head jerked to the side, wrenching her neck. She stumbled, lost her balance, and fell to her knees. For a split second, her eyes met the nurse's. "I told you," he said.

A grinding, metallic sound filled the air, and then Izzy was free. She jumped from the table just as the door banged open and a security guard appeared. Izzy launched herself at him, her hands out in front of her like claws. She went straight for his eyes.

"Izzy, no!" Ethan yelled. He managed to grab her by the shoulders, but not before Izzy raked her nails down the guard's cheek.

The guard grabbed Izzy by the forearms, but Izzy twisted erratically, managing to kick over one of the carts, sending surgical instruments crashing to the ground.

Ethan struggled, finally pulling Izzy into a chokehold. Izzy twisted her head, sinking her teeth into his arm. At the same instant she kicked out with both legs, slamming her feet into the guard's chest. His head smacked the tipped-over cart when he hit the ground.

"Stop! Izzy, stop!" Sarah screamed. The guard bellowed in pain. The arm of Ethan's shirt was soaked with blood, but he was still holding Izzy. Sarah turned to the nurse. "Do something. Don't you have a sedative?"

The nurse ignored her. He had recovered enough to stagger over to the counter next to the computer.

"Let me help. I'm sorry I kicked you," Sarah said in a rush. "I can give her the shot."

But he wasn't preparing a hypodermic. He was pulling up a virtual keyboard.

The guard was grunting and bleeding, and Izzy was still screaming and fighting like a cornered cat. "What are you *doing?*" Sarah cried. "We need to knock her out!"

The nurse typed something into the computer, his face grim.

The screaming stopped. Stunned, Sarah spun toward Izzy— just as she went limp in Ethan's arms.

"Izzy!" Sarah gasped.

Ethan staggered back, gently releasing Izzy. She crumpled to the floor and lay perfectly still, her blond hair covering half her face, her mouth hanging slightly open. For a few seconds Sarah wasn't even sure if she was breathing. "Wh-what happened to her?"

"She was a danger to herself and to the rest of us. I told you to leave her alone," the nurse barked.

"Don't talk! Do something!" Ethan shot back.

"Is she okay?" Sarah couldn't take her eyes off her roommate. "Why is she unconscious? What happened?"

The outside door slammed, and a woman in a lab coat ran into the room. She took one look at Izzy on the floor and pulled out a cell phone. "I need transport in Lab One," she said, then she hung up and gestured at Sarah and Ethan. "Take these two to the dean," she ordered the security guard, who was still holding his bloody cheek.

"No. Wait. Are you the doctor?" Sarah asked. "Why did Izzy just collapse like that? Is she hurt?"

"Answer her!" Ethan yelled.

The woman walked briskly over to the computer and began examining the information on the monitor, ignoring both of them and Izzy lying on the floor. The nurse, still hobbling, picked up the strange wire that had been attached to the port in Izzy's neck. Neither looked at Sarah.

The security guard moved toward Sarah, ready to drag her off to Dean Farrell.

"Izzy, wake up!" Sarah commanded, throwing herself on the ground next to her friend. "Iz! Are you okay?"

Izzy didn't move a muscle. Her arm felt warm, but the stillness frightened Sarah. Was she dead? Sarah brushed her hair out of her face to get a better look. Izzy's eyes were open, staring lifelessly at Sarah like two cold blue marbles. It was like gazing into Karina's eyes after she was shot. "Iz?"

"Give her a minute," Ethan said as the guard reached for her.

Sarah slid her hand down to Izzy's wrist to check her pulse. It was there, strong and steady. But while her body might still be working, Izzy just wasn't in there.

"Let's go," the security guard muttered, hauling Sarah up to her feet. She shook free, and she and Ethan followed the guard quietly. She couldn't help Izzy anymore. She just went along with the guard, as numb on the inside as Izzy seemed to be.

"Ms. Merson, Mr. Steere. Do you want to explain to me what you were thinking?" Dean Farrell barked the instant Sarah's butt hit the chair in her office, Ethan taking the chair next to her. "You were in a restricted area. More than that, you *assaulted* a nurse."

"A nurse who had Izzy strapped to a table doing who the hell knows what to her," Ethan shot back.

Sarah automatically looked at the dean's shoes. Red soles. Louboutin. Completely inappropriate for work. Sarah felt tears prick her eyes. That was Karina's voice, Karina's thoughts. She always did a Farrell Shoe Inventory for Karina, because her roommate loved that kind of stuff.

She pushed her thoughts of Karina away. Right now she had to focus on Izzy. "She was screaming. She never stopped screaming."

I can still hear the screams . . .

The dean sighed. "I'm sure that was terrible to see. But what you did was incredibly dangerous, for you as well as the staff in the room. And, more importantly, for Isobel. She suffers from a very serious emotional disability—"

"PTSD. I know," Sarah cut her off. "She was going for therapy, she told me. But I've had a few hours of state-mandated therapy, and it's sitting in a chair talking about your behavior. It's not being tied down and brutalized."

"Sanctuary Bay Academy is known for its cutting-edge psychiatric treatments," Dean Farrell said. "Many of our students would not be able to function in a regular high school, regardless of their high intelligence. Frequently families will petition to have their children sent here for that reason alone."

She sounds like a catalog, Sarah thought. "Izzy has always been perfectly functional," she said aloud, though her voice wasn't as confident as she wanted it to be. Izzy-in-the-woods flashed through her mind. Izzy-the-murderer.

"That's because our treatment works," Dean Farrell replied.

"Is that what you call it? Treatment?" Sarah shook her head.

"It looked like torture," Ethan added.

"It's experimental," a new voice said from the doorway. "Sorry it took me a few to get here." Dr. Diaz came in and sat on the couch. "Izzy was just brought to my office, and I wanted to check her over."

"Is she okay?" Sarah asked anxiously.

"All her vitals were strong," Dr. Diaz answered.

"That's a stroke of luck," Dean Farrell said. "Interrupting the treatment midstream is . . . well, frankly, it's never happened. When Dr. LaSalle called me from the site, she was afraid that Isobel might have suffered brain damage."

Sarah exchanged an alarmed glance with Ethan. "All we did was unstrap her," she explained. "Izzy pulled out that . . . tube . . . herself."

"Which is precisely why she was restrained to begin with," the dean pointed out. "And her reaction to your interference was violent."

"She was violent the whole time," Sarah argued.

"As soon as Sarah got one hand free, Izzy started clawing at her," Ethan jumped in. "It wasn't our fault."

"She was terrified by what was being done to her," Sarah said. "I'm not sure she even recognized us. I don't think she meant to hurt me—or anyone. She just wanted to get free."

"That must have been hard to watch," Dr. Diaz said. "Have you ever seen a patient being treated, Dean?"

Dean Farrell shook her head.

"I've only read about the protocol myself," Dr. Diaz went on. "I know the patients have no memory of the treatment afterward. But I can't say I blame these two for wanting to put a stop to it." It felt good to have an adult taking their side. Sarah still wasn't used to that.

"I don't understand why Izzy had some kind of chemo port in her neck—" Sarah began.

"We can't discuss a patient's medical situation with anyone other than their parents," the dean interrupted. "You've already compromised the treatment so much that we may have to end it." She looked from Ethan to Sarah, disappointment creasing her face. "And that's a shame, because it was proving to be extremely effective."

"I'm sorry," Sarah said, especially if she'd ended up hurting Izzy worse. "I am. But I don't get what you were doing to her."

"And you don't need to 'get' it," Dean Farrell said. "It's none of your business, and you weren't supposed to be anywhere near that room anyway. And once there, you ignored the warnings of a medical professional, and you attacked him."

Sarah slumped back in her chair, feeling sick. The dean was going to kick them out of Sanctuary Bay. She'd never find out if Izzy was okay or what really happened to Karina. Ethan would never find out what happened to Philip. They were done.

"I didn't attack him." She tried to keep her voice calm as she explained. "He grabbed me to pull me away from Izzy, and I kicked him so that I could help her. I thought he was hurting her."

"And the security guard?" Dean Farrell asked.

"Izzy did that. I tried to pull her off him," Ethan put in. "She bit me." He gestured at the blood on his sleeve. "And she kicked him. Knocked him back into a medical cart she'd tipped over. She took out half the office before she, uh, went unconscious."

The dean sighed heavily. Her mouth crooked as she chewed on her lip, destroying her bright red lipstick. What was she thinking? Was she about to call Sarah's social worker and tell her to make arrangements for a new foster home? Would it go in her record that she'd attacked someone? Who would take her if it did? "Ramon, are you sure Isobel will be all right?" Dean Farrell finally asked.

"Yes. She's resting comfortably," Dr. Diaz answered.

Dean Farrell nodded decisively. "Sarah, you know we here at Sanctuary Bay have always believed in you. Ethan, we believe in your potential too, although you seem to find that hard to stomach," she said. "But today's behavior is utterly unacceptable."

"Sarah was only trying to help," Ethan protested, not mentioning himself.

"And that's why I'd like to give her a second chance. You too, Ethan," the dean said. "But only on the condition that you stop this sort of nonsense immediately. You must respect the privacy of your classmates, do you understand? The treatment area is strictly off-limits. You're not even to speak of it."

"Of course," Sarah replied. She wasn't used to being given second chances, but now that she had, she felt oddly ungrateful. She couldn't shake the feeling that Dean Farrell was hiding something. Why had Izzy's treatment seemed like torture? Wouldn't such harsh tactics make someone with PTSD even worse?

"No more leaving campus for any reason," the dean went on. She turned to Ethan. "I know you've continued to do so, even though we've spoken about it before. If you want to stay here at Sanctuary Bay, you have to follow the rules. *Both* of you."

"Okay," Sarah said. She shot a worried look at Dr. Diaz.

"I'm sure she will," Dr. Diaz added, putting his hand on Sarah's shoulder.

"And you? Are you going to behave?" Dean Farrell asked Ethan, eyebrows raised.

Sarah expected him to say no, to take this chance to get thrown out, but he just gave a quiet "Yes."

"Very well," the dean said, clearly dismissing them.

Sarah started toward the door with Dr. Diaz and Ethan. "One more question, Sarah," Dean Farrell called.

They all turned back. "I'm concerned about your roommate Karina. Her cell has been offline for more than twenty-four hours. I checked with her teachers, and she hasn't been to class. When was the last time you saw her?"

Sarah took a deep breath. She could tell the dean everything. That she'd seen Karina shot, maybe a prank, maybe not. That her friends seemed to be experiencing some kind of unshakable mass delusion. That Nate had begun talking nonsense. That she had no idea where else to look for Karina.

She needed help, more help than Ethan and Dr. Diaz could give her. Dean Farrell could order the whole island searched, for starters.

But Sarah didn't trust her.

"I can't remember exactly," she said. "When I woke up yesterday morning, she was already gone. I haven't seen her since then. But we're both busy. I don't always see her that much." She sounded like all the other members of the Wolfpack. Vague. Unworried.

Dean Farrell held her gaze for a long moment. Sarah forced herself not to look away. Finally, the dean relaxed and smiled.

"All right. I'm sure there's nothing to worry about. Her cell is probably malfunctioning. If you see her, tell her to come to me for a replacement."

Dean Farrell gave her a little wave, as if they'd just been having one of their check-in chats.

As if everything were normal.

"Just don't strap me to the table, okay?" Ethan said as they walked into the waiting room of Dr. Diaz's office. He had insisted on taking a look at the bite on Ethan's arm, because "human bites can be nasty."

Sarah sat down in one of the chairs. There was really no reason for her to be there, but she wanted to strategize with Ethan when they were done.

"Don't you have a *Vogue* or something for Sarah?" Ethan asked.

"Are you scared I'm going to give you a shot? Quit stalling," Dr. Diaz said, heading for his office.

"One sec." Ethan rifled through the magazines on the end table and pulled out an old issue of *Car and Driver*.

Sarah shook her head. "Funny."

Ethan leaned over to hand it to Sarah, whispering, "Try to find Izzy's medical files while I'm in there."

Sarah gave a little nod as she flipped the magazine open. She wanted to see those files too. Maybe they'd explain what the Bromcyan was for. As soon as Ethan and Dr. Diaz disappeared into the office, shutting the door behind them, she jumped up. There were two other doors off the waiting room. The first was the bathroom, and the second was the records room.

She darted inside, and closed the door quietly behind her. The room was really just a large closet. The walls were lined with filing cases from floor to ceiling with barely enough space to stand in the middle. She scanned the labels, trying to figure out how the files were organized. Alphabetically by year? Or everything together?

"Don't you know it's illegal to look at private medical files?" a gruff voice demanded.

Sarah jerked her head toward the door and then immediately relaxed. Ethan. He stepped inside, pulling the door shut behind him, which pushed him so close to her that they were practically hugging. "My Izzy bite is fine, thanks for asking," he breathed into her ear.

Sarah jumped, realizing that she hadn't moved away from him. For one brief but charged moment, she stayed pressed against him, his body warm. She knew she had to step away, but somehow couldn't force herself to do it.

He's Karina's boyfriend, she thought, and that got her feet to move.

"Diaz is still futzing around in his office. If we're quiet, when he comes out he'll think we both left," Ethan told her. "I want to see what the files say about Izzy's so-called treatment. I don't care what the dean says, it was like something out of a horror movie." He pulled open one of the file drawers. "Do you think we convinced the dean we're going to be model students from now on?"

"I hope so," Sarah answered, checking a drawer, then closing it. "When I had my first meeting with her—and that wasn't even two months ago—I never would have thought I'd be lying to her. All I wanted to do was impress her. But now I've turned into you, all paranoid and mistrustful."

"Which is why I'm a good influence on you," Ethan said with a little smile. "Although you've always been mistrustful—just not of the school. You never trusted me."

Sarah hadn't realized Ethan knew. "It wasn't just you. I didn't trust anyone here, not until I joined the Wolfpack." But after Karina, she'd gone straight to Dr. Diaz and ratted them out, so maybe she didn't really trust the Wolfpack, either. "Not trusting anyone is pretty much how I've survived," she said quietly. "I was trying to change that here, to let go of all my old crap."

"Doesn't sound like crap to me," he replied. "But after what we just saw, anyone would be, *should* be mistrustful here. Gotta say, I'm not surprised Sanctuary Bay finds a violent medical treatment acceptable. Along with denying students access to help from outside. Oh, and disappearing them."

"*I'm* surprised," Sarah said. But after what she'd seen happening to Izzy, she found it a lot more believable that Philip didn't drown.

"What was that thing going into the back of Izzy's head?" Ethan asked. "Farrell said pulling it out might've caused brain damage, but she might've just said that to scare us."

"I have no idea. And why does she even need a medical port? It's not like Izzy has cancer," Sarah said. "Do you think it's a coincidence that right when Izzy's acting crazy and forgetting about shooting her roommate, the school is pumping drugs into her head?"

"She's been in therapy ever since she got here, though. The memory issue is new," Ethan pointed out. "And your entire *precious* Wolfpack also has a convenient memory lapse about Karina. They're not all in therapy."

Sarah sighed. "True. It's just that one of the meds they had going in to her was Bromcyan. As part of my Wolfpack initiation,

I was thrown into one of the POW cells under the school. The word "Bromcyan" was carved into the walls over and over. I had no idea what it was, then I saw a bottle of it when we were in the asylum."

"And you decided not to mention it?" Ethan burst out. "What the fuck, Sarah!?"

"I know, I know," Sarah said quickly. "See? Trust issues. I hadn't told you yet that I was in the Wolfpack. And it didn't seem important anyway, just weird, until I saw it on that computer monitor attached to Izzy."

Ethan turned back to the file cabinets. "We really need her file. And I want to look for Philip's. And while we're at it, why not Karina's. Yours too."

Mine?

"Don't you wonder, Sarah?" he asked. "You're the only one who remembers what happened. Your memory is resisting whatever they've done to the rest of the Wolfpack."

"But you just said yourself that the whole Wolfpack isn't in therapy," Sarah said.

"Yeah, I know . . ." He sighed, frustrated. "I'm just trying to think it through."

Sarah frowned. "Dr. Diaz said Izzy wouldn't remember her therapy. He said it looks scary but that the patient doesn't remember it. You don't think . . ." Her words trailed off.

No, that's too insane.

"That the school is using the treatment on other people to erase their memories?" Ethan suggested.

"But, it . . . it sounds crazy," Sarah said.

Ethan didn't answer. He was staring at an open file. "I can't find Philip. And my own file is empty except for the time I broke my arm. I'm going to grab Karina's."

"If you're at the 'S' files, Izzy's should be near there. She's a 'T.'" Sarah moved over to his side and stood on tiptoe, scanning the letter stickers on each file folder. Ethan put his hand on the small of her back, helping her balance.

She swallowed, forcing herself to ignore the little zing of electricity his touch gave her, trying to focus on finding the file quickly so she could move.

"Izzy's isn't here," Sarah said. "I guess they must have it with her in the infirmary."

"I don't see Karina's either," he replied. Just the sound of him saying Karina's name was enough to make that electric tingle evaporate. She shook off his hand a little faster than she meant to, and Ethan's eyebrows shot up.

"Everything okay?" he asked.

The door flew open before Sarah could answer. Dr. Diaz stood there, glaring at them.

"Crap!" Ethan cried, wrapping his arms around Sarah's waist. He kicked the door closed. "We're not, uh, entirely dressed."

Dr. Diaz pushed it open again.

"Don't you knock, man?" Ethan complained.

Sarah was too stunned to move. Dr. Diaz rolled his eyes. "Do you think I'm an idiot? Sarah's got better taste than to make out in a closet with you, Mr. Steere."

Sarah squirmed out of Ethan's arms. "Are you going to take us back to the dean?"

"No, although I don't approve of you going through private medical records," he answered. "Are you looking for Izzy's?"

They nodded.

"Listen, I owe you guys an apology. What I said about Izzy in the dean's office—I don't quite know if it's true."

"What?" Ethan exploded.

"I wanted to get you two out of there, so I tried to sound

knowledgeable about Izzy's treatment, hoping the dean didn't know more about it than I did," Dr. Diaz said. "I've never been given actual details about the procedure."

"What do you mean? You're the doctor," Ethan said.

"Not for the treatment," Sarah reminded him. "That woman who came in was the doctor in charge, right?"

"Exactly. I'm just here to give out antibiotics and pump stomachs," Dr. Diaz said. "For anything else, the school brings in specialists."

"But still, you're the one in charge of Izzy's health," Ethan pressed. "You knew she was getting some crazy experimental therapy."

"Yes, but I don't administer it. Nor do I know any of the specifics," Dr. Diaz insisted. "It's not under the control of Sanctuary Bay. It's a Fortitude project."

Sarah shot Ethan a questioning look. He shrugged.

"There wouldn't be anything about Izzy's treatment in these files, anyway—Fortitude keeps their own," Dr. Diaz said.

"What about my brother?" Ethan asked suddenly. "Why aren't Philip's files here?"

"When students graduate, we put their files in storage." Dr. Diaz's forehead creased as he thought about it. "I'll take you. Follow me."

He took off so quickly that Sarah had to jog to catch up with him. They went out through the empty waiting room and down the hall to the closest stairwell. At the bottom were two doors—one leading outside and one that was marked FACULTY ONLY. Dr. Diaz pressed his finger against the keypad to the faculty door and it clicked open.

The stairwell heading to the basement wasn't nearly as well lit as the one above. Instead of marble, the steps were made of cement. At the bottom of the stairs was a short, nondescript hallway with three doors along the sides. Diaz went over to the second one on the right and opened it.

"More unlocked doors," Ethan murmured in Sarah's ear as they followed.

"Well, the whole stairwell is locked," she pointed out.

"It's a mess," Dr. Diaz told them, gesturing around the room. It was surprisingly large, with stacks of boxes and about twenty big, old-fashioned wooden filing cabinets. "Generally, the newer files are in the boxes, but every few years I make an attempt at organizing things alphabetically instead, because that's how the ones in the file cabinets are. So then I end up shoving newer files in with the older ones and vice versa. I should probably stop doing that."

Ethan went over to the closest box and began digging through it. Sarah turned to Dr. Diaz. "What's Fortitude?"

"It's a company, the Fortitude Corporation. They're a private contractor."

"What does that mean?" she asked.

"It means they developed a treatment for PTSD and other mental disorders, and they're in the testing phase. They partnered with Sanctuary Bay to do the trials," Dr. Diaz replied. "Or, rather, Sanctuary Bay hired them to do the trials. The school gets a lot of mileage with wealthy parents because they offer cutting-edge solutions to psychological problems. We can't do the research and development ourselves, so the school looks for promising companies to do it for us. Then we partner with them for clinical trials."

"But you're a scientist," Sarah said. "Don't you want to be involved in any kind of—what is it, psychopharmacological?—experiment?"

"I do," he agreed. "But that's not up to me. The Fortitude

Corporation has its own protocols, and that doesn't include school doctors."

"So, Dr. LaSalle, the woman Ethan and I saw, she works for Fortitude?" Sarah asked.

"I guess. I've never seen her, or the treatment room." He sighed. "Honestly, I've never given it much thought. They operate so separately from us. But the way you described Izzy's therapy . . . it doesn't sound right."

"You mean because she was strapped down like a victim on *Dexter*?" Ethan said with a snort.

"Yes, but it's more that. Sarah said there was a port in her neck. That's extremely odd. Usually that sort of thing would only be used for chemotherapy or something similar, and it wouldn't be in her neck."

"How do you know she won't remember it? Or was that just something you said for the dean too?" Sarah asked.

"I'm positive. I found traces of midazolam in her blood work. Midazolam is a drug that's used to induce amnesia after medical procedures," he replied.

"What about Bromcyan? Is that a drug that messes with memory?" Sarah asked. She quickly gave him the rundown on the three places she'd seen the name.

"Never heard of it," Dr. Diaz answered. "But I can look into it."

"So what do we do now?" Sarah asked. "If Karina's alive, then where is she? If that treatment is supposed to help Izzy, then why does it seem like she's suddenly lost her mind? And why is the entire Wolfpack acting insane? They repeated a meeting last night word for word and they didn't even realize it."

"What the hell is this?" Ethan's voice was quiet, but something about his tone made Sarah nervous.

"Did you find Philip's file?" she asked.

"No," he said. "But I found my father's." He held up a thick brown file folder. "Gregory Steere. And there's another one right next to it. Elizabeth Lanning. Except somebody wrote in another last name after that, so it would be filed in the right place, I guess. Elizabeth Lanning *Steere*. My mother."

Sarah's eyes widened. "I didn't know your parents went to Sanctuary Bay," she said.

"That's the thing," Ethan replied. "They didn't."

15

"Let me see those," Dr. Diaz said, reaching for the files in Ethan's hand. "Maybe they're just medical histories for enrollment purposes. We don't do that currently, but it's entirely possible there used to be a family history taken."

"Yeah, especially if it has your mom's married name," Sarah said.

"See for yourself." Ethan handed the files over and turned away. From the look on Dr. Diaz's face, he wasn't looking at a simple medical history. His eyes moved back and forth, scanning the records, his forehead creased with concern.

"Ethan . . ." Sarah wasn't sure how to approach him.

"They met at Harvard," he said without turning around. "Sophomore year. They have this whole story about it. She sat next to him in philosophy class and he immediately started annoying her by asking to borrow a pen. Every time she'd tell the story, she'd say the same thing: Who comes to a philosophy class without a pen? But that was all it took. Love at first sight and all that. At least that's what they always said."

"Maybe they just meant that they started dating then, but they knew each other in high school," Sarah suggested.

"They're my parents. I know when they met," he snapped, looking at her.

"Okay, sorry," Sarah said. She started back toward Dr. Diaz, but Ethan grabbed her hand.

"No, I shouldn't yell at you. Obviously I don't really know." His expression was so sad that every fiber of her being wanted to draw him in for a hug. "I don't know anything about my family at all."

"These records indicate that your parents spent all four years of high school here at the Academy," Dr. Diaz said.

"That would explain why it seemed normal to them to send Philip here, if it was their high school," Sarah said.

"There's nothing normal about any of this," Ethan muttered.

"When did the school first open?" Sarah asked, looking around the big room. "There's a lot of stuff in here, and the classes aren't that big."

"In the early fifties," Dr. Diaz replied. "But you're right, there does seem to be a lot. I wonder if there's more than just medical records—it could be old student academic files, I suppose. I've actually never made it to the back of the room."

"I'm going to look." Sarah climbed over a carton and inched her way toward the old filing cabinets along the far wall.

"Why?" Ethan called after her.

"I don't know. There's just something bothering me." Sarah pulled open a drawer and blew the dust off some ancient, yellowing file folders. She glanced at the date on one or two of them. "These are from the sixties," she said. She shut the drawer and moved on to the next huge old cabinet.

"What's bugging you?" Ethan asked, coming over to her.

Sarah hesitated.

"Is this a memory issue?" Dr. Diaz guessed.

"Kind of. Maybe." She shrugged. "The table Izzy was strapped down to, it had these metal bars across it to hold her legs down. Is that normal?"

"Not really. Typically if you were going to restrain a patient, you'd use something made of padded foam and mesh," Dr. Diaz replied.

"Guess metal bars are the more cutting-edge Sanctuary Bay way to go," Ethan said sarcastically.

"The operating table in the old asylum was the same," Sarah said. "It had the same kind of metal straps. Only rustier."

Both of them stared at her, baffled.

"And there was a filing cabinet like this one in that same room," Sarah went on. "It had a drawer missing, and there was water damage to the wood. But it was the same kind. I saw a few of them at the asylum. So I guess I want to see if they brought over any of the stuff from the asylum when they started the school. I thought maybe there'd be a mention of Bromcyan."

Dr. Diaz frowned. "That asylum was closed decades before the school was founded. The POW camp was here in between."

"But Bromcyan was carved in the POW cell too, remember? I saw it," Sarah told him. "I was down there for my Wolfpack initiation."

"Fine. Let's look." Ethan went over to the farthest cabinet, tucked into the corner of the room, and yanked open the top drawer.

"What year?" Sarah asked.

He raised his eyes to hers, shocked. "1924."

"Sanctuary Bay didn't exist then," Dr. Diaz said.

Ethan pulled out a handful of folders and handed one to

Sarah. She opened it up and scanned the fading words. "It's still a medical record, though."

"This one too. And this one." Ethan kept flipping through the files. "They're patient files."

"From the old asylum?" Dr. Diaz took a few folders and began looking through them. "I never looked at anything but the names when I jammed new files in, but I assumed they were all from the school. There'd be no reason for us to keep files for the asylum patients."

"Who owns the island? Maybe when the school bought it, they became responsible for everything," Sarah guessed. "So they technically own everything at the old asylum and the POW camp."

"That could be. They would have had an obligation to maintain the patient files, so maybe they just moved them all here. This is deep storage," Dr. Diaz said.

Sarah couldn't take her eyes off the file in her hand. "This is for a girl who was only fourteen, and it says she had hysteria. Doesn't that mean she just had really bad PMS?"

"It could mean a lot of things. Mental illness wasn't well understood back then," Dr. Diaz replied.

"But still, to be sent away to an insane asylum . . ." Sarah could hardly imagine it.

"This guy thought he was Rudolph Valentino," Ethan said. "Oh, and sometimes he thought he was a two-year-old."

"You're making that up," Sarah frowned. "Stop being insensitive about this."

"I'm not! He suffered from dementia, and the two most common delusions were of Valentino and infancy." Ethan held up the file as proof.

"Schizophrenia," Dr. Diaz put in, his voice quiet as he scanned the file in his hand. "This poor boy suffered terribly. There wasn't any real treatment." He sighed. "Sad as it is, I have to admit a certain professional curiosity in reading these files. I can't believe I never knew they were here."

Sarah opened another one, her gaze skimming over the long list of drugs and treatments, looking for anything that would let her see what this man's life had been like. Did his parents come visit him in that awful asylum with its dark rooms and its grand hall? Were the doctors and nurses kind to him, or were they the kind of horrific figures that always showed up in insane asylum movies?

" 'Mania,' " she read aloud. "So maybe he was actually bipolar. But they had him so hopped up on drugs that the medicine itself may have caused the symptoms!" She ran her finger down the list of meds. "Opium, paraldehyde, Bromcyan." She looked over at Ethan. "Bromcyan," she repeated. "It's listed here as one of the meds they gave this man for his mania. Sedatives and Bromcyan." Her hand that held the paper was shaking.

"The file is from the early twenties?" Dr. Diaz asked. "Maybe it was an experimental treatment that fell out of vogue quickly. They were flying blind back then. Bromcyan. Huh." Dr. Diaz suddenly sat down on a nearby file box. His face had gone pale, and the files he'd been holding fell from his hands without him seeming to notice. He was lost in thought.

"Dr. D? Are you all right?" Sarah asked.

Dr. Diaz stared straight ahead, his eyes unblinking.

"Dr. D?" Sarah bit her lip. "You're freaking me out."

"I'm okay. I didn't recognize the name of the drug at first, but it's starting to feel familiar," Dr. Diaz answered in a strange, low voice. "I can't quite place it though."

"Well, we know it was being used to treat mania in the nineteen twenties," Ethan said. "And we know it's being put into Izzy's blood. And somebody at the POW camp knew about it."

"I wonder if that's the experimental part of the treatment that Dean Farrell was talking about," Sarah mused.

"How experimental can it be if they were using it almost a century ago?" Ethan took the file from Sarah and flipped through it, reading. Sarah sank down onto another box. It was disorienting when memories changed. The details about Bromcyan hadn't shifted, but things she hadn't consciously cared about had suddenly become important. The prisoner who'd gone mad wasn't what mattered; the word he'd scratched into the rock was what mattered. The strange tube attached to Izzy wasn't what mattered; the drug inside it was.

"Cheer up, Sarah. This one has a happy ending," Ethan said. "Listen: 'Patient response better than expected. Episodes of dementia nil.'"

"Really?" Sarah asked. "But it said he was a pretty bad case."

"Apparently the Bromcyan worked." Ethan grabbed another handful of files from the drawer and held them out to Sarah. "Let's see if it worked for anyone else."

"There's a mention here," Dr. Diaz put in. Sarah was surprised to see him studying another file, back to his usual self. He'd seemed so out of it just moments ago. "This one is also schizophrenic, or that's what I would think, reading between the lines. They describe it here as delusions, mania, and dementia—the girl told them that angels were talking to her. Anyway, they treated her with Bromcyan and it seems like it was a miracle for her. Oh!" he exclaimed suddenly, grimacing.

"What?" Sarah asked.

"Uh . . . it worked to calm and order her mind for a short period. Then she jumped off the bluffs after saying she wanted to fly like the angels."

"Oh, god," Sarah cried, covering her mouth. The story about a patient hurling herself off Suicide Cliff was true.

"The doctor notes that he'd decreased dosage of the Bromcyan and he suspects it may have allowed her dementia to return."

"When's that dated?" Ethan asked.

"October 1924," Dr. Diaz replied.

"This one's from 1926. They changed their mind about the Bromcyan, I think. It says they've been using a low dosage with great success when combined with a sort of suggestive therapy. It says that the Bromcyan 'renders the patient calm and suggestible,' so they drug up the patients and suggest they do healthy things. And it works."

"Maybe the angels suggested that poor girl should fly," Sarah said.

"But this doctor thinks it's only useful with low doses. High doses cause more of an unpredictable effect," Ethan said.

"What's the doctor's name?" Dr. Diaz asked.

"Herman Wissen," Ethan replied. "The man had impeccable handwriting, by the way. I've never met a doctor who could even form a single intelligible letter. No offense."

"None taken. There's a reason I use the Smart Board instead of writing," Dr. Diaz said with a smile. "It's the same doctor for this file."

"So this Dr. Wissen was treating mentally ill people with something called Bromcyan ninety-something years ago, and it worked like a charm," Sarah said. "Why haven't any of us heard of it? I know about lithium and penicillin and Prozac and all the other old-school drugs that were revolutionary. Why not Bromcyan?"

"Maybe it has a different brand name we all know," Ethan suggested.

Sarah jumped as her cell buzzed in her pocket. She glanced

at it. "Emergency. Suicide Cliff." What now? She could almost feel the adrenaline rushing through her body. "I have to go. Something's wrong. The pack."

"What happened?" Ethan's voice was sharp. "Something with Karina?"

"I don't know. I'll call you when I find out."

Sarah left them both sitting among the old files. As soon as she got out into the hall, she started to run.

Sarah saw a crowd already gathered at Suicide Cliff when she rounded the west wing of the main building. But she couldn't see what they were looking at. She put on more speed, even though her lungs and the muscles in her calves were already on fire.

"Oh, thank god you're here! Maybe you can talk to him. He won't listen to us," Hazel whispered to Sarah when she skidded to a stop next to the group. She moved aside to let Sarah get closer.

And that's when Sarah saw him. Nate. Pacing about two feet from the edge of the cliff, the robe he wore as the Jager billowing around him. Her heart lurched into her throat. He would never come outside in the middle of the day in that robe. He would never endanger the Wolfpack that way. What was wrong?

Izzy pushed her way up next to Sarah, and Sarah almost fell over from the shock.

"Iz! Are you okay? What are you doing here?" she cried.

"The text said it was an emergency," Izzy replied.

"But . . ." Sarah couldn't deal with Izzy now. All her attention had to stay on Nate.

"A storm approaches," he called in his strong, clear Jager voice as he continued to pace confidently along the edge.

"Nate, you have to come away from there," Sarah told him firmly, fighting to keep the panic out of her voice.

It was as if he didn't hear her, or even see her. He stopped suddenly and stared at the ocean.

"There's a storm coming," he said, this time in a small, thin voice Sarah had never heard before. He sounded young. And scared. "Do you see it?"

Sarah moved a little closer. She didn't like the height, but as long as she looked at the ocean and not the spiky rocks she was fine. The water was a deep greenish-gray, and the swells were high. The sky above them was a bright, cheerful blue, but out toward the horizon darkness spread, the gray clouds matching the gray water. Sarah blinked, trying to fight her sense that the darkness was growing.

"Yes, Nate, I see the clouds," she told him. "Maybe . . . maybe we should get inside."

A gust of wind blew the hood away from Nate's face, and Sarah finally saw his eyes. They were fever bright, darting around the crowd. "We're not all here," he said. "Our number is wrong."

"Nate, you're way too close to the edge." Sarah wanted to grab his arm, but the vision of them both tumbling down to those rocks stopped her. "Come back. Come over here to me."

"Where's . . . where . . ." Nate's voice had lost all its Jager authority. He didn't even sound like his usual self anymore. The cocky self-assurance was gone.

"We can't be out here like this. People will see us," Grayson told him, voice trembling. "Let's go back to the den. Where it's safe."

He didn't respond. "Where is the blood?" Nate asked. "Where . . . where is the girl?"

No one answered. Sarah heard Izzy give a little laugh under her breath. But it wasn't funny. Nate began to work at the belt around his waist, picking at the teeth tangled in the seaweed, agitated.

"Are you talking about Karina?" she asked.

Nate's face blanched, and he spun toward her immediately. Sarah winced. She was relieved he had responded, but that was the wrong thing to say. Nate shook his head . . . and didn't stop. Faster and faster, flinging his head from side to side.

"Okay, this is getting stupid," Izzy said.

Pushing away her fear of tumbling over the edge, Sarah stepped forward and took Nate's face in her hands, forcing him to stop shaking his head. "Nate. What's going on?" she asked softly.

"Where is the bone?" Nate replied. "Blood and bone." Suddenly his self-possession, that laser focus of his, returned. He gave Sarah The Grin, but it looked like the frozen grimace of a skull.

Repulsed, Sarah let go of his face, and he stepped backward—right toward the edge. Sarah grabbed him by his elbow.

"He's lost it," Izzy said.

"Yeah, let's get out of here," Logan put in.

Sarah heard the others moving behind her, murmuring to one another, trying to decide if they should stay or go. But she couldn't take her eyes off Nate. His eyes were wild now, a ring of white showing all the way around his irises.

"Nate?" she said. "I think you should— Maybe you should just sit down for a minute."

"Don't bond us won't be blood," he told her. "Wax poetic. Not poetic, pathetic, peripatetic." He pushed his hand into his short dark hair, and managed to grab a chunk of it. "Stop!" He yanked his hand away, hair and skin and blood coming with it.

"Holy fuck," David burst out.

Kayla screamed.

Nate threw back his head, knocking his hood completely off, and howled, the chilling sound turning into a hysterical, coughing laugh halfway through. He twisted his fingers into his hair again, ready to pull.

"Oh my god. Nate—" Sarah rushed toward him, but he danced away from her, screaming. No words, just blood-curdling shrieks. The others were screaming now too, or crying. Kayla shook with sobs.

"Stopstopstopstop," Nate began to chant. It was quieter than the shrieking, but freakier.

"Nate?"

He looked at her, his eyes fixed on hers. There was no sign of gorgeous, intense Nate in those eyes. They were the eyes of a panicked animal.

He stepped over the cliff.

"No!" Sarah screamed.

But it was too late. Nate was falling, his black velvet Jager robe flapping wildly as he plummeted. She rushed to the cliff, throwing herself down on her belly so she could hang over the edge.

Far below, on the jagged black rocks in the water, lay Nate. Blood poured from his head. His body was shattered, limbs protruding from the robe at horrifying angles. He was dead.

"Wow," said Izzy, peering over the bluff. "Just like that German soldier."

16

Everybody ran.

Sarah heard them, their panicked sobs, their fearful hushed voices, and finally their pounding footsteps. She heard it all, but saw nothing—her eyes were glued to the horrific image below her, to Nate.

Tears streamed down her cheeks. They blurred her view of his poor, broken body splayed on the rocks, the dark ocean lapping at him.

"He was right about one thing, there *is* a storm coming," Izzy said, casually sitting down next to Sarah. "If they don't get him out of the water soon, he'll be pulled in and be gone for good."

Of course Izzy would stay. Just like last time, Sarah thought. *Izzy's the only one with the balls to stick around after a violent death. And the only one psychotic enough to not be crying or freaking out.*

"We need to tell the school. Can you call for help on your cell?" Sarah asked, her eyes on Nate.

"I can't. I left it . . . somewhere." Izzy sounded confused. Her cell must have been lost in the treatment room during her rampage. But Izzy wouldn't remember that.

Sarah rolled onto her side so she could get her hand into the pocket of her jeans. She pulled out the cell and said, "Emergency on the bluffs."

"System offline," the cell announced.

"That's been happening a lot lately," Izzy commented. "They need to upgrade."

"Can you go get help?" Sarah asked. "I'm going to stay here with Nate."

"Why?" Izzy's voice dripped disdain. "He's not very nice to look at. And he doesn't even know you're here, Sarah. He's dead."

"I'm not letting his body out of my sight," Sarah said. "I refuse to let somebody else just disappear. They didn't find Karina, but they are going to find Nate."

The ocean rose higher than before, sending a wave over Nate's entire body.

"Go now. Go *fast*," Sarah said.

"Okay, okay, I'm going." Izzy got up and took off across the lawn. Sarah was relieved to hear that she was running instead of ambling the whole way.

Alone, she stared at Nate's body, willing the water to stay calm until help arrived. Not so long ago, he'd been kissing her. His lips were warm and alive, his eyes were filled with that intensity that only he had . . . and now he was a corpse on a pile of rocks.

"Nate," she whispered. "How could you do this? What went wrong?"

But Nate would never answer her again.

The water had pulled him halfway off the rocks by the time Sarah heard footsteps returning. She didn't move, keeping her eyes on Nate.

"Holy shit." It was Ethan's voice. "What happened? I saw Izzy running by and she said you needed me out here."

"Nate killed himself. I think." Sarah could barely hear herself over the pounding surf, so she raised her voice. "He had some kind of breakdown. He was rambling, speaking nonsense, and it got him started on Karina. He noticed that she wasn't there, and it really upset him, and then he just . . ."

"Oh, god. Poor guy." Ethan sat down next to Sarah and rubbed her back. "I'm sorry."

"I won't look away from him. I can't let him disappear like Karina, or Philip. But the water's really rough." Her voice broke.

"Sit up, Sarah," Ethan said. "Come on. You can't be comfortable lying half over the edge like that."

"It's the only way I can see his whole body," she said. "If I sit up and lean over, I get scared of the height. Look at Nate—that's what happens if you fall."

"But I'm here now. I'll watch him. You sit up." Ethan pulled her into a sitting position, and she collapsed against him, crying. He wrapped his arm around her shoulders and held her, keeping his head turned toward the water the whole time.

"Can you see him?" Sarah asked hoarsely.

"Yeah." He sighed. "Nate always seemed like such a happy guy—it really annoyed me. I can't believe he's dead."

"Where were you going when you ran into Izzy?" Sarah asked, wiping the tears away with the back of her hand. Crying wouldn't help. Not now.

"I was looking for you to tell you what I found out."

"What?" Sarah asked. Now that Ethan was here, his eyes on Nate, she felt like she could let herself think again. Someone else had seen Nate's body, someone she trusted. She wouldn't be surprised if later Izzy and the rest of the Wolfpack told her they had no memory of Nate dying. But Ethan wasn't like that. Ethan would remember, and he would keep her sane.

"I was working my way through the old medical records, trying to piece together the mentions of Bromcyan. But then it occurred to me to look for newer files, so I could figure out how it was working after they'd been using it for a few years."

"That makes sense," Sarah said.

"And I hit the mother lode. The bottom drawer had legal files."

"I don't get it. Legal files about what?" Sarah pushed her messy hair out of her eyes, but it blew right back. The wind was picking up, and the howling seemed to hold an echo of Nate's voice.

"Seems Dr. Wissen wanted to patent Bromcyan—apparently he's the one who created it, right here at the Sanctuary Bay asylum. So he filed all kinds of paperwork."

"That's fantastic. He would have had to describe its formula and all its uses. We can find out everything we need to know." She fought to tune out the wind with her words.

"Yes and no." Ethan's eyes widened and he leaned out a little farther. Sarah shuddered, knowing another wave had overtaken Nate's body. "He's still there, but they'd better get here soon," he said.

Sarah nodded. There was nothing to say.

"Dr. Wissen wanted a patent, but then the drug was banned under the Food and Drug Act," Ethan continued.

"Why?"

"No explanation. One minute the guy is claiming it's a miracle cure for several different forms of mania, and the next minute there's an official government ban."

"There must've been damaging side effects."

"Maybe. The only one he talked about was suggestibility, but that seemed more like a selling point to him—he used it to 'suggest' healthy behavior. I don't know why the Feds would ban it. Either way, Wissen didn't fight it. The asylum closed after the big market crash in the twenties, and by 1930 Bromcyan vanished from the record."

"No, it didn't," Sarah said.

"I Googled it, and Diaz searched all the medical histories. Not a sign of Bromcyan," Ethan said.

"But it was carved into a POW cell. And it was in Izzy's treatment," Sarah insisted. "It absolutely did not disappear."

"Well, not on this island, anyway," he agreed.

Sarah shoved her curls out of her face again, her cheeks stinging from the cold wind. "You're saying that the school is giving Izzy an illegal drug then."

"The Fortitude Corporation," Ethan corrected her. "Who knows if Sanctuary Bay is even aware of it? Diaz hasn't been given any information about this so-called experimental treatment."

"Hold on, are you *defending* the school?" Sarah asked.

"Maybe just this one time." Ethan smiled, his eyes flicking momentarily from the water to Sarah's face. He glanced quickly back at Nate.

"They're not going to come for his body, are they?" Sarah whispered.

"I'm still not taking my eyes off him," Ethan told her.

Silence stretched out between them, the only sound the waves lapping at the rocks. At Nate.

Finally, Sarah heard the roar of an engine.

An ambulance sped toward them, followed by two golf carts driven by security guards. Then a boat appeared in the choppy water—the same sleek black one that brought Sarah to the island—shining a searchlight on the rocks where Nate's body lay. Before she knew it, she and Ethan were being pushed out of the way by the rescue team.

"Are they going down the cliffs or sending divers from the boat?" Ethan asked.

"Honestly, I don't care," Sarah replied. "As long as they get him out of the water." Tears filled her eyes again at the thought of Nate's wild expression right before he stepped off the edge. "He said there was a storm coming. I hate the idea of him being swept away in it now."

"Don't worry, they'll pull him out." Ethan held out his hand. "Let's get you back to your room, Sarah. You're freezing."

Sarah took his hand and let him lead her toward the school, leaving Nate behind.

The next morning, Sarah got up at the normal time, put on her normal clothes, and went off to a normal breakfast with Izzy. The most normal thing about all of it was that everybody— teachers, students, even the groundskeepers—was upset about Nate's suicide.

This is normal. People react this way, she thought. *When someone young dies tragically, everyone mourns. They don't just shrug and say they don't remember, like with Karina.*

Sitting across the dining table from Izzy and Tif, Sarah found herself unable to think of a thing to say. Tif's eyes were red from crying, Izzy's nose looked swollen, and Sarah knew she looked just as bad.

Taylor shuffled over with a tray heaped with melon balls. Nobody even had the energy to tease her about her weird new diet, or ask her why she was back at their table.

"I just can't understand how anyone could do that," Tif finally said. "Especially Nate. He was so popular."

"That doesn't mean he was happy," Matthias pointed out.

"Did he say anything before he jumped?" Tif asked Izzy.

Izzy shook her head. "I don't know, I was too far away from him." She didn't meet Sarah's eyes as she spoke. They couldn't tell anyone what had really happened without outing the Wolfpack. Sarah was glad Izzy had decided to take the lead in coming up with a cover story. By the time she'd gotten back to the dorm last night, everyone knew that Izzy had seen Nate jump off the bluffs. Izzy had been the one to report it and the one questioned by Dean Farrell. Clearly Izzy didn't remember anything about her treatment or she wouldn't have been able to do any of that.

Sarah picked at her omelet, wondering what to do now. She knew all this "normal" wouldn't last. Under the surface of it all, Karina was still missing, and she, Nate, and Dr. Diaz were the only ones who cared, the only ones who noticed.

"I heard they're going to do an autopsy," Tif said.

"Untrue. What would be the point? We all know how he died," Izzy said. "They'll just send his body home to his parents."

"I don't think he even lived with his parents," Sarah replied sadly. "He never really felt at home anywhere but here." A morbid thought flashed through her mind—what would happen to her own body if she died out here? Would her social worker have to make arrangements for her one last time?

"Maybe Nate was failing a class or something," Matthias said. "You two didn't have a fight, did you, Sarah?"

Tif smacked him. "It's not her fault!"

"I didn't say it was. I just meant maybe he overreacted," Matthias said.

Sarah froze, shocked. It couldn't be her fault, could it? She'd pressed him pretty hard on the Karina incident, and it had freaked him out.

"It's nobody's fault. For whatever reason, Nate did this himself. We'll never understand it." Tif broke into quiet sobs.

Sarah closed her eyes briefly, letting everyone's sadness wash over her. This was how it should have been when Karina disappeared.

"Anyone know where Karina is?" she asked for the hundredth time.

Blank faces stared back at her, even from those who weren't

in the Wolfpack. Sarah sighed. The others kept talking about Nate, but Sarah tuned them out because they didn't have all the information.

I have the information, at least more of it, Sarah thought. *And I still have no clue what drove Nate to do it.*

"Stopstopstopstop."

That's what he'd said. Clawing at his head, pulling his hair out of his scalp . . . and yelling "stop."

Sarah felt a chill run down her spine. Stop what? Why was Nate pulling at his head? What did he want to stop? Had Nate been hearing voices?

"Like angels talking to that poor girl at the asylum," she murmured. Nate had never said anything about mental illness, but that would've been something he would want to keep to himself.

"Did you say something?" Izzy asked, her eyes fixed on Sarah.

"No. I'll see you guys later." Sarah stood up and headed for the exit. It was raining out, and the wind was still strong, but she needed the cold air to clear her head. As soon as she was alone, she pulled out her cell.

"Locate Ethan," she told it. She smiled when she saw the yellow dot. He was on his way to Dr. Diaz's office, which was exactly where she had decided to go.

"Sarah, I wasn't expecting you," Dr. Diaz said when she arrived. The place was empty, and Dr. Diaz was just closing the door to his private office. Sarah caught a glimpse of Ethan inside.

"I was looking for Ethan," she said. "Am I not supposed to be here? You're acting all secretive."

Dr. Diaz laughed. "No, you can be here. In fact, I'm glad you are. But we're still going to be secretive. Come in." He waved her in, glancing around the waiting area behind her before closing the door.

Ethan sat in the only available guest chair. He nodded at her. Sarah picked up the stack of files covering the other chair, plopped them on the floor, and sat down.

Dr. Diaz sat behind the desk. Then he stood up again abruptly, turning to look out the window.

"What's going on?" Sarah asked Ethan.

"Dr. Diaz here asked me to go back to the asylum last night to gather some bottles of Bromcyan. Which I did, and then I went to grab some coffee, and then I came back here to find him acting like a perturbed squirrel."

Dr. Diaz laughed, the spell he was under broken, and sat back down. "Sorry about that. I did something, well, let's just say it's not entirely legal. And that puts me into perturbed squirrel mode. I'm not cut out for a life of crime."

"I'm confused," Sarah said. "As usual lately."

"When Nate's body was recovered yesterday, they brought him to the infirmary. We don't . . . we don't have a morgue." Dr. Diaz shook his head sadly. "Who would've thought we would need one."

"So he's there now?" Sarah felt a painful lump form in her throat.

"His body is being transported to the mainland later today. Which is why I had to act fast to do the test, and luckily Ethan likes to prowl around the island in the middle of the night."

"What test?" Ethan asked, leaning forward in his chair.

"I used the traces of Bromcyan you found to reverse engineer a test that would show its presence."

Sarah felt the skin on the back of her neck prickle. "Why would you want to do that?"

"Because we won't understand what happens in Izzy's treatments unless we know—*really* know—whether the Bromcyan is responsible for her amnesia concerning Karina. And then I wondered . . ."

"You wondered whether the rest of the Wolfpack was being dosed too," Sarah put in. "Because they have the same memory block when it comes to Karina."

"I had a Wolfpack member right here, one who would never tell the dean I was testing his blood," Dr. Diaz said slowly.

"Shouldn't you have tested Nate's body for drugs, anyway?" Ethan asked.

"Yes, of course, and I did. But the police lab is on the mainland, and the results won't be back for six weeks. But the Bromcyan test is one I wanted the answer to right away. I snuck a sample of Nate's back to the chem lab and processed it this morning. It was positive."

"Nate had Bromcyan in his body?" Sarah cried out. She turned to Ethan. "I told you it was like he was hearing voices right before he jumped. Dr. Diaz, was Nate mentally ill? Was he getting the same treatment Izzy did?"

"I can't breach any student's confidentiality," Dr. Diaz said. "But I would have been surprised to hear that Nate was receiving such a treatment."

"So he wasn't." Ethan slumped back, blowing out a frustrated breath.

"Then how did he get Bromcyan?" Sarah asked.

"That's the question," Ethan gave her a little half smile. "We don't know how anyone in the Wolfpack got it. Kinda feels like we're chasing our tails."

Suddenly all their cells lit up with a school-wide message. "There's an assembly in ten minutes in the theater. A memorial for Nate," Sarah announced, reading it. "Mandatory."

"That means it's mandatory for me too." Dr. Diaz pushed his chair back and shooed them away. "You two go ahead. Don't tell anyone what we discussed."

No one would believe us anyhow, Sarah thought.

Rain lashed at the window, and the wind howled. The room smelled acidic, like evergreens that had been burned. Sarah couldn't tell if she was just imagining it or not. She could barely tell if she was awake or asleep. It had been such a strange day, with a long memorial service in the morning, and a sort of gigantic group therapy, antisuicide workshop in the afternoon. All the talk had been sad.

Nate was gone. They'd watched the black boat push off with his remains, bobbing on the choppy water. Nate had loved that boat, with its sleek power. It made Sarah feel a little better to think of him getting another ride on it.

It had rained all day, which was appropriate. *But enough is enough*, she thought, turning over again, unable to sleep.

"Stop thrashing around," Izzy complained, her voice muffled with sleep.

"The wind is really loud."

"Yeah, well, there's a nor'easter coming. We're on a tiny island in the ocean. This is how it sounds." Izzy rolled to face the wall, and within minutes Sarah heard her steady breathing. Karina would've gotten up and sat with her, talking about the Ferocious Beast. Karina would've cracked jokes about how the wind sounded like a bad effect in some lame horror movie. Sarah sighed. When Karina was here, everything had been so great. Life at Sanctuary Bay had been beyond anything Sarah could have imagined.

Sarah had been happy.

Her bed felt like it was whirling around her. She was so tired. The air smelled of oranges and limes now, with only a hint of the burned scent from before.

I'm sleeping, she thought. *I'm dreaming about being asleep.* She didn't know when she'd fallen asleep, but she must have, because a man was in their room, and she hadn't seen the door open.

Sarah watched him glide across the floor, fascinated by how quiet his movements were. The man wore black, and he was thin. In the darkness she couldn't tell his race or his eye color, but he was coming closer so maybe she'd see then.

Her eyes closed, and she smiled, thinking about how weird it was that you could go to sleep in a dream. She was dreaming now, but she was dreaming about closing her eyes. Could she dream about opening them?

Her eyes popped open. The man stood directly above her bed with his hand on her arm, holding it still. Something in his hand flashed a dull silver in the moonlight. A word formed in Sarah's head: "syringe." He plunged it toward her arm.

Izzy's entire body slammed against him, knocking him over. The syringe clattered to the floor.

Sarah bolted upright, her heart pounding. This was no dream. Never had been.

"Get out! Get away!" Izzy was screaming. She'd straddled the guy and was slamming her fists into his face, over and over. He grabbed one of Izzy's wrists and twisted until she cried out in pain.

Sarah jumped out of bed and snatched the syringe from the floor, holding it like a weapon.

The guy shoved Izzy off him and got to his knees. Izzy grabbed Sarah's bedside lamp and hurled it at his head. There was a sickening thump as it hit him, and he stumbled against the bed.

Without hesitation, Izzy picked up the lamp again, yanked the cord from the wall, and wrapped it around the guy's neck.

Lights, Sarah thought, stunned. *It's too dark.*

"Turn on—" Her voice was a croak. Sarah swallowed hard and tried again. "Turn on lights!" Spots danced in front of her stunned eyes as the overheads came on. Izzy had her knee on the guy's chest, pinning him against the bed while she tightened the cord around his neck. His eyes bulged, and his boots scraped against the floor as he tried to get free.

"Izzy, no!" Sarah screamed.

Izzy jerked her head toward Sarah, and Sarah gasped. Her roommate's eyes were lit with excitement. This was Izzy-in-the-woods. Izzy-the-murderer. So many times, Sarah had wondered if she'd imagined that girl, but here she was again.

She's going to kill him.

Sarah rushed toward them, lifted the syringe, and plunged it into the man's arm, pushing down the stopper. The guy's wild eyes—brown, Sarah saw now—turned to her for a brief second. Then his eyelids fluttered and he stopped fighting.

Sarah left the syringe in his arm and grabbed Izzy, prying her away from him, forcing the cord out of her grip. "Izzy, stop it. Stop! He's sedated. He's out."

Izzy stared down at him, breathing hard. "He broke into our room," she said. "He deserves it." She reached for the cord again.

"You can't kill him," Sarah insisted, tightening her grip.

"Yes I can," Izzy growled.

Izzy-the-murderer. It's who she really is, just like I thought after that hideous night at the Pine Tree.

But this time Izzy-the-murderer had saved her life.

"Let's go," she said, taking Izzy by the arm. "We have to get out of here before someone else comes." She didn't wait for an argument, but yanked her roommate to her feet and dragged her out the bedroom door. Sarah jumped when her eye snagged on a dark shadow, but it was just the black tree decorating the living room wall. She kept a tight hold on Izzy as she crept to the door, inched it open, and peered out into the hallway.

"What are we doing?"

"There will be more. He came from the school. He must have," Sarah said. "Come on." She hauled Izzy out into the hall and they both ran.

Sarah had no idea what time it was. The corridors were empty, the whole place silent except for their loud breathing. But Sarah felt as if there were eyes on her every step to Ethan's room.

She pounded on his door. It felt like forever until he yanked it open, angry. One look at Sarah and Izzy wiped the glare off his face. "What happened?"

Sarah pulled Izzy inside as Ethan closed the door quickly behind them. "There was a man in our room. He had a syringe, and he tried to inject me. Izzy—"

"Izzy beat the shit out of him," Izzy cut in. She smiled at Ethan, plopping down on his bed.

"What?" He gaped at Sarah.

"She did. She saved me—I thought I was dreaming when I saw him. It was strange. Maybe because I was so exhausted," Sarah said. "Then Izzy almost killed him."

"But she didn't?" he asked in a low voice.

"No. I stabbed him with his own syringe," Sarah explained. "I guess it was a sedative. He passed out immediately."

Izzy picked up a magazine from the nightstand, and calmly started flipping through it.

"Why would someone want to sedate you in your room?" Ethan's voice held all the fear that Sarah had been avoiding feeling.

"I don't know." Her legs buckled from under her, and Ethan grabbed her.

"It's the school. Who else could it be?" he muttered. "We have to go."

"Where?" Sarah cried. "If the school is sending people to attack us, we're dead. There are no police here, nobody to save us. The school is the only authority."

"If the school is sending people to attack *you*, then I'm next," Ethan pointed out. "We've been nosing around, and they noticed. So we have to get out of my room. Now."

"I'm with him, since killing seems not to be acceptable. We need to get out of here," Izzy said, tossing the magazine aside. "But I'm wearing pj's. Ethan? Jacket?"

"Of course," he said, rushing over to the closet. He grabbed a few sweatshirts and jackets and tossed them to Sarah and Izzy, then pulled a thick sweater over his own head.

Sarah hadn't even realized she was still in the yoga pants and T-shirt she used as pajamas. She pulled on Ethan's sweatshirt, the smell of him washing over her.

"What about shoes?" Izzy asked. "I'm in socks. So are you, Sarah."

"Mine will be too big on you," Ethan said.

"Well, we can't go back to our room," Sarah replied. "Just give me some sneakers."

Ethan threw them each a pair, and Sarah tightened them as much as she could. She would just have to hope they stayed on.

"Do you have your cell?" Ethan asked.

"No. I don't have anything. We just ran," Sarah replied.

"Izzy?"

Izzy shook her head.

"Good," Ethan said. He tossed his cell onto the bed. "No cells."

Sarah felt a cold, numbing dread seep over her, replacing the panic and fear of the past ten minutes. Ethan was right. The cells could be used to track them, and they were running for their lives. Running away from Sanctuary Bay.

"Let's go." Ethan held out his hand to her.

"Go where?" she whispered, but she already knew the answer.

"We have to get off this island," Ethan said. "Now."

17

"How are we going to get off?" Sarah asked through chattering teeth. The rain was freezing, and the wind whipped the words away so fast that she had to yell just to be heard.

"There's an old dock down at the beach in front of the asylum," Ethan yelled over the storm. "The security guys keep a dinghy there sometimes."

"So why didn't you ever steal it and leave?" Izzy asked. Her blond hair flew around crazily in the wind.

"It was always guarded, sort of." Ethan bent over, peering closely in the dark at the ground to follow the thin trail that led to the asylum. "Every time I went, there were security people asleep in it, or smoking, or having sex."

"We can't steal their dinghy if they're always watching it. They'll catch us," Sarah protested.

"I doubt they'll be out in this storm," Ethan replied. "It's our best hope."

"Even if someone's there, they won't be expecting company. And there are three of us," Izzy said. "We can take them out and steal the boat. Of course . . . we'll drown in this weather. Nor'easter. Dinghy."

Sarah wrapped her arms around herself and focused on following Ethan. She didn't want to know how she would fare in a fight with trained security guards, and she didn't want to think about being in a dinghy on the giant storm swells. She wasn't even sure what a dinghy was. In her mind it sounded like a rowboat.

"I'm hoping we can put it on the other side of the island somewhere and wait 'til the worst is over," Ethan said. "If they don't know where to find us, they're not going to come after us in this weather. Then we can escape as soon as it's calm."

"Do you know how to control a boat enough to get around the island without being pulled out to sea in this?" Sarah asked.

"I guess we'll find out," he said grimly.

"If you don't, I do," Izzy put in. "I learned to sail before I could even ride a bike. A little rain doesn't change that."

Sarah shook her head. Sanctuary Bay had been her ticket to becoming a person like Ethan or Izzy or Karina, someone who knew things like how to sail and how to use the right fork. But now it was a scary, violent place she had to flee. And even running away from it, she didn't have the skills everyone else did.

In spite of the rain pelting her and the dread coursing through her cold body, the thought of Karina made her wonder. "Hey, Iz?" she asked. Izzy turned and looked at her. "Do you remember shooting Karina?"

Izzy raised an eyebrow. She was Izzy-in-the-woods now, Izzy-the-murderer. She had to remember. She had to know what happened to Karina.

"Karina?" Izzy began. She opened her mouth to say more—and then she collapsed.

"What the hell?" Ethan cried.

"Izzy? What happened? What's wrong?" Sarah dropped to her knees next to Izzy in the wet, overgrown grass. "Izzy."

Her roommate was slumped over in a heap. She didn't answer or even look at them. Her head hung limply, her chin resting on her chest. Ethan knelt next to Sarah. "Izzy, get up. We have to go."

Izzy didn't move. Sarah grabbed her wrist and checked her pulse. "It's slow, but steady." She lifted Izzy's chin up. Izzy's eyes stared back at them blankly, like blue marbles. "Oh my god, it's the same thing that happened after her treatment," Sarah gasped. She shook Izzy, hard. But her dead eyes just kept staring, unseeing.

Dead eyes, Sarah thought, filled with horror. First Karina's dead eyes and now Izzy's.

"We can't carry her. It's too hard in this wind and rain, too slippery," Ethan said. "Obviously she can snap out of this, because she did before. You said she was at the cliff when Nate—" He didn't finish. "And that wasn't too long after she collapsed in the treatment room."

"But we don't know how they revived her. Maybe they gave her something to wake her up after the guard took us to the dean's," Sarah said. "She was still out when we left."

"Okay, well, what made her collapse in the treatment room? I had her in a chokehold, but not one tight enough to make her pass out. Suddenly she just went limp. Did you see anything?"

"No. I was trying to get the nurse to give her a sedative, because she was attacking you and that guard. That's all I remember," Sarah cried, hands still on Izzy's shoulders.

"There must be something." Ethan took Sarah's hands in his. "Sarah. Try to remember the details. Everything that happened. In the treatment room, Izzy was going crazy before she collapsed, but this time she wasn't. This time she was just talking."

"All I saw is that she dropped to the floor unconscious," Sarah insisted.

"There might be an element you're not thinking of," Ethan said. "You're the one with the amazing memory. Like when we were in the asylum. You said that you cried out because you remembered something and it was like a vision. You said it was completely real, with smells and sounds and everything. Do that."

"I can't just *do that*!" Sarah cried out. "That's not how it works. I don't control those kinds of memories. I just sort of get kicked into them by something."

"Like what?"

"I don't know. Like a sound or a feeling. In the asylum, it was a flash of light reflected off a piece of glass. It was the flash from the gun muzzle, and suddenly I was right back in the clearing, seeing Izzy shoot Karina."

"Okay, so focus on something you saw when Izzy collapsed yesterday. Or something you heard or whatever," Ethan urged.

"I said it didn't work like that!" She jerked her hands away, frustrated. He didn't get it. Nobody did.

"Just try, Sarah." Ethan wiped the rain off his face. "That's all I'm saying."

"Her eyes! I thought her eyes looked like marbles then, and just now." Sarah lifted Izzy's face again. The cold, dead blue eyes stared back at her. She brushed Izzy's hair out of her face, forcing herself to look into them fully. Izzy's eyes stared back lifelessly like two cold blue marbles.

And she was in. The treatment room in disarray. The smell of disinfectant and sweat and blood. Something else, something chemical she didn't recognize. Ethan saying "Give her a minute." The faint hum of the fluorescent lights. Izzy's skin, warm beneath her fingers. Sarah sliding her hand down to Izzy's wrist. The pulse, strong and steady. But looking in Izzy's eyes told Sarah everything she needed to know. Her body might still be working, but Izzy wasn't there.

Go back. To before she collapsed. Was there anything happening like today? A vague awareness came over Sarah through the memory. For a moment she felt sick, unsure of which time she was in: the treatment room with Izzy? Or the stormy field with Ethan?

Let the memory be, and just watch. Hold yourself out of it.

Sarah forced the thought into the back of her mind somewhere, a place she had never known she had, one where present-day Sarah could observe.

The treatment room, the nurse crouching down, holding his abdomen in pain. A grinding, metallic sound filling the air, and then Izzy jumping from the table. The security guard appearing, and Izzy going straight for his eyes, her hands like claws. The security guard and Ethan grabbing Izzy. Izzy raking her nails down the guard's cheek. The coppery smell of blood.

Izzy twisting like a mad thing in the guard's grip, kicking over one of the carts, sending it crashing to the ground. Tinkling, jangling as surgical instruments flew across the floor. Ethan wrapping one arm across Izzy's neck in a chokehold. Izzy sinking her teeth into his arm. Izzy kicking both feet into the guard's chest with a meaty thump. A metallic clang as his head bounced off the tipped-over cart when he hit the ground.

Her screaming, "Stop! Izzy, stop!" The guard bellowing in pain. Ethan's bright red blood soaking into his blue-and-white checked flannel shirt. Ethan still holding Izzy.

Sarah-in-the-treatment-room turning on the nurse. "Do something. Don't you have a sedative?"

The nurse ignoring her, staggering over to the counter next to the computer. He wasn't preparing a hypodermic. He was pulling up a virtual keyboard.

I have to pay attention. The nurse never sedated her, but she collapsed anyway.

The guard grunting and bleeding. Izzy screaming and fighting like a cornered cat. A clicking sound. The nurse typing something into the computer, his face grim. Izzy's screaming stopping abruptly.

I have to go back. I passed it. Sarah-in-the-treatment-room was panicking, confused. But Sarah-in-the-field was watching calmly from that place deep inside herself the sensations of the memory couldn't touch. Both there and not there.

She heard a clicking sound. *Look.* Sarah-in-the-field let her attention drift from the guard's grim face to the source of the sound. The computer keys clicking as the nurse's fingers hit them, letters and numbers appearing on the screen.

Xk32R. Standby.

The screaming stopped. Izzy going limp in Ethan's arms. Izzy crumpling to the floor.

That's it. And she was out. Sarah drew in a deep breath and fell back onto the wet grass. For a moment she was so stunned she barely even noticed the pelting rain or the howling wind. All she could think about was that nurse.

"What just happened?" Ethan asked.

"I saw how they sedated her. Or something. I think," she answered. "But it can't be right."

"Thanks for being so clear," Ethan said sarcastically, then immediately muttered, "Sorry."

"I told the nurse to sedate her. But he didn't. He just typed something into the computer, and she collapsed."

For a long moment, the only sound was the whooshing of the wind and the thunder in the distance. Izzy sat hunched between them, perfectly still. Finally, Ethan spoke.

"Are you saying that him using the computer is what made Izzy go catatonic?"

Sarah nodded. "I know it's impossible and I sound like a nut. But I . . . I paid more attention now than I did when it was happening. I saw what he typed."

Ethan looked at her appraisingly. "You can pay attention in your memories?"

"Well, I never did before." Sarah admitted. "But you said to try, so I did. I was there—the way I usually am in one of my freaky memory surges—but I was also here, watching. Is this really the time to be discussing my memory?" she asked, exasperated.

"No. No, it is not," Ethan said. "What did the nurse type?"

"A string of nonsense, and then the word 'Standby.'"

"Standby." Ethan glanced at Izzy, who hadn't moved even though the rain had now plastered her long hair over her face. It was creepy. Sarah reached out and tucked Izzy's hair behind her ears.

"I think the nonsense was a password. And 'Standby' was a command," Sarah said. "I know how that sounds . . ."

"But he did this and she collapsed right away?"

"Right away."

"So he was controlling her actions with the computer?"

"Ethan, I'm not crazy." Sarah shrugged. "Why else would she just shut off like that, right at that second? The nurse didn't even try to get a sedative, he just ran for the computer."

"Yeah, that is weird," Ethan agreed. "And if it was a coincidence that she shut off the instant he typed into the computer, he would have been surprised. Did he seem surprised?"

Sarah shook her head.

"Okay. So let's assume that the doctors are somehow controlling Izzy," Ethan said. "Is it the school, or is it that Fortitude Corporation Dr. Diaz talked about?"

"Fortitude. The doctor was from Fortitude," Sarah said.

"So they turned her off because she was freaking out. And they turned her off right now because . . ." His eyes met Sarah's. "Because she's running away."

Ethan jumped to his feet and grabbed Sarah's arm, pulling her up too.

"They know what she's doing," Sarah said. "Does that mean—"

"It means they can see where she is," Ethan cut her off. "If they know she's running, they're tracking her. They're coming after us, and we're sitting ducks."

"We can't leave Izzy here. She saved me. She wants to escape with us," Sarah protested.

"We have no choice! She won't wake up." He bent over, slapping Izzy lightly across the face. She didn't move. "Even if she did, she's got a tracker on her somewhere. I doubt she even knows about it. If she came with us, they'd find us."

"But—"

Her words cut off when she saw a beam of light bounce across the wasteland. A flashlight, dim through the rain, shone in the distance near the hedge. Sarah's heart began to pound.

"These are people who are using a student as some kind of remote-control robot. Do you want to get caught by them?" Ethan asked urgently.

"No." Sarah took his hand. "Let's go."

Ethan took off running, and Sarah did her best to keep up in the oversized shoes. She didn't look back. Izzy remained, the cold rain pouring down on her.

"I can't go fast enough," Sarah panted. "How do we get down to the dinghy, anyway? The asylum is on a bluff."

"There's a way down through the basement of the asylum," Ethan replied. He glanced over his shoulder at the flashlights. "We won't have enough time to get there." He swerved to the right, running toward something dark in the distance.

"Where are we going?" Sarah asked.

"There's an old hunting blind in the woods. I think that's what it is, anyway," Ethan replied. "It's hard to see, because it's under the trees. If we hide, hopefully they'll think Izzy was alone."

They ran silently until Sarah thought she might pass out, the wind and rain slapping at her face, her giant shoes bogging her down in the mud.

"Here. It's right inside the tree line." Ethan slowed as they reached the edge of the woods that covered half the island. Sarah had never been to this part of the forest before, but it was as thick and tangled as the area around the Pine Tree clearing. The rain felt less oppressive here, and for the first time all night, Sarah was able to wipe the water from her face and stay dry under the thick canopy of branches.

"How did you find this place?" she whispered.

"Same way I found every place," he replied. "There! It's between these two trees." He led her to a tiny shack entirely overgrown with ivy. Sarah could barely even see it in the dark, but Ethan led her to one end, pushed aside a bush, and crawled inside. Sarah followed.

For a few minutes they sat in silence, completely soaked through, listening to the thunder as it grew louder. Sarah's teeth chattered as she hugged herself, trying to get warm now that they were out of the wind.

"Come here." Ethan pulled her into his arms and held her against him.

"What do we do now?" Sarah asked.

"We still have to try for the dinghy," Ethan said. "In the asylum's basement there is a stairway down to the beach where the dinghy is. Maybe when they find Izzy, they'll just take her back to the school. If we wait for half an hour, we can try again."

"No," Sarah said. "We can't leave. We have to find out what the hell this is, Ethan. Do we seriously think that some school contractor is controlling Izzy's mind? That's what we said. And we're just going to leave?"

"We can send help once we get away from here," he said. "Telling the authorities is our best chance."

"Telling the authorities that our friend's brain is being controlled?" she asked sarcastically. "Really, Mr. I Don't Trust Authority?"

Ethan shoved his wet hair off his face with his free hand. "I guess it would be pretty hard to convince them we weren't making it up."

"It would be hard to convince them we weren't mentally ill," Sarah replied. "The school won't take our side on this—they cover up things they don't like."

"And they're the ones who gave Fortitude permission to test their so-called experimental treatment on the students. They'd be liable too." Ethan sighed. "I still don't see what good it does us to stay here. We can't fight them."

"But maybe we can find proof," Sarah said.

"Of what?"

"I don't know. But we have to try. If we ever want to find out what really happened to Izzy, to everyone, including your brother—"

"We have to try," Ethan said.

"That way! You're fifty feet off course," a man's voice shouted from nearby.

"I cant see a fucking thing in this rain," a second man called back. "You carry her for a few."

Sarah could hear her pulse in her ears and feel it with her whole body. She hadn't heard anybody approaching, but these men had to be within a few yards of the hunting blind. Ethan put his finger to her lips, then he took her hand and pulled her over to a slit in the blind. They both peered out at the flashlights bouncing through the dark.

"I'm not carrying her. I'm the only one who knows the way, dipshit," the first guy said. "Just follow me."

Two huge men were attached to the flashlights. One of them had Izzy flung over his shoulder like a sack of grain. They were so close Sarah could smell the scent of cigarettes wafting off them.

"It's this way. You don't go into the woods," the first one was saying.

"I like it better under here, less rain," the other guy grumbled, but he followed his partner, roughly throwing Izzy from one shoulder to the other to get a better grip.

"Where are they going?" Sarah whispered into Ethan's ear.

"Wherever it is, we're following them," he replied.

18

They were heading straight for the old asylum, which meant walking right across the open grassland. There were no trees to give them cover, and if one of the security guys happened to turn around, he'd catch Sarah and Ethan for sure. Sarah kept her eyes on the flashlight beams, ready to hit the dirt if one of those beams suddenly turned.

"We can't follow them down that rickety old staircase," Sarah whispered, pulling Ethan close enough so she could talk in his ear. "They'll see us."

"There's no reason they'd be taking her to the asylum. I don't get it," he whispered back. "Maybe they're just searching for the path back?"

At that moment, the two guys stopped. Ethan and Sarah exchanged a panicked look, and as one they dropped to the ground.

There was a clanging sound, and something creaked in the darkness. The flashlights started away again, so Sarah moved to follow them, but Ethan grabbed her arm. "Wait," he murmured.

"What was that sound?" she asked.

"The fenced-off building is over there. The ruin," Ethan said.

"You said that was the old doctors' quarters or something," she remembered.

"Right, but since it's up here on the bluffs, it's been completely destroyed over the years. Why would they take her in there?"

"I don't know. Let's go look."

They got up and moved as quietly as possible toward the flashlight beams, which were getting farther and farther away.

After a minute, the lights disappeared entirely. Sarah saw a ten-foot-high chain-link fence loom up from the darkness.

"They locked the gate behind them." Ethan shaded his eyes, peering up into the rain. "It's too high to climb, and the top arches over this way to keep people out."

"You sure it's just an old ruin?" she asked.

"Not anymore, I'm not," he said. "I can't believe I fell for that all this time. It's the only part of the island I haven't checked out. The place looks ready to disintegrate any second."

"I don't get it. They're dragging Izzy into a crumbling building?"

"I have an idea. Come on." Ethan took her hand and headed along the bluffs toward the asylum. "We can't get over the fence, but maybe we can get under it."

"Through the asylum?"

"Yeah. Remember the basement I told you about? There's a hallway—a sort of tunnel—off of it. I went down that way once, but it was collapsing, so I stopped. I figured it went under the ruined building."

"So we're going through a collapsed tunnel?" Sarah asked. "Great."

The staircase down to the asylum was terrifying in the storm. The rainwater made the wooden steps slick, and the wind threatened to blow the entire structure off of the wall. This time Sarah couldn't wait to get to the bottom and jump off the final missing steps—anything to get off the stairs.

"It'll be dark in there," Ethan said as they approached the grand old building. "My watch lights up, but that's not enough. Once we get down to the basement, I don't know how we're going to see anything."

"There's lightning," Sarah said, gesturing out to the sea as a fork of light shot down.

Ethan chuckled. "Yeah, that'll work well." He went over to the hole in the brick wall and helped Sarah through into the wardroom. They both stopped for a moment, shaking the rain off as much as possible.

"Wow, it's darker than I thought it would be," Sarah said. She bit her lip, thinking. "You know, they left a lot of chemicals behind here—all those bottles you brought to Dr. Diaz."

"Yeah?" he said.

"Well, maybe we can find some sodium," Sarah said. "Back in the twenties, they would've used it to make sodium chlorite for bleach, and sodium nitrite for food preservation."

"So you think they left some pure sodium around and it hasn't exploded by now?" Ethan asked skeptically. "Water hits that stuff, it goes boom."

"We would only need a tiny bit. You know, it was still dry in the sterilization room upstairs. The roof and walls on most of this building are intact. If they had sodium, they would've known to keep it in something safe."

Ethan nodded slowly. "There's a room at the other side of the lobby, at the very end of the downstairs hall. It was a storeroom or something. I didn't bother looking at it too closely, but I know it has metal cabinets locked up tight. If there are explosive chemicals down here, that's where they'd be."

He took Sarah's hand and led her through the dark to the storeroom. He used an empty fire extinguisher to break the lock on the nearest cabinet. They both leaned forward to study the fading labels on the bottles, which were nearly impossible to make out in the light of a watch.

"Alcohol," Sarah said, grabbing a bottle. "We can use it to make the torch." She left Ethan to keep searching, and went back out into the lobby. The huge windows gave her a little more light to go by. She rooted around, searching for something to burn, finally finding some decaying sheets in the wardroom. She began wrapping the rags around a broom handle. She could pour the alcohol over it, and as long as they managed to make a spark, they'd have light.

"Outrageously dangerous light," she muttered. "But light."

"You ready?" Ethan called. "I've got a tiny chip of what I think is sodium, and a beaker filled with rainwater. I'd really like a pair of goggles right about now."

"Bring it out here," she called back.

Ethan appeared, his face apprehensive. He set the beaker down on the marble floor in the middle of the lobby. "Here goes nothin'." He dropped the small chunk of sodium into the beaker, and they both jumped back as a flame shot straight up three feet in the air. Sarah shoved the makeshift torch into the flame. It exploded into a bright fire that startled her so much she almost dropped the handle.

"Yup, that was sodium," Ethan said drily. "We'd better go before this thing burns out." He took the torch from her and led the way to the stairwell that went underground. At the bottom was a thick door. Ethan pushed it open and they stepped into a pitch-black basement.

"That way is the staircase down to the beach." Ethan held the torch out in front of them, and Sarah could just make out the vague outline of another door in the distance. "It leads to an inside stairwell of about fifty feet, and then you're on the outside stairs the rest of the way down."

"Sounds scary."

"Actually that staircase is pretty well maintained, because security uses it," Ethan said. "That's where the dinghy is." He started to the left across the dark basement. The main room narrowed quickly into a hallway, and after a hundred feet or so, the walls became rougher, and the floor matched.

"This part isn't really finished," she said.

"It's carved out of the bedrock of the island. My theory is they used it to get back and forth from the patient areas to the doctors' housing when it was too cold outside," Ethan said. "Or it was for the servants to get back and forth with laundry and stuff for the doctors. They didn't bother to pave it over with anything."

After another few minutes of walking, a sudden gust of cold air hit them, and the torch sputtered. Ethan stopped.

Sarah gasped. A pile of rock lay covering almost the entire tunnel, and on the right, the wall was gone, revealing nothing but open air.

"Here's the cave-in," Ethan said.

"Thanks, Captain Obvious," she replied. "We're still pretty high up." She gazed out over the ocean, its waves crashing loudly somewhere below. She couldn't even see the beach. Without the wall, they were standing on an open shelf halfway up the sheer bluff.

"The only way through is to climb over the rocks," Ethan said. "I have no idea how big a cave-in it is. I couldn't see the other side even when I was here in the daytime."

"Let's go, then, before the storm blows out the torch." *And before I have time to rethink this*, she silently added. If she slipped on the wet rocks, she would fall all the way down to the beach. She would end up like Nate.

Ethan handed her the torch, then he began slowly climbing along the pile of rubble in their path. Sarah watched where he put his hands, where he found footholds, and how he balanced, memorizing every move he made. When he got five feet away, he turned and carefully reached back for the torch. Then he held it for Sarah while she climbed after him, re-creating each step he'd taken.

And then they did it all again. And again.

By the time they crested the heap of rock and the wall between them and the ocean reappeared, Sarah couldn't tell if they'd been climbing for ten minutes or three hours. Not one of the more enriching experiences the school had to offer, she thought wryly as they began inching their way down the other side of the rock pile. But maybe she could write her college essay on how she—and her sidekick—brought down a corrupt corporation.

"The tunnel is intact here," Ethan spoke up, pulling her out of her stress-induced fantasy. She handed over the torch and forced herself to concentrate on the last few steps.

"I've never been so happy to see a long, dark, creepy hole in the ground," she breathed, sinking to the cold floor.

"I hope I'm right that this leads under that collapsed building." Ethan was joking, but she could hear the strain in his voice. He was as exhausted as she was.

"That torch doesn't have long left," she said after they'd rested a few moments. "We better move."

They dragged themselves up and started through the tunnel again, the makeshift torch burning lower with each step. Within two minutes, they were completely in the dark.

"Okay, we're on watch light from here on out," Ethan said. The glow from his watch only managed to illuminate about six inches in front of them, but they walked quickly. Sarah didn't care if she tripped over something in the dark; she just didn't want to be trapped down here with no light at all.

"Look," she whispered after a few minutes. "Up ahead."

Ethan shut his watch off and they both peered into the darkness. "Yeah, that's light," he said.

"What are we even expecting to find?" Sarah asked as they

inched toward the dim glow. "The basement of the wrecked doctors' building?"

"I guess. Though why Izzy would be there, I don't know."

"You don't think . . . you don't think they brought her there to kill her, do you?" Sarah asked. "If they don't want anyone to know their student experiments are so fucked up, they might get rid of her to hide the evidence."

"It's possible. But there would be easier ways to kill her—they could've just tossed her off the bluffs," Ethan said.

The light grew stronger and stronger, and suddenly Sarah realized that the floor wasn't rough stone anymore. The walls were finished with drywall. And the glow came from soft green emergency lighting running along the ceiling.

"This is not the basement of an abandoned ruin," Ethan said.

"There are windows up ahead." Sarah pointed. Along the wall of what was now a hallway ran a series of long windows. But the windows were on the left, away from the outside of the island. Away from the bluff and the beach. "If they're not windows to the outside, what are they?" she asked.

"I don't know, but there's light coming from inside. Those two guys might be close. We need to be quiet." Ethan eased up to the first window and dropped to his knees underneath it. Sarah followed suit. They slowly raised themselves up until they could look over the bottom edge.

Sarah couldn't understand what she was seeing.

A huge room spread out beneath them, the floor at least twenty feet below. It was the size of an auditorium, and along the far wall were large monitors, one right next to the other in a straight line from one end of the room to the other. A second row of monitors ran right beneath them. Under each pair of monitors was a workstation, and at each workstation sat a person.

"Holy crap." Sarah dropped back down, her heart hammering in her chest. "There are a lot of people in there."

Ethan crouched down next to her. "What the hell is this?"

"That room is huge, and it's *inside* the bluffs," Sarah said. "This hallway must be an emergency exit or something."

"There's got to be a door to stairs along this hall somewhere. We're lucky it's empty up here. There's no place to hide." Ethan shook his head in amazement. "The whole thing is underground. It's built into the rock just like the POW camp was."

"Ethan. Did you see the monitors?" Sarah asked.

"Sort of. I mean, I saw them but I was distracted by the people."

"There are people on the monitors, too," Sarah said. "We have to take another look."

They inched back up and peered into the room. "Every monitor has a different face on it," Sarah said.

"That's Logan," Ethan gasped. "He's asleep."

"Oh my god. The next one is Kayla," Sarah said. A feeling of revulsion crept up inside her as she scanned the other monitors. "And Harrison. And Luke, and Hazel, and Cody . . . It's almost the whole Wolfpack. All of them asleep in bed. What the fuck? What's going on?"

Ethan clapped his hand over her mouth. "Quiet, we can't get caught."

Sarah nodded, and he moved his hand. "These people are watching them. They're in their dorm rooms, thinking they're in private, but somehow these people are spying on them," Sarah whispered.

"It's not just the Wolfpack. There's that walking block of granite from the Lobsters. And that other walking block of granite

270

from the Lobsters," Ethan said. "I never bothered to learn their names."

"And there's Maya!" Sarah exclaimed softly. "Ethan, look at the monitors on the bottom. They're scrolling information."

Ethan squinted, studying the monitors. "Numbers, chemicals . . . they're monitoring hormone levels or something."

"It's the same information I saw on the computer in Izzy's treatment room," Sarah said. "Where I saw Bromcyan listed."

"No wonder they brought Izzy here. This whole place is some kind of observation center, built underground so nobody would know about it." Ethan sounded stunned. "And you know what? I bet if we'd gone out the other side of that treatment room, we would have ended up someplace in this complex. It's where that people mover under the Admin building goes. It makes sense that they wouldn't tromp across the fields every time they wanted to bring somebody over here."

"Gotta be," Sarah agreed, but she was more interested in what was on the monitors. Her gaze traveled from the sleeping faces of her friends, down over the monitors scrolling biological information about them, to a sign on the wall over each workstation. Numbers and letters. Over Logan's workstation was the number Xk48B. Kayla's was Xm01Q. Harrison's was Yk88L.

Those are their ID numbers, Sarah realized, remembering the number the nurse had used to put Izzy on standby. I thought it was a password, but it wasn't. It was Izzy's ID number.

"All these people are like Izzy. They're all being controlled somehow. Those signs are their identification numbers." As the words left Sarah's mouth, she stopped being afraid.

Now she was angry.

"Come on. I want to see what else they're hiding down here," Sarah said. She crawled along the hallway, keeping below the windows, and Ethan followed. They came to a door, but Sarah ignored it. It would lead into the big monitor room they'd just seen. But the hallway was so long she couldn't even see the end of it. There had to be more. Once they'd passed all the windows, they stood up to walk.

"That room had at least twenty people in it, easy," Ethan said. "Why is it so quiet in this hall? You must be right, it's an emergency exit."

"There's a door up there on the right," Sarah said, pointing. "The only thing to the right of us is the ocean."

"Open that door, you'll find stairs down to the beach," Ethan said. "Maybe I was wrong about how the security guys got out to that dinghy. Maybe they just came from here."

"It's good for us," Sarah said. "If they don't use this hall much, we have a chance of finding Izzy and getting her out without being caught."

"And what then?" Ethan asked. "Sarah, they're controlling her. What do we do with her?"

Sarah grimaced. "I don't know. But we can't leave her here to be tortured."

Ethan nodded. "More windows," he said, gesturing ahead.

They inched up to the new set of windows and peeked through. It was a different room, but just as big. This one had a series of modular clean rooms set up in rows, each with an elaborate filtering system set up on the top. There were enough rooms for many scientists to work here at the same time. Right now there were only three people—two in white clean room suits that covered their entire bodies, working with an electron microscope, and one woman on her own operating a mechanical arm inside of a smaller Plexiglas box.

Sarah found herself so fascinated with them that she didn't pay attention to the equipment in the lab. She could see in a glance that it was hundreds of millions of dollars' worth of machinery. But she couldn't tear her gaze away from these three people, who got to play with all this stuff. In another life, these three would have been like rock stars to her—people doing cutting-edge research, using state-of-the-art equipment, making life-changing discoveries.

"How can they stand there acting like it's a job when there are people being experimented on without knowing it?" Sarah exploded.

"I don't know. But this is all biotech equipment. Microarray scanners, CO_2 incubators, I see at least five different centrifuges. And there's a 3-D printing setup over there that's . . . honestly, I can't even imagine what that's doing."

"I don't care." Sarah stormed on down the hallway, barely even caring if one of the scientists happened to glance up at the windows and see them. She stopped in surprise when the hall suddenly took a left turn.

"Looks like the fun continues deeper under the island," Ethan said. "Have we seen enough?"

Sarah shook her head. "We still don't have proof. Without our cells we can't take any pictures. And we haven't found Izzy."

"Every minute we stay here we risk getting caught," Ethan pointed out.

But she kept going, and Ethan followed her reluctantly. The hall ended in a staircase down, so she followed it. At the bottom were a series of small rooms—testing rooms. MRI machines, CT Scanners, X-rays, and three different state-of-the-art operating rooms.

"And to think, we all considered the dinky little infirmary to be a phenomenal setup," Ethan said drily.

Sarah shivered. "It's freezing."

Ethan was in front of her now, peering through a window in

the door at the end of the hall. "It's the servers. They have to be kept cold."

Frowning, she walked up next to him and looked through the window. This room was so vast she couldn't even see the back wall. It was entirely filled with servers. The only lights were the same greenish emergency lights that ran along the hallway, and something about the tall black servers in the darkened room gave her the creeps. Why would the Fortitude Corporation need something like this? They'd clearly spent billions of dollars building this place and hiding it from everyone. For what? Not innovative therapy treatments, that was for sure.

"Biotech equipment, student experiment subjects, a Google-worthy server room. Why?" she asked despite knowing Ethan was just as baffled.

"This is the end of the hall," Ethan said. He gestured to the stairs that led up. "Do we go up or go back?"

"Go up," she told him.

He took her hand and squeezed it, and Sarah felt a rush of gratitude. Whatever was happening, they were in it together. She left her hand tightly grasped in Ethan's as they climbed up the new stairs. This flight was longer than the one they'd taken down. Sarah wondered if they were climbing all the way back up to the surface.

At the top was a small landing. A narrow corridor ran off to the right, and a shorter flight of stairs led to a metal door in front of them marked EXIT. A small, hysterical laugh escaped Sarah at the normalcy of the sign amid the utter insanity surrounding them.

"I hear something." Ethan turned to the small corridor. "Down here."

Sarah could hear it, too. Voices. "People. Should we turn around?"

A shrill, loud scream cut through the low hum of talking. Sarah and Ethan exchanged wide-eyed glances before sprinting toward the sound.

A door swung open in front of them, and they skidded to a stop just as a woman dressed in scrubs stepped out. She looked at them, mouth open in shock.

Sarah punched her in the face.

When the woman hit the floor, Ethan jumped on top of her, covering her mouth with his hand. "Find something to tie her up with," Ethan said frantically.

Sarah didn't stop to think. She grabbed the door and pulled it back open. Inside was a wardroom filled with patient beds, almost all full. At the far end of the room, a guy in scrubs fought to restrain someone, so Sarah took a chance and dropped to the ground behind the closest bed.

She looked up at the patient, and had to bite her lip to keep from screaming. It was an old man, white-gray hair, one eye. Where the other eye should be was just a socket filled with ropy white-and-pink scars. His good eye—brown—stared at her lifelessly, and he was laughing soundlessly. Or was he trying to talk? Sarah couldn't tell. She crawled away quickly, scanning the area for rope or medicine. The screaming from the far end of the room kept going.

The next bed held a large woman, black, maybe forty, with a shaved head and a gash above one ear. Her left leg was missing below the thigh, and she was asleep, drooling. Sarah saw that she was hooked up to an IV, and even though she was restrained, she didn't seem likely to wake up.

Carefully, Sarah undid the strong Velcro restraint around her arm, hoping the shrieks would cover the sound of it ripping open. She took the restraint and started to move away—just as the woman's eyes opened.

Freaked out, Sarah stood up. The whole ward was filled with mutilated people—missing limbs, missing eyes, covered in scars. Every single one of them was tied to their metal bed. Over each bed hung a number, just like the numbers in the monitor room. The place reeked of urine and feces and blood and bleach, and the screaming hadn't stopped.

Sarah looked at the patient fighting off the guy in scrubs. Blond hair flew everywhere as her hands raked at him like claws. He'd gotten her legs clamped down under the metal straps like they had in the treatment room, but her arms were free. She grabbed his forearm and sank her teeth into it. He grabbed a handful of her long hair and jerked her away, slamming her down onto the bed. She kept screaming, white spittle flying from her mouth.

Izzy.

Sarah turned and ran.

In the corridor, Ethan sat on the nurse, desperation in his eyes. "Here." Sarah grabbed the nurse's hands, pulled them behind her back, and wrapped the restraint around her wrists. "I still need a gag." She took hold of Ethan's shirt and tore off a long strip of fabric, then tied it around the woman's mouth.

"What are we going to do with her?" he asked.

"Throw her outside the exit. The other nurse will find her eventually."

Ethan raised an eyebrow questioningly.

"They've got people tied to the beds, hacked to bits in there. God knows what they're using them for, but it's nothing good and it's nothing legal. And they have Izzy in there," she snapped, glaring at the nurse. "This one can handle being out in the rain for a bit."

"You're the boss." Ethan picked up the nurse, slung her over his shoulder, and hurried back to the door. Sarah opened it just enough to get a brief glimpse of the rain on the crumbling ruins above them. A short cement staircase led from the door up to the ground outside. Ethan propped the nurse on the stairs, and Sarah pulled the door shut, locking her out.

"You've been right all along. We have to get off this island," Sarah said. "It's like a horror movie in there. We'll just have to figure out how to convince the cops to come back."

Ethan didn't answer. He simply took off running.

Sarah followed.

Back down the stairs, past the server room and the MRI machines. Up the next staircase, past the bio lab and back toward the monitor room. The outside door loomed up on their left, and Ethan hurled himself against it. Sarah followed him out, barely even noticing how slippery the metal stairs were on the way down. She just hung on to the railing and prayed that nobody would find that nurse until they were far away from here.

On the beach, reality caught up with her. The wind was still strong, and the waves pounded with frightening strength against the rocky shore. "We can't get on a boat in this," she yelled.

"We have zero options," Ethan yelled back. He was already running down the beach toward the old asylum. Sarah followed, struggling to run through the mix of wet rocks and sand. Before they'd gotten too far, she made out a battered dock jutting out into the water. Upside down on the dock, tied with a thick rope, was a tiny rowboat.

"No. No no no no," Sarah cried. "That is a rowboat. This is the ocean in a huge storm!"

"Do you want to end up like Izzy? They're going to find that nurse any second, if they haven't already," Ethan yelled over the roaring of the waves. He unwound the rope and turned the rowboat over.

Sarah closed her eyes, forcing herself to push the panic down. Panicking wouldn't help.

"Sarah." Ethan's voice was quiet, close. She opened her eyes, finding his face inches from hers. He leaned forward, resting his forehead against hers. "I know you're scared. I am too."

"This is suicide," she whispered.

"But if we stay, it's worse than death," he said. "I don't know what happened to Karina, but I'm willing to bet she was in that room with Izzy. Maybe Philip is too. I don't want to end up there, Sarah."

"Me either."

"If we can get to the floating wind farm, we'll be safe. The worst of the storm is over," he said. "We just have to get to the wind farm."

Sarah nodded. "Okay."

"The hardest thing is going to be to keep off the shore," he told her. "The waves will push us back in. There's a motor, but I don't know if it'll be strong enough."

He pulled her into a quick hug before hauling the boat up and dropping it into the water at the end of the dock. Shaking, Sarah climbed down the wooden ladder and managed to get her feet in the boat. She sat down fast, clinging to the sides, trying not to retch from the motion of the waves. Ethan jumped down after her.

"Ready?"

She felt tears on her cheeks, warm against the cold wet of the rain, but she nodded. She'd thought she had no choices growing up, but those people in the lab truly had no control over their lives. Ethan was right. She'd rather die than live with every movement dictated by some demented scientist.

Ethan pulled the motor, turning it on with a sputter that seemed pathetic against the roaring wind. "Look!" Sarah yelled, pointing at lights on the bluffs. Flashlights in the darkness, pointing in every direction.

"They're too far away to see us," Ethan yelled back, steering the boat out to sea.

Sarah held on tight to the sides and kept her eyes on the lights. The swells were high, and almost immediately began pushing them back toward shore, just like Ethan had said. "Hold the tiller!"

Sarah scrambled over next to Ethan and held the tiller the way he showed her. He grabbed an oar and struggled to keep them off the rocks. They made it free and got out to open water—

Only to have the waves hurl them back into the rocky stretch near the shore again. And again.

At least we've moved away from the asylum and the Fortitude lab, Sarah thought. *If we could survive being slammed back onto the shore, maybe we could hide on the island for another few hours before they found us. We could try again when the weather's calmer.*

The third time they made it to open water, the motor cut out.

"Damn it!" Ethan struggled to make it turn over, but it didn't work. They both picked up the oars, fighting against the tide. Sarah knew it was a losing battle, but that didn't mean she was going to stop trying.

Suddenly a spotlight shone on them, so bright that it dazzled her eyes. It bathed the entire boat in light. She slowly put down the oar. Ethan did too, defeated. They were caught.

"Stay where you are, we're throwing a rope to you," a voice announced through a megaphone.

"Maybe we should jump in the water," Ethan said.

"No way," she replied. "You obviously don't know this, but poor black girls don't learn to swim."

He gave a crooked smile. The rope splashed into the water next to them, and Ethan leaned over to fish it out of the ocean. He tied it to the boat, and Sarah felt them being reeled in toward the bright light.

When they banged up against the bigger boat, somebody tossed down two life jackets. Sarah put one on, her fingers shaking with the cold. There was a rope ladder, and Ethan gestured for her to climb it first. She forced her hands to hold on, forced her legs to bend and climb. Her entire body felt like it was going to shut down, and her mind wanted it to. What were these people going to do to her?

At the top, a pair of strong hands grabbed hers and pulled her over the side. Sarah looked up, trembling, into the eyes of the guy in the uniform.

"What in god's name are you kids doing out here in this storm?" the guy bellowed. "You're lucky we found you!"

Sarah stared at him, weak-kneed with relief. "You're . . . you're the Coast Guard."

"Who were you expecting, the Tooth Fairy?" he asked.

Sarah laughed, turning to see Ethan as he was hauled on board. "It's the Coast Guard!" she cried, hurling herself into his arms. "We're saved."

"And we didn't even have to make it to the wind farm," he laughed, hugging her back.

Ten minutes later they were wrapped in blankets, huddled inside the cabin of the rescue boat. Their rescuers had given them hot coffee, and Sarah finally felt her body stop shaking. Her mind was whirling, but she wasn't sure they could talk about the island in front of the crew.

"Should we tell them?" she murmured, moving closer to Ethan. He lifted his blanket to put his arm around her so they'd be closer. "We don't have any proof."

"Which is why we need to think very carefully about how to report them," Ethan said. "We can go to my house and figure things out from there. My parents know a million lawyers."

His house, Sarah thought, shocked at the sudden return to real life. *He has a house, and parents, and buckets of money. I have my muddy pajamas—and nothing else.* She pushed the thought away.

"Will they help us, though? They never told you they went to Sanctuary Bay," Sarah said.

"But there's no way they'd be okay with all this Fortitude stuff," he replied.

"Okay, kids, we're here," the captain said, sticking his head into the cabin. "All ashore."

Ethan got up and smiled down at Sarah. "I've been trying to get home for years. I can't believe we really did it."

"I'm happy for you," she said, covering her own worries with a smile.

The captain climbed down first, then Ethan, and Sarah followed slowly after them. Her clothes were still wet, and Ethan's too-big shoes made it hard to find her footing on the ladder. When her feet hit the ground, she realized it was made of familiar smooth stones.

A chill of terror ran up her spine.

She was standing on the same jetty as when she'd first arrived at Sanctuary Bay. Sarah turned around to find herself staring at Dean Farrell.

"Welcome back, Ms. Merson," the dean said.

19

Sarah whirled back to the Coast Guard captain, who was already halfway back up the ladder after escorting them down. "What are we doing here? You were supposed to take us to the mainland."

"Your school called us and told us to search for you," he replied. "If it weren't for them, we wouldn't have been out in this storm. You should be grateful."

"You can't leave us here," Ethan said. "The school is experimenting on students."

The captain laughed. "That's a new one." He disappeared onboard without another glance.

The two security guards behind Dean Farrell stepped forward, and Sarah felt as if she'd fallen back into a nightmare. "Take them to my office," the dean said. She turned her back on them and clacked away down the dock in her completely inappropriate low-heeled leather boots. *Karina would be appalled*, Sarah thought, feeling sick at the thought of her roommate. Was she going to end up like Karina? Or Izzy? Or even Nate?

One guard took Ethan roughly by the arm and the other one took Sarah. She didn't have a chance to speak to Ethan again until they were deposited at the door of Dean Farrell's office.

"Maybe she doesn't know how bad it is," Sarah said to him in a rush. "She thinks Fortitude is running a medical trial, she probably doesn't know about the rest."

"Then she's about to find out," Ethan replied, as one of the security guards opened the door.

Dean Farrell wasn't there.

Instead, there was a man sitting behind her desk, grinning from ear to ear. Midforties. White, dark hair, brown eyes, two-thousand-dollar suit.

"Well, well, look at this!" the guy crowed. "You're alive, even after braving the Atlantic in a nor'easter!"

Sarah and Ethan just stared at him, baffled.

"Sorry, where are my manners? Have a seat," the man said. "I'm Mr. Carothers, senior vice president of the Fortitude Corporation, but you can call me Dave. We're going to be friends."

"What are you doing in the dean's office, *Dave*?" Sarah asked. "Where's Dean Farrell?"

"Oh, she's really more of a figurehead, Sarah," Dave replied. "I'm the actual dean. Hmm. Maybe I should add that to my title, what do you think? SVP of the Fortitude Corporation, Dean of Sanctuary Bay Academy. Sounds great."

"What are you talking about?" Ethan asked. "Fortitude is a contractor."

"Well, not so much." Dave gave him a wink. "It's more like Sanctuary Bay is a front."

Sarah sat down heavily in one of the guest chairs, a strange buzzing feeling seeping through her. She wasn't sure she could take any more surprises today. "A front for what?"

" 'Front' might not be the right word," Dave said thoughtfully. "Technically, the word would be 'subsidiary,' but we do use the school as a front. So I guess it's an okay term. Though we also use it for recruitment and training and placement . . . I have to say, kids, after consideration I'm not comfortable calling Sanctuary Bay a front. It's much more than that."

Ethan sat down next to Sarah looking grim.

"I guess the best way to put it is this: Sanctuary Bay Academy is the public face of the Fortitude Corporation," Dave went on cheerfully. "See, we own the school. The school is us. It exists for no reason other than to complete our mission."

"Your mission is to give kids illegal drugs and do mind-control experiments on them and then strap them down to metal beds and torture them?" Sarah asked edgily.

Dave looked offended. "There's nothing illegal going on here, Sarah. Why would you say that?"

Did Call-Me-Dave not hear the word "torture"? Sarah thought wildly.

"Bromcyan was banned, but you're using it on students," Ethan said.

"Ahhh, I see the confusion," Dave replied. "You're right, Ethan, Bromcyan *was* banned . . . but not for us. You could say that the government placed a ban on anyone else exploiting the drug called Bromcyan."

"It was banned before the school even existed," Sarah argued. "Before the asylum even closed!"

"Riiight . . ." Dave said. "About that: The closing of the asylum wasn't entirely a closing. It was more like a retreat from public view. The 1930s were all about research for us, and the 1940s brought a really wonderful new supply of test subjects. You see, we'd been testing the uses of Bromcyan on the nutbars at the asylum. Oh, I'm sorry, Sarah. You don't like those kinds of terms." He smiled warmly at her. "You're very compassionate that way."

He'd been watching her? Listening to her? Of course he had, she realized. Lab rats were always observed.

"Instead, let's say that we were testing Bromcyan on the mentally ill patients. We were able to retain many of them after the official closing of the asylum. On the down-low, you understand," Dave continued.

Sarah found herself staring at his teeth. They were blindingly white, and there was something mesmerizing about the way they moved when he spoke. She couldn't bring herself to look at anything else as his words washed over her.

"But the fact is, we didn't so much care how Bromcyan affected the loonies. We wanted to know how regular people would tolerate it. And in the 1940s, there was a war—that's World War Two for you kiddies."

"Yeah, we know about World War Two," Ethan snapped. "We know there was a POW camp here."

"You experimented on the prisoners," Sarah said. "That's why that German soldier went crazy. Why someone carved the word 'Bromcyan' into the cell wall."

"Exactly! It was a real stroke of luck, let me tell you. We found out that Bromcyan's effects on those of normal intelligence were everything we could have wanted," Dave said. "You see, it works like a charm on the mentally ill—it orders their minds, if you will. It calms the mania and makes them open to suggestion. Give them talk therapy, suggest a new pattern of thinking, and they do it! It's really a shame it will never be available to them."

"You are such a bastard," Sarah muttered.

Dave went on as if he hadn't heard. "But on regular people, well, it renders them extremely suggestible, as well. The trick is, you have to use a much lower dose. In high doses, it helps the mentally ill but destroys the mind of a healthy person. In low doses, though, the healthy mind becomes putty in our hands."

"What you're saying is that you destroyed the minds of a bunch of German prisoners to find this out," Ethan said, a low growl in his voice.

"Well, sure. But they were Nazis," Dave said with a dismissive wave of his hand.

"I don't understand. Bromcyan was discovered by Herman

Wissen at the asylum. You keep saying that Fortitude did all this, but Fortitude wasn't there. It was an asylum and then a government POW camp," Sarah said.

"Technically you're correct, of course. It wasn't until after the war that the Fortitude Corporation officially came into being," Dave replied. "When the POW camp closed, the government decided to create some distance between themselves and our work with Bromcyan. Plausible deniability, I believe it's called."

Sarah closed her eyes, not wanting to hear more, but unable to stop herself from asking, "Fortitude is the government?"

"No, no," Dave said. "Fortitude is a government contractor. Did you miss the part about plausible deniability?"

"Who founded Fortitude?" Ethan asked.

"Why, Dr. Wissen, of course," Dave said. "Though he was pretty old by then. He died a few years later. But it was his brilliant idea to create Sanctuary Bay Academy. The school was founded nearly as soon as Fortitude was. Think about it: What better setting for controlled psychological testing?"

"It's never been a school?" Sarah asked. "Not even at the beginning?"

"Nope." Dave grinned. "What we like about Bromcyan, as I'm sure you've realized, is that it lets us explore the idea of mind control. The drug itself tills the soil, so to speak. It renders the mind open to suggestion, to influence. And teenagers are all about influence. I mean, everything in high school is based on peer pressure, am I right?"

"You're talking about the Wolfpack," Sarah cried. "All those missions! They were psychological tests."

"Yup." Dave beamed. "The Wolfpack, the lacrosse teams, the student government, even the debate team and math club! Everything can be a test. It's fantastic. See, the Wolfpack drinks the Blutgrog, that's Bromcyan. The lacrosse players have their special protein drinks, that's Bromcyan. The cheerleaders suck down homemade alcohol and diet Sprite, that's Bromcyan. Hell, we even put it in the food sometimes."

"The entire school is a giant petri dish? It's not just some students," Ethan said. "It's all of us?"

"Well, of course," Dave replied. "We're not just testing Bromcyan anymore—we know how *that* works. I mean, we've had eighty years to research it!" He laughed loudly. "No, at this point we're mostly testing the people, the candidates. We try out various types of stimuli, gauge reactions to psychological stress, anything the scientists want."

"Candidates," Sarah repeated.

"We're talking about brain chemistry here, Sarah. You're good at chemistry, so you understand how tricky a subject this is— everybody reacts differently to a drug. We need to make sure a candidate is able to handle the Bromcyan both mentally and physically before we proceed."

"Proceed with what?" Ethan asked. "Candidates for what? Why don't you just skip the history lesson and tell us what you're talking about, *Dave*?"

"Okay, if you want. Proceed with implanting the tech. Candidates for usage in the field. Happy?" Dave asked.

"No," Sarah said. "What tech?"

"Ooh, I'm glad you asked. Right now, we're running a pilot program for our new nanotechnology," Dave said. "Back in the day, we injected operatives with Bromcyan and used hypnosis to give them their orders. Then we graduated to implanting a device to pump out the Bromcyan, which still required hypnosis, of course, but made it easier to maintain the proper dosage levels. That lasted for a long time—I mean, we'd upgrade the implants from time to time. Originally they were very crude, but then we learned to equip them with sensors that could send back readouts, and eventually the sensors were able to analyze the results themselves, and adjust dosage accordingly. Technology is something, huh?"

"All the biotech equipment in the underground lab," Ethan said, turning to Sarah. "It was producing this."

"Not anymore. Now it's producing nanites," Dave corrected him. "See, we first developed the smart chip—that was an implant that monitored enzyme levels, controlled the Bromcyan dosage, *and* produced Bromcyan right there in the body. Basically, it was a tiny factory that used the body's own chemicals to create Bromcyan. But the problem was that we still needed hypnosis to give orders."

"Now you just do it wirelessly," Sarah said. "We saw that with Izzy. You figured out a way to have your smart chip send electrical impulses to the brain to create the behavior you desired."

"I knew you were a keeper, Sarah," Dave said. "That's exactly right. Only now it's not one smart chip anymore. Now we're using a bunch of nanites that move through the bloodstream and operate in unison. The idea is that this will give us a more precise control of hormone and Bromcyan levels, and a more sophisticated interface with the brain commands."

"What kind of commands?" Ethan asked.

"That all depends on what we're using them for," Dave replied. "If the operative is a soldier, we're giving them military commands. If it's a diplomat, we'll be giving them commands to act in whatever way advances our political agenda. If it's a business executive, the commands will be to help us further our financial goals. If it's an assassin, well, that one's pretty obvious."

Sarah just stared at him.

"You know what a sterling reputation Sanctuary Bay has,"

Dave said teasingly. "Our students go on to become leaders in almost every walk of life. Presidents, ambassadors, tech gurus, rock stars, you name it."

"And you're controlling them," Sarah whispered.

"Have been for years!" Dave crowed. "I told you, this school was a stroke of genius. It gives us the perfect setting for testing, and the perfect vehicle for placing our operatives." Dave frowned. "There are bumps in the road, of course. Right now the nanotech is in the initial testing stage, and unfortunately that always means a higher incidence of mistakes. We run a lot of tests before we move on to implanting the nanotech—we like to be sure how a candidate will react before we make the investment. But sometimes it still goes wrong. You can never tell how a host body will act."

"Like Nate. Nate was a mistake," Sarah guessed. "Something went wrong with him."

"Yes, unfortunately that was a mess," Dave agreed. "You know, that was a little bit your bad, Sarah. No guilt, but if you hadn't pushed him so hard about the Karina situation, he would've been fine."

Sarah was stunned.

"It was basically a domino effect," Dave went on. "We told Nate that he spent Halloween getting down and dirty with you, so that's what he believed. When you kept needling him about it, he got stressed. His hormone levels went nuts, pumping out a cocktail of glucocorticoids, catecholamines, prolactin . . . It got out of control. The nanotech tried to keep his Bromcyan production regulated, but eventually it was overwhelmed. Still, though, Nate's experience gave us a lot of information to work with. Sometimes you have to get it wrong before you know how to get it right."

"I hate you," Sarah snarled. "You sit there smiling like it's funny but you're playing with people's lives. I'm not the one who killed Nate, *you* are."

"But I'm not!" Dave cried, insulted. "Nate had had the tech for more than a year. We were finishing up his post-implant testing. Everything had been stellar until you came along. Now Izzy, that's another story. She just flat-out rejected the nanotech. Well, *you* know, Sarah. You saw her getting the little guys pumped into her head."

"That treatment? When she was screaming," Sarah said.

"Yeah. We hoped it was just a short-term reaction, but nope. The nanites have trouble regulating her adrenaline levels. Whenever we increase her Bromcyan, she becomes unpredictable and violent. When we decrease the levels, she doesn't follow commands. It's really too bad. I was convinced she'd be a perfect candidate for an assassin. I mean, did you see the way she shot Karina? Stone cold."

"Screw you," Ethan growled, jumping from his seat. "You let Karina get killed as part of some experiment?"

"Whoa, whoa! Calm down, tiger." Dave threw up his hands. "Don't you remember the wax bullet? You weren't supposed to find that, by the way. But Karina's fine. Look."

He grabbed Dean Farrell's cell off her desk and typed in a command. Two seconds later, the door opened and Karina walked in. Her long black hair was as lustrous as ever, her dark eyes bright, and her smile happy.

"What's up?" she said. She beamed at Sarah and Ethan. "Hi! I'm Karina."

A rock seemed to settle in the pit of Sarah's stomach. There wasn't a trace of recognition in Karina's eyes. Sarah had no idea who they were. She glanced at Ethan worriedly.

His face was pale, his expression haunted. "How . . . how long?" he choked out.

"What, the nanotech?" Dave asked. "Karina's had that since before you ever met her. Her primary mission was to convince you to join the Wolfpack, Ethan. You're such a nonjoiner that we've had trouble testing you! Anyway, you turned down the chance once, so we put Karina on the case. She can be very persuasive."

With a grin, he typed a few more words into the dean's cell. Karina's smile grew wider, and she walked over to Ethan, plopped herself down in his lap, and kissed him.

Ethan shoved her away so hard that she fell to the carpeted floor. "You don't even remember who I am!" he cried.

Karina picked herself up, her pretty face puckered in a wounded expression.

"Don't be so hard on her, you big bully," Dave protested. "She's our greatest success story. You want to talk about influence. A pretty girl has it in spades, am I right?" He input another command, and Karina went to the couch in the back of the room, sat down, and zoned out. Her mouth hung slightly open, and her eyes stared blankly. Cold brown marbles. *Dead eyes.*

"She's in standby mode," Sarah said. "You just turned her off."

"Yup," Dave said.

"When Izzy shot her with the trick bullet, that's what happened. You put Karina into standby."

"Exactly," he replied. "It's a fantastic test. We wanted to see how the rest of you would react to the killing. And then afterward we wanted to test your memory, Sarah, to see how well that total recall of yours would withstand the Bromcyan and the influence of your peers. Most of all, of course, the whole mission was designed to find an assassin. Sometimes nobody is willing to pull the trigger, but usually there's one who works up the nerve to do it. Izzy, though, she didn't even hesitate! Bam! No one has ever been so willing to kill before."

"How many times have you done that test?" Sarah asked. "You tried to do it again the next day."

"Oh, we do it whenever we want," Dave replied. "It's easy enough to wipe everyone's memory—sometimes the Bromcyan alone works for that, and if not, we use midazolam. Then we just start over. In that particular test, Karina always makes the best victim—so sweet and funny and pretty, such a nice girl. Anyone willing to kill her has to be a real badass. Or a sociopath, which I think was the case with Izzy." He sighed. "I'm usually very good at matching a candidate with their eventual line of expertise. It's important to have a basic inborn compatibility between the operative's psychological makeup and the types of commands they're expected to follow in the field. The better fit they are, the less likely they are go against the suggestion. Less fighting. Less stress hormones. A higher success rate. I mean, we've got spies, policy makers, seducers, hackers . . . whatever a client needs. We can't just plug any operative into any job; it still comes down to who they really are. You can't expect a hacker to turn into a ninja."

"Do you even hear yourself?" Ethan asked. "These are human beings you're talking about."

Sarah felt a pang of sadness. She'd said something just like that to Ethan once about the patients at the asylum. In a normal world, she would be happy that he had finally learned to be a decent person.

But the world would never be normal again.

"I'm just helping them realize their full potential," Dave said, unperturbed. "I tell you what, though, you kids are really putting me through the wringer lately! First you, Ethan, refusing to do what we expected. Half the time we couldn't even manage to dose you with Bromcyan! And then Izzy turning out to be an uncontrollable killing machine. And *you*, Sarah! We really got you all wrong. After you promised Dean Farrell you'd be a good little girl and acted like you hadn't seen Izzy shoot Karina, I thought you'd passed the test. I thought you were malleable enough to doubt your memory after some peer pressure, that you'd be a candidate we could control without any glitches. We were all ready to install your nanotech—I couldn't wait to see how it would work with that brain of yours. But you were lying. You're a liar."

His friendly eyes had turned mean, finally. It had always been there, the ruthlessness, but now it was on the surface.

Ethan reached out and took Sarah's hand. "I couldn't have imagined a better partner than you, Sarah," he said softly. "No matter what they put us through now, I want you to know that."

"Aw, so touching," Dave said smarmily. "Why would I put you through anything? I'm not the bad guy."

"You just sat here for twenty minutes and told us *everything* about Fortitude's sick behavior. And you know Sarah's memory won't let her forget. The Bromcyan doesn't work on her. So there's no way you'll let us live after that," Ethan said. "But I think I'd prefer to be killed than to be pumped full of your precious tech, so it's okay."

"You'll get away with killing me," Sarah told Dave. "I'm an orphan. Nobody to give a shit. But if Ethan turns up dead, you'll have a world of trouble. He's got a family. His parents are well known and wealthy. They've got connections—"

"And heads full of nanotech," Ethan cut in. "Right, Dave?"

Dave winced. "Busted. But it's not nanotech. Your parents kick it old school with the smart chip, and theirs are too old to be very smart, frankly. The nanotech is first generation."

"Oh my god, Ethan," Sarah gasped. "Your parents?"

He nodded, his face set. "It's okay. It at least explains why they sent me here, why they never cared about what happened to Philip. Fortitude probably killed my brother. They'll have no problem killing me too."

"You two are so melodramatic," Dave said, shaking his head. "No one's getting killed. Well, unless you refuse to cooperate." He typed something into Dean Farrell's cell, and Karina popped up off the couch with a smile on her face.

She didn't even glance at them as she walked across the room, out of the office, and disappeared. A moment later she appeared outside, walking across the wet grass in the first gray light of dawn. Sarah felt a shock realizing that the entire night had passed—somehow she'd felt that the darkness would never end. The rain had stopped, but the wind picked up Karina's long hair and sent it flying about her face. Sarah didn't know what to think as she watched her old roommate through the window. Karina had that same old bounce in her step and a calm smile on her lips.

The dorm door swung open, and Kayla appeared, followed by Tif and Maya. From the other side, Harrison and Logan joined them. Then they all followed Karina, walking straight across the lawn.

Toward the bluff.

"What are you doing?" Sarah demanded.

"They're heading toward the edge," Ethan said in a strangled voice. "He's going to make them walk off the bluffs."

"Just like Nate," Sarah cried. "They'll die, just like Nate!"

"Sadly, yes, they will," Dave said. He came over and perched casually on the arm of Sarah's chair, watching through the window as Karina and the others got closer to the edge. "I hate to lose so many assets. Especially Karina. She's good. Right, Ethan?"

"What do you want?" Ethan asked through gritted teeth.

"Why, I want the two of you to play nice," Dave cried. "What else?"

They were ten feet from the edge of the cliffs now, all of them walking right toward it without even slowing down.

"No? Okay. Then we'll just sit back and watch your friends commit suicide," Dave said. He leaned over and spoke softly in her ear. "This time, you'll know for sure it was your fault, Sarah." He patted her on the knee, and a silver ring flashed on his finger.

A silver bird stared at her from the ring. Stared from a horrible little black eye.

Sarah's body went cold, her heart giving a lurch. She'd seen that ring before—on the finger that pulled the trigger of the gun that killed her mother.

Dave. Dave had murdered her parents. He was going to murder her friends.

"Fine," Sarah snapped. "Just make them stop."

Dave typed quickly into the cell, and all six kids stopped walking. As if nothing had happened, they turned around and started back toward the dorms, talking and laughing like normal.

"Oh, I'm sorry. I assume Sarah speaks for you, too, Ethan?" Dave asked.

"Yes," Ethan growled. "What do you want us to do?"

"Here's how it will work," Dave replied, walking back around to sit behind the big desk. Every move he made, every word out of his mouth made Sarah feel physically ill. His fake friendliness, his delight in all the disgusting things he was telling them . . . it paled in comparison to her memory of him. Shooting her mother. Chasing her father down like a dog and shooting him too. Everything wrong in her life, everything awful that had ever happened, was his fault.

"The two of you are going to put your little noses to the grindstone, work very hard, and get excellent grades," Dave was saying. "You're going to finish your education here at Sanctuary Bay. And then you're going to go out into the world and take advantage of all the extraordinary opportunities that a degree from this school will afford you. It sounds like torture, doesn't it?" he added sarcastically.

"That's it? We just graduate and leave?" Ethan said.

"No, no, no. You graduate, leave, and have an outrageously successful life," Dave corrected him. "Which you might have had anyway, Ethan. But you wouldn't, Sarah. Let's face it, you'd have been lucky to stay off the pole." He stood up. "Do we have a deal? Or should I murder some of your buddies?"

There's no choice, Sarah thought. *He could make anyone here kill themselves with a keystroke. Or kill one another. Hell, for all I know there's tech in Ethan and he'll turn on me. But someday I'm going to find a way to get Dave alone, and I'm going to kill him.*

Just like he killed my parents.

"Can we just go back to our rooms now?" Ethan asked in a flat tone. "Just forget any of this ever happened?"

"Nothing would please me more," Dave replied.

"Fine, then. We'll be good," Sarah agreed. "We'll do whatever Fortitude wants."

"Excellent! I knew you'd be reasonable," Dave said. He pushed an intercom button on the dean's desk. "Our friends are ready to go back to their rooms." He gave them both a huge smile.

Like a shark, Sarah thought, staring at the white, white teeth.

"I trust I'll never have to see either of you again," Dave said. "Because if I ever do, it's not going to be as pleasant for you."

The security guards appeared, and Sarah and Ethan went with them without a backward glance. Nobody spoke as they walked back to the main lobby. As they were about to part ways, Ethan to his room and Sarah to hers, Ethan suddenly grabbed her and pulled her close.

Over his shoulder Sarah saw the guards roll their eyes at each other.

"We have to bring this whole place down," he whispered, pressing his lips against her ear as if he was kissing her. "They'll probably try to implant us tonight. We won't get another chance to escape."

Sarah ran her lips over his cheek, bringing her mouth close to his ear. "Fire," she whispered. "If the school is burning, fire-fighters would have to come from the mainland. Dave won't let his whole lab burn down."

"All right, that's enough," one of the security guys interrupted. "Let's go."

"We're supposed to meet with Dr. Diaz before chemistry, remember?" Ethan said.

"Right," she replied. "I'll see you there."

20

"Dr. Diaz?" Sarah said, knocking on the door of his office. The doctor's waiting room was empty, as usual, but she could hear him moving around inside the office. "It's Sarah. Can I come in?"

The movement stopped, and for a long moment there was silence.

"Dr. Diaz?"

"Not here," Dr. Diaz called.

Again, silence. Sarah wasn't sure if she was supposed to laugh. It was a strange joke. "Um, I can hear you," she finally said.

The door creaked open a tiny crack, and Dr. Diaz peered out at her, squinting.

"It's me. Ethan's meeting me here. Do you think it's safe to talk?" she murmured. "Should we go down to the deep storage room?"

Suddenly his eyes opened wide, and he pulled her inside and shut the door. "No need," he said in a rush. "I've brought the relevant files up here. They were watching me down there but no one ever comes here." He gestured to his desk, which was covered with papers. "They thought they could hide the truth but the truth doesn't hide, the truth shines."

"Okay." Sarah studied his face, finally understanding what Ethan had meant by "perturbed squirrel." Dr. Diaz wouldn't meet her eye. "Are you all right?" she asked.

"Stop staring at me!" he yelled.

Sarah was so shocked that she didn't answer, and he turned away and began rifling through the papers on his desk.

"Hey, Dr. D," Ethan called, opening the door.

Dr. Diaz jumped in surprise, then stumbled back into a corner of the office as if he was frightened.

"What's going on?" Ethan asked. "Sarah, did you tell him what happened?"

"No," she said. "He's . . ." She struggled to find the words, then gave up. "There's something wrong."

"It's the Bromcyan, that's what's wrong," Dr. Diaz whimpered. "They hide it, they put it in all the files, all the people, but they never say the truth." He ran his hand through the papers on his desk. "I arranged them every different way but the truth isn't there. It's in here." He tapped at his head.

"Did they get to him?" Ethan asked, alarmed. "Is Dave making him this way?"

"This time I hid. This time I got away. This time I spit it out. I know what it is now, I know. I made the test for it. I figured it out." Dr. Diaz sounded agitated, and he grabbed a file folder from the floor, clutching it to his chest like a teddy bear.

"Nate was a little like this before he jumped," Sarah murmured to Ethan. "But Diaz doesn't seem like he wants to hurt himself."

"Dr. D? Can I see that file?" Ethan asked.

"It's Bromcyan. That's the answer," Dr. Diaz said, looking intently at Sarah.

"I know it is," she agreed. "Is there something in that file about Bromcyan?"

"Yes," he said, relieved.

"Let me see." Sarah reached for the file in his hands, and he slowly relinquished it. She glanced down at the light brown cover. "It's a student file from the eighties. Ramon Diaz."

Shocked, her eyes flew to Dr. Diaz's face. "Ramon Diaz."

"I won't let them in again. I spit it out," Dr. Diaz whispered. "I made the test for it."

"Were you a student here?" Ethan asked.

"I won't let them in," Dr. Diaz muttered.

Sarah opened the folder and glanced at the top page of the thick file. Right away she saw a word that made her heart stop. "Schizophrenia," she said. "Dr. D, are you schizophrenic?"

"It's the Bromcyan," he replied.

"Nate's Bromcyan levels were going haywire when he died, that's what our good friend Dave said," Ethan put in. "And he told you he was hearing voices in his head."

"But don't you think that's because there were voices in his head, literally?" Sarah asked. "I mean, commands from Fortitude. His brain being lit up against his will, it pretty much *is* voices in his head."

"Not voices, songs," Dr. Diaz said. "But I won't let them, not again."

"This says Dr. Diaz was diagnosed at age fifteen, which is very young. He's . . . he's severely impacted by the disorder." Sarah's eyes filled with tears as she skimmed through the medical records detailing psychotic breaks, suicide attempts, and severe depression. "If he wasn't at Sanctuary Bay, he would've had to be in an institution."

Dr. Diaz began keening, rocking back and forth in his chair.

"They treated him with Bromcyan," Sarah read, flipping through. "It took two years to get the dosage right. It's really high. There's a note that says to never go below there or he'll be at risk of another episode. But otherwise he's symptom free. The last page says 'Do Not Recommend Civilian Life.' "

She put down the folder and Dr. Diaz stopped keening long enough to snatch it back. He held it to his chest again, and it seemed to calm him down.

"Dr. D, have you been here ever since high school?" Ethan asked.

"I have a doctorate," Dr. Diaz replied, his voice steady. "I had a friend."

"Someone who came with you to college? Who gave you the Bromcyan?" Sarah asked.

"I spit it out."

"They stabilized him, educated him to suit their needs, and brought him back here. He's like a slave," Ethan said. "Fortitude has been drugging him his whole life, just like my parents."

"I don't know," Sarah said slowly. "He has a good life here, Ethan. Better than he would otherwise. He's free of the schizophrenia. Remember what Dave said—it's like a miracle cure for the mentally ill. Maybe it's not so bad in his case."

"I won't let them in again. They said medicine, these files are not medicine. It's the Bromcyan, it's the answer to our questions," Dr. Diaz said, anger in his eyes.

"We know, Dr. D," Ethan said gently. "The thing is, there are two uses for Bromcyan. One is bad, and that is the answer we were looking for. But the other use is good, and that's the way the school has been helping you."

"You didn't take your last dose," Sarah said. "You spit it out? Do you take a pill?"

"I spit it out."

"A pill? That's remarkably low-tech," Ethan muttered.

"It really is just medicine for him. They're not controlling his mind. It's just meds and therapy, like Dave said. Why waste money putting tech in a chem teacher?" Sarah shook her head. "But you have to take that medicine, Dr. D. It's what makes your mind clear."

"No, no. I won't let them in again."

A frightening thought hit Sarah. "Ethan, he needs Bromcyan. It's the only way he can cope. If we succeed, if we burn this place down and he doesn't have it, he'll be stuck this way."

"Dr. D, where do you keep your medicine?" Ethan asked.

"They bring it to me every morning, but I won't let them." He shook his head hard, and tears ran down his cheeks.

"Damn. They bring it from someplace else." Ethan bit his lip, thinking.

"They'll have a store of it in the underground lab," Sarah said. It was what they were both thinking, she knew. Neither one of them wanted to say it. "We have to get some for him before we get off the island."

Ethan sighed. He looked at Dr. Diaz and nodded. "As much as we can carry. When we're safe, and he's stable, he can figure out how to make more of it. It really is the answer."

"So . . . we start it all, and then we go to the lab during the chaos?" Sarah asked.

"We're not going to get a better chance," Ethan said. "At least we can catch a ride through the tunnel this time."

She nodded, tension already tightening her muscles. "Let's get this over with." Sarah knelt in front of Dr. Diaz. "Dr. D, it's going to be okay. You trust me, right? I'm your friend."

He licked his lips. "Yes," he whispered.

"Good. Everything will be all right. We're going to fix things around here. I just need to borrow your cell." She had the codes. Maybe she could use the cell in ways Dr. Diaz couldn't.

His brow furrowed. "I promise it will be okay," she said.

Dr. Diaz held out his cell, and she took it from his shaking hand. She glanced down at the screen. "It's totally different from ours."

Ethan took the cell and studied it. "Dave just seemed to type a command. Give me a number," Ethan said.

"Logan is Xk48B," Sarah said, closing her eyes to help herself picture the sign near his monitor.

Ethan chuckled. "It's like the ancient locks on places we're not supposed to go. Fortitude is so sure they've got us all controlled that they don't bother with security on things we're not supposed to touch. They're cocky."

"Why? What do you mean?" Sarah asked.

"I just typed in Logan's number, and that's all I needed to do. No password or anything." Ethan handed her the cell. On the screen was the ID followed by the word "Command." Underneath it was an image of Logan in the dining hall, laughing and talking. Along the bottom, information scrolled—hormone levels.

"Is there anywhere they're not monitoring us?" she asked. "They can probably see us right now."

Ethan took back the cell, and his thumbs flew over the keys. "No, they only monitor the ones with nanotech this way," Ethan said. "I just checked myself. Everyone else is still only a potential candidate. They probably only want to spend the money on the confirmed ones, the ones they've implanted."

He hit a few more keys and handed it back with Logan called up. "I guess if they could see us, they would've been onto us sooner than this," Sarah said. Her finger hovered over Logan's face. "What command should I give?"

"You said the command for standby was just 'standby,'" Ethan replied. "Keep it simple."

"Here goes, then." Sarah typed one word into the command box: Burn.

Next came Kayla. Xm01Q. Burn. Harrison. Yk88L. Burn. The first lacrosse player. Xm33G. Burn. The second lacrosse player. Yl20H. Burn. Maya. Xl48F. Burn.

Sarah floated somewhere in between reality and her memory of the monitor room—green emergency lights shining down on her, the smell of the ocean mixing with acrid chemicals, her heart pounding with fear and anger, the sleeping faces of students on the monitors. She read their ID numbers in the memory, and typed them in reality. Then she switched to the numbers she'd seen in the horrible ward room where they'd put Izzy, the numbers over all the beds. One after another, until she'd done them all.

Burn.

Last, she typed in Izzy's number. Xk32R. Sarah hesitated for a moment, and then she wrote a different word.

Fight.

21

The first fire started two minutes later. Sarah heard a rushing sound outside the office window, followed by shouting.

Ethan locked eyes with her. "That's our cue."

Sarah turned to Dr. Diaz. "We have to go now. You need to get out of the building and go down to the jetty. Can you do that, Dr. D?"

He nodded, a short, frightened nod. She wasn't sure he'd be able to handle it, but there was nothing else she could do. She kissed him gently on the cheek. "We'll meet you there, and it will be okay. I promise."

"Another fire in the hallway," Ethan said from the door. "We have to go."

Sarah ran over, not letting herself look back at poor Dr. Diaz. The hall was filled with kids running and screaming, and smoke poured from a room way down at the other end. The fire alarm started to blare, and she and Ethan rushed from the building as part of a frightened crowd.

"I hope nobody gets hurt," she panted as they hurried down the long narrow steps that led to the passageway between the Admin building and the secret lab.

"Me too. But we have to just stay focused on getting the Bromcyan," Ethan replied. He jerked open the door, and they got on the people mover. It probably was going about twenty-five miles per hour, but it felt like they would never get to the other end

"Hold up. Who knows where the fires are on this side?" Sarah said when they finally—finally, finally—reached the other end, jumped out of the pod, and ran to the door. "I don't know if any of those patients could follow the command. They were all restrained. And we don't even know if any of them had the nanotech."

Ethan pressed his palm flat against the door. "It's not hot."

When they entered the room, Sarah could almost hear Izzy screaming, as if the walls had absorbed the hideous sounds. She bolted to the door on the opposite side of the table where Izzy had been restrained. This time she was the one who felt the door. It wasn't warm. Cautiously, she pulled it open. The sounds of terrified cries immediately hit her, and when she pulled in a breath, smoke filled her lungs.

"The ward!" Instinctively, she turned in the direction of the cries and shrieks, thinking of those people strapped to their beds. If a few of them had managed to set fires, the rest of them were sitting ducks. Why hadn't she thought of that? She started to run again, the smoke thickening, burning her eyes.

"We don't have time to do anything but get the Bromcyan," Ethan protested.

"We can't just leave them there! They'll die. And the bio lab is close to the ward," she answered.

A door to the left burst open, and a nurse flew out, her face a mask of fear. The sounds of the screams intensified, and now Sarah could hear the roar of the fire. "Untie me!" someone begged, while someone else let out a howl of sheer panic. The nurse had to have come from the ward. "Turn around!" Sarah yelled. "Get the restraints off your patients."

"She's killing people," the nurse screamed back, without slowing down.

"Who?"

A shrill scream pierced the air as Sarah reached the open

door. She was right. It was the ward. A few beds were empty, and burning, their occupants gone. The rest of the people lay strapped down, moaning and coughing. All except Izzy.

Sarah's command had worked. Izzy had gotten free of her restraints, and she was beating a nurse with an IV pole. The guy was on the floor already, and his head was bloody. "Oh my god," Sarah said. Next to the nurse lay a security guard, his eyes open and unseeing. Another guard crawled, wounded, toward the door.

Sarah ran to the closest bed and freed one of the patient's wrists. "We can't untie everyone. We have to get to the Bromcyan," Ethan urged, coughing. "And Izzy will kill us if she catches us."

As if she'd heard him, Izzy's head snapped toward them. Her blue eyes lit up with rage, and she dropped the pole. Screaming again, she rushed in their direction.

Ethan yanked Sarah out a door near a bank of monitors and slammed it closed. There was an old dead bolt on the top, and he shoved it into place.

"We can't leave her there," Sarah cried.

"She's beating people to death. That's the command she's following. And she's hopped up on adrenaline. This door won't hold her for long," Ethan retorted. "Sarah. We got her free, and that's all we could do. She. Will. Kill. Us."

"You're right." Sarah thought she spotted a staircase through the smoke. "The lab should be down there." She started down the hall. She was moving so fast when she hit the stairs that she stumbled down the first few steps before she could catch herself on the railing.

"Sarah?" Ethan called. The smoke was too thick for them to see each other.

"I'm here," she called back. "Meet at the bottom of the stairs."

She made her way to the bottom. "We have to hurry. There will be better ventilation in the lab area," he said when he joined her. "I still don't even know what's burning."

"If we need to, we can use the beach exit in this direction." Every step they'd taken the last time they were in the building was locked in her brain. They ran past the server room and the medical machines. Through the safety glass of the window, they saw that one of the MRI rooms was filled with flames, the only thing containing them the thick fire door.

They ran faster. Up the next staircase and down the hall to the bio lab. Sarah's nostrils and throat felt singed by the smoke. Ethan shoved open the lab door after a fast check, and they hurried down the stairs into the clean room area. There were so many ventilators in here that the smoke wasn't as bad, but Sarah still couldn't see any kind of storage room.

"There's the front door," Ethan said, pointing ahead. "We didn't see the main part of this complex, we only stayed in the service hallway. Maybe there's storage out here."

"Worth a shot," she replied. They pushed through the main door of the lab and found themselves in what looked like a hospital hallway. An alarm was blaring, and the overhead fluorescent lights were harsh compared to the green emergency lighting they'd come from. People ran, coughing.

"This way." Sarah spotted a door with a biohazard symbol and ran for it. She opened the door, glanced inside, and knew she'd found the right place. Rows of metal cabinets lined the room, thick Plexiglas windows showing what was inside. It only took a minute to locate the Bromcyan. There were hundreds of bottles of it.

Ethan grabbed a metal transport case from a shelf and began

stuffing it with Bromcyan. Sarah did the same. "It's not refrigerated," she said. "It should be okay to transport, don't you think?"

"Who knows?" he replied, then broke down into a coughing fit. "I can barely breathe, Sarah. We have to get out of here."

"We just left the lab. The monitor room was the next one down," Sarah replied. "We need to go there first."

She didn't wait for him to reply, she just ran. A hundred yards down the hall was the entrance to the huge room where Fortitude kept track of their test subjects. It had been abandoned, because the far side of the room was on fire. Flames leapt to the ceiling, engulfing the metal stairs that led up to the emergency exit hallway. "Crap," Sarah muttered. She raced over to the nearest workstation, praying that it would still function.

The computer awoke at her touch, and Sarah frantically typed in the ID numbers of all the people she'd ordered to burn. After each one, her fingers flying over the keys, she added a new command: Escape.

With a horrible creaking sound, the wall on the far side collapsed, taking part of the high ceiling with it.

"We're done," Ethan said. He grabbed Sarah's hand and hauled her away from the computer, out of the monitor room, one step ahead of the billowing black smoke, and back down the hallway past the lab. "Follow the running people," he gasped. "The lab is next to the monitor room. Once the flames reach it, this whole place will blow. We have to find a way out."

The smoke was so dark that Sarah couldn't make out any running people. Heat hit her like a body blow. There were screams in the blackness, and someone was crying. She let go of Ethan's hand to grope in front of her, the other hand clinging to the case of Bromcyan. Finally a red light pierced the smoke. Red means exit, Sarah thought, moving that way. She stumbled, wheezing, a few more feet, and then she was outside, the door propped open, a cement staircase in front of her. Sarah climbed it on her hands and knees. The sudden influx of cleaner air made her feel light-headed, but she knew she had to get to the surface.

Finally, exhausted, she reached the top of the steps and crawled up onto the grass. "Ethan?" she croaked.

"Oh, he's right here," said a voice that she had never wanted to hear again.

Sarah sat up, blinking to clear her aching eyes. Ethan stood about five feet away, the case of Bromcyan at his feet, and a gun at his head.

Horrified, Sarah looked up into Dave's face. His suit was just as expensive as the last one, but his tie was askew and his face was smudged with soot. The gun in his hand shook a little as it pressed against Ethan's temple.

Sarah rose to her feet, her hands out pleadingly. "Dave, no . . ."

"Was this your doing?" Dave spat, his pretend friendliness gone, his expression filled with fury. "Do you have any idea how much money you've just cost us?"

"Money?" she repeated in disbelief.

"You know what, you little brat, we aren't done here," Dave spat. "I can't kill you because your father would be pissed, but Ethan is another story."

"*What?*" she cried.

That got Dave's attention, and he lowered the gun slightly. "Oh, that's right. You don't know. Did I forget to mention that dear old dad works for Fortitude, Sarah? Surprise!"

"My father's been dead for years," she whispered. "You killed him, you son of a bitch."

"Wrong," Dave snapped. "Of course, he doesn't know we found you, Ms. *Johnson*. You stayed off the radar for years with that fake name. Too bad you couldn't keep your brilliant memory from outing you."

Merson, she thought, her head spinning. *Tell them your name is Sarah Merson. Merson.* Her father's voice saying that to her. Her father's rules for what to do if something bad happened. Her father.

"You can't save your boyfriend here, but if you play nice maybe you can have a tearful reunion with Daddy—after I beat the crap out of you."

Dave pressed the gun back against Ethan's head and cocked it, jerking Sarah out of her shock. She saw Ethan's blue eyes filled with fear and love. She couldn't move, couldn't breathe. Dave was going to kill another person that she loved, and she would have to watch. Again.

Izzy flew out of the smoke-filled stairwell like she'd been shot out of a cannon. Her chest was heaving, but she was on her feet, her hands covered in blood, a scalpel in her grip. Her face was wild. She turned on Sarah, who was closest to her.

She's going to kill me, Sarah thought.

"Izzy, no!" she yelled. "It's not me, it's him." She pointed at Dave, hoping with all her might that some scrap of the real Izzy was still there inside this wild animal. "He's the one in your head! He's the one doing it!"

Izzy's crazed eyes moved to Dave. Her lips twitched like a dog getting ready to bare its teeth.

Dave's brow furrowed, and dread flitted across his face. Suddenly Ethan grabbed Dave's gun hand and jerked it down toward the ground. With a cry, Dave fell forward, struggling to keep his grip on the gun. Ethan let go, ducking free . . . just as Izzy hurled herself at Dave.

He tried to raise the gun again, but it was too late. Izzy snarled, tearing at him with one hand, stabbing him with the other. Dave shrieked and tried to fight her off, but she was freakishly strong. The scalpel plunged into him again and again, and Sarah stumbled away, Ethan by her side, as blood spurted into the air.

She refused to look back. The sounds alone were horrifying enough. With the screams and moans and cries filling her ears, she threw up on the grass.

"Izzy, stop." Ethan's voice was steady, and when Sarah spun around she saw him holding the gun. It was pointed at Izzy, holding her at bay.

Izzy smiled. It was a wide, crazed grin, nothing like the pretty smile of the posh girl Sarah had first met. Blood dripped from the scalpel in her hand. Her cheek was slashed, but she didn't seem to notice. She just smiled . . . then turned and headed for the stairs.

"Izzy, no," Sarah cried. "It's on fire down there. You'll die."

Izzy kept walking, straight toward the stairway. Black smoke billowed around her, and flames licked at the cement.

"Izzy!" Sarah screamed.

But Izzy was gone. She'd taken the only true escape possible.

EPILOGUE

Sarah gripped the railing of the upper deck as the ferry plowed through the ocean, leaving firefighters behind to battle the flames that devoured Sanctuary Bay Academy. Soon there would be more ruins on the island. Added to the remains of an insane asylum and a POW camp would be the remnants of something that had appeared to be a school but wasn't, and a high-tech underground lab most of the world didn't know existed. She didn't want to think of what might be built there next.

In the distance, she heard a sound that reminded her of the centrifuge in the chem lab. "News helicopter," Ethan said from beside her. "Fortitude won't be able to cover up what happened to the school. They can cover up a lot, but not the fire."

She shivered, thinking of Izzy, thinking of Karina, thinking of Nate, and Ethan put his arm around her. At least Dr. Diaz had made it onto the boat. He was inside with an EMT who'd had to tranquilize him to get him on board. He had his supply of Bromcyan and Sarah had explained to the EMT that the medication was necessary to treat Dr. Diaz's schizophrenia.

"Parents will hear about the fire on the news," Ethan continued. "They'll come to get their kids. At least we saved some of them, Sarah."

"Yeah," she murmured, but all she could think about was the ones they hadn't been able to save.

"My parents might even come," Ethan said. "But I can't—" He shook his head. "I can't trust them. My mom might give me a hug, then turn me over to Fortitude. Same with my dad."

"I can't believe my dad is alive," Sarah said, wrapping one arm around Ethan's waist, wanting to be even closer to him. He pressed a kiss onto the top of her head. "But he works for Fortitude. How is that possible? What if he's . . ."

"Like mine," Ethan finished when she didn't continue.

"Like yours." A head filled with nanites. No will of his own. "Or worse, like Dave."

"You're going to look for him," Ethan said, studying her face.

Sarah nodded. "I know he was a scientist, at MIT, I think. I remember we lived in Boston before all the hotels, all the rules. And Dave said my name was Johnson. My real name, I guess. So that's my father's name."

"That's enough to start with," Ethan said. "But Sarah, if he's one of them . . ."

"I'll take him down," she cut him off. "I'm going to take them all down."

"Okay. Then we're agreed. Fortitude can't be allowed to rebuild." Ethan turned toward shore. "We're getting close to the dock." There were people waiting, more EMTs and locals eager to help, to offer thermoses of hot chocolate, blankets, beds for the night, phones that could call anywhere. "We can't trust anyone to—"

"I know," Sarah interrupted. A few houses dotted the shoreline, windows glowing with welcoming light. But behind them lay dark, dense woods. "We'll go to the forest."

"Good," Ethan agreed. "We've handled worse than mosquitoes

and raccoons. Come on." He took her hand and they headed for the gangplank. People were already gathering there.

When the gangplank lowered, she and Ethan walked off with the rest of the crowd. They headed down the dock, surrounded by their friends and classmates and teachers. But when they reached the end, they veered away from the group and let themselves disappear into the shadows, and then into the woods beyond.

Once they were shielded by the thick branches of the pines, Sarah turned back. In the distance, the island burned. But here, other figures were gliding into the shadows of the forest, melting into the darkness, following the last command she'd given them: Escape.